1901

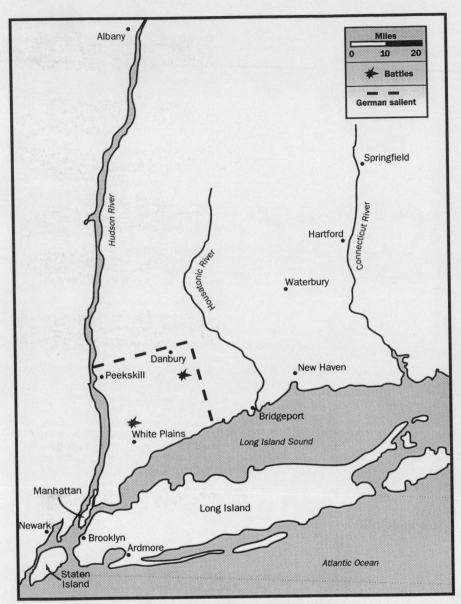

Area of the German invasion, 1901

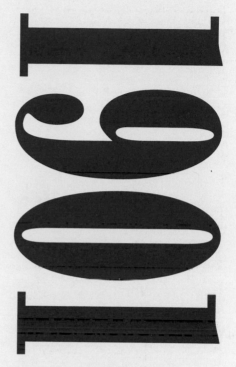

a novel by

Robert Conroy

LYFORD
Books

Some of the characters in this novel are fictitious. Any resemblance between these characters and actual persons, living or dead, is purely coincidental. The dialogue and specific incidents described in the novel are products of the author's imagination and creativity. They should not be construed as real.

LYFORD Books
Published by Presidio Press
505 B San Marin Dr., Suite 300
Novato, CA 94945-1340

Library of Congress Cataloging-in-Publication Data

Conroy, Robert (Joseph Robert) , 1938–
      1901 : a novel / Robert Conroy.
          p.   cm.
      ISBN 0-89141-537-8
      1. United States—Foreign relations—Germany—Fiction.
2. Germany—Foreign relations—United States—Fiction. 3. United
States—History—1901–1909—Fiction. I. Title.
PS3553.051986A614   1995
813'.54—dc20   94-24791
                                                              CIP

Typography by ProImage
Frontispiece map by ProImage
Printed in the United States of America

Acknowledgments

I am very grateful for the support given me by my wife Diane, my daughter Maura, my mother, and other family and friends who always encouraged my writing efforts.

I would also like to thank Bob Kane and Dale Wilson of Presidio Press for their willingness to take a chance on a new writer, along with Bob Tate, who edited and shepherded both the novel and the author.

1901

Chapter 1

WAR, THOUGHT THE kaiser, was the natural order of the world, and only fools thought otherwise. It mattered not whether one was referring to animals, as Darwin had, or nations, as he now was. War was the lubricant that drove the successful to greatness and condemned the weak to a deserved obscurity. A nation that did not grow was doomed to shrivel and die. A nation that did not take from the weak was forever doomed to be weak herself. With so much of the world already under the jurisdiction of other powers, it was obvious that the essential growth that would spur Imperial Germany into the twentieth century could come only at the expense of others. Bismarck had understood that, but only to a point. To Kaiser Wilhelm II, it was a picture seen with utter clarity. For Germany's sake, he thanked God it was he who ruled the empire for the past twelve years. He was the grandson of the man who had, with Bismarck's help, formed the state of Germany. He was the descendant of Prussian kings whose military skills were feared; nevertheless, he had not yet fought a war. Worse, he knew that his English relatives thought him inadequate and had mocked him since his childhood. They would learn, he seethed; the world would learn.

The kaiser squinted and tried to see out the rain-streaked window of the small office on the second floor of the chancellery. On the street below, a handful of people out on the ugly night scurried for cover from the cold wet rain that had originated in the North Sea. They had, the kaiser smiled to himself, just lost a minor war with the elements. He tapped his fingers impatiently on the window ledge. He was always impatient of late. If he hadn't been so impatient, he would have convened this meeting in the more convivial atmosphere of one of his residences and resolved matters over brandy and cigars. But no, he was in this dismal and sparsely furnished little room that would have better served as the office of a postal clerk than an emperor.

Yet perhaps this way was more advantageous. The pomp of a formal meeting would have attracted the noses of the swinish liberal press, or, worse, the Socialist creatures who inhabit the Reichstag.

Behind him, he heard the door open and close and the last of his invitees take one of the uncomfortable wooden chairs. He turned and confronted the handful of men. In the poor light of the small office, they looked nothing like the powers who ran the empire in his name and at his call. All of them, however, had "von" preceding their surname. This indicated their stature as Junker nobility who came from that bleak Prussia their forebears had conquered from the Slavs so many centuries ago. Prussia was the military soul of the new German Empire.

Of the four men, the kaiser controlled three. They were all older than he by at least a decade. That fact made him slightly uncomfortable, and he often had to fight to control his insecurities.

Alfred von Tirpitz was the architect of the expanding navy they both wanted to be second to none, not even England's. Bald, burly, and grim, his face obscured by a long and full forked beard, he burned with an ambition for an overseas empire the kaiser shared with a passion. Their navy was now the second largest in the world, although still dwarfed by England's.

Count Alfred von Schlieffen, a slight, gray-haired man who looked more like a scholar than a soldier, was chief of the Imperial General Staff and led the Imperial Army, which was already second to none in quality and fighting ability, and second only to the Russian army in size. Since the Germans considered the Russians to be little more than barbarians, the difference in the size of their armies was not considered important. It was significant, however, that the mighty Imperial Army, with the exceptions of the short war against

Denmark and the punitive expedition against China, had been underoccupied for almost thirty years. That was far too long. An army that does not wage war can soon forget how to fight.

For that matter, he reminded himself, his navy had never fought in all its existence.

Mustachioed Bernhard von Bulow was the kaiser's choice for chancellor. Although some considered him a sycophant and a toady, the kaiser thought him loyal and cooperative. Replacing other chancellors, particularly Bismarck, who had balked at implementing the Imperial ideas, Bulow was ideal for Kaiser Wilhelm.

The fourth person was the heavyset, enigmatic, and mysterious Friedrich von Holstein. Nicknamed the Jesuit because of his secretive ways and a preference for manipulation rather than confrontation, he had run the foreign affairs of the German Empire from his office in his home on the Wilhelmstrasse for more than a decade. The oldest of the four men, Holstein was both feared and respected, even by the kaiser. Holstein's favored way of deterring the will of the kaiser was to avoid receiving orders. Thus it was rumored that the two had met face to face only a handful of times over the last dozen years, and it was only the veiled threat of a level of force that saw the angry and uncomfortable Holstein present at this meeting. Even so, Holstein was a loyal German. If the kaiser commanded, Holstein would obey. In his younger days, he had been the protégé of the subsequently dismissed Bismarck. This, too, caused the kaiser to deal with Holstein cautiously.

The kaiser cleared his throat and began his prepared comments. "Gentlemen, the empire is at a critical point in its young history, and direct action is needed in order to ensure that the German nation continues its inexorable journey to its destiny."

The two military men appeared interested, Bulow looked enraptured, and Holstein seemed puzzled.

"The recent war between the United States and Spain has left the United States with an oceanic empire and a position on the world stage as a major player. The United States is neither ready nor worthy of such honor. It is my firm belief that what the United States has taken from the stupid, corrupt, and incompetent Spaniards rightfully belongs to Germany."

Now he had them, Wilhelm exulted; even Holstein looked intrigued.

"Consider the German Empire. Unlike England's, ours is land-locked and confined to continental Europe. Of course, we have a few square miles of useless desert or jungle in Africa and a rock or two in the Pacific, but hardly an empire when compared with the overseas possessions of England, Portugal, Holland, Spain, Belgium, and, now, the United States.

"Yet we have the greatest army in the world." He bowed to Schlieffen, who smiled. "And the fastest-growing navy in the world that is now second only to England's." He nodded to Tirpitz, a man of powerful build who hid a stern visage behind his beard. He never smiled in front of his kaiser. Tirpitz was also aware that second to England was an extremely distant second, and that the German navy was only slightly larger than those of France, Italy, or the damned United States.

The kaiser continued. "The great Bismarck did not understand this. He cared nothing for overseas colonies and let many opportunities slip through his fingers. Fortunately, it is not too late. We are building a great navy to protect our overseas interests. But we do not yet have many overseas interests to protect. It is even more appalling that our warships must refuel and resupply in British-controlled ports. We do not have enough coaling stations to permit our fleet to sail without begging permission to dock from some other European power. If the time ever came that Britain decided to deny us entry to their colonial ports, we would be unable to leave Germany. That, gentlemen, is intolerable!"

Holstein stifled a yawn as the kaiser recited a litany of perceived slights by the United States, culminating in the failure of the quiet and unofficial negotiations to purchase the Philippines along with Puerto Rico and other lands. Good lord, Holstein thought, suddenly chilled, what was the kaiser planning to do?

The kaiser paused dramatically and rose to his feet for effect. When the men started to rise with him, he waved them down with his good right hand. The withered left one he kept permanently resting on a sword handle or in a convenient pocket. It was the only flaw in his physique, and he had spent a lifetime hiding it. It was particularly difficult for him to ride a horse, since his weak hand somehow affected his sense of balance. Daily he cursed the fool doctors who had hurt him with carelessly applied forceps at his birth.

"Gentlemen, let me conclude. Some time ago, the Imperial General Staff was directed to develop plans for war against the United States. It is my wish that those plans be updated immediately and implemented as soon as possible. We will be ready to commence war against the United States in the late spring or early summer of 1901 at the latest."

Holstein spoke. "We will declare war?"

"No, Holstein, we will present them with an ultimatum. Our fleet will then announce war with its presence off New York and its guns firing. The United States has had enough warnings."

"All Highest, the United States is huge, larger even than all of Europe. We could never conquer it."

"Such is not the idea, von Holstein. The plans that were developed so long ago called for attacks at the American jugular. As predators, we are entitled to go for the throat." Wilhelm smiled at the picture. "We will land near New York City, take it—thus damaging their economy—and move eastward into Connecticut. If the Americans do not see reason and refuse to concede to our demands, our army will continue in that easterly direction and take both Hartford and Boston."

The kaiser laughed quickly. He pictured his invincible armies overrunning frightened Americans. "We do not feel that it will be necessary to march all the way to Boston, although that is included in the plans. We anticipate a quick and limited war and an early peace. General von Schlieffen's preliminary estimates call for only three or four corps and other supporting units—all in all, less than two hundred thousand men. Admiral von Tirpitz has assured me that he can land at least one corps of thirty thousand without difficulty as our initial attack force, and both sustain our army and enable it to grow through a continuous stream of reinforcements protected by our fleet. Our ability to transport a major force to China last year proved that beyond a doubt."

Holstein was persistent. "But I seem to recall that the Americans, at the end of their Civil War, had almost a million men under arms and more than a thousand warships."

Tirpitz snorted in exasperation. "First of all, von Holstein, it took them almost four years to reach those levels, and even then, those million men were a rabble with rifles. Our army would devastate them. As for the thousand ships, the majority were converted merchant ships, coastal vessels, or small craft designed for going up rivers. No, their navy will not overwhelm us. But they are now building a number of major ships, and many others are authorized to be built in the coming years. When that construction is finished, the United States will no longer be vulnerable."

Holstein looked at the others in the room. The military minds were intrigued by the possibilities of the first taste of combat in more than a generation. Bulow, of course, was looking at the Kaiser in much the same way a spaniel looks at his adored master. Holstein was cornered and would have to acquiesce in his kaiser's desire for his first war. But one more thought.

"And what about England? As you say, All Highest, she has been the enforcer of the Monroe Doctrine, not the United States. Will England stand by?"

This time it was Bulow who countered him. "The English are preoccupied with wrapping up their war in Africa against the Boers. They will not like it, but they will not interfere."

The kaiser smiled at Holstein. "My beloved grandmother Victoria is gravely ill and likely dying. When she does pass on, I shall grieve and miss her. But with her passing, the empire will fall to her overweight and corrupt son, Edward, my uncle. No, England will not oppose us. They are too busy elsewhere, and," he laughed harshly, "my kingly uncle is more interested in parties than in warfare."

"How long will our war last, All Highest?" Holstein asked.

Kaiser Wilhelm recognized the shift in attitude and smiled. Holstein would not oppose him. "It will be over within three to six months. Along with the lands in question, we will also insist that the United States not build a navy. After all," he laughed hugely, "without all those islands, why would they need one?"

They all laughed with their kaiser. The meeting concluded and they departed with their instructions. Holstein walked the dark corridors of the chancellery alone and in thoughtful silence. What if the kaiser's first war lasted longer than the kaiser anticipated? Was an army that had not fought in so long really up to the endeavor? And how would the kaiser's shiny new navy fare? Only a little more than a generation past, there was no such thing as a German navy. The army would certainly win battles, but it would be the navy whose success or failure would determine the course of the campaign. Holstein could see a land war in North America as a pit into which the wealth and manhood of the Reich would plummet.

Holstein also knew there was no dissuading the kaiser from this unhealthy scheme; nor would he wish to try. That could be very dangerous indeed. He could be dismissed and banished as abruptly as Bismarck had been. Banishment from the court would be a devastating fate. What to do? Although he had avoided personal contact with the Kaiser, a coterie of aides and informants had kept him abreast of events. He felt he had a clear picture of his kaiser: the man was desperate to reinforce his image as a warrior king in the grand manner of his Prussian ancestors. Also, he wanted to show the English, whom he both admired and hated, that he was their equal. His kaiser, Holstein thought ruefully, was insecure and lethal, and he needed to prove his manhood to a world he felt did not take him seriously. As a result, thousands would pay. What to do, what to do?

Chapter 2

FOR PATRICK MAHAN, the first Sunday of June in the year of 1901 would be recalled as a day of many surprises. Some of them were trivial, some were climactic, and others were decidedly unpleasant, but all were surprises nonetheless. First was the unexpected presence of Doctor Palmer, the aging alcoholic who administered the malaria patients. He was actually present in the hospital on a Sunday morning. The good but very shaky doctor looked puzzled and disconcerted, and seemed to be worried about something behind him.

"We're releasing you today," he told Patrick. "You are to get packed immediately."

Patrick was confused. Even though the doctor was nominally a colonel and he was two ranks lower at major, the directions were unusually peremptory.

Already dressed and ready for a morning walk, Patrick looked down at the smaller man. "Why the change? Don't get me wrong; I'm more than ready to leave this charming place, but wasn't this supposed to happen on Monday?"

Now the poor doctor looked really concerned. When he hesitated to answer, another man, this one much younger and very fit looking, entered Patrick's room and motioned Palmer to leave. The doctor scuttled out as if relieved to be going.

"Now, just who might you be?" Mahan asked, trying to take the measure of his visitor. The man appeared to be in his late twenties and was well dressed in a conservative business suit.

"Sorry, Major. My name is Welles, and I'm with the Secret Service." With that, he displayed his credentials. Impressed, Patrick examined them. The Secret Service was the security arm of the U.S. Treasury and was getting more and more involved in the personal safety of the president.

Patrick forced a smile and beckoned Welles to be seated. Welles declined. "I've been directed to inform you that President McKinley would like to see you at two in the afternoon in his office at the White House."

"And for what reason would that be?" asked Patrick.

"Sorry, sir. I don't know, and even if I did, I don't think I'd be allowed to tell you."

Well, Patrick thought, it didn't sound as though he was going to be arrested or anything. He'd never met McKinley, although he had more than a passing acquaintance with the vice president, Teddy Roosevelt, from their days in Cuba. That relationship was enhanced by the fact that he, Patrick Mahan, was distantly related to the noted naval theorist Alfred Thayer Mahan, and Roosevelt, as ex–assistant secretary of the navy, was fascinated by war at sea. Patrick recalled Roosevelt's initial disappointment that he knew little about naval theories, rarely spoke to his distinguished cousin, and even pronounced his last name differently. Patrick pronounced it "Mann," whereas his famous relative pronounced it "ma-HANN." Even so, Patrick and Roosevelt became friendly, although they were not actually close friends.

Welles, it seemed, was not quite through. "Major, it would also be appreciated if you wore civilian clothes."

Patrick nodded. Fortunately, he had one suit, although it was in rather bad shape. Since he hadn't planned on getting malaria again, he hadn't brought that much clothing with him. When Patrick mentioned this to Welles, the man's stern face softened considerably. "Major, from what I understand, no one is going to be concerned that you aren't dressed like some ambassador or potentate." He reached into a pocket and pulled out an envelope. "This contains your pass into the White House. You are to present it a few minutes before two at the side entrance indicated. It's probably just as well you aren't going to be all that gussied up. I think they would like you to look as inconspicuous as possible."

"I may look like the White House gardener."

With that, Welles actually laughed. "I'm certain, very certain, that both the president and vice president are well aware of your predicament. Major, if you'd like, I'll take your bag with me and you can pick it up when you leave the president."

"That way I won't look like some uninvited weekend guest, will I?"

Welles again smiled. Taking Patrick's bag further assured that he would show up, as if there were a doubt. Patrick finished packing and let Welles take the grip. The cloth bag wasn't very heavy, but, even so, Welles flipped it as if it were no heavier than a feather.

When the agent departed, Patrick sat on his cot and tried to sort out his thoughts. Who was he that McKinley would want to see him. Even in the small American army there were several thousand officers, so why him? He cast through his largely indistinguished military career for a clue. He had graduated from West Point in 1885 with a solid class ranking of fifteen. This was followed by a series of short assignments out west where he was primarily involved in helping track down groups of Apaches who, with great justification, resisted being returned to reservation life and the degradation and starvation that would inevitably follow. Patrick did not remember these years as pleasant.

In order to pass the time—most days were a study in monotony—and to help further his chances for promotion, he read voraciously about military history and the development of the modern army. This led him to an interest in the German military machine that had scourged several of the nations of Europe and now dominated the Continent. He found that the German army both fascinated and repelled him.

A senior officer noticed his interest in the German army and mentioned it to Gen. Arthur MacArthur. By coincidence, MacArthur had just been asked by the War Department if there was anyone who could be spared for an assignment to Germany as an observer of their army. Since Patrick was both interested and without a proper billet on the frontier, he was promoted to captain and instructed to spend the year of 1895 in Europe at the government's expense.

After a stop in England, he devoted a number of months to observing the German army. He was stunned at first by the size of it—casual maneuvers involved more soldiers than existed in the entire U.S. Army—and by the precise way it was organized. This led to virtually flawless maneuvers by incredibly well-armed and -drilled units. In a way, it made him ashamed of his own army. He knew that the Germans he associated with looked down upon him and other Americans as military bumpkins.

Upon his return to the United States, Patrick was assigned to West Point in order to write about his experiences in Germany and to teach classes on the German army. With his report completed, and doubtless filed in some government archive, he settled down to continue as an instructor for as long as he could. After being shot at by Apaches and awed by the Germans, he enjoyed teaching future officers. He prided himself that his lectures were extremely well received. They were popular because, after the overwhelming German victory over France, the military world was mesmerized by the success and apparent invincibility of the German war machine.

The war with Spain intervened, and Patrick was assigned to General Shafter, directing an administrative support staff. When the battle of Santiago began, Patrick slipped out and attached himself to Roosevelt's Rough Riders—with Roosevelt's permission, of course—and joined in the charge up San Juan Hill, which those who participated in knew actually took place on nearby Kettle Hill. During that bitter fight, Patrick had been greatly impressed by the personal courage and leadership of Teddy Roosevelt. The man was among the first up the hill, and he gunned down at least two Spanish soldiers with his service revolver. That heroism had helped endear him to the American public.

In 1900, Patrick was sent to Hong Kong to observe a German expeditionary force that had been sent to China to assist in putting down the Boxer Rebellion and lifting the siege of the European legations in Peking.

In order to give Patrick status with the rank-obsessed Germans, he was promoted to major. Since the promotion was premature, some professional jealousy had manifested itself, and he was confident that his next promotion would not be for a very, very long time, if ever.

Both he and the Germans arrived in Hong Kong after the siege had been lifted, but he spent the next couple of months watching the Imperial German Army function in a "real" environment. On his way home from that task, he stopped in the Philippines. His malaria, previously caught in Cuba, flared up again and he was sent to Washington to convalesce.

Patrick stood and stretched, deciding he had time for breakfast. Had anything else occurred that would justify his summons? Teddy Roosevelt had visited him a couple of weeks ago, but that meeting was purely social. In fact, Patrick was certain that the vice president had been in the hospital to visit someone else and had simply noticed his name on a list upon arrival and decided to be polite.

Several hours later, a crumpled and sweaty Patrick Mahan found himself on a bench across the street from the White House quietly cursing the summer heat and stifling humidity that made Washington in the summer more like a Cuban swamp than a nation's capital. Whatever creases and folds his clothes had once possessed had disappeared, and he felt himself to be little more than a soggy, sweaty lump. His tie hung limp and his starched collar, except where it chafed his neck, had collapsed. As always, there were scores of tourists staring at the famous building, and he wondered just how so many of them managed to look even slightly comfortable. Several adults were taking photographs using Mr. Eastman's new box camera, and a number of children were crying to either go home, go to the bathroom, or eat. Maybe the tourists weren't that comfortable after all, he decided.

He pulled his watch from its pocket and again checked the time. Almost 1:30. In about twenty minutes he would walk leisurely across the street and present himself. Then, for the first time in his life, he would meet a president of the United States.

For about the hundredth time, he questioned himself as to why he had been summoned. No use speculating, he finally decided; he would find out soon enough.

"Patrick Mahan."

He turned quickly and looked up, blinking in the sunlight that caused the man standing to his left to be a silhouette. "Excuse me?" he responded confusedly.

"Patrick, don't you recall me?"

The voice was British, educated, and very familiar. Recognition finally came. Patrick jumped to his feet and grabbed the other man's hand and pumped vigorously.

"Ian! Ian Gordon! What on earth are you doing here?"

Ian Gordon, a smallish, wiry Scot with thick black hair and a neatly cropped and equally black beard, grinned. "Goodness, Patrick, is there a law against my being here?"

"Of course not, but you have to admit it is quite a coincidence." Then another memory intruded. "Ian, it is a coincidence, isn't it?"

Gordon smiled gently. "Good, so you do remember. Why don't we both be seated and chat."

Patrick quickly tried to recall as much as he could about Gordon, whom he had met in Europe the year he was to observe the Germans. Prior to reaching Germany, however, Patrick was directed by the War Department to meet with certain people in the British army, and Ian Gordon, then a major himself, was high on the list.

It didn't take long for Patrick to find that Major Gordon, for all his affability and good humor, was not an ordinary military officer. Gordon's admitted specialty was military intelligence, and his particular focus was the military might of Germany. Although not a spy himself, Patrick was certain that the pleasant Scot controlled a number of spies and received much information from them.

Their assignment had not been all work; their mutuality of interests resulted in a number of social nights at plays, pubs, and private gambling clubs. As a minor member of the aristocracy, Gordon was welcomed virtually everywhere, and Patrick tagged along for the very pleasant ride. There had also been a standing invitation to visit the Gordon castle, which Ian assured a disbelieving Patrick stood atop a bleak, rocky crag that jutted into the North Sea.

Patrick again pulled out his watch as a means of both gathering his thoughts and actually checking the time.

"Don't worry," Gordon said. "Your secret meeting isn't for another half an hour."

Bastard, Patrick thought. "Actually I make it twenty-five minutes. That assumes there actually is a secret meeting, which, if there were, I wouldn't admit to anyhow."

Gordon chuckled. "Wonderful. Nothing's changed you. How's your malaria?"

"Fine, thanks. I think I am now completely cured, although I am going to do my damnedest to avoid the Tropics from here on in." Good lord, he thought again, he knows about my malaria. Does he know whether my bowels move regularly?

"Ian, can I assume your being here with me this lovely summer day is no coincidence at all?"

"Of course, although the fact that I am assigned to the embassy here is a coincidence. When it was decided to arrange a meeting with you prior to your meeting with McKinley, I thought it logical that I be the one to talk with you."

"About what?"

"Do you know the purpose of the meeting with the president?" When Patrick shook his head, Ian continued. "Then I will also presume you know nothing about the problems with Kaiser Wilhelm. Don't feel left out, very few people have any inkling that the situation between the United States and Germany is so very critical—perhaps even more critical than your government realizes." He took out a thin, dark cigar and lit it, oblivious to the angry stares of a mother who promptly yanked her young son away from the offending object.

Well, Patrick thought, that means the subject of the president's meeting is doubtless going to be Germany. "Good lord, I am hardly the ranking expert on Imperial Germany. I admit I know a good deal, but there have to be others who know more."

"Don't belittle yourself. You probably know as much about the kaiser and his incredible army as anyone in Washington at this time. And timing is most critical.

"Let me clarify the crises for you. Germany is outraged that the United States has an overseas empire, whereas she has none. In short, Germany wants your newly acquired overseas possessions."

Patrick was angry. "The hell you say! We paid for them in blood. She cannot have them."

"That is precisely, but more politely, what the Germans were told. They then responded, all through unofficial channels, that they were willing to purchase them. When that offer was also rejected, they informed your president, just a few days ago, that failure to turn over those lands was a grievous insult and Germany would consider taking those lands by force."

Gordon expertly blew a smoke ring and watched it drift slowly skyward. "Over the past few months, the Germans have managed to gather both a sizable fleet and a portion of their immense army without anyone knowing that it was for anything other than routine maneuvers or internal purposes. Patrick, that force numbers perhaps thirty thousand soldiers and it sailed in our direction almost two weeks ago. We believe it will land tonight."

Patrick was stunned. "Thirty thousand! How astonishing, and how like them. My God, Ian, our garrison on Cuba is so small. It'll be slaughtered. And the one on Puerto Rico is smaller yet. What a disaster!"

"Why do you think they would land on Cuba or Puerto Rico?" Ian asked softly.

The question puzzled him. "Why, because those are the places Germany wants. Why on earth would they go elsewhere?" As Patrick said this he saw the expression on Ian's face and knew there was something even more dreadfully wrong than he had first surmised.

"Patrick," Ian continued in that same soft, whispering voice. "My government wants you to know about this, and we would like to keep you supplied with additional information as we receive it. All of this has to be unofficial and deniable, of course, which is why I am sitting here with you like this. By the way, don't worry too much about your comrades in Cuba, or anywhere else, for that matter. They're safe. Cuba isn't the target. Germany will attack where you have virtually no effective defenses to hinder them."

In shock, Patrick could only whisper as well. "Where?"

"New York City, Patrick. New York City." Ian put a hand on the other man's shoulder. "Now go and meet your president."

Ian Gordon rose and quickly strode away, almost immediately losing himself in the crowd. Patrick also stood and wondered if the startling information he'd just been given was written on his face and readable to all around him. As he walked across the street toward the side entrance of the White House, his shock waned. Was Gordon telling the truth? If not, why on earth would he lie? What should he do with the information? Obviously, he was supposed to tell McKinley, but would he be believed? He couldn't just walk up to McKinley and say that a man he hadn't seen for some years just met him on a bench in front of the White House and informed him that the city of New York was going to be attacked tonight by Germany.

And again, why him? Was this whole thing a dream? If so, he thought wryly, he would like to wake up as soon as possible.

Inside the slightly cooler White House, Patrick handed his pass to a black porter who directed another black servant to take him to the cabinet room on the second level. All of this took place under the watchful eyes of the Secret Service detachment that protected the president during the day. Uniformed city police watched him at night.

When they reached the second-floor cabinet room, the servant knocked, announced Patrick, and gestured for him to enter. Inside, President McKinley sat behind a large dark wooden desk; Theodore Roosevelt stood beside him. McKinley rose and extended a hand.

"Ah, Major Mahan, thank you for coming."

The grip was firm. Although he appeared tired and strained, the clean-shaven president looked very much like his pictures and radiated warmth. McKinley, reelected only the fall before, was extremely popular and obviously easy to like. It did not strike Patrick as odd that while the profile was the same as the campaign art, the body was somewhat different, softer, even overweight. In addition, McKinley did not dress with an eye to fashion. His suit was old and there were fray marks on the cuff.

"I'm honored by your invitation, sir."

Roosevelt laughed. "Invitation? Patrick, the malaria's affected your mind and you're deluding yourself. It was an order and you damn well know it."

Patrick chuckled and took the vice president's hand as well. Roosevelt seemed not to have changed from Cuba and now resembled nothing so much as a middle-aged little boy who was having a wonderful time. Unlike the president's garb, Roosevelt's was crisp and dapper.

McKinley smiled tolerantly at his vice president. Patrick wondered if a degree of friendship had developed between the two men who were so unalike. Political rumors had them intensely disliking each other before the Spanish war, which Roosevelt had wanted and McKinley had adamantly opposed. Now, of course, that war was won and so was the reelection, and Roosevelt was McKinley's vice president. Winning does take the edge off of past differences.

Patrick was gestured to a chair and the three sat. After refusing offers of refreshment, Patrick waited for the president to get to the reason for this gathering.

Roosevelt spoke instead. "Patrick, I daresay you are curious about this summons, or invitation if you'd prefer."

"I am."

McKinley spoke. "It concerns your experiences in Germany, Major."

"Sir, I am hardly the most qualified person in the army to discuss Germany."

Roosevelt laughed loudly. "You certainly are not, Patrick. But what you are is here, right now and today. Not only are most of our senior officers in the Philippines or serving in some fort in Arizona, but virtually everyone else with your knowledge who resides within a hundred miles of here is away for a nice summer weekend. No, my friend, you were selected not only for your expertise but because you were the only one around."

McKinley softened the comment. "Theodore assures me that you are intelligent and discreet as well as in possession of at least much of the information we now need."

Patrick nodded, having been quietly put in his place. Yet how did he now tell them of his conversation with Ian without looking like an utter fool?

He was pondering how to do that when McKinley leaned over and stared intently at him. "Major, let us come to the primary reason for your visit. Please tell us about your experiences with the kaiser."

It was both a reprieve and an opening. While in Germany he had indeed met the German kaiser and gotten to know him fairly well, or at least as well as anyone in his position could. The first meeting took place at a birthday party for one of the kaiser's relatives. Patrick, as an eligible and reasonably presentable young bachelor officer at the U.S. embassy, had been invited.

The kaiser was intrigued by Patrick's American uniform and spoke to him briefly in the receiving line. Afterward, the kaiser summoned him and they discussed the state of the American military and Patrick's purpose in visiting Germany.

"Patrick," said Roosevelt, "I was not aware you spoke German."

"I don't. At least not enough to hold a good conversation. The kaiser, however, speaks excellent—no, extremely fluent—English. Please recall, sir, that both his mother and grandmother were English, and English was possibly his first language. I also think he enjoyed picking up American slang and other phrases from me. For a despot, he can be quite charming when he wants to. Although, sir, it was a hypnotic sort of charm. Unlike you as president of the United States, the kaiser has absolute and total power over the lives and deaths of millions. It was a chilling realization."

Patrick went on to explain that there had been more contact with the emperor. Since he was openly there to observe the German army, the kaiser invited him to be his own guest during the coming maneuvers. It was a marvelous opportunity, and he jumped at it. For two weeks he watched and marveled at tens of thousands of Imperial Germany's elite forces marching and countermarching while artillery thundered and cavalry charged. The force and power were staggering, and the kaiser was delighted with his ability to show off his magnificent and murderous toy to his American guest.

"Gentlemen, I must tell you about a curious incident during the maneuvers. At one point, the kaiser decided to get directly involved, and he took over command of a brigade. I went with him while he ordered them about. The German High Command wasn't too pleased, but they didn't toady up to him either. Within a few hours he'd led his brigade into an ambush, and the referees ruled it defeated. He sulked for hours. It didn't get any better when his own senior officers later analyzed his performance and pointed out his many mistakes."

Roosevelt chuckled. "Good grief. I assume he had them beheaded or something appropriate."

"Hardly. Even he would never do that to one of his own class. No, he would have banished his critics. They later softened the blow by acknowledging that affairs of state and the need to run an empire had doubtless prevented him from keeping his military skills up to date."

"He accepted that?"

Patrick laughed at the memory. "Like a child being forgiven a minor transgression and allowed to play outside again. Gentlemen, the kaiser is a very immature fellow, in many ways just a forty-year-old child. A very dangerous child, however. He is the absolute ruler of a militaristic state, and the military supports him utterly. Some people may think him ludicrous, but not his generals. To them he is the descendant of Frederick the Great, and they think he will lead them to glory. Bloody glory."

Roosevelt started to say something, but McKinley shushed him. "Tell me about their army."

"Sir, it is huge—almost half a million men on active service with again as many in reserve. It is modern, efficient, and brutal."

"Brutal?"

"Yes, sir, brutal." He told them that although he'd been impressed with the army as a whole, it was their behavior in China that had stunned him, even sickened him.

"Sir, they were told by that same childlike Kaiser Wilhelm that they were being sent to China to save white men and women from the evils of the yellow race. The kaiser told them that the Chinese were descendants of the Huns and his soldiers should remember that, and be even more brutal than the Huns in order to impress them with German superiority."

McKinley was clearly shocked. "And that is how they behaved?"

"Yes, sir. Their command was furious that the siege of the legations in Peking was over when they arrived, so they amused themselves with punitive marches about the countryside. Sir, they burned, looted, raped, and murdered! It was barbarism, it was savagery, and it was inhuman! And it was so unnecessary. The rebellion was over and all they did was slaughter innocent peasants."

Patrick sagged back in his chair at the memory of the stacked dead, the maimed, and the black smoke pouring from the pitiful Chinese hovels while the survivors wailed and screamed. "It was then I decided that my continued presence in China served no earthly purpose, so I requested permission from our attaché in Peking to leave."

McKinley nodded solemnly. "And well you did. And these obscene orders came from your charming friend the kaiser?"

"Yes, sir."

"Major, is he capable of further erratic behavior?"

"President McKinley, he is a person who is extremely willful, and he can be totally irresponsible. It may be that power has corrupted him. It is a tragedy that he is in total control of a country as strong and militaristic as Germany. There are no checks on him. Their parliament, the Reichstag, has no real power."

Patrick paused and took a deep breath. What was the saying—in for a penny, in for a pound? "Is he capable of something erratic and tragic? Yes, gentlemen, without question. He is capable of something as gigantic as declaring war on the United States and launching an invasion if he thought he'd been insulted."

There was silence in the room. McKinley and Roosevelt stared at him. Finally the president spoke, his voice icy and calm. "I thought you said you knew nothing about your summons here."

Now I'll tell them, he thought. "Mr. President, while waiting and biding time before this meeting, I had a most unusual conversation."

In a rush, Patrick told of his meeting with Ian Gordon and his friend's prediction that an invasion of the United States was not only imminent, but would occur that very night.

When he finished, the silence in the room could have been cut with the proverbial knife. McKinley looked gray and pale; his hands gripped the edge of his desk so that the knuckles turned white. Roosevelt's reaction was almost ludicrous. His mouth was open and, set as it was in his round face, he looked like a nearsighted fish. His pince-nez had tumbled from the bridge of his nose and dangled about his waist.

"Nonsense," Roosevelt rasped as he finally got his breath. "Cuba. It has to be Cuba. Great God, Cuba's what they want, isn't it?"

Patrick shook his head. "I can only tell you what Mr. Gordon told me—New York City."

When Roosevelt started to argue further, McKinley shushed him. He then rose and turned his back on them, and stared out the window before responding.

"There are several things that concern me," commented McKinley. "The most obvious question is whether or not the information is true. If it is true, then why are the British informing us? Again, if true, and the invasion is tonight, how long have they had that information? It seems just a little too convenient that such a discovery should occur and we should be told with just enough time left on the clock for us to be grateful for the information yet unable to do much about it."

He turned and confronted them. His mouth was set in anger and his jaw outthrust. "And if it is the truth, then the action by Germany is an outrage. We shall thank Great Britain and not look a gift horse in the mouth. I do believe they truly want us to have the information as an indication that they are not in the German's camp. We shall also respect their desire for secrecy."

"Sir." Roosevelt's voice was almost a wail. "New York is my home. What shall we do?"

Even Patrick was surprised. Usually strong, confident, almost arrogant,

Theodore Roosevelt suddenly looked lost. McKinley patted the younger man's shoulder.

"Theodore, what we shall do is what we can. First, should we notify the governor of New York? The mayor? Sadly, I think not. First, we don't know if the information is indeed true. If it is not, then we shall have initiated a panic and made ourselves look like fools. If it is true, what can we accomplish in the few hours left to us?"

The president walked out of the cabinet room and across the hall to the war room with the others following. Inside, Patrick stared at the maps on the walls with pins still stuck in them to designate units in combat in Cuba and the Philippines. There was also a large map of the United States.

"Again," the president continued, "if the Germans do attack New York, precisely where shall it be? Major, with polite deference to my esteemed vice president, I believe you are the true professional among us. What are your thoughts regarding what they specifically might do?"

Patrick walked to the map and stared at the East Coast, focusing on New York harbor.

"Sir, the message said the goal of the attack would be New York City. I do not believe that necessarily meant the attack would be directly upon the city. Frankly, I think they would consider it foolish and risky to get involved in a street fight while attempting to land directly onto the piers.

"If I were the Germans, I would land either on the New Jersey coast or Long Island and advance overland to take the city, or that portion of it they feel will give them effective control. If you wish my specific opinion, they will land limited forces on Long Island, as the British did in the Revolution, and advance to a point where they can dominate the harbor, seize some docks, and deposit the remainder of their forces, their artillery, and their supplies."

McKinley nodded, then glanced at Roosevelt, who concurred. Patrick was gratified to see that the younger man had regained his composure.

"Theodore, I believe the major's outline makes sense."

"It does, sir. It is also remarkably similar to what we did in Cuba, landing at a smaller town and marching overland to Santiago."

"Which, gentlemen," said the president, "brings us back to the case at hand. Specifically, what do we do?"

After further discussion, it was decided that the governor of New York, one Benjamin B. Odell, had to be informed of the grave situation and of the possibility of an invasion. White House clerks were called in to make telephone contact with the governor, with hopes that spoken conversations would be more private and controllable than the telegraph and cause less damage from public furor if the reports turned out to be in error.

It was then that McKinley, Roosevelt, and Patrick realized the scope of the situation. It was a summer Sunday, the governor was unavailable, and no one in Albany had the foggiest idea where the lieutenant governor was. The presidential party then tried to reach the mayor of New York City and was informed that he was at a party given by his Tammany Hall colleagues and he wouldn't be back until Monday morning at the earliest, and, no, he could not be reached.

Frustrated, they tried to reach the coastal fortification at Sandy Hook, on the New Jersey side of the harbor, and were informed there was no telephone line and the telegraph was out of order. The telephone company and Western Union were apologetic and assured the callers that the situation would doubtless be rectified in the morning, but, after all, both were fragile and emerging technologies and these things had to be expected.

The telegraph was out of order? At this particular time? The coincidence chilled them. How convenient that the lines should be down on this night. None of them believed very much in coincidence.

The duty officer at the War Department, a captain who was much older than Patrick, was brought in, briefed, and told to try to contact any of the forts in or along the harbor. Captain Hedges, a portly man in his fifties, was obviously put out by the fact that the younger Major Mahan was in quiet and intimate conversation with both the president and vice president. Tight lipped, he nevertheless did as he was told.

An hour later, Hedges returned with the unfortunate information that there seemed to be a major problem with the telegraph all along the eastern seaboard. Further, telephone lines to New York City were also starting to have problems.

With evidence of sabotage mounting, they decided to contact other military areas. Hedges suggested they simply warn all coastal military facilities that labor anarchists might be planning sabotage this night, and that all locations should be on extreme alert. The idea was approved and Hedges departed, carrying with him orders to try to find the secretary of war and the secretary of the navy.

Patrick Mahan slouched in a chair in the war room and stared at a map of Cuba. How easy it had been then. How frustrating it was now. White House servants brought in tea and sandwiches, and Patrick realized he was hungry. A quick check of his watch told him the reason—it was after 6:00 P.M.

After Captain Hedges departed, there were attempts by the Secret Service to bring Ian Gordon to the White House. These met with failure; the British embassy reported he was away for the weekend. So, too, was the British ambassador and everyone else of importance. Everyone, it seemed, was away. More coincidences.

That also included the Germans in Washington. The German ambassador had recently retired and a new one had not yet been named. The other key people at the embassy, Roosevelt recalled, were in Germany for conferences and holiday.

"Funny," Patrick thought out loud. "Germans usually take their vacations in August, not June."

The president nodded grimly. "Patrick, it gets even more suspicious. Did you hear of the labor strife that virtually halted all German shipping? No? Well, there hasn't been a German passenger ship or freighter out of German harbors for a couple of months. Wouldn't a fabricated general strike be a wonderful way of gathering together all the shipping necessary to transport the men and supplies needed for an invasion? To think," he said heatedly, "I once felt sorry for them and the fact they were losing so much in commerce as a result of the strike!"

Patrick could only agree with him. The evidence, even though only circumstantial, was adding up. In spite of the gravity of the situation, however, a small part of him was pleased that the president of the United States had just referred to him by his first name.

McKinley picked up a sandwich and chewed nervously on it. "We're stuck. We're completely helpless and cut off. If Britain meant to inform us with too little time to react, then she's been fabulously successful."

Patrick was shocked. "Sir, I cannot imagine they would be deceitful regarding anything this important."

McKinley laughed. "The British are the most subtle and devious

people on the planet. They could easily have decided that war between the United States and Germany is in their best interest, and
that it is also in their best interest to appear to be our saviors. The
point, however, is irrelevant. What is truly relevant is whether a
landing will take place tonight, on Long Island or anywhere else.
Gentlemen, this night will be a long one. I will have a cot brought in
here for you, Major. Theodore, you will bed down in the Lincoln
Room." McKinley smiled wanly and thought of Roosevelt's un-
abashed political ambitions. "You always wanted that, didn't you?"

The president lifted his cup of tea in a mock salute. "Gentlemen,
I pray for an uneventful dawn."

Chapter 3

ARDMORE, LOCATED ON the southern shore of Long Island about twenty miles from New York City, was a town of about five hundred people. For more than two centuries, it had been a slow-growing and not very prosperous place to live, depending as it did on small farms and a handful of professional fishermen.

In recent years, however, subtle changes had begun to occur. The growth of the metropolis to the west had started to bring people to the area for the purposes of rest and recreation. They found the soft beaches, fishing, and quiet ambience of Ardmore a compelling reason to return on an annual basis. This brought a new level of prosperity, which resulted in a hotel, a new rooming house, and a restaurant that was open in summer only.

It also meant more people and more problems, which resulted in the town of Ardmore hiring a policeman. He was called the chief, which was a private joke, since he, Blake Morris, was the only member of the Ardmore police force.

One of the chief's recurring annoyances was Willy Talmadge, who, this warm night in June, was doing what he did best—sleeping off a drunk.

This time, however, he was sleeping it off on the beach and not in the small jail, as he had the night before. He was sharing the beach with the crabs and other creatures that came out at night. Willy

Talmadge was frankly delighted that he had eluded Chief Morris, who, in Willy's opinion, was getting to be a bit of a shit regarding his behavior. Willy was half Indian and half Irish, and the attraction to alcohol was permanent and overwhelming. Not overly fond of work, Willy supported his habit by petty thievery. This antagonized Chief Morris, who would punch Willy in the stomach and kidneys when he caught him with something that belonged elsewhere. The punches, although hard and painful, caused no visible wounds and no serious damage. Chief Morris, Willy decided, was well on his way to becoming a serious cop.

Willy rolled over on the sand and stared at the cloud-speckled sky and the fading stars. Screw Morris. No, he smirked, screw his wife.

With dawn almost on him, his view of the ocean was clear, and there was no fog or mist to confuse him. His eyes widened as he took in the panorama before him. He saw a huge ocean liner just offshore with other, smaller ships almost alongside the liner. He quickly realized that the smaller ships were warships!

Stunned, he lurched to his feet and ran to the center of the little town until he was at the fire alarm bell, which he commenced ringing as quickly and as hard as he could.

Almost immediately, windows opened and voices shouted their concern. Some, when they realized it was Willy Talmadge on the bell, presumed he was still drunk and having some stupid sort of fit. He hushed them by waving out to sea where the ships were now plainly visible.

Just about the first person to actually arrive was Chief Morris, grim-faced and angry. "Goddamnit, Willy, you are about to spend a long time in my jail for this." Then he saw the ships. "Oh, Jesus."

Willy knew when he had the upper hand. "Yeah, looks like that big liner's in some kind of trouble and the others are gonna help it out."

Morris quickly agreed with the evaluation. The liner was obviously aground; although he thought there was plenty of water where the ship was, maybe a sandbar had shifted. What was the damned thing doing so close to shore in the first place?

"Wow, what a sight!"

The comment came from Homer Walls, the owner of the hotel and publisher of the summer weekly. Homer also had the town's only telephone.

Morris grabbed his arm. "Homer, I think you ought to call some-one in the big city and tell them what's happened."

Homer smirked. "Did that already. Called the *New York Post*." Then he looked a little chagrined. "They weren't as excited as I thought they would be. Seems there were a bunch of explosions and fires all over the city last night and everyone's in an uproar about them. The *Post* seemed to think they were caused by labor agitators or something and didn't particularly give a damn about a ship aground off Ardmore."

Morris grunted and continued to watch. By this time a number of the townspeople had gathered, and others were coming as quickly as they could. It was apparent that the sight was drawing people from as far away as they could run to the beach. Chief Morris's wife and four-year-old daughter joined him and brought his telescope. He noticed a number of other spectators using telescopes as well.

"Hey, Homer," Morris said. "Guess what? That isn't an American ship. Looks like a German flag."

"Yeah," Homer replied. "And those don't look like American flags on the warships either."

After further discussion they decided there was no reason why a German ship couldn't have run aground. As to the German ships helping out, well, why not? Only thing was, the liner didn't look aground; instead it seemed to be floating freely and held in place by its anchor.

The crowd grew even more excited when the warships lowered boats and sent men over to the liner. Shortly after, the lifeboats on the liner filled with men and were lowered to the water.

"Chief, are all those people on the boats wearing the same thing? Like uniforms?" asked Homer.

"Yep, and those look like rifles they're carrying."

"Holy shit," yelled Homer. "Now I am going to get those assholes in New York to pay attention!" With that, he ran off toward his ho-tel and the telephone.

The lifeboats gathered in a group and commenced to row toward shore. It was obvious that the sailors from the warships were work-ing the oars while those who seemed to be soldiers sat and waited. For what? Chief Morris wondered.

As the boats rowed closer to shore, the crowd, now quite large, drew nearer to the beach, almost by instinct. On board the closest German ship, the light cruiser *Gazelle,* the captain looked on that movement with dismay. What had once been a lonely stretch of sand was now packed with people. Were they armed? Of course they were! All Americans were riflemen, and wasn't this part of the country the home of the Minutemen?

The captain of the *Gazelle* looked at the soldiers huddled helplessly in the little boats, jammed so tightly they couldn't raise their arms and fire back if they wished to. Almost three hundred men being rowed toward shore and all of them possibly heading for a slaughter. He couldn't take the chance. His duty was clear.

"Open fire on the beach!"

Within seconds half a dozen of his ten 4.1-inch guns roared, sending shells into the packed humanity at virtually point-blank range, while machine guns on the deck clattered and scythed the human crop on the beach. The explosions hurled sand and bodies into the air. The survivors swirled, like leaves in a vagrant wind, not knowing what to do, then turned and ran away from the ships and toward the town. A second broadside was fired with the same deadly results: the gun captains had calculated the retreat and sighted their weapons accordingly.

Inside the hotel, Homer had indeed made contact with New York and now they were interested, very interested, particularly about the soldiers. When the ships opened fire, Homer screamed in disbelief into the open phone and, sobbing, described the carnage on the beach. He was still trying to report when a shell from the third volley crashed into the hotel, destroying it and blowing the life out of his body.

Instead of fleeing inland with the others, a panic-stricken Willy Talmadge screamed and ran down the beach as fast as his thin legs could propel him. He was unharmed.

Blake Morris turned and ran from the beach as soon as he saw the guns fire. The concussions hurled him to the ground and momentarily deafened him. He rose quickly and looked for his wife. She too was running from the beach. Her skirts were hiked up around her hips, and she was carrying their screaming daughter in her arms. Morris automatically figured them to be about a hundred yards ahead, and he started moving faster than he ever thought possible to reach them.

There had to be screams, perhaps even his own, but he could hear nothing. He tried to yell for her to hurry, prayed for her to hurry.

Suddenly, the earth about her opened up and a mountain of dirt leaped for the sky. Later, he would desperately try to recall if he saw her and the child in that explosion, but he could never be certain.

He lurched forward to the smoking crater. There was nothing. He looked about and saw pieces of cloth on the ground and bits of things that were red. He screamed, and this time he could hear it.

On board the *Gazelle,* the German captain called a cease-fire. The mob on the shore was no longer a threat. The lifeboats were on the sand and the soldiers already disembarking and fanning out in open skirmish formation. He peered through his telescope at the lifeless bodies on the beach and elsewhere, ignoring the fleeing survivors who were fast disappearing into the nearby woods. Search as he might, he could not see any weapons. His heart filled with a sickened dread. There had to be weapons. Dear God, there had to be weapons. Please.

Patrick Mahan stretched his six-foot body on the stiff cot. After so many years in the military, he still found it difficult to get comfortable on one of the damned things. He was surprised that he had slept at all, but he obviously had.

The clock on the wall told him it was 6:00 in the morning of Monday, June 3, 1901. He remembered that he was in the war room on the second level of the White House.

He stood up, and his rustling alerted a servant, who came in with a bowl of water and a cloth to refresh him. Equally important, he directed him to the little room down the hall where he could relieve the suddenly intense pressures on his bladder and bowels. The same servant told him they had taken the liberty of cleaning and pressing the uniforms and clothing in his baggage.

Mind and body clear, he changed into a uniform and sipped a cup of coffee. He had to admit that the service was excellent; he could easily get used to staying at the White House. If only they provided something better than cots.

He turned at the sound of footsteps. Teddy Roosevelt entered, his face grim. "I hope you slept well." When Patrick assured him he had, Roosevelt continued. "It appears things are happening. The phone lines to New York came up a few moments ago, and the New York papers are saying there've been fires and explosions in both the city and the harbor. They also say a number of strange ships have been sighted either in or approaching the harbor."

Roosevelt stared at the silent phones and telegraph in the war room. "Of course, no one thought to tell us first." He sighed. "Perhaps they assumed we already knew. After all, we are the government. By the way, I have not told McKinley. Let the man rest while he can. That is also why I didn't waken you."

"What about landings?"

"Nothing yet. Thank God."

There was a clatter of footsteps on the stairs and a half-dozen soldiers entered the room with a young and very nervous lieutenant. Roosevelt waved off a salute and the men took up stations by the communications equipment. "One of Captain Hedges's ideas," explained Roosevelt. "He also sent a platoon of infantry to provide additional security for the White House. Other units are being quietly scattered throughout the city. The ones here will be housed in the conservatory for the time being and simply be a standby reserve."

Stand by for what? Patrick thought. Before he could comment, the phone rang and was answered by one of the young soldiers, who listened and appeared to spasm slightly before gaining control of himself.

"Sir," he said, directing his comment to the vice president, "the caller is saying that unknown soldiers are landing on beaches along the south shore of Long Island. He also says there's been a lot of fighting and many casualties. He's also heard something about a massacre somewhere."

William McKinley chose that moment to enter the room. The information appeared to stagger him, and Roosevelt grabbed his arm. Patrick was shocked by McKinley's appearance. The man who was so imposing a physical specimen that he had been described by some as a statue now appeared to have lost all color and life. The vibrant, angry man of yesterday seemed but a shell. Patrick quickly recalled that McKinley had served in the Union army in the Civil War as well as having been commander in chief during the Spanish war, so this was his third war. And this for an old man who professed an abhorrence and hatred of violence.

Roosevelt took McKinley to a chair and tried to make him comfortable. It was questionable whether he succeeded.

From that point on, the day became a blur. Calls and telegrams poured in, confirming the worst. Soldiers, now positively identified as German, had indeed landed on Long Island and were advancing along the shore toward the Brooklyn side of New York, where a flotilla of German warships was now in plain sight. Behind them were scores of merchant ships and liners, all obviously full of soldiers and materiel.

Governor Odell called out the National Guard at about ten in the morning and reported that a handful of German nationals had been taken into custody and were being charged with sabotage. The governor also asked where the hell the rest of the American army was.

McKinley sipped a glass of water. Some of his color seemed to be returning. "It is a good question, is it not? What do we have that can assist them?"

Roosevelt shook his head. "Nothing. Not a damned thing. There may have been a navy ship or two in the harbor, but I doubt it. There is no army post of any size within hundreds of miles, and the coastal fortifications appear to have been either taken by surprise or blown up by saboteurs. Of course," he added ruefully, "our coastal forts were a farce anyhow."

About noon, Secretary of State John Hay arrived, along with Lt. Gen. Nelson Miles, the commanding general of the U.S. Army.

General Miles was a vain and bristly man who had a deserved reputation of presuming slights at the drop of a hat. John Hay, on the other hand, was a courtly gentleman who had begun his government service decades before as the assistant personal secretary to Abraham Lincoln during the Civil War. He accepted his introduction to Patrick with a warming grace, whereas Miles simply glared. Hay, at sixty-three, was a year older than Miles.

"John," said McKinley to his secretary of state. "Should we have expected this? Why have we been so surprised?"

"In all my life, sir, I have never been so totally shocked. I thought I had seen all manner of strange things when dealing with the Germans, but this tops them all. I knew they were upset with us for insisting that they stay out of the Western Hemisphere, but never, never did anyone at the State Department even remotely anticipate what they are doing! And they have us so helpless!" He turned to Miles. "Have they not?"

Miles looked as though he had swallowed something sour. As commanding general, he surely took the question as a rebuke. "Totally," he said finally. "The state militias and the National Guard are all there is. Even if they succeed in making contact with the Germans, they will be defeated. They have had little training and less in the way of necessary equipment. No, gentlemen, the bulk of our regular army, such as it is, is well away from New York."

Patrick knew that the major units of the regular army, and the better-trained units of volunteers, were, in large part, in the Philippines, fighting the Moro insurrectionists. The remaining regular units were located primarily in the West, near the Indian reservations and along the border with Mexico.

With that the issue of the army was resolved, although to no one's satisfaction. They then turned to the status and whereabouts of the navy. Unfortunately, neither the secretary of the navy nor any ranking naval officer had yet been located. Roosevelt, however, had once been assistant secretary of the navy and, with his continued interest in naval affairs, had a fair idea of its whereabouts.

"One squadron is in the Philippines," Roosevelt said. "With another squadron in or about Cuba, and a handful of remaining ships at Norfolk, Boston, Brooklyn, San Francisco, or on solo cruises."

Hay sat back in a comfortable chair. "So, what do we do now?"

Before anyone could answer, another telegram was handed to McKinley, who read it and passed it to Roosevelt. "German infantry are now in Brooklyn and appear headed for the waterfront. The German ships are heading for the docks as well." The German army in Brooklyn? It seemed almost ludicrous, Patrick thought. Might they stop at Coney Island?

Miles stood. His face was florid. "Well, now it becomes obvious. They are going to take the docks and disembark a major force under the protection of their naval guns!"

To Patrick, it sounded very similar to what he had suggested might happen the day before. He caught Roosevelt's eye and, despite the tension in the room, the man winked slightly. Patrick realized that it is sometimes a shame to be proven right.

McKinley waved a limp hand. All the weakness of the earlier part of the day appeared to return. "Theodore, what should we do?" His voice was almost a whine, and Patrick shuddered.

Roosevelt put his hands behind his back and puffed out his chest.

"Do? We must defeat them. But first we must find out more precisely what is occurring. The only reports we are getting are from hysterical politicians and irresponsible newspapers. I propose we send our own observers to New York to report back on the facts and not on the rumors. In the meantime, I suggest we ask the states and Congress to give us control of the local National Guard units before something awful happens to them. At the same time I would like General Miles to take command of the guard and alert what regular units we have to be available and ready for a possible move to New York."

Hay nodded. "And what about those observers? How many and who?"

Roosevelt grinned maliciously. "For the time being, one." He laughed, more of a bark than a laugh, and pointed at Patrick. "Him!"

The others looked at Patrick, who had been silent for some time and who could only nod agreement. It was logical. He had no command responsibilities and would not be missed. He was also intrigued at the thought of heading north to where the action was.

Roosevelt quickly sent a messenger to the train station to commandeer an engine and a caboose for a high-speed run to New York, about two hundred miles away. They hoped Patrick could be there in about ten hours, allowing for the inevitable turmoil.

Roosevelt was concerned about the rumors of panic and chaos within the city, and he gave Patrick the names of friends to contact who could provide places to stay. "I think the hotels will be in a state of uproar. Besides, I wish you to remain an anonymous observer for as long as possible. That reminds me, I think it best you travel in civilian clothes."

Isn't this where I came in? Patrick thought. Civilian clothes again? Perhaps this time they'll be more presentable, thanks to the White House domestics. Of course, clothes are a silly thing to be concerned about under the circumstances. Interesting the way the mind works.

"One last thing, Patrick, and I think the president will concur. My own experience tells me that a mere major will not be taken seriously when it comes time for him to identify himself as a presidential emissary. Since I also believe that the military will be greatly expanding, I propose you be the first beneficiary of this sad fact. Mr. President, I suggest you promote Major Mahan immediately to the rank of full colonel. Temporary rank, of course."

McKinley looked at General Miles. "Your thoughts, General?"

When Roosevelt first made the suggestion, Miles looked as though
he would explode. But then logic set in and he quickly realized what
could happen to the current commanding general of an army that
might just grow many times its current size. He smiled, almost benignly, as he contemplated the possibility of a grateful Congress and
the president granting him the fourth star of a full general. It would
be the crowning achievement of his long career. "I concur, Mr. President. Congratulations, Colonel Mahan, and godspeed."

Chapter 4

IN THE SCHUYLER apartment, four floors above the East River, Patrick sipped a cup of excellent coffee and took in the scene below where a German cruiser insolently and unbelievably patrolled, its turreted guns pointed skyward from its sleek gray deck. The white-uniformed crew was in plain sight, and walked about the decks as if on a holiday.

It was Wednesday; the supposed short and quick run to New York City on a commandeered train had taken more than twice as long as anticipated, presidential orders or not. Transportation in and out of the city was chaotic. Many unscheduled trains fled filled with the first rush of what were bound to be many refugees, while stationmasters along the way tried to juggle rights-of-way to avoid disaster. Patrick knew of at least one head-on collision and many dead and injured. It sobered him and made it more logical that he arrive safely and alive rather than early.

He recalled that yesterday, Tuesday afternoon, had found him in Jersey City, his view of the events largely blocked by Manhattan. He did think, however, that some of the silhouettes on the water were those of the enemy. The Jersey shore was full of people craning their necks to see the wondrous and terrifying event: the Germans had invaded.

The ferries that transported mobs of people from Manhattan Island to New Jersey had to return to pick up more passengers, so finding transportation across the river was no great chore. Once Patrick was on Manhattan, however, getting to his destination—the residence of Jacob Schuyler—proved impossible until the driver of a carriage succumbed to the temptation of a ten-dollar gold piece. For the duration of the ride, Patrick sat in the back with his right hand firmly around the handle of a revolver, which he let the driver glimpse on · more than one occasion.

The narrow city streets were filled with angry, sullen people, and fights broke out frequently. The carriage wheels crunched through broken glass; many store windows had been smashed and shops plundered. He was glad he had not worn his uniform. It likely would have made him a focus of the crowd's anger, which, justifiably, centered on the government's inability to prevent the travesty occurring before their eyes.

He saw a body lying facedown in a puddle. Two small children stood by, fascinated. "Looter," said the driver.

"Where in God's name are the police?" Patrick asked.

"Protectin' the rich people. Where the hell else would they be?" He laughed harshly. "Don't worry none. You'll be safe where you're goin'."

When Patrick had arrived the night before at the Schuyler apartments, armed with a letter of introduction from their good friend Theodore Roosevelt, he was disappointed to find that Jacob Schuyler was out of town. His daughter, Katrina, was at home and assigned him a room that overlooked the East River. When he was told the Schuylers had apartments, he hadn't known what to expect. Certainly not the thirty rooms they occupied, along with their several servants.

Nor was Katrina what he had expected, given such a totally Dutch name. He'd thought of her as a blond dumpling with blue eyes and a vapid, giggly personality. But instead of being plump, Katrina was slender, almost thin. She stood slightly over average height but appeared taller because of her thinness and because she carried herself very straight, with almost military precision, and dressed quite primly. She was also a little older than he had expected. He guessed that she was in her late twenties or early thirties, a spinster and well over marriage age. She appeared distraught, tired, alone, and concerned.

At least he'd been right about the blond hair and the bluish eyes,

Patrick thought as he sipped his morning coffee and wondered what the new day would bring.

"Good morning, Colonel. Is the view to your satisfaction?"

Patrick placed his coffee cup on a table and turned. "Hardly, Miss Schuyler. I find it most depressing."

She nodded. "Now you know how I've found it over the past couple of days. To be honest, I am delighted you are here even though I might not have shown it very well last night. There was that horrid feeling that we—that is, everyone in New York—had been abandoned. What with the explosions of Sunday night and the invasions and the mobs of looters, my world has been a nightmare."

Of course, he thought, and that would have accounted for her distracted and confused behavior of yesterday. He had to admit she looked far less unattractive, although now, rested and under control, there was an air of formidability that he hadn't noticed. While she was far from a beauty—her face was thin, her nose a little long, and he hadn't yet seen her smile—he found her looks interesting. Interesting—now there's a word to be damned with, he thought.

"And what ship is that?" she asked, looking at the German cruiser.

"Her name is the *Hela,* a small cruiser."

"Not a battleship? Are we so insignificant that we don't even rate a battleship?"

He told her the larger ships were doubtless out at sea or in the harbor keeping a watch for the American navy.

She gestured to the table. "You've read the morning papers, I see. Anything of note?"

"Other than a level of vitriol against things German, there is a wide divergence of opinion. The Hearst paper wants us to invade Germany, while the others call for the army to do its job immediately. They seem to forget we don't have that much of an army. There are hints that McKinley should resign or be impeached for letting this happen to us."

She pulled an envelope from her pocket and handed it to him. "This is for you."

Surprised, he opened it. Inside were the insignia of a colonel in the U.S. Army. "They belong to my father," she explained. "He wore them against Spain, although he never left the city." She laughed, and he saw she did have nice teeth and a pleasant smile. "You said last night how quickly you'd been rushed here, and I thought you might find these useful when it comes time to show your true colors."

He stammered his thanks.

"So, sir, now that the army's here and in full control, what are your plans for disarming the Germans and driving them off? I wish to tell Mr. Hearst."

Damn, was she making fun of him? Her mouth was set again but her eyes were laughing. He drew himself to his full height and stood at attention. "Miss Schuyler, I intend to rent a small boat, paddle over, and inform them that they must leave or pay the consequences. The American army shall not be trifled with.

"Seriously, my plans are to go to the waterfront and observe what I can. I will be leaving shortly and, with your permission, hope to return early this afternoon. I already used your telephone to contact my superiors in Washington."

"Is that safe? Using the phone, I mean. Couldn't an operator overhear you?"

"Yes, but it's a chance we have to take. There were some precautions to at least forestall that. For instance, the number I call is answered as the Windsor Hotel, even though it goes directly to the White House war room."

That struck both of them as just a little funny under the circumstances. Katrina, however, became serious very quickly. "When you go observing, I will go with you." When he started to protest, she waved him silent. "Please note that I am not asking your permission, Colonel, I am telling you what I will do. We will take my carriage, and two of my servants, armed, for additional protection. Believe me, sir, it is very important that I see what is actually happening. My family has been in this town, in this area, for many, many generations. I feel so angry that I will not be deterred."

Patrick resigned himself to her company and, shortly, they began moving down streets that paralleled the East River. He was gratified to see that the hysteria of the preceding day had subsided and that the crowds, although excited, were not in a state of panic. It was also, he realized, far too early in the day for them to be liquored up.

A number of armed men in uniform, obviously local militia, had taken control of the streets and were enforcing order. A couple of quick conversations between Katrina and officers whom she appeared

to know told them both that at least three regiments were bivouack-
ing in Central Park and were trying to anticipate the Germans' next
move. One young officer also added that many heavy wagons were
being assembled and, once loaded, would be sent under the heaviest
possible guard to the ferries and across to safety in New Jersey. Their
contents would be the money and bullion from the banks as well as
the stocks and other valuables necessary to keep America's financial
world operating.

The officer was not thrilled at the prospect. "I'm afraid the same
people who've done so much looting will realize what's in the wagons, and a mob will try to overwhelm them." He shook his head.
"Even though the governor has ordered at least one regiment to
guard the wagons, I'm afraid there will be fighting and rioting before
we get them to safety. A lot of people could be killed."

Patrick agreed. "But we can't leave all this for the Germans to
take if they come across or decide to seal off the island, can we?"
responded Patrick, who was appalled that a junior officer knew of
the plans and was so blithely informing people of them. There was
no secrecy.

"No, we can't, mister. Lord, what a mess." With that, he excused
himself and let Patrick and Katrina continue on.

The first point of note was, of course, the Brooklyn Bridge, which
connected Manhattan to the very place where the Germans were
landing. The Manhattan side was barricaded by a miscellany of carriages, carts, barrels, and anything else that could be put in place
quickly. What appeared to be several hundred policemen were augmented by a horde of civilians and others in militia and National
Guard uniforms. There were even several old men in what could only
have been Civil War uniforms. Patrick again was glad he hadn't worn
his own uniform. Despite that, there were a number of hollered requests for him and Katrina's two servants to join the defenders. He
lied easily, saying they'd be back later when they returned the lady
to safety. For her part, Katrina smiled demurely and they drove on.

Pathetic, Patrick thought, that a few hundred unarmed or half-
armed and undisciplined men could even think of halting the German
army should it decide to cross the bridge. They'd be brushed aside in
minutes and the lucky ones merely humiliated.

Finally they reached a point near decrepit old Battery Park, near the stinking and immigrant-filled slums of the Lower East Side where they had a good view of the harbor. Before them lay the vast panorama of invasion. Hundreds, perhaps thousands, of other New Yorkers gathered to watch, mainly in silence. Stretched to the horizon were scores of freighters and ocean liners waiting to disembark their cargo, human and materiel, at the Brooklyn docks. Protecting and screening them were at least a dozen large warships, which, thank God, appeared to be unconcerned about the crowds of spectators watching the show.

After a while, Patrick, Katrina, and the two servants went to the roof of a building and observed further. Using field glasses, Patrick could easily see the lines of gray-clad soldiers leaving the ships and marching inland. It was a precise and awesome performance. On a nearby rooftop, he noticed two men with what he recognized as a movie camera, probably from Mr. Edison's Biograph Laboratory in New Jersey. He wondered what they would do with the pictures, where they would show them. After observing for a while, Patrick suggested they leave. Saddened and silent, they returned to the Schuyler home.

Once there, he excused himself to use the telephone and, to his surprise, had little trouble getting through to the "Windsor Hotel" for his report.

A moment after he disconnected, Katrina tapped on the door, entered, and took a seat on a luxurious couch. Yesterday's look of anguish had returned, and she appeared to have been crying. "What now, Colonel?"

"I'm going north and east across the Hudson before Manhattan is cut off." Patrick shrugged and smiled wanly. "I wouldn't be able to do much observing as a prisoner, would I?"

She paled. "You think that will happen?"

He explained to her calmly that cutting off Manhattan was very likely, that indeed it was the only logical thing for the Germans to do. They had, he estimated, landed the better part of an entire division and appeared to be picking up the pace. They could land about five to six thousand men a day, with their heavy equipment taking a little longer.

He told her to visualize the area. Manhattan, as so many seem to forget, is indeed an island, even though the Harlem River to the north is not much of a barrier to traffic or commerce and is crossed at a number of points. However, a military force could turn it into an extremely effective moat. Thus, he explained further, the Germans would likely head north and off Long Island, which would logically carry them along the Harlem River, thereby severing Manhattan from the rest of the world. The city would then be under siege and easily invested. Sieges, he told her, were grim and cruel events. He quickly recounted the horrors of the siege of Paris by the Germans in 1871 and, of course, Vicksburg and Petersburg in the Civil War. As sieges inevitably wore on, the besieged were always confronted by disease, starvation, and the likelihood of sudden and violent death. Death, he told her, was often preferable to being wounded in such an environment.

"I've only read about sieges, I've never actually seen one. And, Miss Schuyler, I don't ever wish to. What I've read of them is enough. Starvation and disease are the rule, not the exception."

"The Germans would do this?"

"They really have no choice. They came here for a purpose, and that purpose is not to sit on Long Island and be trapped there by an American army. No, they will move off to the interior as soon as they are strong enough. It would not surprise me at all if advance units have already taken some of the crossing points. Therefore, I must get out of here as quickly as possible." He looked at an ornate bronze clock on the mantle and automatically wondered how much it cost. More importantly, it told him it was just after noon. He would have thought it much later. "With regrets, I will leave very soon."

"Again, I will come with you."

He started to object and changed his mind. Why shouldn't she flee the horrors of siege and conquest? "All right. Be ready quickly and be prepared to travel light. Will your two hired hands be available? We may need them."

They would. She quickly explained that they could take a carriage or horses north over the Harlem River where it met the Hudson and continue north from there. They both agreed that horses would be more advantageous than a carriage simply because a horse could go so many more places. With the possibility that roads might be blocked, the ability to travel cross-country might prove important.

"Colonel, since we are going to be traveling companions, I would appreciate your calling me Katrina, or Trina. Miss Schuyler sounds as though I am your teacher. And I will call you Pat or Patrick. Which do you prefer?"

"Either, but most wind up calling me Patrick. Now, what will you do when we reach what we feel is safety?"

"Simple. With all the refugees and a war on, there will be many opportunities to help. I'm certain the Red Cross will be out in force and I will volunteer to help them. Who knows, perhaps Miss Barton herself will be there."

He winced again. She was correct in her implication that the Red Cross would be on duty well before the army could even dream of arriving.

She left and returned in a few moments with a small traveling bag full of clothing and other essentials. "For your information, Patrick, we also have a home in Albany. If volunteering is not an answer, I will go there."

He was about to say something when a series of loud noises and explosions shook the room and jostled vases on the shelves. They ran to the nearest window and looked out. Along with the explosions there was what Patrick quickly recognized as the distinctive rattle and pop of rifle and machine-gun fire. Were the Germans attacking and crossing the bridge?

Mercifully, whatever was occurring could not be seen from their observation point, although clouds of dark smoke quickly emerged from the Brooklyn side.

"Patrick, what has happened?"

"Who knows? Anything and everything. Perhaps some well-intentioned fools made an attack on the Germans."

The cannonading continued with a fury like nothing he'd ever heard and without letup for the better part of an hour. By this time plumes of smoke trailed into the sky from many points, and it was obvious that a number of major fires had started.

"Katrina, we must leave right now." When she started to say something, he stopped her. "Look at the fires. Who on earth is going to put them out? That is a catastrophe beginning over there and nothing can stop it! There are going to be more refugees than you ever thought possible as soon as they figure out that running is better than being shot or burned to death." She swallowed and concurred.

When they left the apartments, the streets were filling rapidly, and many other people were headed north. Some were grim-faced and determined; others showed signs of panic. A cart in front of them overturned and they were forced to urge their horses over someone's well-kept lawn in order to pass it. Free of the obstruction, Patrick looked behind and saw his worst fears confirmed. The multitude of individual fires across the East River had coalesced into one great cloud of smoke through which he could see occasional tongues of flame.

"Patrick," Katrina said, "check the wind."

He did and nodded confirmation. It was from the west. No ashes would fly over and onto Manhattan, but Brooklyn would doubtless be scorched.

When they finally reached the Harlem River, it was a scene from Dante. Mobs of people, rich and poor, walking and in wagons or carriages, pushed or were trying to push their way onto the bridges that connected Manhattan with the Bronx. Even on a good day, the traffic was heavy; this day it was impossible. The river was little more than a narrow and muddy stream, but it was not crossable by foot. Scores of boats of all sizes ferried people back and forth, and Patrick and Katrina saw riders and their horses swimming the muck. At Patrick's urging the four of them formed a compact mass and pushed their way through the mob, oblivious to the curses hurled at them. Finally they reached a small boat whose owner, a grinning little man in filthy clothes, demanded fifty dollars to take them across. Patrick thought about arguing, but others behind him were shouting that they would pay. Patrick handed over the money and the four were ferried across with the guards holding the reins of the horses, which swam easily alongside.

They had barely remounted when they heard the sound of shots and screams. An expensive carriage with a well-dressed family had tried to bull its way onto a bridge and had run someone over. Friends of the injured person then stormed the carriage and shot the driver, who was dragged bleeding from his seat and disappeared into the crowd. While they watched in horror, the mob turned on the family inside, plucked them out one by one, and hurled them into the river, where they were pelted with rocks and debris until they disappeared under the dark water.

Katrina's mouth was open in shock at the sudden violence. Neither of them had ever seen anything like it in their lives. "We've become animals," she said finally.

With much of the fleeing throng still trapped on the wrong side of the river, the roads were not crowded and they were able to urge their horses to a trot. They had barely gone a mile when they saw a score of horsemen in dark gray uniforms. The Germans rode with the insolence of conquerors as they idly scattered the refugees in their path like a flock of chickens.

"Patrick, they don't even care about us, do they?" The grinning Germans passed within fifty yards of them.

"No, we're nothing to them. They're just scouting the area."

"Patrick, this nightmare isn't going to end, is it?"

No, he thought, not for a very long time.

Chapter 5

LUDWIG WEBER, A private in the kaiser's Imperial 4th Rifles, gripped his usually clean and well-oiled Mauser with an unholy fervor and wished he were someplace else than this city of hell. Sweat dripped down his face for many reasons. First, it was hot, and his uniform wasn't intended for the steamy weather. Second, he had just survived his first encounter with an armed enemy intent upon killing him, a fact that also accounted for the dirty and smudged condition of his rifle. Third, he was only a few hundred yards away from the sea of flame that seemed to be consuming the city of Brooklyn.

What a change, he thought. Was it only a year ago that he, a teacher of English in a private school just outside Munich, had been conscripted to serve the Prussians in the Imperial Army? God, what had happened to him? First they took away his dignity and made him a private soldier, an automaton, a nobody, and then they taught him how to march and kill for the glory of the emperor and the Reich.

Then they took him away from his home and placed him in a large, cramped, oceangoing vessel where he spent almost two weeks in unwashed and unwanted intimacy with thousands like him. The passage had been horrible, and he'd spent much of it covered with puke. The whole ship and its human cargo smelled of shit and piss. If he hadn't vomited so much from seasickness, the unholy stench generated by his comrades would have made him ill. Was this why he had educated himself? He was twenty-two years old. Would his life end here?

To consummate his problems, a vengeful god had also given him to Corporal Kessel. Otto Kessel was an illiterate and hulking blond-haired brute who hated with a passion anything better than himself. He was a bully, a sadist, a murderer, and a rapist. Weber had heard with horror of Kessel's so-called adventures in China where, apparently with the blessings of senior officers, he had behaved like a pig, rutting and killing. Weber found it difficult to believe that anything like Otto Kessel existed on an earth that God made.

Worse, Kessel hated Weber. Or did he love him? For the two months since Kessel's assignment to the company, Weber was the primary focus of Kessel's actions. He bullied him verbally, punched him and kicked him when he thought he could get away with it, and robbed him whenever any relative or friend sent Weber something of value. Whenever possible, of course, Weber would try to avoid Kessel, particularly when Kessel was drunk, which was a good deal of the time. Weber could see that the other officers in the company, especially Captain Walter, were puzzled by Kessel, but since they had no reason to do otherwise, they largely ignored him.

On board the ship, Kessel had tried to molest Weber, and the thought of it made him even more nauseous. Weber recalled a time during the voyage when, thinking himself safe and alone on a secluded part of the deck, he'd suddenly found himself imprisoned in the man's immense arms while Kessel's hands roamed and groped his body. The chance sound of approaching voices made Kessel release him and depart. Weber was fully warned now and even more careful. He tried to never be alone.

However, his and everyone else's spirits lifted when they splashed ashore on the clean, sandy beaches of America. Their landing was unopposed, although rumors spoke of places where skirmishes had been quickly won.

Once ashore they'd quick-marched down country roads in what Weber realized was the direction of New York. The fact that they were tired and cramped from their time on the ship was of no concern. Their destination was an urgent one. They could all see from the lines of gray-clad soldiers that thousands of others were also involved. For the first time he realized this was an invasion and not a raid.

After several hours of hard marching, a brief pause for water turned into several minutes, and Weber realized the entire exhausted and hungry company was alone. Up front he could see Captain Walter and the other officers and senior noncoms talking animatedly. He edged himself closer and could see that the captain, a young man only a few years older than he, who seemed to be really quite a decent sort, was getting agitated. Then it dawned on him. They were lost.

"Hey, asshole!" Kessel yelled behind him. "Get your sweet butt back to the squad." Weber sighed. It was an opportunity that he had to take no matter what the consequences. He dusted himself off and walked up to the knot of men, came to attention, saluted, and announced himself.

"Captain, Private Weber requests permission to speak, sir."

Captain Walter looked annoyed, the other officers looked shocked, and the company first sergeant looked as though he would strangle him. One major rule for survival was to not piss off Sergeant Gunther.

"Not now, Private," the captain said gently. The first sergeant moved as if to propel him back to his place, and he was aware of the utter silence behind him. Not even Kessel had anything to say. No one in the Imperial Army spoke to an officer, particularly one with as exalted a rank as a captain, without first being ordered to.

"Sir," Weber persisted, a slight note of panic growing in his voice. "Please excuse my impertinence, sir, but I teach English. I both read it and speak it fluently." To his relief, he saw a flicker of interest in the captain's eyes and continued. "I also have studied much about this area and have relatives here." As a youth he had spent a summer in New York with an aunt and uncle, but he saw no reason to divulge that information at this time. "If you are looking for a quicker way into the city, I may be of assistance."

Captain Walter blinked and smiled slightly. "A quicker way? Yes, that's one way of putting it." Weber saw the others relax and take their cue from the captain. Yes, Weber was right. They were lost.

In a few words and gestures and with only a quick look at the inadequate maps the captain had, Weber guided them in the correct direction and they soon caught up with other German columns. When he was certain they were no longer lost, he asked the captain if he should return to his squad.

"Do you really read and write English? I mean the English the Americans speak?" asked the captain.

"Yes, sir."

"Well then, you are the only one in the entire company who does. I will be damned if you are going back to any squad. I need you here. First sergeant! Have this man transferred to my headquarters. I don't care what regulations say, I now have another clerk." Then he laughed. "No, make him the company translator."

The first sergeant cuffed him on the shoulder and parted his mouth in a gap-toothed leer that might have once been a smile. "Good lad. When the captain's happy, everyone's happy."

And so am I happy, Weber thought, and a hearty fuck you, Corporal Kessel.

The happiness had lasted until about two hours ago. For a couple of days they stood perimeter guard while the ships in the harbor unloaded their cargoes. Then, when the perimeter got too tight, they were ordered to advance from the docks farther into the city itself. They were not going to do anything but expand their area a few dozen blocks to alleviate the cramping of men and supplies. But unlike the march into Brooklyn, where the crowds had seemed stunned and cowed by the presence of armed, marching soldiers, this slight move was resisted.

When the Germans moved out in skirmish formation to clear the streets and nearby buildings, the shouting began, and crowds gathered with astonishing quickness. From rooftops and windows the obscenities and challenges were hurled, along with an occasional and inaccurately aimed brick or bottle. Nevertheless, the populace retreated, albeit cautiously, as the soldiers advanced.

Soon, however, the soldiers were confronted by barricades. Wagons and other conveyances were turned on their sides and stacked in the streets with people behind them. To Weber's horror, he could see that many Americans were armed with rifles and shotguns.

The Americans opened fire when the Germans were about a half block away. The exposed German infantry ducked and tried to take cover under the hail of bullets, most of which went wild. Even so, there were casualties. A man next to Weber went down with a scream. Weber saw a large hole in the man's leg and blood gushing onto the ground.

"Fire!"

The order came and Weber obeyed. He shouldered his Mauser and began pumping bullets into the barricade, which seemed to explode in splinters and chaos. There were screams and howls of pain and rage as people were hit.

"Fall back!"

Why? Weber thought. Despite the fact that he didn't want to be here, his blood was up. Those stupid people had tried to kill him! How dare they? Didn't they know he meant them no harm? And now they had to be killed. How foolish they were to even try to stop the Imperial German Army. My God, he thought, I am beginning to sound like a soldier.

When the Germans reached their original start point, Weber understood why they had been ordered to fall back as he heard the warships opening up with their great cannon. He realized that it was much better to let the big guns chew up the barricades than to storm them in the face of rifle fire. Along with the others, he exulted as this ultimate display of German might raged against the enemy.

Of course it had never been anyone's intent to burn the city; it was just another example of how things race out of control when people start killing each other. It hadn't taken long for Weber's pride to turn to horror as he watched the flames roar through the crowded buildings. He waited in vain for the fire brigades to come and put them out even after the bombardment had finally ceased. How naive, he thought. There will be no fire brigades. The clean and lovely city of Brooklyn—no, it is called a borough now—will burn until the fires run out of things to burn.

For the rest of the day and the night he and the others watched in stunned disbelief while Brooklyn was largely destroyed. Their horrified eyes saw sights that they would never forget. They saw the tightly packed brick buildings erupt with people carrying whatever they could, often just bundles of clothing, sometimes not even that, as they tried to flee. They saw the eager flames lick at and take the tardy, turning them into running, screaming torches. They saw panic as the Americans trampled the slow and the weak in their efforts to get out of the way of the implacable and malevolent fire.

At one point, Weber may have cried. He didn't know. He saw the captain and realized that the man also felt the sadness of the terrible event.

But he didn't see Kessel. He looked around and saw the others from his old squad, but not Kessel. He asked one of his friends, who said he hadn't seen their corporal since the order came to fall back from the barricade.

Good grief, Weber thought. Could Kessel have been killed? He grinned slightly at the thought of such rough justice. What a tragedy for mankind. Perhaps now the bastard is roasting in the fires of Brooklyn in preparation for the eternal fires of hell. For the first time, Weber felt some relief. Perhaps something good would come of this awful incident.

As Molly Duggan slowly regained consciousness, the first thing she became aware of was the pain that racked portions of her body. Then she noticed she was lying on a cold floor in a strange room. She forced her eyes open through her swollen lids and looked about. Where was she? She tried to roll over onto her side, and the pain in her groin caused her to gasp.

Then she remembered. She and her brother, Cormac, had gone beyond the barricades to harass the stupid Germans with their pointed helmets. Cormac, at twenty, was four years older than she and her caretaker following the recent death of her father. Cormac was a wild one; the idea of tormenting an armed army was lunacy, but Cormac convinced her and a number of others to join in the wildness.

With whoops and hollers they approached the cowlike Germans and threw rocks and horse shit at them, then laughed when the hurled turds struck home. It stopped being funny when the Germans started moving on them with their bright bayonets flashing in the sun. The tormentors had run back to the barricades, where, with an unladylike leap to the top of an overturned wagon, Molly yelled an obscenity she'd heard an angry customer in her father's butcher shop exclaim over the price of a cut of meat. Cormac looked shocked, then laughed.

In a burst of sound the world ended and Cormac's head exploded in a froth of bone and gray meat as the Germans opened fire. Molly screamed and fell off the wagon she was using for a platform as more gunfire swept the crowd, now trying to run from the barricade that had once seemed so strong. German soldiers, firing from the waist, clambered over it and the crowd scattered. Molly took shelter in a storefront that was empty and being rebuilt. As the Germans prowled the streets, looking for more prey, she hid behind a counter, not daring to breathe.

She heard footsteps crunching on the debris of the building and closed her eyes, as if the act would render her invisible. Suddenly, she was jerked upward by her long brownish red hair, and she found herself looking into the grim, ruddy face of one of the largest men she had ever seen. He said something in a guttural voice, which she took to be German. When she shook her head, he slapped her, dragged her to a back room, threw her to the floor, and, while standing on her wrist, laid aside his rifle and pack.

She screamed and tried to struggle, but it was no use; he was much too large and so much stronger. He laughed and hit her until she was barely aware of him ripping her clothes and arranging her for his convenience. She screamed again when he forced himself inside her, and he hit her again.

For a while she lay there, half conscious, in shock and pain, hoping he was gone. He wasn't. When he returned, he was more than a little drunk and even more vicious as he repeated the performance, punching her and slapping her as she tried to writhe away. Finally, he hit her hard and she lost consciousness.

But now she was conscious and remembered his savagery. She curled herself into a fetal ball and tried to think. She still was wearing some of her clothes, and the rest, although torn, were lying about. But where was the German? Could she move enough to escape? She sniffed the air. What was burning?

Molly got to her hands and knees. For a moment she was dizzy, but it passed. The pain in her face, her breasts, her ribs, and her thighs did not go away, but she realized it could be endured. She sniffed the smoke again. If something nearby was burning, then any pain she might be feeling had to be ignored!

She reached out for the rags of her clothing and lurched to her feet, relieved to find she could stand. She arranged herself as best she might and started to walk to the front room of the store. The mumbling sound of a human voice stopped her. Carefully, she peered in. There was her German. Fear and nausea nearly overcame her; then she realized the German, squatting on the floor with his back to her, was soddenly drunk. His rifle was on the other side of the room. There were two empty bottles by his haunches, and he was swaying back and forth to an unheard rhythm.

He was also between her and the door, and the smell of smoke was getting worse. She glanced about and saw some workmen's tools, including, thankfully, a hammer. She grasped the hammer in both her small hands and, as hatred and rage overwhelmed her, brought it down on the German's head. In her pain she stumbled and her aim was bad. Although she struck only a glancing blow on his forehead, she still heard the sound of something crunch and felt the German's blood spray her. He growled like an animal and tried to get up. She swung from the waist and hit him above his left eye. He screamed and grabbed his face and she hit him again, this time squarely on the forehead. He dropped like a sack of meal. With horror, she saw that his eye was dangling from its socket and appeared to be staring at her. She hit him a couple more times, until her fury was replaced by the realization that she had better get out of there. But to where?

Her mind told her that her once-tidy world had become fearful indeed, and all the memories of home and security were gone. Cautiously, she reached for the German's rifle and picked it up. It was much heavier and more ill balanced than she expected, and she thought about leaving it. But then she grimly recalled that she'd been raped twice this day and had no inclination to have it occur again. She hadn't the foggiest idea how to use the damn thing, but it was a fearsome-looking weapon, and the bayonet looked absolutely evil.

She experimented for a moment and found she could handle it in one arm with a degree of ease. Then, clutching her tattered clothes to her with one hand and the rifle with the other, she headed out the door. She must get away from the flames she could now see advancing. She had taken but a few steps when she realized she hadn't made arrangements with Father Connelly to bury Cormac. She looked back at the churning smoke and fire that seemed to be moving closer down the abandoned streets, and sadly realized that there would be no funeral, and that Father Connelly was doubtless prudently running away as well. Good-bye, dear Cormac, she thought. She would leave him behind along with the dimming memories of a father who'd brought them from Ireland to a new world that was supposed to be clean and safe. God damn the Germans.

Patrick Mahan took steady aim at the man who held the knife to Katrina's throat. Cautiously, carefully, he tried to gauge the situation and ignore the look of stark terror on Katrina's face. How foolish they'd been to think that three men and a woman were safe once they'd cleared the mobs. Three bandits had leaped from the bushes and clubbed down the two servants, smashing their skulls, before anyone had a chance to react. In a motion that seemed to take forever, Patrick had reached for his revolver while kicking at the thug who grabbed at his leg. Finally the pistol came free and he shot the man in the face.

But now they were at an impasse. He had the gun and they had Katrina.

"Let her go," he said with as much firmness as he could muster.

"Fuck you!" said the man with the knife. "Give Charley there the gun and you both can leave."

Patrick almost smiled at the incongruity of the request. Give them the gun? Trust them? Not bloody damn likely. He turned the revolver on Charley, who was inching toward the horses. Had Katrina packed another gun in the bags? Patrick didn't think so, but he was uncertain.

He gestured to Charley. "Take whatever you want and let the girl go. Then you can leave."

The man with the knife laughed. "You got it all wrong. We're taking what we want and the girl. If you're lucky, you'll find her later when we're through fucking her and release her. And don't wave that goddamn gun around like you're actually gonna shoot. You won't take a chance on hitting the bitch."

The knife man was right. But if Patrick let them leave, then all he could do was follow them and try to get a clear shot before they got too far away. Charley had the horses and was now rummaging through the saddlebags. Shit, Patrick thought, if they ride off and leave me on foot, I'll never be able to follow, and God help Katrina. He could see by the look on her face as her eyes followed the byplay that she was aware of this as well.

Until the moment the bandits had attacked, the trip from New York had been relatively uneventful. Once they had crossed the Harlem River, it had been almost a pleasant ride in the country with Katrina and the two servants. He had found the young woman—she was younger than he—to be both pleasant and intelligent. In point of fact, she was extremely intelligent. Almost better, he discovered she had a wicked sense of humor. He enjoyed her company, however strange the current circumstances.

Now she stood a good chance of dying a violent, degrading, and painful death if he couldn't come up with some way of resolving this brutal dilemma.

"Hey," yelled Charley, "lookit this shit. Pretty boy is a sojer. Lookit the uniforms."

The knife man looked at the blue uniform held up by Charley. "That true, hero? You a soldier? You gonna fight the Krauts?"

"I am trying to report for duty, yes. Now let her go and let us go on."

The knife man sneered. "Then why ain't you wearing the fuckin' things? Know why? Cause you a deserter!" He laughed. "Now I know what you and your woman are doin'. Shit, you're running away. You ain't gonna do nothing about me and Charley 'cause you'll get hung for desertin' if you do." He found this very funny and laughed loudly.

"I am not a deserter," Patrick said grimly. "And I will kill you if you don't let her go."

The knife man used his other arm to give Katrina's breast a painful, hard squeeze, which caused her to utter a small scream before she was able to stifle it. "Hero boy, we're gonna ride out of here on your horses and, when we're far enough away, we're gonna take turns ridin' your other mare." He thought that witty and laughed again, as did Charley, who by now had the horses over by Katrina and the knife man. "And, like I said, when we're through we'll leave her for you to find." He slid his hand from Katrina's breast and let it wander down below her belly.

With a scream that came from the bowels of hell, the devil emerged from the bushes by the trail. In this case, Satan took the form of a half-naked woman, her hair singed frizzy, her face red and burned where it wasn't bruised blue. She hurled herself forward with, instead of a pitchfork, a rifle and a long bayonet.

Charley turned and opened his mouth to say something, but before he could utter a sound, the bayonet entered his throat and came out the back of his neck. He fell to the ground as the rifle did an obscene dance with his body. As the knife man turned to face this new threat, Patrick raced the few steps that separated them and yanked Katrina away before the knife man could gather his shattered wits. Patrick jammed the revolver in the knife man's side and pulled the trigger twice, with thunderous explosions. The knife man howled and fell to the ground as dead as Charley.

The sudden silence was as shocking as the violence. "Are you all right?" Patrick finally and inanely asked Katrina. She stammered that she was.

"Where'd she come from?" asked Patrick. The apparition was facedown on the ground, her back heaving as she moaned and sobbed, hollering for her father and someone named Cormac.

Katrina knelt beside the woman's side. "She's hurt rather badly. She's very young, only little more than a child." She put an arm around the sobbing girl's shoulder and tried to comfort her. After a bit, she succeeded, and the girl calmed down enough to volunteer that her name was Molly and she had no idea where she was.

As Katrina helped Molly fix her clothing into something resembling decency, she also took stock of the girl's injuries. She determined that neither the burns nor the bruises, although unsightly, were as serious as she had at first thought. Then the girl moved and her torn skirts parted. Katrina saw the additional bruises on her inner thighs and quickly realized what had happened.

"We will have to take her with us," she said grimly. "She's in no shape to be left alone."

Patrick had the rifle and was examining it. "A bright, shiny German Mauser. I wonder how she got it."

Molly Duggan raised her head and fixed him with a glare of hate through her swollen eyes. "I took it offa German. Hope I killed the fooker."

Chapter 6

TEDDY ROOSEVELT PACED nervously. It was nearly midmorning and nothing had been resolved. It was as if President McKinley didn't want to confront the fact that the nation was at war. This was worse, he thought, than the vacillations that had so delayed America's entry into the war with Spain.

And now the oppressed were not Cubans but white-skinned Americans who lived in his home state of New York. At least he had convinced McKinley of the need to call Congress into emergency session. Representatives and senators were converging on the capital with a briskness and a sense of urgency they rarely displayed. Roosevelt's contacts on Capitol Hill told him there should be enough for a quorum by early this afternoon.

John Hay entered the president's office unannounced, carrying a large and official-looking envelope. "Gentlemen, I just received this from the Italian ambassador."

"Received what?" asked McKinley in a weak voice. "What does Italy have to do with our problems?" At least, Roosevelt mused, he acknowledges that we do have problems.

Hay continued as if the response had been totally adequate and normal. "This is an official message from the German kaiser that was given to the ambassador in Rome several weeks ago. The ambassador is quite embarrassed. He had no idea that what he would be bringing over was such a critical and infamous document. He assures us that he had no wish to be put in such a compromising position, and that his young nation is a friend of the United States' and not allied with either the kaiser or his aims."

Roosevelt's impatience showed. "John, you're not negotiating another treaty. Please finish the preamble and get on with it."

Hay waved the papers. "This is an ultimatum from Germany. It was supposed to arrive here and in our hand no later than the Saturday before the invasion, so the Germans could say we had fair warning. But the fates intervened and the Italian ambassador's crossing was delayed by faulty engines in the liner he'd taken; therefore, we just received it. Since he had no idea what he was carrying, he also gave it little urgency."

Roosevelt gave up. "Will there be a time in the near future, say this year, when you might tell us what the ultimatum contains?"

Hay smiled and allowed that he would. Then he summarized the lengthy document.

Germany needed colonies for what she viewed as the legitimate expansion of the Reich.

Germany was a major world power and the United States was not.

Germany was better suited to govern the hitherto Spanish colonies than the United States. The fact that the United States was talking of freedom soon for Cuba and somewhat later on for the Philippines was a betrayal of the white man's prerogative to govern the nonwhite races, who were, of course, incapable of governing themselves.

Germany was angry that the United States did not see the logic behind this argument.

Germany's invasion was to show the United States the weakness of her position and the strength of the Imperial German military machine and, thereby, to put her in a better mood to negotiate the transfer of the requisite territories.

Germany would take from the United States the following: Cuba, Puerto Rico, the Philippines, the Hawaiian Islands, and Guam. From this time forward, Germany would be exempt from the Monroe Doctrine and would establish spheres of influence over the Isthmus of Panama and the republic of Venezuela, which, not coincidentally, owed Germany substantial sums of money and were in default. Of course, any prior arrangements regarding independence for either Cuba or the Philippines were cancelled.

Germany required that the U.S. Navy, upon completion of the hostilities, be reduced to a coastal defense force. Thus all battleships and cruisers were to be either scrapped or sold to Germany for a nominal amount. Germany was not particularly concerned about the size of any American army as, without a navy to transport it, the American army was of no consequence to Germany.

Germany would be paid the sum of one hundred million dollars in gold for the expenses incurred in the actions against the United States.

If Germany did not receive total acceptance of these terms by July 15, 1901, the amount of indemnity would rise by the amount of five million dollars per week.

For a moment, there was stunned silence. Then President McKinley looked up. "Is there any room for negotiation?"

Roosevelt jumped to his feet, his face a furious red. "Negotiate! What the hell is there to negotiate for? We've been attacked by a tyrant and a pirate. I say we raise the largest army this country's ever seen and wipe Germany off the face of the earth."

"How?" McKinley asked. "You seem to forget we have no army. No navy."

Before an astonished Roosevelt could respond, Hay spoke. "Mr. President, there may indeed be room for negotiation. I have it on good authority that they really don't want Cuba or the Philippines, but are dead set on getting Puerto Rico. Of course, that was before they attacked. God only knows what their real minimum demands will be now that blood has been spilled and their sense of greed inspired."

"Damnit, sir, I say we wage war!" Roosevelt was consumed with rage.

Hay blinked at the anger and fury in Roosevelt's voice. As a diplomat he knew how important it was to maintain calmness and rationality in even the most trying of circumstances. Now it was even more important than ever. His country could not afford emotional responses that could be tragic mistakes. "Mr. Roosevelt, I suggest that we wait until today's meeting with the military leaders to discuss feasible responses."

"Yes," said McKinley, rising to his feet. Both men noticed that the president held on to the back of a chair to steady himself. "This afternoon. We will discuss things then. I feel I must rest." With that he turned and left the two astonished men alone in the cabinet room.

Wherever William McKinley walked, the waist-high grass and crop of young summer corn had been pounded down to nothing. Worse, the sun-baked Maryland field was covered with the dead and wounded from the tragic battle that had just taken place. Even though only a couple of hours had transpired since the guns mercifully ended, the dead were already blackened and bloating, some of them emitting noxious gases as their bodies rejected themselves.

Along with the dead, some of them lying as if asleep and others lying in bloody bits, there were a number of wounded. McKinley had to watch where he placed his feet lest he step on someone and cause even more pain. Or worse, have them reach out and cry for him to help them, which, of course, he could not do. "Mother, mother," seemed to be the constant but weak chorus. He looked about for doctors, for stretcher bearers. Where were they? They were overwhelmed by the immensity of the day's events, he realized, and they would be a long time coming, if ever, with their blood-drenched wagons. There was nothing to help them.

His ears took in a heavy buzzing, humming sound and he tried to place it. Then it dawned: flies. All about were flies. Flies by the hundreds, by the millions, by numbers uncountable, a living, moving cloud that hovered a few feet above the ground. They covered every corpse and every living wounded and buzzed and munched their disgusting way to contentedness.

What horror, he thought as he gazed about. The entire field covered with bodies dressed largely in Union blue, but with a speckling of Confederate gray. Antietam, another name for horror.

"Now this, William, is a war. A real war!" Teddy Roosevelt stood in front of him, his wide-brimmed cowboy hat rakishly back on his head, his face a wide grin. "Not like what I saw against those Spanish pussycats!"

"Theodore, do you actually enjoy this?"

"Certainly, and so do you."

McKinley was shocked. "No, I hate it," he said vehemently.

Roosevelt laughed derisively. "Then why do you keep getting us involved in wars?"

"I didn't start the Civil War."

"Of course you did. You and millions like you from the North and South who wouldn't see reason and the reality that the other side would fight. And you are certainly responsible for the Spanish war."

Sadly, McKinley accepted the latter point. He had allowed himself to be manipulated by yellow journalists like Pulitzer and Hearst, and the other Manifest Destiny warmongers like Roosevelt, into accepting the dubious verdict that the explosion on the *Maine* was sabotage.

"William, don't forget the Germans."

"You blame me for that?"

"William, you are the president, the captain of the ship of state, and the invasion occurred on your watch. Of course you're responsible."

"But you're the vice president!"

Roosevelt shrugged and stepped over an armless corpse. "People will forget. In normal times, the citizenry doesn't even know, or care, who its vice president is. Besides, would you have listened to me?" McKinley agreed he would not have. "Oh, look," Roosevelt said, "Spaniards."

They had walked to a different portion of the field. Now it no longer looked like Maryland. The farm grass had been replaced by thicker and more luxuriant vegetation, more evocative of the Tropics. And these dead wore white and had sombreros and darker, Latin skins. But they were just as dead, just as maimed.

Then it dawned on him. He was dreaming. He laughed. A dream. Of course. Dreams were often terrible things and this certainly was one of the worst he'd had since he'd been a lad in Ohio.

"William, the Germans are coming."

Despite himself, he started. "Where?" Then he saw the line of men clad in dark gray that was almost black. They wore funny helmets with spear points on the top and they were marching toward him rapidly.

"William, run! Hurry! Run!"

McKinley tried to turn but his legs wouldn't respond. He knew the unreasoning panic of a nightmare when the evil cannot be avoided. The line of Germans was only yards away, and one man in particular had his bayoneted rifle pointed directly at him. He tried again to run

but his legs were leaden and unresponsive. A dream, he thought, it is
a dream! This creature, now upon him and grinning, cannot hurt. Despite this thought, he screamed and tried to thrash himself free. It's a
dream, he said, as the bayonet entered his chest. It cannot hurt me.

The pain began in the center of his body and it felt as if his chest
would explode. The German was gone, replaced by visual waves of
red ocean that sought to engulf him. It can't hurt, he continued to
think as further torrents of agony continued to rack his body. It's a
dream. It can't be hurting, he continued as the red waves were replaced by black. After a bit, he could no longer hear his own voice
protesting that it was only a dream.

They stood around the table in the Red Room, a shocked and confused group. Theodore Roosevelt entered and nervously took the
place of honor at the head of the table. His normally ruddy complex-
ion was pale, and he looked as if he might have been crying.

"We shall begin," he said, "with a moment of silence for the soul
of the late William McKinley. Although many of us, myself included,
disagreed with him, often vehemently, we all respected him. His un-
timely death this afternoon leaves a void that will be difficult to fill.
For those who did not witness it, I was sworn in just a few moments
ago by Chief Justice Fuller. The late president will lie in state in the
rotunda for two days; then he will return to Ohio, where his widow
says he will be interred. Canton, I believe."

After McKinley had gone to his rooms for a short nap, Hay and
Roosevelt grew concerned when he did not return at the scheduled
time. Thinking that he had overslept—a logical assumption because
of the strain he'd been under—they waited a little longer to allow the
man to rest. When he still didn't come out, they had one of the servants enter the president's private quarters to awaken him. That poor
man's screams sent them running down the hallway, where they
found McKinley dead on the floor, his face blue. He was the victim
of an apparent heart attack, doubtless brought on by the stress of the
situation.

Now Theodore Roosevelt, at age forty-two, was the twenty-sixth
and youngest-ever president of the United States, and he fervently
prayed for guidance. It was one thing, he realized ruefully, to be the
vice president, the gadfly, the tormentor. Now he had to make the de-

cisions, and he was more than a little frightened. The fate of the nation was his to decide. As he prayed, he begged the Almighty for the guidance to do the right thing, and to do it bravely and well.

Roosevelt raised his head and the others followed suit, unconsciously affirming his primacy. He had a war to plan.

"Gentlemen, now to the task at hand. Today is Tuesday, the eleventh of June, and we have been at war for a little more than a week—a week during which, I might add, we have accomplished damn little." His voice was harsh. "First, General Miles, what is the latest situation in and around New York?"

Miles seemed oblivious to the implied criticism. "As expected and anticipated by Colonel Mahan's reports, the Germans have indeed moved off Long Island. The massive fires in Brooklyn may have delayed them a day or so, but a large contingent, perhaps a division, has moved toward White Plains and is likely to cross the border into Connecticut in a couple of days. They have met virtually no opposition, nor are they likely to. They have also moved a blocking force on the north side of the Harlem River. Thus, with naval units in the Hudson as well, Manhattan is now cut off and under a state of siege. The Germans have called for its surrender."

"Mr. President," interrupted Elihu Root, the secretary of war, "there are at least three regiments of New York National Guard trapped on Manhattan Island. If they surrender, which I'm afraid is inevitable, the Germans will have at least five thousand of our boys as prisoners, not to mention possession of the largest and most important city in the United States."

Roosevelt nodded. There was nothing he could say at this time. "And the war at sea?" he asked as he turned to the secretary of the navy, John Long, who was present with his intelligence expert, Capt. Charles Sigsbee.

"Sir," responded Long, "we have been inundated with ship sightings in such copious quantities as to make one believe the Spanish armada was off our shores. Quite frankly, every old lady who sees a fishing boat has reported it as a German battleship, creating panic everywhere along the coast. Sorting out the wheat from the chaff has been difficult, but we now estimate at least six German battleships and twenty or so light and heavy cruisers in and about New York harbor. Although that itself is not a huge fleet, we assume there are other vessels out of sight of land and, since our navy is nowhere near, it might as well be the Spanish armada."

"Are you trying to gather our fleet?"

"Yes. However, there are several difficulties. First, the problem of notifying those ships currently at sea that hostilities have commenced. We will have to wait until many of them reach port or are hailed by another ship that is aware of the war. Even for those we can reach, there is another problem: what specifically do we ask them to do? Gather certainly, but where and for what purpose? Frankly, sir, we need not only direction in that regard but a safe haven for the fleet to gather. A sanctuary, if you will."

There was a buzz of general agreement. An army could be accumulated in safety almost anyplace on the continent. A navy, however, needed ports. Safe ports. If the fleet were forced to do battle piecemeal, it would be destroyed piecemeal. No, the fleet had to be gathered in its entirety. There was no answer, so they settled for a compromise in which those ships currently in American ports would remain where they were until they received further instructions, along with those that would subsequently return to the United States as word of the war spread. Somehow they had to find sanctuary.

However, the army could be gathered. Directions were given that the scattered regular units would be brought eastward together from the dusty forts and camps they'd occupied in the West for more than half a century of warfare against the Indians. Even though the Indians were long subdued, no one had ever thought to move the army. It would have cost money.

"Mr. President."

"Yes, Elihu."

"Guard and militia units from a number of states are accumulating around the New York area. For all intents and purposes, they are leaderless, as each consists of an independent brigade or regiment. There is no cohesion, no direction. I suggest that you appoint regular army generals for that area and make them responsible for the gathering up of those units before disaster strikes. For a start, I recommend simply establishing geographic lines of demarcation and control and letting our generals sort out who's in their area."

"Who do you have in mind? General Miles?"

Root smiled. "No, sir, he's much too valuable right here." A small sop. Root neither liked nor trusted Gen. Nelson Miles. "I propose sending Joe Wheeler and Fitzhugh Lee up there immediately. They are in town and I've got them standing by. Baldy Smith has been contacted. He will get there in a little while and, with your concurrence, will assume tactical command for the time being."

John Hay leaned back in his chair and looked to the ceiling in mock prayer. "My lord, our first line of defense is two aging Confederates to be followed as soon as possible by an old Union general."

Roosevelt hushed him. "It could be worse. At least they're skilled soldiers." There was a pause as a messenger entered with a sheet of paper. Roosevelt scanned it and looked up. "Well, Congress didn't dally. They've approved a declaration of war and given me control over state units."

"Well, sir," said Hay, "where does that put us regarding a response to the German ultimatum?"

"Tell them," Miles snarled, "to shove it up their Teutonic asses!"

Roosevelt laughed and slapped the table. The irascible and unpleasant Nelson Miles, who had spent much of his career fighting rivals for his own personal glory, had focused on yet a new enemy and this time the correct one. Bully! thought Roosevelt. "Well, General, I think Mr. Hay and I can formulate a response that will convey the sense of what you just said."

Miles handed Roosevelt a thick envelope, bypassing the very surprised Elihu Root. "Sir, since we are going to war with a major European power, it will necessitate a major increase in the size of the American army. I have some thoughts and recommendations I am confident you will find interesting."

Roosevelt took the envelope and tried not to look at Root, who glared at Miles and appeared as though he wished to strangle the man. "I think we have accomplished much that is necessary here today, and we will accomplish much more in the days to come. We must make an army and gather our fleet. Then we will wring that puffed-up little bastard kaiser's neck."

To a chorus of "hear, hear" they started to rise in dismissal, but the young lieutenant who'd been overseeing the telegraph operations in the war room above burst through the door. "Mr. President," he gasped. "There's been a battle!"

Chapter 7

PATRICK MAHAN REGRETTED the delay in his journey to the front, but there was little he could do. With the death of the two servants in the attempted robbery, he had assumed responsibility for Katrina Schuyler and the refugee, Molly Duggan. The first thing to do was see to Molly's health. They found a doctor who treated her physical wounds and assured them she would be all right with time. What mental wounds she'd incurred were beyond anyone's estimate. It sometimes seemed to Patrick and Katrina that the whole ugly incident with the German soldier had been blotted from Molly's mind once she told them of it. But then something about Germany or the Germans would arise in conversation and they could see her hatred. Nevertheless, with the resilience of a youth who was still almost a child, she soon became relatively cheerful and talkative, and assumed the role of assistant to Katrina. Patrick almost thought of her as Katrina's maid, but that wasn't quite right. The girl was very bright and reasonably literate, considering her tough urban background and her history as an immigrant. Until recently, she had been well cared for.

Katrina accepted the inevitability of the situation and seemed to enjoy Molly's company. Although Katrina had been shaken by the attempted robbery, she seemed to have put it behind her. She was, however, aware that she was growing more and more dependent on Patrick, and she wondered about it. He certainly did not resemble

what she had once thought a knight-errant should look like, but he
was quite attractive. He was tall, about six feet, and surprisingly
muscular. And, as befits an officer, he had a commanding presence.
But it quickly melted when they talked quietly together. He had a
slightly receding hairline, and she imagined he would be bald in a
decade or two and decided it might suit him. There was a small scar
on his cheek and she wondered what caused it. A Spanish bayonet?
She was also pleased and surprised to find him almost as well traveled and educated as she was. She had a strong dislike for stupid men
and men who thought Katrina Schuyler was stupid. Patrick Mahan
did not possess either flaw.

All three of them, while relieved to find the escape portion of their
journey over, were saddened at breaking up. The women would stay
behind while Patrick rode on to find the armies. To no one's surprise,
there was a Red Cross camp north of Stamford, Connecticut, where
Katrina's and Molly's services were gratefully accepted. When they
parted, Molly gave Patrick an impulsive hug, and Katrina felt compelled to follow suit. Although amused at Molly's embrace, Patrick
seemed a little taken aback at Katrina's. His response amused her.
Brave soldier!

Patrick was thinking of that hug and the surprising warmth and
strength of Katrina's slender body, and how involuntarily monastic a
soldier's life often is, while he rode westward alone toward White
Plains, New York. He halted as the distant sound of thunder rumbled
from the hills to his front.

Thunder? Thunder, hell! That was artillery! He spurred his horse
to a gallop and rode in what he thought was the right direction. What
had Napoleon said? Ride to the sound of the guns! At least and for
once, he was wearing a proper uniform.

He had heard disturbing information that a number of militia units
had been called up by the governors of at least three states and were
converging westward in the general direction of the rumored location
of German outposts, just east of White Plains. What in God's name,
he asked himself, were they going to attempt? Was there a plan? A
leader? He doubted the existence of either. If the militia's dismal
performance in the Spanish war was any indicator, the best that
could occur would be chaos, and the worst, disaster.

Patrick had passed a number of poorly armed and poorly dressed militia units heading in the same direction as he was, but he had also seen others heading north, which further reinforced his conclusion that no one was in charge and that there was no coherent plan.

After a while, he slowed his horse to a trot and listened as the cannonading became sharper and was punctuated by the distant rattle of rifle and machine-gun fire. Then it seemed to cease altogether and the land became eerily silent as the sounds of birds and buzzing insects returned.

The first soldiers he saw were individuals running in panic. He made no attempt to stop them. They were the first casualties and they wouldn't be useful until their terror abated. God only knew what they'd just seen, but they were through for at least this day.

Even so, he yelled at them and tried to get information. "Boys, what the hell's going on? Why're you running?"

One skinny, terrified lad who looked little more than fifteen stared at him, eyes wide with fear. "Everybody's dead. Germans killed 'em all. You better run too!"

Patrick rode on to a fork in the dirt road that commanded a good view. After a while he was able to discern groups of men coming through the brush and trees. As he saw more, he realized that some were coming back in relatively good order, whereas others appeared leaderless and confused, separated from their units by the shock of whatever battle had just transpired.

No use going after individuals, he decided, and urged his horse over to a group of a hundred or so men led by a stocky and sweaty-faced major who slogged along on foot.

"Major, who is in command here?" Patrick asked.

The major, who looked to be in his midforties, responded without raising his head. "Colonel Blaney of Massachusetts, if the dumb shit is still alive, that is." The major was angry, his face reddened by exertion.

Patrick leaned over in the saddle. "And who are you?"

"Jonathan Harris, Connecticut Militia. Now, who the fuck are you?"

"Major," Patrick snarled, deciding to take immediate control of the situation, "as of this instant I am your commanding officer, and unless you wish to be shot for insubordination as well as for running from the enemy, you will acknowledge that simple fact and commence obeying orders."

Major Harris blinked and took in the fact that the man on horseback was not only his senior but regular army and immediately decided to obey. "Yes, sir," Harris said as he smiled slightly and actually saluted. "What'ya have in mind?"

Patrick ordered Harris to take his men and fan out in a screen to gather in as many of the retreating soldiers as possible. They were to direct them to a large and reasonably open field, where officers were to identify themselves and begin rounding up men in their units.

Patrick watched for a few minutes until he was confident that his orders were being obeyed. He was puzzled by the absence of actual casualties. Had everyone run before the guns could do much damage? There was only a handful of wounded, but most of the men looked scared. It did not appear to have been a good day for American arms.

Patrick then galloped hard down the dirt road and repeated the performance every time he found a good-sized group of men who appeared to have a leader. He was surprised at how readily he was obeyed, the major's first reaction notwithstanding. The men were, of course, confused and in desperate need of direction.

"Colonel Mahan, sir."

Patrick turned. Who the hell besides Harris knew his name? The speaker was a stocky black man with the uniform and insignia of a sergeant major in the 10th Cavalry. "You know me, Sergeant?"

"Yes, sir. Esau Jones, battalion sergeant major, 10th Cavalry, sir." Jones saluted.

Patrick returned it. "Good to see you, Jones," he said, although he couldn't remember the man. He had spent only a few months as a young lieutenant with the 10th, and later they were the "other" unit that stormed San Juan Hill. History immortalized the Rough Riders and conveniently forgot the black soldiers of the 10th Cavalry who charged alongside them.

"Jones, steal a horse and come with me."

Jones simply took one from a confused private and rode on with Patrick as he tried to halt the flow of men. After a while, they returned to the field where Major Harris, his face even redder than before, was trying to bring order from chaos. There were now several thousand men in the field, and dozens of officers marched back and forth hollering the names of their units and trying to attract followers. Had it not been so tragic, it would have been farcical.

Patrick saw casualties and realized that Harris's group had been lucky. There were scores of moaning, crying wounded lying in rows and being attended by volunteers who did their best in the face of horror. Some of the silent had already died. Patrick could only nod when Harris told him he'd sent to the nearby towns for medical help and to find permanent places to care for the wounded. There was nothing else to be done.

It was beginning to look as though Patrick had gathered up the greater portion of the "army" that had taken part in an abortive attack on an advancing German column. He could count six militia regiments represented on his field: three from Massachusetts, two from Connecticut, and one from New York.

In conversations with Harris, Jones, and others, Patrick learned that the major culprit was indeed a Massachusetts colonel named Charles Blaney. Blaney, whose brother-in-law was a congressman, had arrived from his home in Springfield, Massachusetts, at the head of his local regiment and was deferred to by the other Massachusetts officers because of his political influence. In all fairness to the man, Patrick realized he must have also been a natural leader who saw a job that needed to be done and tried to do it.

Upon being informed that a force of Germans was to his front, Blaney had prevailed upon all three of his state regiments and at least three others to advance against the enemy. He had foolishly believed that his force would prevail and he would be able to drive back the German force.

"Of course," said Harris, "we did no scouting and had no artillery. We moved out for about an hour when we saw our first Germans. Skirmishers. We shot at them and they moved back. We stupidly thought they were retreating, then we stumbled onto the entire German column. Shit, they cut us to pieces."

Sergeant Jones agreed. "Colonel, it was awful. One minute we were runnin', whoopin', and hollerin', and the next minute machine guns and rifles we couldn't see were cutting our men down. Then they started firing their cannon into us. Nothing missed. Some of us fired back for a few minutes, but it was too much. Then we all just ran." He shook his head sadly. "Wasn't nothin' like Cuba. Nothing at all."

Jones's part of the tale had an even sadder ending than the simple defeat. He, along with three others from the 10th, had been in the area to recruit from the sizable colored population and had had the bad luck to be there when Colonel Blaney decided to forge an army. Blaney thought it appropriate for the four regular army men to accompany him as he led the assault. Although they didn't think it right, they also knew better than to disobey the orders of white officers.

"Blaney stood there for a minute when the Germans opened fire," Jones said. "It was like he never expected nothing like it. He wasn't no coward, not at all. He just stood there until he took a bullet in the gut and started screaming. Then the others ran off and left him. He has to be dead by now."

German skirmish lines moved out to take the field back from the retreating Americans. It was then that Sergeant Jones realized the other three men weren't with him. "I looked back and saw all three lying there. Two weren't moving, but one was trying to get up. I started to run to him but I stumbled. When I got back up I saw that a couple of Germans had reached him and were sticking him with their bayonets. You know what? They was laughing. Then someone blew a whistle and the Germans pulled back."

Patrick wished the story had never been told. But then, was it so different from Cuba, where victorious Americans had killed Spanish wounded? He looked at the lengthening shadows and realized that night would come shortly. He gave orders to expand the area and form a defensive perimeter, with the wounded and unarmed men inside. Even though they had no digging implements, he told them to prepare such barricades as they could. If nothing else, it would give them something constructive to do and take their minds off the debacle.

He also had each unit send out reliable men as scouts and pickets to warn of any German advance. If the enemy came, Patrick would gather his flock and retreat in the general direction of Bridgeport, Connecticut.

The night was one of little or no sleep for most. Medical help finally began to arrive, and the wounded—those who could be transported in wagons—were sent out; the slightly wounded were patched up and returned to duty or left to rest through the night. The gravely wounded were given comfort; they would either get better or they would die.

On a more mundane level, there were the questions of food, water, and ammunition to resolve. Although the soldiers could go a little while without food, they desperately needed water to fill canteens gulped dry during the warm day. Units were assigned to bring back as much water as they could from nearby springs and wells. The food they would have to find tomorrow.

Ammunition was a problem—there wasn't any. Each man had about ten rounds for his single-shot Springfield rifle. Both the rifle and the ammunition were old. The Springfield was totally outclassed in rate of fire by the five-shot magazines of the German Mausers. Worse, the Springfield used only black powder, which gave away the shooter's location. In a duel with a Mauser, a man with a Springfield was at a serious disadvantage. Again Patrick realized that little had changed since the war with Spain.

Patrick was now better able to get a grip on the numbers of soldiers involved. According to senior officers remaining, the six regiments totaled about 8,500 officers and men. They could account for 116 definitely killed, including Blaney, and 170 wounded. There were almost 2,000 missing. Most of these, however, were simply runaways like the frightened boy he'd first seen. Some, however, were doubtless uncounted dead and abandoned wounded who would die if they were not found and treated. Patrick could only wonder if the Germans had taken any prisoners.

Morning finally came and with it reports from the scouts that the Germans had pulled back west of White Plains, although certainly not as a result of the fight. The Germans who had mauled the raw militia were probably only part of a large scouting force who had gathered all the information they needed. The American scouts also reported the disquieting news that there were no wounded on the battlefield, only dead—another eighty or so—and some appeared to have been executed.

More positively, additional runaways had started returning, often reduced to shamefaced tears by the hoots and curses of those who had stayed the course. Patrick allowed each regiment to send men to their prior encampment to retrieve supplies and gear left behind, and he tried further to get his little army organized.

It was near noon when they received the stunning news that president McKinley was dead of a heart attack and Teddy Roosevelt was now president of the United States. It seemed appropriate and comforting to have brief prayer services, and each regiment held its own.

Patrick stayed quietly to himself and wondered about the man he'd met just a few days ago, and the startling fact that brash, young Teddy Roosevelt was now the president.

It was after the last service that Patrick finally took stock of his own personal position. Without authority, he had assumed control of what amounted to a brigade. The officers, many older and more senior in state rank and grade, readily accepted him. Apparently, they believed he knew what he was doing. He also showed no urge to lead them again to the slaughter, and he didn't hold it against them that they'd run so quickly. It later occurred to him that they would be quite willing to blame him for whatever foul-up might result from his leadership.

He was now in charge of more than six thousand men. Although he was a career officer, he had never commanded more than a company. His senior officers had always thought of him as the perfect staff officer, literate and well organized, rather than a leader of men. It was intoxicating and fulfilling to be in command.

One of the returning work parties brought with it Colonel Blaney's large and elaborate tent as well as his camp furniture, and they insisted Patrick use it. There was no reason not to. It was a perfectly acceptable alternative to sleeping on the ground, even though the weather remained warm and dry.

The next day, a captain from the New York regiment brought with him a trunk of clothes and a little man he identified as a tailor. "Frankly, sir, we kinda noticed you didn't have any baggage with you and figured you might need some changes of clothes before you, ah, get too gamey. These belonged to one of our people who, uh, isn't going to need them again. He was kinda your size and, if you need some tucking and sewing, the corporal here is a real good tailor." The captain grinned. "Only reason we keep the little shit."

Ever practical and never prone to look a gift horse in the mouth, Patrick accepted. At least now he didn't have to worry about the unlikely possibility of his baggage ever catching up with him.

If it hadn't been for the omnipresent concern about the now-sedentary Germans, the next couple of days might have been pleasant. Patrick continued to organize, patrol, and drill, and was bemused by the almost worshipful way the men looked up to him. In their minds he had arrived at just the right moment to save them and, so far, had done all the right things. He could only wonder just how long the acceptance would last. If the Germans moved on them in any force, they would have to retreat. His six regiments were armed with only single-shot rifles. They had no machine guns and, of course, no artillery. That they were poorly trained to use what equipment they had was almost irrelevant.

Finally there was a small break. Sergeant Esau Jones, patrolling alone, actually located the Germans. They were digging in and fortifying an area about ten miles away and showed no signs of moving. Now that they were located, they could be observed, and Patrick set about organizing it. He also found from Jones that there seemed to be only a single regiment of Germans. Patrick realized sadly that his brave little army had been whipped by a German force one-fifth its size.

There had to be more Germans. They wouldn't leave one regiment hanging out to dry.

Theodore Roosevelt lit a small cigar and eyed the golden hue of a well-aged brandy in a crystal goblet. "Well, Elihu, what do you have to tell me?"

Secretary of War Elihu Root put down his own goblet. Once he had wanted to be president himself and had campaigned shamelessly for the office. A brilliant lawyer and a solid Republican, he thought it the next logical step in an outstanding career. But as he looked at the younger and more vigorous man before him, he knew his time had passed. Perhaps it had begun to pass when, years before, he had defended some Tammany Hall Democrats in a criminal trial. Ah, well, hindsight. Now all he could do was to make as great an impact as he could in his loyal support of a president who was young enough to be his son.

"Sir, I—we—have a problem."

"And that is?"

"Lieutenant General Nelson Miles."

Roosevelt chuckled. "Ah, the charming and lovable commanding general."

"It's more serious than that."

"Elihu, do you want him replaced?"

"It may come to that. I do not have much confidence in his skill should he command against the Germans. I doubt that he is capable of commanding the large force we both know will be needed. Worse, his ideas about combat are considered by many to be archaic."

Roosevelt pondered. He knew that Root—who wanted very much to change the way the army commanded itself, did business, and fought—was opposed by an old guard, led by Nelson Miles. They wanted to retain the status quo of a small frontier army.

"Elihu, is this the proper time? Miles is a distinguished old soldier who has served his country well. And, after all, he is the commanding general. Who would replace him? Wasn't he a great Indian fighter?"

"Sir, it took him three thousand men and several years to capture a score of Apaches. And Lawton, not Miles, actually captured Geronimo."

"And Lawton's dead, killed in the Philippines, if I recall. A shame. But what about Puerto Rico? He took that, didn't he?"

Root knew he was being tested. "Hardly a campaign, sir. His five thousand men took four casualties. The whole Spanish island garrison surrendered virtually without firing a shot. But that's not the point. He actually thinks that fool Blaney's a hero. He wishes to attack the Germans in overwhelming numbers as soon as the army is large enough. He doesn't realize the current qualitative differences between the German soldier and ours—in training, in equipment, and in leadership. It will be a worse slaughter than Cold Harbor or Marye's Heights," he said, referring to Civil War incidents where thousands of Union soldiers had been killed in futile attempts to dislodge well-dug-in defenders.

"What do you propose?"

"Sir, I have seen Miles's list of suggestions for expanding the army. In all fairness to the man, many of them have merit. I propose we act on those with which we concur and defer on the others. In particular we must avoid giving Miles overall field command. In the meantime, we can commence with his basic suggestions, which are to enlarge the number of available generals to command the larger army, and go about getting the modern equipment needed to outfit that larger army."

"Does he wish himself a fourth star?"

"Not in so many words, but the implication is clear. Indeed, sir, someone may have to have a fourth star if the army is to be as large as we think will soon be necessary."

Roosevelt grunted and asked for the list of names. He read it and grunted again. His cigar was out and he lit it. Then he took a pencil and began making notations, his brow furrowed in deep thought. "Elihu, don't we have any young officers?"

For Patrick Mahan the next several days were notable only for their similarity. The weather remained constantly sunny and un-threatening, and the encampment took on the convivial look and feel of a boys' camping ground. Had it not been for the weaponry, the constant patrols, and preparation for defense that he insisted upon, most of the men could almost be described as having a good time. He tried to drill them but not too hard, as he was well aware of the volunteer soldier's long-standing antipathy toward close order drill. He did find them receptive to combat training. That was something they could see a purpose to. But to expect them to act like spit and polish soldiers was more than he could reasonably expect.

At least, however, he could keep them busy and prevent them from brooding over the defeat. The drilling might just turn them into decent soldiers someday, but the digging of defensive works was pure make-work. It tired the men's bodies, and the sight of the dirt walls gave them the illusion of safety. Patrick declined to tell them that news of a sizable German advance would cause him to call an immediate retreat. He had no desire to lead his army in a slaughter.

He had now amassed about ten thousand men under his highly unofficial command as other states called up their militias in re-sponse to a presidential order. Additional units from states as far away as Ohio had arrived in his area as a result of the battle and the general knowledge of his encampment. Still more stragglers had re-membered their duty and found their way to what most were calling Fort Blaney, in derisive salute to their fallen first leader.

The Germans continued their policy of inaction. They had been spotted in several regiment-sized locations about a day's march away and so heavily dug in that they were easy to observe. This lack of aggressive pressure brought a semblance of rude civilization to Fort Blaney. First came the merchants selling all manner of goods and services, from clothing to liquor to sex. Although Patrick was a long way from being a prude, he chased out the hookers and rationed the liquor. He informed his senior officer that if the men wanted sex, they would have to get leave and go to a city. Brothels would not come to them. There was grumbling, but most saw the sense of it. Besides, his prohibition against whores wasn't that effective; all it did was keep things quiet and out of sight, which was exactly what he wanted.

This was soon followed by the inevitable visits by friends, relatives, and other loved ones whose shrieking and often tearful presence further lightened the atmosphere. At times it seemed there were so many private carriages on the roads about the camp that the army couldn't move. These visits were encouraged as long as they didn't interfere too much with training and defense requirements; they definitely increased morale.

Communication with the outside world came in the form of newspapers, some only a day old, from nearby towns. These the men devoured immediately; given the lack of any real command structure in the area, newspapers were the only reliable source of information. Through newspapers they learned of the fall of Manhattan and the imprisonment of thousands of American soldiers. They also learned that their battle, although acknowledged as a defeat, was praised to the skies as a valiant effort to rid the country of the invaders. This was a great boost to their morale. The reading and passing around of newspapers became an afternoon ritual not to be trifled with.

Patrick was walking about and simply observing when several men, lolling and reading their papers, noticed him.

"Hey, Cunnel, come here a minute."

Patrick winced. In a real army enlisted men do not summon their commanding officer so cavalierly. But he had to remind himself for the hundredth time that day that these were volunteers and not regulars, and their training in such arcane matters as saluting was, at best, negligent. Doing as he was bid, he tried not to laugh.

"What's up, boys?"

"Just a question, sir." The speaker was a young private with glasses and a stringy beard. He had obviously been reading aloud for the benefit of the others. "Is your first name Patrick?"

He was puzzled. "Yes, why?"

"Well, according to the Hartford paper, you've just been made a general."

Patrick swore and grabbed the offered paper. Yes, there it was, Patrick Mahan, brigadier general, U.S. Army. The rank was temporary, of course, but temporary or not, he was a general! He scanned the list and saw the names of a score of others both appointed and promoted. At last, something was happening.

The men gathered around and offered handshakes, which he took eagerly. They pumped his arm and pounded his back. Somewhere in the back of his mind he recalled that enlisted men don't do this in a regular army. But the front of his mind didn't give a damn, and he exulted in it. The private who had first summoned him insisted on his keeping the newspaper as a souvenir. Why not? he laughed, and stuffed it in his pocket.

Later that afternoon and following congratulatory drinks, he and several other officers were gathered in his tent—the one he had inherited from Blaney—to discuss the next day's training and patrol routine. On his collar he wore the star of a brigadier, courtesy again of the little tailor from New York.

The men paused when they heard the sound of a horse outside and a man dismounting. Through the thin wall of the tent a voice bellowed, "Where the hell is that ignorant Yankee asshole who thinks he's a general? Jesus Christ! Did the army run out of qualified Southerners and have to promote ignorant Michigan farmers who don't know how to wipe shit from their boots?"

The others in the tent froze in astonishment and shock, but Patrick flushed and grinned and found his own loud voice. "The Confederacy lost! Damnit, why do slow-learning rednecks who never figured out how to spell Confederacy have to be told that simple fact over and over again?"

Patrick rushed outside. "General Wheeler!" He gave a salute, which the other, much older and smaller man returned. Then, never one for formality, he grabbed Patrick's hand and slapped him on the shoulder. Major General Joe Wheeler of the U.S. Army, hero of the Spanish-American War and ex–Confederate States of America, grinned happily. The man his soldiers called Fighting Joe had arrived.

After quick introductions, Patrick chased the other officers out and sat down with Wheeler, who looked in amazement at the elaborate tent. "Boy, you don't have anything to drink in this canvas whorehouse, do you?"

"I sent Blaney's personal effects back home," Patrick said, reaching into a trunk. "I did not consider his liquor to fall in that category."

"Spoils of war," said Wheeler, taking a glass. "To your promotion, my command, and death to the goddamn Germans."

Patrick took a swallow. It was good whiskey and a mighty toast. Joe Wheeler was sixty-five years old and had served the Confederacy as a brigadier general himself almost forty years ago. Later, he'd been resurrected and given command of a division against Spain in what had been described by some as a sop to the South to show that the Civil War was really, once and for all, over. It had worked. Wheeler, white bearded and in his sixties but still wiry and spry enough to look like a jockey, had performed well and inspired his men. But what was he doing here?

"Patrick, lad, I hope you aren't too fond of these troops, because your talents are required elsewhere. Washington, to be precise. Your president calls you for more help, anticipating what the nasty shithead Germans might do."

"And what about my little army?" The whiskey was starting to warm him. With Wheeler here, he frankly felt better, further assured that people elsewhere were aware of what was going on.

"I'm going to take it from you and make it part of my division. I've got one division. Funston and Pershing have been promoted to major generals and will each get a division. Baldy Smith will command the entire corps."

A good choice, thought Patrick. Major General William Smith, forever known as Baldy, had served under Grant in the Civil War and with Wheeler in Cuba. It was an interesting reunion of two old protagonists. But the appointment raised a question.

"Not Miles?" Patrick asked.

Wheeler poured each a generous refill, looked at the glasses, and added some more. "Nah. Our beloved commanding general will remain in Washington for the time being, overseeing the entire operation in his own unique and lovable manner."

"How soon do they want me in Washington?"

"Leave in the morning. Show me around this evening and introduce me to your key people. Later we can have dinner and see if there's any more of this liquor around. It ain't bourbon, but it'll do." It was Scotch and quite expensive. "By the way, you got anyone on your staff who speaks German?"

Patrick grinned sheepishly and confessed he didn't. It was an embarrassing oversight, but one that Patrick thought was immediately correctable. There was an Ohio regiment nearby with a number of German-speaking men in it. There had to be one who would qualify. Wheeler agreed. "And get yourself a German-speaking aide as well. Hell, you're a general," he laughed, his wrinkled face breaking into a smile. "You might as well start acting like one."

Later that night, Brig. Gen. Patrick Mahan looked up from where he was seated and stared at the hulking young man standing nervously at attention before him. The note handed him earlier had said the man's name was Heinz Schmidt. He was from Ohio and had been recommended for duty as Patrick's aide. With only a few hours before he left for Washington, there wasn't much time to be choosy.

"You are literate in German?" The question seemed superfluous, given the man's name and recommendation, but he asked it anyhow.

"Sir, it was my first language. My parents are both from Cologne, 'Köln' to them. I was born here but all I heard for my first six years was German. I didn't learn English until I went to school. Then my parents insisted I keep my German skills as I grew up. It was a fortunate decision. I have found myself in the position of helping new immigrants get settled, and that is very satisfying."

The general nodded. "And what were you doing before this war?"

"Going to college, sir, at the University of Cincinnati. I wish to be a lawyer."

The general grinned. "I took you to be smarter than that."

Heinz responded with a small smile of his own. The general was younger than he thought and seemed to be fairly well educated himself. Not a lard-ass like so many of the senior officers in the militia. "Sir, despite what Shakespeare said about killing all the lawyers, a quote that is usually taken entirely out of context, there may be room for a few. Frankly, sir, I've seen too many of my relatives bilked of their money and property because they didn't understand American laws. I am confident I will be useful there."

"After the war, that is."

"Yes, sir, after the war. I am committed for the duration."

The strapping youth did not look much like a lawyer. Or a clerk.

With his brawn he could easily be mistaken for a laborer or a
farmworker. Yet he seemed intelligent enough. "All right, you're
hired as my aide. I'm giving you an immediate rank of second lieutenant. I wasn't going to do that, but my good friend General
Wheeler reminded me that generals do not have privates as aides."

Heinz was stunned and could only stammer his thanks. An officer?
Perhaps this assignment wouldn't be as bad as he had feared. Now he
felt embarrassed that he had complained to the colonel, his uncle,
about leaving a fighting unit to become a glorified clerk. A lieutenant, hot damn!

Chapter 8

IAN GORDON LOOKED about the well-furnished room for the tenth time to make sure everything was in place and, once again, found it all satisfactory. The farm had been rented more than a year before by his predecessor through an American intermediary. It was used by the British embassy for meetings where discretion, if not outright secrecy, was essential. It was a small, non-working farm about five miles south of Washington, in Virginia, consisting of a good-sized and comfortable house, a barn, and a stable. There was also a driveway about a hundred yards long leading from the road to the house; thus the armed guards he'd posted would be easily able to see and identify anyone attempting to enter by that very obvious route. Other guards were stationed to prevent more clandestine intruders.

Gordon sat in an overstuffed chair and thought about the last time he had used this safe house. It had nothing to do with the needs of the empire, but with his own biological needs and those of the young wife of an older mining baron from Colorado. He could not help but smile as he recalled her naked body and the way the flames from the fireplace created erotic shadows across her abdomen. If only he could recall her name. Ah, well, he was certain she had one. It was the only time he'd used the farm for such a tryst, although it had hardly been the first for others, and he'd had to put a halt to it. Too much traffic would attract attention from the nosy locals.

Ian's assistant, Charles Bollinger, a slight and bookish young man who looked like a law clerk, entered the room. "I believe our guests are arriving."

Ian looked out the window. A small carriage carrying two men was stopped where the drive intersected the road. The men were in conversation with a field hand who was actually another of Ian's men. There were two others, armed with rifles, in the barn. He presumed they were watching the byplay.

The field hand removed his hat, a signal that everything was all right, and waved the carriage on. "Charles, I think it's just about time for you to disappear."

"Of course, Ian." Charles smiled and took himself upstairs, where he could listen with the aid of a stethoscope and take notes in shorthand. An earlier attempt to use a phonograph had been a dismal failure.

The carriage pulled up in front of the house and Ian opened the door, gracefully waving his guests in. When he saw their identity, it took a great deal of willpower to maintain his composure. He had asked for representatives from State and the army. He had not expected John Hay himself and Maj. Gen. Leonard Wood.

"Mr. Secretary, General, so good of you to come."

Hay barked a laugh. "When His Majesty's Imperial representatives say they have something important and confidential to discuss, I consider it well worth my time. Besides, Mr. Gordon, I am very curious."

"As am I," added General Wood. "Your reputation is that of spymaster extraordinaire for England, and we are both very intrigued."

Gordon rubbed his hands. "Sirs, I am but a humble functionary, a commercial attaché, within the embassy of Great Britain."

"Balls," said Wood, in good humor. "If you are a commercial attaché, then I am the grand vizier of Turkey."

They entered the living room and took seats. Gordon offered brandy, which was cheerfully accepted despite the summer heat. As he poured, he thought about the two men. Hay he knew for a skilled and admired diplomat. Leonard Wood, on the other hand, was almost an enigma. A Yale graduate, he was both a competent surgeon and a general, having risen in rank as a result of military skills acquired on the frontier. More important, he was a close friend of Teddy Roosevelt's, and it was Wood who had nominally commanded the Rough Riders in Cuba when formal command was denied Roosevelt.

Like Roosevelt, Wood was in his early forties, and he was now considered an administrator rather than a field commander. His presence was almost as interesting as John Hay's. Ian was not displeased.

As the senior American representative, Hay spoke first. "Your message stated that you had items of import and urgency to discuss with representatives of the United States government. Since the only event of note occurring at this moment is the unfortunate war, I will assume that is why we are here."

Ian nodded. "It is."

"Then let us get on with it. The ride, however pleasant, was rather long and we will doubtless not get back before late tonight. Regardless of the security provided by the men in the barn and the fellow you have upstairs, I would prefer to be home." Hay smiled to soften the implied rebuke.

Ian quietly regretted having Charles Bollinger at a listening post. It now seemed faintly unsporting. However, it was too late, and Hay had a fair idea how these games were played and didn't seem to be offended.

"Mr. Secretary, General Wood, I meet with you today in a dual capacity: first, an unofficial one as a representative of a newly developed commercial firm called Caligula, Limited, and second, as a messenger from His Majesty's government.

"Caligula's stock is privately held by a number of important Britons who feel strongly that there are opportunities to make a substantial profit while tweaking the nose of the damnable and insufferable little kaiser."

Hay stroked his full beard. "May I interpret that to mean that Great Britain is displeased with Germany's military adventures?"

"'Aghast' would be a better word," Gordon responded. "The last thing we wish is German hegemony in the New World. No, gentlemen, although my country does not wish to directly confront Germany, we do wish her progress impeded, if not stopped altogether. My country is sick of war. The campaigns against the Boers have been so debilitating that it will be a long time before we are ready to fight again; therefore, we must use indirect means against the kaiser.

"And that brings us to the purpose of Caligula, Limited. With the Boer War winding down, we find ourselves in a war economy with no war to fight. We have whole industries geared for military production and warehouses bulging with equipment and supplies of all kinds, shapes, and colors." He saw that General Wood had put down his glass and was eagerly leaning forward. "Caligula is in the process of buying up this so-called war surplus in hopes that the United States government might be interested in purchasing it. Please note that I said 'purchase.' We are not talking about gifts or grants, although we might be creative in our methods of financing and payment, should that be advantageous. As you have doubtless surmised, I am Caligula's commissioned representative and a minority stockholder."

"And what equipment and supplies do you have?" asked Wood. "What prices?"

"Gentlemen, without getting into a litany of specifics at this time, I guarantee you the prices will be fair. Surplus weapons will cost a fraction of their retail price. The cost of new weapons, of course, will be higher. As to specific items available, here are some examples. First, we recently replaced our excellent Lee-Metford rifles with even better Lee-Enfields. Thus we have many, many thousands of Metfords lying about gathering dust, along with many millions of rounds of ammunition. The Metfords have ten-shot magazines, which compare favorably with the five-shot magazines for the Mauser and are incomparably superior to your Springfields, which have no magazines and cannot use smokeless powder. Would you be interested in one hundred thousand rifles and, for starters, ten million rounds of ammunition? Smokeless, of course."

Wood gasped. "Good lord, yes." Arming the army was one of the many quandaries facing the military. This would be a major step toward resolving the problem. The only difficulty would be the mindset of Nelson Miles, who thought repeating rifles were unnecessary. But Roosevelt would take care of Miles.

"On receipt of the rifles," continued Gordon, "I would suggest you adapt our method of prone aimed fire rather than the Prussian method of firing rapidly from the hip while advancing. A good English rifleman can get off between fifteen to thirty shots a minute and actually hit something."

"I'll make a note of it," said Wood.

"On short notice, we can provide you with five hundred Maxim machine guns and an appropriate supply of bullets. We can also get, new, some of those wonderful Swedish 1-pound pom-pom guns that are such quick-firing mankillers. The French will sell Caligula some of their new 75mm rapid-fire cannon, which are useless against fortifications but will do a marvelous job on men in the open. We also have a number of now-redundant 15-pound Long-Tom long-range artillery pieces with which to soften up their fieldworks."

"Marvelous," said Wood. "When can we get them over here?"

Now it was Ian Gordon's turn to smile. "My associates and I were so confident you would be interested that we took a calculated risk and have already begun shipping some of the smaller and lighter items. These are now on the high seas. They will make port in Halifax or Quebec and be shipped overland."

"Mr. Gordon?" asked Hay.

"Yes, Mr. Secretary?"

"How will you handle Germany's reaction to this?"

"Sir, His Majesty's government will remind the kaiser that England is a democracy, and that its people are free to do what they wish. Thus, and to its eternal regret, the government cannot stop them unless it is specifically illegal. Caligula will offer to trade with the kaiser as a sign of good faith."

Both Wood and Hay guffawed.

Gordon continued. "Would your government be interested in warships?"

"You are joking!" exclaimed Wood.

"Certainly not. As a budget-cutting device we laid up more than a hundred older warships a few years back. Although they are certainly obsolescent, you might consider whether they would meet your strategic and tactical needs, and whether you can find enough men to crew them."

Wood scribbled on a notepad. "I will inform the Navy Department."

"Gentlemen, I also said I was here in an official capacity. My government will be notifying the kaiser that, in the spirit of neutrality, German warships will not be allowed in Canadian waters. These will be defined as the Canadian shore extending twelve miles out from the mainland and the islands. Thus the entire Gulf of Saint Lawrence as well as Hudson Bay will be off-limits to Germany."

Ian smiled. "We will not prohibit American ships of any kind from fully using those waters for the same reason of neutrality. Your ports coexist with ours in that area, so we would be showing bias if we were to forbid your ships from entering their own home waters. Indeed, sir, we will be initiating a convoy system in order to protect our shipping, and American ships will be welcome to join those protected convoys for the same reason."

Hay's face remained impassive while inwardly he rejoiced. Without specifically saying so, the Brits had offered the American navy a desperately needed sanctuary. The ships could gather in the Saint Lawrence and remain until they were strong enough to sortie.

"And what do you suppose the kaiser's reaction to that will be?" Hay asked.

"He shan't be given a choice," Gordon answered. "After all, doesn't Britannia rule the waves?"

"And waives the rules?" Hay asked impishly.

"Touché."

"Mr. Gordon, I have only one other question," said Hay. "Why on earth did you decide on Caligula as the name of your corporation?"

Ian Gordon kept a straight face. "Sir, we decided to commemorate yet another mad emperor."

The kaiser was not amused. Once again he had convened his supreme war council for the New World venture, and he did not like what was happening. He had expected to be crucified by the world's liberal press, and he had also expected statements of dismay and official protests and disclaimers from other countries, but he had certainly not expected ridicule.

Chancellor von Bulow was extremely uncomfortable. "All Highest, it is clearly apparent that the United States has no idea how to conduct itself in the sophisticated world arenas of statecraft. Diplomacy, even during war, is an art that must be continually perfected. I am afraid that we must expect similar indiscretions from them in the future."

The kaiser simply glared. In his hand was a copy of the London *Times* with the entire ultimatum that the Italian ambassador had belatedly given the United States. Now the whole world knew what Germany wanted. Didn't the fools understand that such correspondence was the basis for negotiation, not for publication?

Holstein, the Jesuit, folded his hands across his ample lap and smiled his snake smile. "Sire, I am afraid I must agree with the chancellor. The new American president is youthful, immature, and inexperienced." He watched as his kaiser started to flush in anger, then added, "The fact that he is your age is irrelevant. You have had the good fortune to be raised in an Imperial and European environment, whereas Roosevelt is little more than a rich cowboy."

The kaiser wadded the newspaper and hurled it in the general direction of a trash receptacle. "Cowboy? Is it his wild west mentality that has led him to offer a reward for my arrest—ten thousand dollars—for highway robbery and murder? At least he had the sense to insist that I be taken alive, instead of setting off a spate of assassination attempts. And who is this Wyatt Earp he has told the newspapers is coming to get me?"

This time Holstein could not suppress a smile. "An aging western gunfighter with a dubious reputation of somewhat epic proportions for shooting, drinking, and fornicating—although in what order I'm not certain. Would it not be an amusing sight to see the old man traipsing bowlegged down the Unter den Linden with his six-guns drawn?"

The kaiser considered it for a moment and then nodded. It would be amusing indeed. Quickly he changed the subject. "Enough of the American's political stupidity. What of the British? What is this nonsense I have been hearing?"

Bulow almost squirmed. "All Highest, I am afraid it is true. The British government will sell war surplus to private enterprises who will then sell to the Americans."

"Stop them!"

"We cannot, sire, and they will not help us. I was very unsubtly reminded that we helped arm the Boers and that their army is still fighting them. The British take shelter behind their laws prohibiting government interference in private enterprises. They also say that raising money through the sale of surplus will help pay the war debts that we caused them to incur. They are, of course, lying hypocrites, but there is little we can do." At this time, Bulow thought but did not add.

The kaiser sagged. "And Canada?"

Holstein, the foreign secretary, responded. "The British proclaim themselves neutral and say that the Dominion of Canada, as a part of their empire, must also be neutral. Their conclusion that American ships cannot be denied access and egress via the Saint Lawrence and its gulf has some legal validity. The practical effect of this is that the arms the Americans are buying have a safe conduit into North American waters and, hence, into the United States. Unless we wish a war with England—a naval war that we would quickly lose—we cannot prevent this."

The kaiser fumed. Damn the British. Their turn would come. Once this American venture was over, then it would be time to settle with the damned British. The kaiser sometimes found it hard to believe that the English royal family was of German stock and closely related to him. Why couldn't they be reasonable like his cousin the czar?

"Well," he said finally, "at least we have had successes on the military fronts, have we not? And was I not correct in demanding that we attack at New York instead of Provincetown or even Washington, as our previous plans suggested? And the shipping strike ruse? Brilliant!"

Schlieffen, chief of staff, smiled tentatively. He seemed to recall that it was his plan, and his ruse, but he too remained discreetly silent. "Yes, All Highest, we have. At this time we have landed one complete corps of three divisions. A second corps is approaching the harbor and will begin disembarking shortly. We have moved out of New York and into Connecticut, after taking all of New York City in a relatively bloodless manner. The unfortunate fires that destroyed Brooklyn have delayed us slightly, but we will make up the lost time."

"Yet our armies have stopped advancing."

It was an accusation, not a question, and Schlieffen responded carefully. "Yes, All Highest. Please recall that the initial force is now spread quite thin because of its myriad responsibilities. Sire, we have only about fifteen thousand men confronting the American General Smith's large but inept force."

"A shame so few were available. With more we could have crushed them," said the kaiser. He knew that a large percentage of the initial force was tied down in occupation and administrative duties and in guarding other portions of the perimeter. Further reinforcements, however, would largely rectify that problem.

The kaiser nodded, apparently understanding. "Prisoners," he said suddenly. "We have large numbers of American prisoners who can be used to unload the ships, can't they?"

Schlieffen shook his head. "It has been discussed, but they are a sullen and mutinous lot. We are afraid they would work at best very slowly and, worse, sabotage whenever they could. We would also have to detail larger numbers of our soldiers to guard them while they perform their tasks."

The kaiser persisted. "If they commit sabotage, or refuse to work, shoot them!"

"Certainly, sire, but our people there are afraid that some heroic martyr might still do something catastrophic to our efforts if given an opportunity. Perhaps some demented fool might even blow up a munitions ship. That, sire, would be a disaster."

"And the navy?" Here the kaiser looked and spoke more deferentially to the imposing bulk of Tirpitz.

"Sire, we are still attempting to locate the American fleet. It is scattered but is doubtless trying to collect itself in a force that will enable it to attempt a fleet action. We have small units searching for it, but so far with little success. Other major naval forces are busy protecting the harbor around New York and our reinforcement convoys as they cross over. We have also sent several cruiser squadrons south to cause havoc in the American ports by bombarding them. We are confident that that will tie down many army regiments which might otherwise be sent north to fight us. In the meantime, our main battle fleet is ready and able to sink theirs, whether we find its hiding hole or it shows up to challenge us."

"Do you think it will?" asked the kaiser hopefully. He had spent a fortune developing his new navy as an instrument of Imperial expansionary will. Now it was time to reap the dividends from that investment.

"Without a doubt," assured Tirpitz.

Tirpitz too had read the work of the most prominent naval theoretician of the age, Alfred Thayer Mahan. Mahan's beliefs were based on the primacy of the capital ships of the main battle fleets and the need for one navy to aggressively seek out and destroy an enemy's main battle fleet. Tirpitz and the other senior officers in the German navy looked forward to the likelihood of the slightly smaller American fleet challenging the might of Germany.

The kaiser slapped his good right hand on the table. "Now that is what I like. Good, aggressive attitude. It has been too long since anyone challenged the British on the oceans. When we have destroyed the American fleet, we will be battle hardened and wise, and the British must respect us."

The kaiser rose, signaling that the meeting was over. He shook hands and departed, as did the military chiefs. Bulow was left alone with Holstein, and he clearly did not like being with the Jesuit.

"Von Bulow." Holstein smiled. "Have you been reading the foreign press? Some of the comments are quite interesting, especially the excerpts from the American papers."

Bulow paled. "I don't know what you mean."

Holstein chortled. "Of course you do. I particularly call your attention to the article in the Hearst papers that refers to the All Highest as a degenerate cripple. It also implies that the All Highest hurt his left arm doing something horribly decadent with it, such as manipulating the Imperial manhood."

Bulow rolled his eyes. "Those articles are horrible, disgusting. Thank God the kaiser does not read such drivel, and I shall ensure that no one mentions it to him. There is no telling what irrational rage the emperor would fall prey to if he were not protected from such things. Frankly, von Holstein, I am surprised you even brought it up. It's lewd and beneath you."

With that, the chancellor whirled and marched out, leaving Holstein alone. Holstein stood silently for a moment, mentally reviewing the afternoon's events. Then he smiled and departed as well.

Chapter 9

F IRST," SAID ROOSEVELT, "on behalf of everyone here, I would like to commend you on the way you took charge of those poor lost New England sheep."

Patrick Mahan nodded his acceptance of the compliment. The others in the room effectively constituted an American war council. Along with Roosevelt was John Hay, Secretary of War Elihu Root, Secretary of the Navy John Long, Gen. Nelson Miles, and, for the first time, Adm. George Dewey. Dewey had disembarked at Norfolk and had just received word to go to the Saint Lawrence. The naval representative at future meetings would either be Navy Secretary Long or Patrick's eminent but distant cousin, Capt. Alfred Thayer Mahan. Patrick noted to himself that it was singularly unfair that he, as a brigadier general, should outrank his cousin, one of the foremost military minds the world had yet known.

Roosevelt continued. "The Massachusetts congressional delegation also praises your efforts, General Mahan, but insists that the late Colonel Blaney be made a hero. Politics, nothing but politics. We are issuing Blaney a posthumous Medal of Honor, which the brave fool's congressman brother-in-law will accept. You will receive a formal commendation from the governor of Massachusetts, as well as our undying gratitude."

John Hay led a brief smattering of applause. "Don't worry, Patrick, posthumous medals are the worst kind."

"Enough," Roosevelt chided gently. It was obvious that the formidable John Hay was no longer just secretary of state. He was now the number one assistant and adviser to the young and inexperienced president. "I have been informed that the British arms will start being available to our soldiers in a few days. At first, it will be only a trickle, then a torrent. When our boys are properly supplied we will drive out the invaders! General Miles has been working on plans for attacks on the German defenses that will accomplish our goals. He will, when appropriate, depart here and lead those endeavors."

Patrick looked surprised. General Miles had certainly risen in the esteem of Roosevelt in the brief time Patrick had been gone. But then Miles was the senior officer in the army, and if he wasn't to lead, then who would? There had to be an effort to drive out the Germans, and for the time being at least, it appeared that Nelson Miles would command the American army.

Roosevelt looked squarely at Patrick, obviously aware that his mind had wandered. "We would like your assessment of what you have seen regarding the German invaders."

As succinctly as he could, Patrick described what he had found out from his scouts and a couple of deserters. The force currently on American soil likely consisted of one corps of three divisions of about thirteen thousand men each. Patrick reminded them that the German army consisted of twenty-two such corps, although many of the divisions were significantly smaller. "They are in the process of reorganizing their total army into larger divisions. This is doubtless one of the newer corps with such large divisions."

Overall, he noted, the regular German army totaled about half a million men, with another half million in active reserve. The average German soldier was a conscript taken for a three-year period of intense training and duty, and then transferred to the reserves for another fifteen to twenty years during which he trained with his regiment for one full month each year. Thus even the German reserves were much better trained than any American force.

The German officers were almost entirely professionals, and many careerists came from the Prussian homeland. They reflected the bleak and harsh environment that their medieval forebears had wrested from the original Slavic owners. The Prussian militarist was to Germany what the Spartan had been to ancient Greece—a dangerous and formidable foe with centuries of experience waging war against the best that Asia and Europe could field against him.

"General Mahan," asked the president, "how many more men will they send?"

"Even though they have the potential to send a million men or more, I don't believe that's likely. There is one corps on our shores and another one about to disembark. I have been informed that two more corps are gathering in Germany and are being prepared for transport. That would bring their force to about 160,000 men." His source was Ian Gordon, who had given him the information less than an hour before the meeting. The British system of gathering intelligence was marvelous, Patrick thought. "Secretary Hay," asked Patrick, "do you think the situation in Europe will allow them to send many more?"

"No," Hay answered. "The situation there is too unstable, and they are so unloved by the other European nations."

"Thank you, sir," said Patrick. "Further, I feel that the two corps still in Germany will consist of reserves. As I stated, however, even their reserves are so well trained we may not notice any decline in their military skills. However, being reservists called up from civilian life, they might not wish to be here. That could affect their enthusiasm and morale. Additionally, the Germans do not wish to conquer; rather, they wish to exact from us just what they have asked for in the way of overseas possessions."

"I agree with Patrick," said Hay. "In Europe, wars are generally fought not to conquer a nation but to attain a goal. The German army will be here only long enough to achieve their goals. I cannot even imagine they would set up a puppet government to rule directly over a hostile population. Ultimately, the United States will rearm and be able to drive out the Germans. In simple math, please remember that the population of the United States is sixty-five million to Germany's fifty-five million. In the long run, this could be decisive."

"Which brings me to another point," Patrick added. "In their past wars with France, Germany has shown little mercy to irregulars or insurgents. Raiders or guerrillas captured by the Germans will be executed summarily. I also think the prisoners of war they've taken will be used as hostages to guarantee our relative good behavior."

Roosevelt's face was stern. "That is a price we may have to pay. I

cannot tell Americans not to strike back or defend their homes. No,
I will not. Mr. Hay, please inform the kaiser through whatever diplo-
matic channels you may wish to use that we will hold his army responsible for any atrocities or massacres, and that we consider any American taking arms against Germany to be a member of our military."

As Hay wrote himself a note, he thought it was an exercise in futility—that Roosevelt had a great deal to learn about his adversary—
but he kept the thought to himself. However, there was a further
point to be made. "Politically, it could be a disaster for the kaiser if
his reservists were to suffer heavy casualties." His eyes twinkled.
"General Miles, you must see to it."

Miles nodded. "I intend to."

"Strange people, the Germans," mused Roosevelt. "And they're all
ours to contend with, although, thanks to Britain, we are not totally
alone. You should also be aware that the British have detached ships
from both their home and Mediterranean fleets under an Admiral
John Fisher. That force will be defending the isolation of the Saint
Lawrence and covering our navy's sanctuary." He smiled thinly at
the brief murmurs of approval. "Gentlemen, this meeting's adjourned. A week from today will be Wednesday, the Fourth of July.
Our Independence Day will be a solemn one, I'm afraid. God only
knows how we'll celebrate it. Patrick, I thank you for your disserta-
tion. I would, however, like you to return to the invasion area and
keep in further touch."

"Yes, sir." That meant he would not have any chance at a command, at least not for the time being. However, he would still be the
president's emissary and be involved as the army prepared for the attack against the invaders. Also, he might have a chance to stop off at
a certain camp and see how Trina was doing.

While the others gathered their belongings to depart, it suddenly
dawned on Patrick that Admiral Dewey hadn't said a word. Why?
Was something occurring that the admiral hadn't wished to comment
on or be drawn into discussing?

As Patrick retrieved his hat and walked toward the door, a Negro
porter called to him. "General Mahan?"

"Yes."

"Sir, a woman called on the White House phone and insisted you
were living here and had to be reached. Fortunately, I overheard our

part of the conversation and I remembered your name on the admission list for tonight."

"Who was she?"

"Sir, she sounded Irish and very upset. She said that someone you knew, a Katrina Schuyler, had been burned in an accident and you should come as fast as you can."

Chapter 10

AFTER HEINZ SCHMIDT was unexpectedly commissioned as an officer, his world became a whirl: getting uniforms, finding out what a lieutenant was to do, whom to salute, whom not to salute, and just what the hell General Mahan wanted of him.

This was followed by a wild ride down to Washington on a commandeered private train where he, a young man who'd never been farther than twenty miles from home, was present in the White House and saw the great leaders of America. These included the high-ranking generals who made even General Mahan stand up straighter than normal. Heinz even saw the president, who seemed to acknowledge him and smile but did not speak to him.

This was followed by an even wilder train and horseback trip back up to New York, because a woman friend of the general's was in some kind of trouble, injured or something. Burned in a fire was what he'd heard.

Finally, the trip ended at a small house outside Waterbury, Connecticut, which he later found out was rented by the woman they'd ridden to see. Patrick pounded on the door, which was promptly opened by a young woman in a drab dress who looked puzzled for only a moment.

"Well, thank God. What the bloody hell took you so long?"

Heinz was shocked. Patrick pushed the woman aside and entered, with Heinz following. "Damnit, Molly, in your message you forgot to say which camp you were at and where Katrina'd been taken. Do you know how many camps there are around here?"

The answer, Heinz knew from recent and frustrating experience looking for them, was a lot.

Molly softened and managed a small smile, which, Heinz realized, made her rather attractive. She had a good figure, full but still trim, and she had a nice smile and the hint of dimples. She was also very young, perhaps even younger than he. He straightened his brand-new uniform tunic and smiled.

Molly cheerfully acknowledged her oversight. "Well, perhaps I could have been a bit more specific, but you're here now so it doesn't matter."

"Right. Now where is Katrina and how is she?" Patrick demanded.

Molly answered in an accented voice that Heinz realized was Irish. "She's in her room and she's resting. Do you want me to tell her you're here?"

"In a minute. First, what happened, and has her family been told?"

Molly sat and gestured the others to do likewise. "She was burned in a fire that started in a storage tent. She was in there with some others trying to figure out how many blankets or some such there were when the tent sort of exploded. There must have been some chemicals or something, and a lamp made them blow up. She was dragged out hurt. Her face and hands were all swollen and red, and her hair was burned off. She was unconscious and cut bad on her head and they had to shave off what hair remained and stitch her scalp."

"Jesus," said Patrick.

"Even so, she was luckier than the others. She turned out to be more scalded than burned. A couple of other people were killed in the fire." Molly looked a little contrite. "I may have panicked, but I didn't know what else to do."

"And her family?"

"When she was unconscious I realized I didn't know anything about her family. When she came to I found out that her father was in Texas and we don't know where, and her brother's at sea in the navy. Didn't matter. Neither was going to be here for her."

Patrick nodded. Her father could likely be located, but certainly not her brother.

"Now, General," she glanced at Heinz, "who is this young giant?"

Patrick quickly made the introductions. He watched incredulously as her face turned from a look of gamine charm to one of venom. "A German? You brought us a fuckin' German?"

He reached over and grabbed her hand. "No, Molly. Heinz is not from Germany. He's from Ohio, which is in this country. He joined the army to fight them."

Her look of hatred passed, at least a little. Molly was uncertain. Heinz seized the opportunity. "Miss Duggan, I am not a German, I am an American. I was born here, in Ohio, which makes me a citizen of the United States. My parents and many other relatives came from Germany, but now they're Americans too. They left because of the German government and its crazy kaisers and its damned army that likes to kill and crush innocent people."

Molly digested this. It had also been a while since a young man called her "miss." "All right," she said quite formally. "We'll see. General, I'll ask Miss Schuyler if she will see you now."

Patrick thanked her. As she disappeared down the short hallway, he made a mental note to give Heinz some idea of Molly's tragic time during the Brooklyn fire and how it had affected her attitude. Perhaps he couldn't change her, but it would help to understand things.

A moment later, Molly beckoned and Patrick entered the small, darkened room and took a chair by the bed. The creature under the covers was a mummy, swathed in soft white bandages so that only her blue eyes were visible. The hands were wrapped in white mittens, and her head was also covered with loose white bandages.

"Frightened, Patrick?" Her voice was soft but firm.

"No."

"Well," she said, carefully adjusting herself so that she could sit up better, "I certainly was."

"How painful is it?"

"Endurable. I've been told I look worse than I am. The burns are healing, although much of my face and hands are red and scabby. I believe I'm all swollen as well. But the doctors tell me nothing is permanent and I'll heal in time."

"How soon will the bandages come off?"

"Anytime I wish. I had Molly wrap me so I wouldn't scare you away."

Patrick laughed, half out of relief. "Scare me? A bold general?" His voice softened. "Show me."

Slowly, and without using all her fingers, she unwrapped her hands, and then her face, and he realized how fortunate she had been. Even though he knew she was healing, she was virtually unrecognizable. She carefully removed her cap and he saw her shaved scalp and the jagged sewn gash that ran down the middle of her head. There was a light fuzz of blond where her hair was just starting to grow in. Her hands and the skin on her face were, as promised, cracked and scabbed. Where her skin was actually visible it was reddened like a bad sunburn. He realized she must hurt something awful.

"I said I can handle the pain and I will. I must," she said. "Do I have a choice?"

"Not really."

"I am very fortunate and I know it. Mr. Morris pulled me from the fire." To Patrick's puzzled look, she continued. "Mr. Morris is our chief of security in the camp. He was a police chief in a town on Long Island. Very sadly he lost his family in a German bombardment of his town. He is a very tormented man. I am, however, eternally grateful that he was nearby at the time."

"As am I. Are you confined to the bed?"

"No. I was just resting. I still tire very easily." She shook her head. "No, that's not quite right. I've spent most of the last several days lying here feeling sorry for myself, which is ridiculous when you consider the true horrors the refugees are enduring." She raised herself to a sitting position. "Please hand me my robe."

He turned and found it draped across a chair.

"Please don't be bashful. I'm going to need your help."

Patrick took her arm, being careful not to touch her hands, and aided her to a standing position. As she swung her legs out of the bed he caught a glimpse of bare calf and tried not to look startled. When she stood, her nightgown modestly covered her from neck to foot. However, it was a light cotton gown and he sensed she had little on underneath.

"You're not going to blush, are you?" she asked as he draped the robe over her and eased her hands through the sleeves. Patrick allowed that he hoped he would not. He helped her into the living room, where a surprised Molly and Heinz were waiting.

"I should have done this a few days ago. Molly, why didn't you make me?" Molly snorted and said she'd tried but Katrina'd been a typical stubborn Dutchie.

Patrick looked at his watch. It was only midmorning. "I've got to get to General Smith fairly soon, but I can spend the rest of the day. If you're willing, I'd like to take you out for a carriage ride and a small picnic. It'd do you some good."

"I'll have to be very careful of the sun."

Molly spoke. "You can wear a bonnet to protect your head and face and I'll fix something to cover your hands."

"Fine, but how will I eat?"

Patrick grinned. "If necessary, I'll feed you. I'll be back at noon. Lieutenant Schmidt, you are free for the rest of the day." He paused. "That is, after you've found a place for you and me to stay."

Molly smiled. "Why General, sir, you and the German can sleep in the stable."

Later, after Patrick and Katrina had departed, Heinz confronted Molly in the kitchen of the house.

"Molly, how can I convince you I am an American, not a German?"

"Heinz Schmidt is not a German name? Perhaps you're one of those Polacks. Or even a dago." There was bitterness in her voice, but also a degree of sadness.

"Molly, General Mahan told me your brother was killed by the Germans and that one beat you badly, and I'm sorry, but I want you to realize that I'm here to fight them, not love them. Look, the general and Miss Schuyler left us here while they went on their picnic, and I don't want to spend the rest of the day with you hating me for something I never did."

She looked at him, a large young man, light haired and open faced. He looked honest and intelligent. And she wanted to hurt him. Or did she?

"You said the Germans killed my brother? They blew his brains out in cold blood when all he did was try to protest them. He was twenty and the insides of his skull splattered all over me! Beat me? Some pig of a German punched me all over with his great fists, and then stuck his ugly thing inside me and raped me. Then, when he felt like it, he did it all over again!" She sagged from the confession and, to her fury, tears came from her eyes and her body began to convulse with sobs. "And it's not just me. We see it every day as new refugees come in. The Germans let them pass, but they rob them, beat and kill them if they refuse, and take the women just like they did me. They are pigs!"

As she tried to regain control of herself, she saw the stricken and hurt look on his face, and saw that he too was near tears. "My father," he said softly, "had two brothers. Now he has one. The oldest, Klaus, was drafted into the German army. It was peacetime and there was no problem. He would serve his three years and come home and resume his life. So would his two younger brothers. But one day Klaus came home in a box. An accident, they said. But we found he'd been beaten to death by a sergeant for not saluting some goddamn Junker properly. They held him down and stomped on his chest with their boots until his ribs were all crushed and he was puking blood."

Heinz took a deep breath and felt some of the pain his father had felt. "When my father and his brother found that nobody was going to do anything about the murder, even laughed at him, they decided they wanted nothing more to do with the kaiser's Reich, and that Germany was no longer their home. This is our home now and, if necessary, I will kill Germans to protect it."

Molly looked at him and managed a small, bitter smile. "Perhaps I already did that for you," she said and told him about the vengeance she'd extracted from her attacker.

"Good," he said when she was finished.

"Young Lieutenant, you may be right. Perhaps I cannot go on hating everyone because of what one did. You are the general's friend and he is Katrina's friend, and they are both my friends. Therefore, I must figure out how and if I can learn to include you."

"Molly, let me be your friend," Heinz urged. "I am your friend whether you realize it or not or want it or not."

"Really? We shall see whether I have a choice or not. Besides, don't we have an assignment from their lordships?"

Yes, he thought, and not all day in which to accomplish it. If he and the general were to remain in the area, they had to find a place to stay. With an overflowing refugee camp only a few miles away, that could be a monumental problem. "You said there was a stable?"

*   *   *

Alone in his White House office, Theodore Roosevelt glared at the
document he gripped in his hand. The handwriting was his own, but
the words and the topic were so strange, so alien, as to be almost inconceivable. But they had to be conceivable now, didn't they? He
could not deny the dark reality of the invasion and the upheavals
throughout the nation that resulted from it. He took his pen and began to read again, poised to make corrections and additions to the
message that would be telegraphed throughout America the next day.

My Dear Americans,
   Today, Wednesday, July 4, 1901, is the 125th anniversary of the
founding of the United States of America, and a day in which the
whole country should be uniting in festive celebration of a century
and a quarter of freedom and prosperity.
   Yet we look about and find it is not to be. For the first time
since the War of 1812, a foreign army has imposed itself on our
soil, and American soldiers are dying in valiant efforts to hurl
them away.
   We did not wish this war. We did nothing to deserve it or en-
courage it. Yet we have been invaded by a tyrannical European
power that wants our wealth, our dignity, our future, and our
freedom. We will not surrender to them! As I write this, our armies
and our navy are gathering to expel them. It will be a most difficult task. Germany is a great military power. We must, therefore,
be greater, stronger, smarter.
   Germany has demanded that we negotiate a surrender. We shall
indeed do that, but the surrender we negotiate will be the kaiser's,
not ours. We will not rest until every German soldier has been
purged from our land, our cities have been retaken, our homes
have been rebuilt and reoccupied, and the diabolical kaiser has
been punished for his grievously evil deeds.
   It will take time to do this and we may have to pay a terrible
price. The cost will include the lives of many young men who will
be called upon to make the greatest sacrifice possible in the cause
of their country. We honor them! We will make those sacrifices
and proudly mourn our fallen and condemn the invader with our
anger.

A word. Please, dear friends, let our anger be righteous and focused only at the German invader. But let us not forget that we are all immigrants, or descendants of immigrants. Either we or our forefathers all came to this fair land from elsewhere in order to be free. This includes people from Germany or of German ancestry. Many of the Germans who came to America did so to be free of that same malevolent kaiser whose marauding hordes have appeared on our shore. The Germans who came to America have already fought bravely in our wars, including the Civil War and the recent Spanish war. Now those same German Americans are uniting with other Americans whose backgrounds include English, Irish, Italian, Dutch, Swedish, and Spanish against a common enemy. Governors of two states, Wisconsin and Ohio, have informed me of their plan to form a German American legion to fight against the kaiser's barbarian army. Therefore, I implore you not to take vengeance against the helpless immigrants. I have been saddened by reports of burnings, beatings, insults, and, yes, lynchings inflicted upon helpless and outnumbered people who happen to have recently come from Germany.

If you are so brave that you wish to fight Germans, then join our army! I guarantee your blood lust will be sated. I further assure you that there are no saboteurs about. They were all captured, they were all German officers, and they will be punished according to the law. So there is no reason to fear someone who talks with an accent or who behaves differently.

So let us spend this day in prayer, reflection, and preparation. Then let us go forth to bear our burden and earn our just victory.

          God bless America,
          Theodore Roosevelt
          President of the United States

                    *   *   *

Katrina Schuyler tried hard not to giggle, but it was impossible.

"Darn it, Trina, how can I feed you if you keep making it so difficult?" Patrick had graduated to using the more familiar form of her first name.

The giggles turned to laughter. "I don't know," she gasped. Patrick had a piece of chicken impaled on a fork and was poised to pounce

with it as soon as her mouth stood still. He was a wondrously ridiculous sight.

"Is this what happened to me when I was a little baby?" Trina
asked.

"Probably."

"Look, I'm bruised, not a cripple. Just cut the food into small
pieces and let me use a knife to navigate the items onto a fork. I
think I can grasp it well enough from there."

"How about a wineglass? Can you maneuver one of those?" He
held a bottle of chilled white wine and a corkscrew.

Trina laughed hard again. "Most definitely," she answered.

How pleasant, Patrick thought, and how misleading. The July sky
was a vivid blue and the meadow that surrounded the shade tree
where they were relaxing was as rich and verdant as could be imagined. A soft breeze weakened the thrust of the sun and made them
comfortable. All around them birds chirped and squirrels chattered
from overhead branches.

And there were no ants. Yet.

But only a few miles away from their idyll was a refugee camp
that teemed with thousands of hurt, lost, and bewildered souls,
huddled under inadequate canvas, many of them damaged both in
body and soul. And only about thirty miles farther, there was war,
and armed people were killing each other.

This was an interlude, an oasis of calm, and it could not last. Tomorrow he would go south, find Baldy Smith's headquarters, and try
to see what was developing. In a few days Trina would be healed
enough to go back to helping the refugees find more permanent
places to stay than a squalid tent camp.

The comings and goings were, she told him, developing into a
cycle. The trains southbound from Springfield and Boston brought
soldiers and supplies and picked up refugees in Hartford. From there
the refugees were shipped to other cities throughout the eastern half
of the United States. Tens of thousands had already departed. Hartford was developing into quite a railhead, and a number of temporary
spur lines had been laid down to handle the dramatically increased
volume of traffic. It seemed to Patrick to be very well organized.

Along with talk of refugee camps, they learned a great deal about

each other. Trina, he found, was extremely well read and well educated, almost intimidating in the depth of her knowledge. She had
attended a number of classes at Barnard. She was also extremely ath-
letic, another point that seemed to bother her peers who felt that a
woman's role was to be docile and physically weak. What Patrick
first took for thinness he realized was a lithe muscularity. She enjoyed cycling, hiking, swimming, and horseback riding. Patrick recalled the horseback ride from New York and had to admit she was
vastly superior to him in that category. He had reminded her he was
infantry, not cavalry.

Trina's younger brother was a recently commissioned ensign in
the navy and was serving on the newest battleship, the *Alabama*. She
had no idea where he was, except that the ship was on a South
American cruise. She hoped it was out of harm's way, although she
knew in her heart that it would not be so forever. Her father was a
wealthy investor, descended from a long line of equally successful
men. He was currently out west buying up oil rights. Jacob Schuyler
had a feeling that the internal combustion engine was going to be
important in the future and wanted to be prepared for that day. He
was, Trina told Patrick, buying up the oil drilling rights to hundreds
of thousands of acres almost for pennies apiece. She had been in
contact with him by telegram, and he was trying to make it back
from Texas, where oil had been found and was beginning to be
drilled in profitable quantities. The first well, she laughed, was something named Spindle-Top.

When she found that Patrick was from southern Michigan, she
asked him if he knew Henry Ford.

"No, I've never actually met him, but I know who he is and understand he's trying to line up investors for a new corporation that will
make cheap automobiles. He hasn't asked my family to invest. Although we're not poor, I don't think we'd be interested in such a
risky endeavor."

He continued. "My family has lived in the Detroit area for a couple
of generations. My grandfather was a blacksmith and gradually ex-
panded from repairing implements into making farm machinery. My
father made the enterprise very profitable, but they wouldn't be interested in Ford. At least not yet and not as investors, although it
wouldn't surprise me if they were interested in working with him as a

supplier. I haven't followed those goings-on very much. I just know what I've read in letters from home. I chose the army, not farm machinery." He laughed. "Why, has Ford contacted your father?"

"Yes, but Father's not interested in a direct investment either. But he did inform Ford that he would like to sell the automobiles if he was able to make them. That and oil are the extent of his interests at this time." She thought for a moment. She had ridden in an automobile exactly once in her life and found it an experience that was both frightening and exhilarating. "If Ford succeeds, do you think the army would ever use automobiles instead of horses?"

"Not for a long, long time. The automobile would have to be made reliable as well as inexpensive. That and it would have to be able to go cross-country over rugged terrain like a horse, and there would have to be fuel dumps to keep the things going. And what about mechanics for repairs? It would take a major reorganization of the army to accommodate automobiles. No, I don't think that will happen for a while. Although," he demurred, "there are other countries that are experimenting with putting machine guns on them and protecting them with armor plate." He did not add that the current U.S. Army was firmly entrenched in the last century and not, thanks to Nelson Miles, very interested in future developments.

She asked him why he joined the army and not the navy and was amused at the response: he got seasick.

Quietly, they got around to the reasons why they both were still single. Trina readily admitted that her wealth had attracted many potential suitors when she was younger, but her fond and doting father would not push her into a relationship she did not want. She had known from early in her youth that she would never be a raving beauty according to the standards of the time. Her intellect and forceful personality scared off potential suitors, however obsessed with money they might have been. Too many men didn't like dominant women or were afraid of them. There were also those who felt her quest for learning and athletics smacked of Bohemianism.

When she mentioned that fact to Patrick, it perplexed him. Since his simplistic view of Bohemianism meant a degree of sexual promiscuity, he found himself wondering about her, and also wondering why he was concerned. Before he could wonder more, Trina answered his unasked question.

"I am hardly a Bohemian. I am probably more conservative than an old dowager." She frowned. "Why do people fear me when I try to be a little different? All I want is the freedom to be me, to learn, to search. Does that make me a Bohemian?"

Her answer relieved him. "Of course not." Now why was he so relieved?

"Do I frighten you, Patrick?"

He lay on the ground, his face looking into the latticework of tree limbs while she sat farther in the shade, her back against the tree trunk. "Naw. After fighting Apaches, Spanish, Germans, and the odd drunk in a garrison town, I'm not frightened of you at all."

Patrick told her about growing up an only child in Michigan, around Detroit, and what it was like being a soldier, moving from place to place and never really being settled. He had a lot of friends and was part of a fraternity, but he had little opportunity for close relationships. As for women, there were very few in a military compound, and those who were there were either already taken or not worth taking. It was, he told her, a strangely monastic existence. Not that he was a saint, but there was no reason to bring up everything.

He told her that for some time he had been considering leaving the military. "I think I may be through with war and killing. I know I don't want to sell farm machinery, but I would like to do something like what I did at West Point—teach. I've friends at the University of Michigan and maybe I can get something there. With what I get from the family business, and a few other investments I've managed to make, I could live there quite comfortably."

Trina nodded. "I wonder now if I could ever go back to living in New York. It's like a phase of my life that's closed. It's occurred to me that I was never really comfortable in the city. For all its cosmopolitanism, it can be strangely restrictive. I don't think I will ever go back there to live. Those apartments I lived in were rented. It's as if we knew we would not put down permanent roots."

Against their wishes, the afternoon passed. As the sun descended, Patrick gathered their belongings and they drove the carriage slowly back to town and her house. When they arrived, Heinz informed him he'd found suitable accommodations with a local farmer a couple of miles down the road. He'd done so by appealing to the man's patriotism and by outbidding another man.

The four of them ate a quick and light dinner prepared by Molly. Both Patrick and Trina were openly pleased that Molly and Heinz had managed to negotiate a sort of unarmed truce. With dinner finished, it was time to depart. Patrick told Heinz to get the horses, which gave him a moment to say a quiet good-bye to Katrina.

As they stood by the open door, Patrick had a feeling of longing. He wanted to touch Trina, but he feared that simply reaching for her hand would hurt her even more than the possibility of rebuff would hurt him. They stood in silence for a minute until Trina solved the problem. She reached up and kissed him softly on the lips. "I'm not afraid of you either, General Patrick. Please come back to me. I would appreciate it very, very much."

Chapter 11

CAPTAIN ROBLEY EVANS, Fighting Bob to his peers and the press, paced the deck of the battleship *Alabama* and peered into the mist. He had a feeling of utter impotence. The *Alabama* was one of the finest and newest American warships afloat; yet with the distant sounds of ships' guns echoing about, she was forced to crawl at less than one-third her rated speed of sixteen knots. He wondered if she was moving at all. It was maddening.

The powerful *Alabama* was designated BB-8, or the eighth modern battleship in an expanding American navy. It displaced more than twelve thousand tons, was more than 370 feet in length, and had a crew of just under seven hundred. The only newer American battleship was the *Wisconsin,* BB-9, currently cruising the West Coast.

"Anything, Mr. Lansing?"

"No, sir. The lookouts think they can see the sky, so the mist may be breaking up, but until then we are well and truly blind."

Evans breathed deeply of the warm, moist air. What on earth had caused a mist at this time and place? It only showed how little control man has over the planet. According to the navigator's best estimate, made less than an hour ago when they could see, the *Alabama* should have been about five miles off Saint Augustine, the ancient city on the east coast of Florida.

Evans dared not speed up lest they blunder into something that might prove fatal or run aground. Evans and the crew of the *Alabama* knew full well that the United States was at war with Germany. Less than two weeks ago, they had been in port in Rio de Janeiro when the word was cabled throughout the world. In immediate contact with the American embassy, they'd been told to wait in Brazilian waters until they were either asked to leave by the Brazilians or given further orders.

A few days later, orders had arrived directing the ship to depart Brazil and steam directly to the naval station at Guantanamo Bay on the eastern tip of Cuba. There they hoped they would be further enlightened. They had steamed carefully and prepared for war by painting the ship gray, discarding unneeded wooden furniture, and practicing their gunnery, which had proven to be a major problem for the navy.

With gun ranges and ship speeds increasing, it was damnably hard to hit anything at all. Worse, the *Alabama*'s secondary batteries, set as they were in the hull of the ship, could easily be rendered useless in a heavy sea, as the waves would crash right over them. There had to be a better way, Evans had thought. That was why he had experimented with the new Royal Navy way of aiming and firing that was being developed by their brilliant young innovator Percy Scott. So far, Evans had been impressed with the results.

Scott's technique was called "continuous aim" and required a telescopic sight for each gun, an elevating wheel to raise the gun so that the target did not become lost in the pitch and roll of the seas, and practice, practice, practice. The result was that a gunner did not have to find his target each time the guns fired; thus the rate of fire as well as the accuracy were increased. Evans had recalled the humiliating misses at Santiago where hundreds of shells splashed all over the ocean but rarely near the Spanish ships. The newspapers had crowed over the terrible shooting by the Spanish but had apparently not noted the almost equally bad American gunnery.

The *Alabama* had made Guantanamo without incident. What had been a bright and gleaming example of American naval pride in Rio had been transformed into a dark and lethal weapon, at least as lethal as Evans could possibly make it. He knew that only a handful of his crew had ever seen battle, and that had been in the one-sided victories against the totally overmatched Spaniards. How would they react?

All the drilling and practice in the world could not compensate for the real thing. For all intents and purposes, his ship was a virgin.

There were other problems as well. The numbers of men in the navy's officer corps had not kept pace with the ongoing expansion. The *Alabama,* like virtually every other ship, was short more than 20 percent of its allotted complement of officers. This resulted in junior officers having serious responsibilities. Evans did not relish the thought of going to war without a full complement of officers or enlisted men.

But Evans had the experience his ship did not. An 1863 graduate of Annapolis, he had been wounded late in the Civil War, at Fort Fisher. His previous commands included the armored cruiser *New York* and the battleships *Indiana* and *Iowa.* The *Iowa* was his during the battle of Santiago. Had the Spanish war lasted longer, there was talk of giving him a cruiser squadron to send against the mainland of Spain. The *Alabama* was not supposed to have been his, but the sudden illness of Captain Brownson had given him an unexpected opportunity for independent command, and he had relished it.

A powerfully built man, Evans was clean shaven in a time of beards and bushy mustaches, and he parted his thinning brown hair directly down the middle. With his strong demeanor and colorful vocabulary, he could intimidate as well as charm. He liked everything about his navy except his small marine contingent. He considered them useless mouths on his ship and quietly urged that the Marine Corps be abolished. In his midforties, he was considered a man with a future.

At Guantanamo they had received a coded message directing the *Alabama* to the Gulf of Saint Lawrence. So totally unexpected was this order that Evans had it decoded several times before accepting it as true. Canadian waters? He had hoped someone knew just what the hell they were up to.

He hadn't planned to be anywhere near Saint Augustine, but one of his crewmen had been badly hurt in a gun-loading accident and needed help that was well beyond the scope of his medical officers. Besides, Evans had rationalized, it would be a grand opportunity to pick up some additional supplies and the latest news of the war. Perhaps someone would cancel the puzzling orders to make for Canada.

And now they heard the sound of guns. His crew had been bending and peering over their weapons for what seemed an eternity while lookouts tried to make visual sense of what they were hearing.

"Mr. Lansing, anything?"

Heavy guns could only mean the presence of the Germans. Yet in what strength? Was the *Alabama* being led to a slaughter? Running away was anathema to Evans, but so was running aground. Thus they prudently kept their speed agonizingly slow.

"Captain, the lookouts say they can now see the horizon."

Evans smiled thinly. "Well, that confirms we are still on this earth!"

There were a few forced chuckles. The captain had made a joke. When Capt. Robley Dunglison Evans made a joke, regardless of the circumstances, you laughed. The lookouts in their cramped platforms above had the best view. There was a school of thought that held that the captain belonged up there as well, but Evans disagreed. Although the view might be somewhat better, the command apparatus was here, on the navigating bridge, twenty feet below, where half a dozen officers and men were jammed into the little lookout post.

Ship-to-ship communication was either by semaphore or Morse flashes, or even the new wireless, but messages were sent throughout the ship by different means. First, there were speaking tubes, which became useless when several people tried to speak at the same time, or when it was windy and the air distorted the sound. Second, there were the recently installed electric telephones, but their signals were weak, scratchy, and often overwhelmed by the sound of the guns. That is, when they worked at all. That left the tried and true means of sending messengers or shouting out commands and hoping they were heard. A wise captain used all means and hoped the men understood exactly what they were supposed to be doing.

"Sir, the lookouts can make out two, no, make that three ships off our starboard side. They, damnit, they are firing into the town!"

Evans pondered. "Are we making much smoke?" Like all major warships, the *Alabama* burned coal, and the finger of black smoke usually pointed skyward, giving away her presence long before she could actually be seen.

"No, sir. Very little." The mist was also doing them a favor by keeping the smoke down on the ship and not letting it rise to the sky.

"And what do the lookouts make them out to be?"

"They say cruisers. One heavy and two smaller and all in line, Captain."

"Very well. Maintain speed and steer in the direction of the enemy ships. Let the lookouts guide us. I mean to run down that line."

Evans stood tensely by his chair and drummed his hand on the armrest. Three cruisers. The *Alabama* had a primary battery of four 13-inch guns in two turrets of two guns each, one forward and one aft. There was a secondary battery of fourteen 6-inch guns in single mounts, with seven on each side of the ship. From what he recalled reading of German cruisers, no one of them could be a match for the *Alabama*. But three of them? The challenge was exciting. If fate smiled, he could wipe out an entire German squadron.

He straightened up. By God, the mist was clearing! He could see the dim shapes of the enemy. "What range?"

"Four thousand yards and closing. Sir, they are coming toward us at very slow speed. They may even have stopped. The heavy cruiser is closest."

Stopped? Not damn likely, thought Evans, but without anyone to prevent them from shelling the town, they were likely moving as slowly as he and enjoying their day's work. "Fire when ready, Gridley. I want the big guns on the heavy. Divide the secondary on the other two."

Lansing smiled. The Gridley comment was an old joke. Within seconds, the ship shook as the forward twin thirteens belched fire at the lead German cruiser, with the smaller 6-inch guns quickly joining in the chorus, blinding them all with the lingering smoke.

The smoke cleared quickly and Evans could see that the lead cruiser was obscured by splashes. Misses, he cursed. "Goddamnit! What the hell's wrong with our gunners?"

Lansing looked up from his speaking tube. "Lookouts report no hits, sir."

Evans cursed again in frustration. Surely all the practice had not been wasted. Or were they firing short in fear of hitting the town behind? He pounded his chair with his fist. Probably the gunners were just nervous. Let them work it out. The big guns fired again, silencing him, and the bridge was again blanketed by the stinking smoke cloud. He gave orders to turn the ship so that the rear turret could also be brought to bear, even though that meant widening the distance slightly. It made no sense to have half of his biggest guns unavailable.

"Hit!"

Evans strained to see. Yes, smoke was pouring from the front superstructure that housed the lead enemy cruiser's bridge. He chilled, thinking of the bloody carnage that smoke hid. The bridge was where his German counterpart held sway. Only now there was a good chance the German had been blown to bits. Evans didn't even hear the rear turret fire.

"Hit!"

Again Evans pounded the chair with his fist, this time with relief and satisfaction. One of the lead German's two funnels had collapsed, and smoke was pouring from her innards, including clouds of white that indicated her boilers had been penetrated. She was now immobile. A cruiser's armor could not stop a 13-inch shell weighing eleven hundred pounds and traveling at more than two thousand feet per second. Cruisers were meant to fight other cruisers, not battleships.

"Sir, lookouts identify her as the German cruiser *Freya*. She has two 8.2-inch guns and a half dozen 6-inchers. Sir, she also has torpedoes."

"Thank you, Mr. Lansing. Let the lookouts watch for torpedo wakes." Evans watched spellbound as his ship passed down the line of three Germans. Their return fire had been slow, very slow indeed. He suspected that virtually all the lookouts had been watching the shore bombardment and not looking to their rear. The smaller German guns were, so far, firing wildly. He tried, but failed, to feel some sympathy for them, tried to visualize their reactions as they saw the *Alabama* emerging from the mist at such close range and with so little time to react.

The *Alabama*'s guns hammered away with a life of their own. He could not help an involuntary cry as the forward single-gun turret of the *Freya* lifted into the air and fell into the ocean with a mighty splash. The sound and feel of the explosion washed over them seconds later. The *Freya* was doomed, seeming to shudder as the life was pounded out of her. Fires raged everywhere. She was no longer returning fire. "Secondary batteries on the heavy. Shift the big guns to the little ships."

"Aye, aye, sir."

"Who are they, Mr. Lansing? We should know their names before we sink them."

Lansing smiled. "They appear to be the *Gefion* and another like her. I don't know how many in that particular class. The *Gefion* has ten 4.1-inchers and torpedoes."

Evans nodded. The lookouts were again instructed to let him know if one of the infernal torpedoes was launched at his ship. The *Gefion* and her companion each had triple stacks and each was flying apart under the bombardment. Pieces of metal flew skyward along with what were, sometimes very obviously, bodies. The last ship, still unnamed, suddenly lifted out of the water and disintegrated as her magazine exploded. Two down.

"Torpedo in the water!"

Evans rushed to the port side of the circular bridge and stared at the blue-green water, straining to see the lethal tracks.

"Captain," yelled Lansing, "lookouts say the torpedo will miss. It may have been thrown off the German ship by an internal explosion and not actually launched." Evans nodded to mask his relief and turned back to the one-sided battle.

The second ship, the *Gefion,* seemed to disappear in a cloud of water and spray as the guns of the *Alabama* bracketed her. She was given a momentary respite as the *Alabama,* having run the Germans' futile gauntlet, turned about. This simply gave the fresh and frustrated gunners on the starboard batteries an opportunity to practice their hard-earned skills in what was now a slaughter, not a battle. In moments, this phase too was over as the last German ship began to settle in the water, blazing from stem to stern. Evans called a ceasefire as he saw lifeboats being lowered and frantic German sailors jumping into the sea. He gave orders for their own boats to be lowered and the survivors rounded up.

"I do not," he added sternly, "want hundreds of goddamn Germans on my ship. Bring only the swimmers and the seriously injured aboard. Gather the lifeboats and direct them to the shore." When an officer started to say something, he waved down the protest. "We will send our own marines ashore to see that the fools aren't lynched, although," he grumbled, "that might not be a bad idea for some of their senior officers. At least it will give the marines something to do for their pay. Now, what about our own damage? Any?"

"Captain, we were hit at least three times, no major damage. However, we do have at least four dead and seven wounded."

Evans nodded and tried to keep the astonishment from showing. In the intensity of the battle, he hadn't been aware they'd been touched.

In the lookout's position high above the *Alabama,* Ens. Terry Schuyler searched his memories. Nothing in his twenty-three years of life had prepared him for the shattering, thundering drama and violence he'd just witnessed from the best seat on the ship. His lookout position was even with the tops of the twin funnels, and, unlike other days when the smoke had blown on him and obscured his view, his vision had been marvelously clear. He'd seen the guns fire and watched the shells hit. How many had died? How many were wounded? His own ship had been relatively unscathed, but what about the Germans? His books told him the *Freya* had a complement of more than 450, and the *Gefion,* if that's what she was, and her twin had crews of more than 300. That totaled about 1,100 men! The presence of the lifeboats meant there were survivors, perhaps many, but he knew there were equally as many dead. The *Alabama*'s own lifeboats had been lowered and were approaching as close as possible to the stricken cruisers without endangering themselves from the fires and the still-exploding ammunition.

There was a shuddering, crying sound as the *Gefion* capsized, her broad hull grotesquely in view, and then began to slip beneath the surface.

"Kinda looks like a fat-ass whore I usta fuck in Hong Kong, if you ask me, sir."

Ensign Schuyler thought about chastising Seaman First Class Winslow but decided against it. Winslow, toothless and wiry, was one of his companions in what would have been called the crow's nest in sailing ships, and he had been in the navy for the greater portion of his fifty-odd years. Schuyler did not think Winslow was chastiseable. Winslow had been up for discipline before the captain's mast, or stick, as it was known in the ranks. Sailor's slang amused him; during idle times, he had been trying to develop a glossary of terms.

Schuyler's hands started to shake in delayed reaction, and he wondered if he would be able to speak coherently. The silence of this moment was as deafening as the roar of battle when the 13-inchers went off below him. He knew he didn't belong in command of this post, at least not yet, and the unexpected responsibility had been awesome. He prayed he had made no mistakes. At least not serious ones.

Winslow grinned toothlessly. "Goddamn, sir, weren't that a helluva show? Quite a way to earn me twenty-four dollars a month, now ain't it?"

Terry sagged to a sitting position. No one was interested anymore in ship identities or speed or torpedoes. He was dirty and exhausted and there were a lot of other places he'd rather be now, like home. "Yeah, Seaman Winslow, one helluva show. One helluva show."

"Tell me, General Mahan, how does one make hamburger?"

Patrick considered both the question and the source. "Well, General Funston, I suppose one would need meat."

Funston chuckled, rolled over onto his side, and laid his field glasses on the ground. The men were well hidden from prying eyes by fresh-cut shrubs. Major General Frederick Funston was a self-made soldier in an American military where you were usually doomed if you were not a West Pointer. He had earlier risen to the rank of brigadier general through skill, tenacity, and a great deal of merit. He had been promoted to his new rank of major general at the same time Patrick had become a brigadier general. A short man, Funston was less than five and a half feet tall. He was in his midforties and had red hair that was starting to gray at the edges. He was bowlegged and pugnacious. As a youthful dropout from the University of Kansas, he'd decided to fight with the Cubans for their independence and joined the American army when war finally came. His abilities brought him notice and rank, and finally he became colonel under Arthur MacArthur in the Philippines.

Frederick Funston, with his slightly silly-sounding name, had the reputation of a street fighter, and now he was in command of a newly formed division.

"Meat?" he snickered. "What kind of meat, Patrick?"

Shit, thought Patrick, why are we playing word games with Germans coming down the pike? "Raw meat, Fred. Dead, raw meat. And don't you need a meat grinder?" The two men had met a couple of days before, renewed an earlier brief acquaintence, and taken a quick liking

to each other. As Roosevelt's observer, Patrick had been invited by
Funston to watch the ambush of a German column. As Funston had
explained, it was time to strike back.

Funston slapped him on the shoulder. "And how do you feed that
raw meat into a meat grinder, smart-ass?"

Despite his tenseness, Patrick had to laugh. "With your hands?"
He began to think he'd rather face the Germans than Frederick
Funston's foolish questions.

"You're hopeless, Patrick. No, you feed it in one piece at a time."
He picked up his binoculars and held them to his eyes. "Now watch,"
he said, all jocularity suddenly gone.

Funston and Patrick were in a woodland that covered several dozen
acres. It fronted on an open meadow that ended in another wooded
area. A wagon road ran down the center and straight toward them.

About in the middle, a small group of armed men, soldiers in civilian clothes, sat huddled about a fire, cooking a meal. They were
the bait for the trap Funston was about to spring.

Patrick and Funston, along with Funston's soldiers, were west of the
Housatonic River near the small village of New Canaan. They were
about twenty miles east of the site of the unlamented Blaney's defeat.
Prudently, the Americans had earlier withdrawn their forces farther
east, almost to the Housatonic, which formed a natural north-south
boundary running from Long Island Sound toward Massachusetts.

Funston dropped his voice to a whisper. "What a wonderful place
for a picnic. You like picnics, Patrick?"

Patrick's mind went quickly to the afternoon with Trina, and how
surprised he was that he missed her. "Yes," he said and tried not to
think of her kiss and the brief but shockingly erotic feel of her body
against his. "But aren't they being foolish out there?"

"Maybe. Look!" There was motion in the trees, a sparkle of sunlight off something shiny. Funston snickered. "Like clockwork. Every three days, rain or shine, they march down this road and then
march back again, a show of force trying to scare us. Goddamn, are
they punctual. Germans probably screw their women to a metronome!"

Patrick thought it very likely and said so, even though he was
more fascinated by the approach of the German column as it moved
toward him from the enemy's lines in the west. It was like watching

a snake slither toward you, evil and ominous yet utterly fascinating. He felt like shouting a warning to the men now casually eating but held it back.

A small group of horsemen emerged from the trees and Patrick gasped. Uhlans! To the casual eye they looked ridiculous with their nine-foot lances and square-blocked helmets, but they were the elite of the German cavalry. And now a troop of them was moving slowly into view.

There was a shout from the campfire as the horsemen were spotted. Men started to run the other way, toward Patrick. A couple of them leveled their rifles and fired. A horse shrieked in sudden pain, which seemed to galvanize the Uhlans. More German horsemen appeared, Patrick guessed fifty altogether, and fanned out on either side of the road. They started forward at a brisk trot and quickly increased the pace to a pounding gallop that ate the ground and closed the distance.

The men on foot, the bait the Germans were swallowing, ran in apparent panic, any thoughts of cohesiveness seemingly replaced by the primal fear of being impaled on one of those fearful lances being lowered in their direction.

Patrick watched in fascination as they ran toward him and his sheltering shrubs. Would they make it to safety, or had they cut it too close? Then, to Patrick's horror, one man fell and couldn't get up right away. Perhaps he'd had the wind knocked out of him. As the others made the safety of the trees and the rest of the trapping force by about fifty yards, a Uhlan caught the straggler and ran his lance into the man's back with the bloody point sticking out of his chest. The man shrieked as, for a moment, he was propelled along the ground by the horse and spear, his arms and legs whirling like the limbs of a deranged marionette. Then he was lifted off the ground and shaken loose from the lance like a leaf by the grim-faced German rider.

From alongside Funston and Patrick, more than a hundred hidden rifles opened fire at once from close range, sending horses and men into jumbled piles. Funston surged to his feet. "Hit the horses! Hit the horses. They can't ride without the goddamn horses!"

The firing continued, men working the bolts of their rifles as quickly as possible. Dozens of horses and men lay on the ground.

Some tried to rise but were quickly dropped by the withering fire. The remaining Uhlans scampered for the other side of the meadow and the protection of the infantry that was coming into view.

Funston was exultant. "I said one piece of meat gets fed into the grinder at a time, didn't I?" Patrick nodded, his eyes glued to the field. "Well, that was the first piece. Now watch."

German infantry emerged from the other side of the field in open skirmish formation. They were followed by several more companies in assault formations that were more dense. They moved with a precision that showed discipline and confidence. Their bayoneted rifles were at the ready, and their helmet points bobbed almost in cadence as they walked. Patrick quickly estimated their numbers at a nearly full battalion.

Funston snickered. "Good. Now they've stuck their heads in it."

At six hundred yards, the Americans opened fire and started dropping Germans. Those who were not hit simply continued on. They must have felt they could overwhelm the hundred or so men shooting at them.

At four hundred yards, the American machine gunners opened up from their hiding places, along with two more companies of infantry. Now the American front was a U, with the open end covering the head of the German column. The volume of fire was deadly and the Germans paused, dropping to their knees to fire back at their dug-in and largely hidden tormentors. The Americans could see the Germans starting to bring up their own machine guns.

"Enough," Funston snapped to Patrick and crawled away from the front line. Patrick followed in undignified haste behind him while bullets whipped and whistled through the branches and whacked off the trees. "Let's get back to the horses," said Funston. "I've got the rest of this fight to direct."

The horses were in a clearing only a few hundred yards away. The two men covered the distance quickly, all the while being passed by hundreds of well-armed Americans heading for the battle. Funston's plan, as outlined earlier in the day to Patrick, was simple. The German force numbered about two thousand men. To combat it, Funston had gathered half his entire division, almost eight thousand. These were now enveloping the head of the column and concentrating fire on the left flank. Recently purchased pom-poms and French 75mm cannon added to the din as they fired from positions where targets had already been registered.

"Like I said, Patrick, the Krauts are so totally and marvelously predictable. Same number of men, same route, but today, a different result."

A messenger ran up to them, breathless and flushed. "Sir, Colonel Martin requests permission to take the road behind them and cut off their retreat."

Funston threw his hat on the ground. "No, goddamnit! Tell Colonel Martin to keep his troops off that road and pay attention to the plan."

He picked up his hat and dusted it off. "Goddamn Martin's too reckless. I don't want them cut off. If that happens they'll dig in and send out for reinforcements, which will come long before we can root them out. If we leave an escape route open, they'll take it and we can maul them all the way back, or at least as far as we want. Jesus, we don't want them to brag about a 'heroic rescue.' I want them to retreat with their tails between their legs and have to tell the All-goddamn-Highest kaiser how they got their asses whipped." He paused and grinned. "You think that's plain enough, Patrick?"

"Wonderfully eloquent, Fred."

They waited out the remainder of the afternoon while the outnumbered and outgunned Germans fought on tenaciously and with iron discipline, inflicting surprisingly severe casualties on the advancing Americans until they finally decided to fall back. Subject to continuous harassment and driven by the nightmare fear of being surrounded, the Germans soon quickened the pace of their retreat. Very soon, units lost their cohesion and thus their strength. Individual soldiers lost their nerve and started to run. This was infectious. Despite protestations from mounted officers, who made wonderfully easy targets for riflemen, the retreat quickly became a rout, with men flowing down the road to the safety of the German lines. First, equipment was abandoned, then the wounded; then the German soldiers started looking for a way of surrendering to end the torment.

Funston called off the chase in the late afternoon. A German relief force had been sighted and was finally coming. It would soon meet the remnants of the retreating column head-on in what Funston hoped would be demoralizing confusion.

As a degree of quiet and normality returned, Funston and Patrick walked their horses down the road, which was littered with packs, rifles, canteens, helmets, and other items. The farther from the field of initial contact, the fewer were the dead. By this time, the wounded prisoners had been gathered and were being taken to field hospitals to be treated. Other prisoners had been marched away.

Patrick and Funston halted their horses. "Well, General Funston, are you satisfied?" Patrick asked.

Funston removed his wide-brimmed hat and wiped his forehead. "By and large, yes," he said softly. The sight of the battlefield had a sobering effect. "I wanted to bloody their nose, and I did. I also wanted my men to get a cheap victory to show that the Germans aren't gods, and I did that too. But," he said, pausing thoughtfully, "you saw how well the Germans fought and how disciplined they were, and look at how many casualties they caused us, even though they were outnumbered and outgunned. We had four times as many men and even greater advantages in artillery and machine guns, and they still hurt us. Had we outnumbered them by only two to one, the results might have been different. If the numbers were even and their commander was not so blazingly stupid, they would have beaten us. No, Patrick, victory or not, what this also proves is how much more we have to learn."

Funston turned his horse back to the American lines. "I just hope we get the opportunity to do that learning."

Holstein entered Bulow's office unannounced and sat down before the astonished man could react. "The kaiser did not wish me at his most recent conference?"

Bulow gulped. What was it about the man that was so damned intimidating? "I did not know you were not invited." The evasion came easily. "I thought your absence was for other reasons. You have not always graced us with your presence in the past, you know."

Holstein accepted the mild rebuke. "The kaiser cannot be happy. The foreign press is making a huge fuss over two defeats on the same day. I notice our tame newspapers are referring to the incidents as only skirmishes and the type of thing that is bound to happen. Is that what the kaiser also feels?"

Bulow leaned back in his leather chair. "Had either commanding officer—Captain Westfall of the second cruiser squadron or Major

General Kirstein of the army—survived their unpleasant days, they would have been court-martialed and shot. The kaiser, to put it mildly, was outraged. The two gentlemen are more than fortunate that they had the good luck to be killed. Other senior officers involved in the debacles are, of course, disgraced."

Holstein grunted and shifted his weight to ease the pressure on his girth. "And I understand these catastrophes have caused changes in our strategies."

"Yes. Even though you were not there, I see no reason you should not know." Holstein would find out anyway, Bulow thought. "We will be sending a third corps of regulars to the United States along with a fourth corps of activated reserves. A fifth and six corps of reserves will be activated and prepared for shipment to America if the circumstances warrant. The kaiser feels, and I agree, that the Americans' little victory in Connecticut will embolden them to take further aggressive actions. We must be prepared for whatever they try to do to expel us. When they fail, as they must, then the kaiser is confident they will be willing to negotiate terms. He feels it is possible that the little defeat will ultimately work to our advantage."

"And the navy?"

Bulow could not stifle a smile. It wasn't often that the overbearing Tirpitz was knocked down a peg. "Our North Atlantic Fleet has been ordered to effect a concentration in force and cease sending squadrons out to bombard and aggravate the Americans."

"Ah."

"Further, the Asiatic squadron at Tsingtao will be directed to leave China and join the North Atlantic Fleet in order to make good the loss of the three cruisers. This is to be a highly guarded secret."

For once Holstein was surprised. "But that abandons the Pacific to the Americans."

"Von Holstein, the kaiser was shocked beyond words by the loss of those cruisers, and von Schlieffen is absolutely beside himself at the possibility of our army being cut off by the Americans. He is confident that our army can overwhelm the Americans, but first it has to get over there to America, and then it has to be supplied. Our navy is larger than the Americans', but not as overwhelmingly so as our army. The American navy is not to be taken lightly, and I'm afraid that is what we did. We may have to face the unpleasant fact that the American navy is, ship for ship, at least our equal, perhaps our superior. The kaiser feels, and I concur, that we cannot afford to have isolated portions of the fleet overwhelmed and defeated. The kaiser is also personally embarrassed by the fact that the first shots ever fired by any German warship against a modern power resulted in such a crushing defeat. It is hardly the stuff of Nelsonian legends! He thinks his Uncle Edward is laughing at him, and he may well be.

"As to the Pacific, the kaiser feels there is nothing there that we couldn't take back later after the war, should we have to. What else is there in the Pacific but the squalid mainland port of Tsingtao and part of the Samoa Islands? Von Tirpitz begged for a couple of old gunboats to be retained at Tsingtao to protect our interests and our tiny garrison from a hundred million or so Chinese who have no reason to love us, and that boon was granted. For the sake of our garrison, I hope the Chinamen never figure out how weak we are. At best we could only hope for a hasty evacuation. At worst, a massacre."

Holstein thanked Bulow for his assistance and departed deep in thought. No German warships in the Pacific? He knew that the Americans had long since left to concentrate in the Atlantic, but now the Pacific was totally deserted by the navies of both combatants, and it was truly pacific. How interesting. How very, very interesting.

Theodore Roosevelt greeted the press in the bright sun on the lawn of the White House. There were about fifty reporters, pencils and notepads in hand, accompanied by a number of photographers. There was a movie camera as well, grinding away while Roosevelt shamelessly beamed into it. He was bubbling and ebullient. Beyond him were Secretary of State Hay, Secretary of the Navy Long, and War Secretary Root.

"Gentlemen, I am delighted to be here and to be able to answer your questions. But first, some news. I have promoted Captain Evans to the rank of rear admiral. Major General Funston, having recently been given his new rank, will have to wait a little while for further advancement. In the meantime, he has my undying gratitude." This brought a few chuckles from the assembled reporters.

Roosevelt continued. "We have waited a long time, more than a month, for even the barest inkling of good news. Now, like the day that our country won twin victories at Vicksburg and Gettysburg, we have two bright and shining accomplishments to set against a long period of failure."

Hay winced inwardly. It was absurd to compare these little incidents with the end of the epic siege of Vicksburg and the culmination of the titanic battle at Gettysburg, both on July 3, 1863. These most recent battles were piddling in comparison. Hay had been with Lincoln when he received the news of those victories, and Vicksburg and Gettysburg meant the end of the war, rather than a new beginning.

Roosevelt put his hands behind his back and thrust out his chest. "Gentlemen, any questions?"

"Sir, can you give us any information regarding the numbers involved?"

"Approximately eleven hundred German seamen were either killed or captured. Many of the captured were also wounded. Our casualties were only a couple of handfuls. Two or three dead—I'm frankly not certain—and a half dozen wounded. There was no significant damage to the ship herself. The casualties appeared to have been struck down by flying objects while they were out on the deck performing their duties."

Roosevelt knew it would do no good to lie to the press about the naval fight. It had taken place in plain view of people on the shore, and the ships' size, speed, armor, armament, and complement were all published information. But the land battle had taken place well away from curious and prying eyes, and he was under no such restraints.

"Regarding General Funston's fine effort, I can only say that the numbers of fighting men on each side were quite substantial, although they did not involve the bulk of either army. The Germans' efforts to trivialize the incident simply will not work. As to their casualties and ours, I will only say that they lost up to a third of their force, whereas our losses were substantially less."

But not that much less. The body counters tallied 117 dead Germans and 209 taken prisoner, about half of whom were also wounded and were unable to flee. Funston estimated that the Germans suffered another 200 wounded based on traditional proportions. Thus the Germans had sustained just over 500 casualties out of a force of approximately 2,000. Not one-third, but high enough. The American casualties had been 88 dead, 264 wounded, and 2 missing. Although low as a percent of Funston's force, the numbers were disturbingly high when his overwhelming numerical superiority was added to the equation.

A hand was raised. "Sir, just to give a sense of proportion to the battle, would you say that more or less than ten thousand were involved?"

"More." That drew whistles, and the scratching of pencils picked up its pace.

"Sir, what will be the impact on naval operations of the victory off Florida? Has this tilted the balance of power to us?"

"The answer to the second half of your question leads to the first. No, it has not tilted the numbers to us. They still have a larger fleet on which to draw. I expect they will replace those ships from their own coastal defense forces if they deem it necessary. Further, no capital ships of theirs were involved. Therefore, their main battle fleet is untouched, as, of course, is ours. That basic fact will influence our future actions much more than the sinking of their three cruisers."

"Sir, I'm confused. Just what was the *Alabama* doing there anyhow?"

"I understand she was on an errand of mercy. It was just plain luck—good for us and bad for the Germans—that she arrived at that particular spot at that time. It was more than luck that she was commanded by Admiral Evans, who knew exactly what to do with the cards he'd been dealt."

The reporter was insistent. "And what about on land? I hear rumors that General Funston was called on the carpet for his independent actions. His superiors said they were irresponsible and might have jeopardized the entire army."

Roosevelt scowled at the reporter, a young man he didn't know. Must be one of Hearst's more vicious puppies. "Major General Funston showed a high degree of initiative and creativity in his operations. If he did not notify everyone in the government of his intentions, it was probably to keep people from blabbing." He treated the young man to a wicked gleam. "He certainly wouldn't want to read about them in your paper before he put them into effect, now would he?"

Another reporter rescued the young man. "Can you estimate or forecast how this will affect future operations?"

"Ah, I might speculate." Roosevelt turned to the movie camera and gave it his best presidential smile with all teeth gleaming. God, these things fascinate me, he thought. "First, we beat the hitherto invincible German at his own game. He thought himself the master of land warfare and now he has to rethink that opinion. The German army is considered the best in the world. To see it, or even only a portion of it, sent running by a bunch of freedom-loving farmers and mechanics who vote for their leaders rather than submitting to inherited tyrants must have distressed them greatly."

"Sir, did you say the Germans ran?"

Roosevelt paused for effect. Let the question sink in. "They ran."

Pencils worked furiously and he continued. "And a number of them surrendered; they were not captured. It would appear that the rank and file's enthusiasm for the American campaign might not be as great as the All Highest kaiser imagines." He laughed and raised a hand to the sky. "I've also been informed that some of our German prisoners have requested to stay in the United States. They have no wish to be exchanged and returned to the kaiser's tender care. We will honor all genuine requests for asylum."

"And what about the future, sir? When will our main army move against theirs?"

Roosevelt mused. This was difficult. Congress had been pestering him for the same information. Yes, we could beat the Germans under the right circumstances, and, yes, the rearming of the military was proceeding even faster than he could have imagined. But was the army ready to expel the Germans through force of arms? Miles said yes. Congress and business leaders said it must be done and soon, before the economy suffered even further and perhaps collapsed. Thus, with extreme reluctance and misgivings, Roosevelt had given in and, even as he spoke to the press in the July sunshine, Gen. Nelson Miles was speeding north to take direct command. His orders were to initiate battle as soon as possible and drive the Germans away.

But that could not be his answer. He had to dissemble. "All in good time, all in good time. We are continuing to build our strength while we are whittling at the Germans'. I know some of you are afraid we might be afflicted with what President Lincoln referred to as the 'slows' in describing General McClellan, but do not worry. We

will strike. Our commanding general is no McClellan and is not possessed by the slows."

But will the attack succeed? He was worried as he waved an end
to the meeting with the press. These gentlemen stood and applauded
and he and his cabinet ministers walked among them and shook
hands, giving away nothing of what they knew. Oh, God, he thought,
let them not fail. I cannot bear the thought of defeat. Miles must win.

Chapter 12

WELL, WELL," SNEERED Kessel as he pushed the dripping helmet off his sweaty forehead with his left hand. His right hand held the rifle to his shoulder as he leaned his body against the wet earthen walls of the trench. "Since you're now an almighty fucking corporal and must know everything, would you mind telling me just why we're standing here in this fucking rain and muck?"

Corporal Ludwig Weber smiled sweetly and tried not to look at either Kessel's rain-soaked and ravaged face or the hate emanating from it. "Otto, if I knew I'd tell you. Unlike what you said, I am only a lowly corporal and the captain's clerk. I don't know shit about what's going to happen and I've been standing here all morning like you. Maybe if I was a general I might know, but I don't." As clerk and translator for the captain, he had not expected to be told to join his old squad, but as the sergeant major had said, every rifle might be needed this day.

Kessel giggled obscenely and turned away. Weber noted idly that Kessel's once-pristine uniform was not only soaking wet but covered with mud from the side of the trench. Ludwig assumed he looked that way as well. It had been a long time since the 4th Rifles had been clean and neat and ready to stand inspection or parade. Virtually all their clothing was filthy and worn. There had been neither the opportunity nor the ability to clean up. He knew he must stink because he could smell the fetid odor of the others. He was also a little hungry. Rations had been slow in arriving lately.

Ludwig reviewed what else he knew. He knew that his regiment had erected earthworks, one of a line of similar constructions that started at Long Island Sound and ran north for some miles into the boggy woods. The fortifications were there in case the Yanks, who everyone knew outnumbered them, attacked from their lines a dozen or so miles to the east. Ludwig also knew he didn't relish the thought of an American attack.

He watched as Kessel hunched over his rifle and half hummed, half whistled a nameless tune. He'd been acting even more oddly than usual since he'd come back on the day after he was reported missing during the Brooklyn fire. Although it was obvious the man had been terribly hurt, Kessel's explanation that he'd gotten lost and confused in the smoke and subsequently injured by falling debris simply didn't ring true. There was now a scar-surrounded, lifeless orb where his left eye had once been. Although he had been issued a patch, Kessel let everyone see his maimed face and raged when they tried not to stare or were nauseated by the sight of it.

Captain Walter had spoken at length with those who'd seen Kessel last in the fire, and he had been informed that Kessel, far from being lost, had strode off very purposefully in the direction of some shops that were well away from the fire. The conclusion was inescapable that Kessel had been looting and had somehow gotten into serious trouble. When confronted with that and given the alternative of losing his rank or facing a court-martial and possible death for desertion under fire, Kessel prudently decided to take the demotion. He had lost his stripes before and would doubtless lose them again.

When Ludwig Weber became corporal in his stead, Kessel's hatred became palpable. Some thought Kessel a buffoon, but Weber knew better. Despite the advantage in rank, Weber still tried to stay out of the man's way and felt that someday, somehow, Kessel would try to kill him. Through the rumor mill, he'd heard that Kessel, in his tormented logic, thought Weber was responsible for his demotion, and the hurt done to his face.

But what were they doing on alert, and how long would it last? It had rained lightly all night and the trench was inches deep in mud and water. If it weren't so warm, they could be in real trouble. Worse, it was still raining and looked as though it would continue all day. The clouds were dark above, and Weber felt he could reach out and touch them. He turned imploringly to Captain Walter, who merely shrugged. Despite the difference in their ranks and social standing, a degree of cordiality, if not friendliness, had developed between them. Walter was not, Weber realized, an archetypal Prussian. Even Sergeant Major Gunther had begun to acknowledge Ludwig with a friendly nod.

About ten in the morning, they heard the distant crackle of small-arms fire. They stiffened and pointed weapons at targets as yet unseen. If the Yanks were about, the 4th Rifles were ready. The regiment held an earthen-walled fort shaped like a five-pointed star with trenches that protected the riflemen's bodies both to the front and rear. On all sides in front of the fort the shrubs and trees had been hacked and pulled out for several hundred yards in what had been backbreaking work. Now it seemed the effort might have been worthwhile. Directly in front of the walls, the ground sloped down to a man-made cut in the ground that not only protected the fort from direct fire, but forced any attackers to stop and negotiate a ten-foot drop. But before they made it to the drop, they would have been confronted by an array of wooden spikes that had been driven into the ground and laced together to break up their formations or delay them.

Machine guns were set in both the points and recesses of the embankments. The whole thing was designed so that overlapping fields of fire could protect the inhabitants. The design had been perfected centuries before and it still worked. Inside the perimeter, a battery of howitzers stood ready to shoot at any target found by the lookouts on the fifty-foot-high wooden tower.

Without warning, one of the howitzers barked. "What the hell?" said Kessel, his face pale. It suddenly dawned on Ludwig that Kessel, for all his bluster, had never been in a real battle. All his exploits in China had been against helpless peasants. Somehow, Ludwig found it comforting.

The other cannon fired and continued to fire as quickly as shells could be rammed into the smoking breeches. Obviously, the Yanks were out there, as yet unseen. Damn the rain, Ludwig thought. He gulped and concentrated on trying to locate his firing lane and the range markers they'd staked out at fifty yards, on which to register their rifles.

Through the sound of the guns he heard distant and undecipherable voices, screeching and yelling. Suddenly, he could see a group of men, maybe a hundred, rushing in the general direction of their fort.

The machine guns opened up and he watched men fall, flopping like puppets with their strings cut. He found it hard to think of them as humans. The Americans stopped and pulled back, clearly stunned by the ferocity of the German defense, and commenced long-range and inaccurate rifle fire.

As yet the German rifles had been silent, and Captain Walter walked among his troops. "Patience men, that was just a probe. There will be plenty more for us." Some men chuckled. Ludwig thought he heard a whimper come from Kessel.

More? He didn't want more. Ludwig sighted down his rifle and tried to ignore the annoying thwacks as American bullets landed randomly in his area.

"Now they're coming," the captain shouted. As if in response, the land in front of them erupted with a solid wave of blue-coated Americans, their bayonets fixed, running forward. "Fire!" Captain Walter screamed, and the trench erupted in fury.

"Steady, men. Aim low. Let them come to you. Watch your markers." Captain Walter walked the top of the trench behind them, ignoring the fact that he made a splendid target.

Ludwig felt Sergeant Major Gunther's presence behind him. "Squeeze the trigger. Don't pull it, squeeze gently. Just like your sweetheart's tit," coached the sergeant major. "That's right, squeeze it like a tit, don't jerk it like you do your cock."

Shut the fuck up, Ludwig wanted to scream as the rifle slammed into his shoulder again and again and his face burned from the powder. The Americans were falling, but they were still coming. They were into the obstacles and ripping them apart with their hands, screeching and hollering while sword-swinging officers urged them on. Ludwig could see faces and he was shocked that they were convulsed and flushed with rage. They wanted to kill him!

Some Americans, unable to get through the spikes, had dropped to their knees and were shooting at German heads and shoulders now visible above the trench wall. Some of the screams came from German voices as the hail of fire inevitably found flesh.

The obstacles were breached and the Americans ran to the ditch less than a hundred yards away from the German trenches. German rifles and machine guns cut the Americans down in quivering bundles, but they still came on. The Americans' rifle fire grew more accurate and more intense the closer they got. Worse, they had brought up their own machine guns. Then American artillery started firing, and their shells churned up gouts of mud as they landed in the fort. As Weber fired back, he was pelted with falling dirt. Oh, God, he hoped it was only falling dirt.

It suddenly dawned on Ludwig that the regimental fort was not impregnable and that the Americans might overwhelm them through sheer weight of numbers and uncommon bravery.

The Americans reached the lip of the ditch and paused while the German guns continued to rake them. Some tried to climb down; others were pushed over the edge by those behind them. Still others tumbled lifeless onto the ground below.

The rain, until then a nuisance at worst, suddenly commenced to come down in torrents, blinding Ludwig and everyone near him. He could no longer see the Americans! Terrified, he wanted to run. At any second a horde of blue-jacketed Yanks would emerge from the sheets of rain that were beating on his face.

"Aim low!" Captain Walter shrieked. "Aim for the wall of the cut. You know where it is!"

The Yanks were on them. Emerging from the rain, they came at the German line screaming like maddened animals. Weber fired and fired again, pausing only to reload. He awkwardly dropped bullets into the mud and lost precious time as he hurried to jam them into the magazine of his Mauser.

A beast was before him—an enemy with wet hair plastered on his head, his red face surrounding an open mouth that vented a primal scream. Ludwig fired and the man dropped to his knees. He fired again and the man rose up and hurled his rifle at him like a spear. It skidded along the rain-slicked ground and came to rest just over the lip of the trench. The man lay facedown on the ground and stopped moving.

It was too much. Later, Ludwig felt he'd heard a sigh, and perhaps he had, but slowly, very slowly, the Americans began to withdraw in the now-slackening rain. As some of them tried to drag their wounded away, others turned to fire at their German tormentors, while German fire continued to reach out and kill.

Finally, the order came: "Cease-fire!" It was not obeyed immediately. The intensity of battle had overwhelmed some soldiers who
continued to fire until they ran out of ammunition or were grabbed
by comrades and stopped. Not caring in the least what the mud
would do to it, Ludwig set his rifle on the parapet and realized he
was breathing convulsively. The Americans had tried to kill him.
Now the enemy had a face. Part of him wanted to go out and look at
the dead man who'd thrown his rifle at him. He knew he'd killed that
one, but had there been others?

As Ludwig's senses returned, he realized he was in a world of
sound and smell, as well as sight. The area about the trench was full
of the stink of blood, urine, feces, and other stenches he couldn't
recognize. He checked his crotch and found to his relief that he
hadn't soiled himself, although others had. He also realized he was
hearing moans and screams that hadn't reached his deadened ears in
the heat of battle. A number of his comrades were hurt, many very
badly. Although the earthen walls protected most of their bodies, soldiers had to raise their heads and upper torsos in order to fire, and
most of the wounds were to those critical areas of the body. A handful of men had been hit by American artillery, which finally shifted
to shrapnel that exploded above the trenches and showered the occu-
pants with maiming shards of steel. For the first time, Ludwig also
saw just what sickening things a bullet can do when it hits a man,
twists inside, and leaves through a fist-sized hole.

The day was not over. The Americans came again and again. The
subsequent attacks, however, lacked the strength and ferocity of the
first one and were beaten back almost easily. Even so, Ludwig's
company and the rest of the 4th Rifles took more casualties. It was
small comfort that the Americans had suffered far worse. The 4th
Rifles had been mauled.

Before sunset and after it was confirmed that the Americans were
indeed withdrawing from the area, a few Americans appeared under
a flag of truce and asked to remove their wounded and dead. The
request was quickly granted. "Let them care for their own," sighed
an exhausted Captain Walter. "We have enough to do with ours."

Ludwig watched as the sad caravan of American carts took as
many of the moaning wounded and dead as they could. He was
deeply saddened and shaken by the cries coming from the blood-

soaked field. He had not truly realized that so many men would call for their mother in such circumstances, and it tore at him. For once, even Kessel had nothing to say.

In the early afternoon of the next day, the mangled company was withdrawn and replaced by fresh troops, who stared at them in disbelief. Do we look so awful? Ludwig thought. Are we the walking dead? Do they not know we are the victors? His uniform was covered with dirt and blood, some his own. He found a small cut on his neck that had probably been caused by a piece of spent shrapnel. He still carried the American's rifle, which he'd shown to the captain. The fact that it was a British Lee-Metford was disturbing. Just where the hell were the Yanks getting British equipment? The captain had no answer, but Ludwig could see that he too was puzzled and disturbed. If the damn Brits were arming the Yanks, there could be real trouble.

As they marched slowly and out of step along the dirt road a few miles from the fort, Ludwig found himself alongside Captain Walter, who suddenly raised his right hand and signaled a halt.

"What the hell?" Ludwig gasped.

In a field alongside the road lay bundles of American dead. Some were in small, neat rows; others were piled in heaps. A troop of dismounted Uhlans idled nearby, and Ludwig noticed their lances had been replaced by rifles. Then it dawned on him. The Americans had been executed.

"Who is in charge here?" asked Captain Walter, his voice almost breaking.

A young lieutenant rose from the ground and saluted insolently. He had a sulky, pouty face and looked upon the infantry captain as if he were some lower order of life. He was a Uhlan, and to a Uhlan all riflemen were shit soldiers. "I command here, Captain. Lieutenant Sigmond von Hoff at your service."

"Are you responsible for this? This murder?"

"An execution, Captain." Hoff smiled benignly. "Nothing more and most certainly none of your concern."

The man's casualness was outrageous. "And by whose orders?"

"Why the kaiser's, Captain, the kaiser's."

Captain Walter seemed rocked by the answer. "It cannot be. What was their crime? When was their trial?"

Ludwig noticed that several of the other Uhlans were gathering around, grinning, while others had turned away, possibly ashamed of what they had done. Ludwig wondered if these were some of the group that had gotten whipped by the Americans a few days ago. If so, that would account for their behavior, although it did not justify it.

"Captain, their crime is treason. They are Germans fighting for the Americans. The kaiser has decreed that one who is born a German will always be a German. A German cannot renounce his citizenship and be justified in taking up arms against the Reich and our beloved kaiser. If he does that, he is a traitor and, by the way, no trial is necessary under these circumstances. Their guilt is obvious." He again saluted, this time even more casually. "If you will excuse me, Captain, my men and I have much to do."

As the Uhlans walked away, Ludwig turned to the captain. "Sir, has the kaiser gone mad, issuing that kind of order?"

The captain's voice was stern, but Ludwig could see the concern and hurt disbelief in his eyes. "Corporal, you will watch your tongue. Our kaiser is surely not mad. He may have received bad counsel, or an order may have been misinterpreted. Do you understand me, Weber?"

Ludwig nodded. Indeed, he understood quite well. One did not call the kaiser insane, no matter what, unless, of course, one wanted to be considered a traitor as well. Ludwig looked at the captain and saw a small, sad smile on his face and he quietly shook his head. Then Ludwig knew that the captain was in complete agreement regarding the kaiser, only he had the wit and discretion not to say it.

Ludwig turned again to the field where so many dead lay in prim formation. What will the Americans do when they find out about this atrocity? His body chilled at the thought of the vengeance that could be wreaked upon them. What if he were captured? Would they kill him as well? Oh, Jesus, what is going to happen now?

It was dark in the president's office. No light had been turned on to dispel the gloom of the darkening summer night. Obviously, that was the way Roosevelt wished it as he sat there, brooding silently in the shadows. Patrick tapped on the door and entered. Without saying a word or receiving one, he sat and waited. Minutes stretched out. Roosevelt's face was hard to read in the shadow, but Patrick sensed the man was on the verge of tears. Perhaps he had already been crying.

Finally, the president spoke. "Patrick, what happened? What went wrong?"

Patrick took a deep breath. "Sir, where would you like me to begin?"

"Anywhere you wish, just don't sugarcoat it. Don't pander to me. Just give me the straight answers I'll need tomorrow when I have to confront Congress and the press. Yesterday, I had a fine new army going into battle to save our nation. Today that army is in ruins. What happened?"

Where to begin indeed? Patrick thought. "Sir, it was a poor plan, poorly conceived, and even more poorly executed." There, he'd said it.

Surprisingly, a low chuckle rumbled from Roosevelt. It dripped bitterness. "And where is General Miles? I assume the plan and the conception were his, were they not?"

"Yes, sir, they were. I believe the general is in Boston, under a doctor's care. He may have suffered a nervous collapse." For the first time, he felt sympathy for General Miles. A brave and honest man, he'd had a long and distinguished career even though he often behaved as a paranoid dictator. The totality of the defeat had crushed him. "Sir, he was in well over his head."

Roosevelt moaned. "And I put him there. Gave him the go-ahead and urged him to strike. Where does that put me?"

"Sir, you are the commander in chief. If you are blaming yourself, you're at least partially right."

There was a strained silence. "Patrick, in the last minute you've criticized both your commanding general and your president. Although I know I asked for frankness, I'm a little surprised at how much I'm actually getting."

"Mr. President, if you're thinking my candor might end my military career, don't worry about it. When this war is over I will resign my commission. Enough is enough." Too many wars, he thought, and too many dead.

"And I will respect that decision. Now, please tell me what you saw."

Freed of the burden of having to be tactful, Patrick described the battle in detail. He reminded the president that the German lines ran from a point on the Hudson just above Peekskill, through a tangle of lakes, ponds, and bogs, stopping short of the Housatonic River, near Danbury. From there they ran generally south to Long Island Sound, a little more than twenty miles away. This twenty-odd-mile front was the only area that could be assaulted by a major force because of the lakes and bad ground to the north, which could be infiltrated only by smaller units. It was, therefore, the area most heavily fortified. Conversely, it was the place deemed most likely for the Germans to attack, so the constraints of geography placed the fighting bulk of both the opposing armies at that point.

"The Germans built about a dozen forts, each containing a regiment and some artillery. They numbered about fifteen thousand men in total, although we think they had another five thousand men in reserve. The forts were so situated that artillery fire from one could help the others on either side. The line of forts was between ten and fifteen miles from the American lines, which ran north-south on the west side of the Housatonic River."

Roosevelt nodded. There was nothing new in what was being said.

"Yesterday, and with very little planning or preparation, between fifty and seventy thousand American soldiers in four divisions and two corps attacked those fortified Germans."

Roosevelt was incredulous. "And failed? How? You're saying we outnumbered them at least four to one!"

"They never had a chance. At least not a real one. I said there was no preparation. They all managed to leave their lines at about the same time, and all were scheduled to launch their attacks at seven in the morning. General Miles's plans, such as they were, totally ignored the fact that the units were at different distances from the Germans and each confronted unique problems in getting there. There were no good roads, maps were poor, and, in trying to reach their objectives in the night, people simply got lost. Not one regiment made the start time. Some few actually did attack before nine, but many didn't start their assaults until early afternoon. By that time, of course, the Germans were fully alert."

"Dear God."

Patrick continued. "The German forts communicated with each other by means of telephone and telegraph. There was no attempt to cut those lines. Thus all of them knew within minutes of the first attack that something was happening."

Roosevelt sagged. Poor Miles. Didn't he understand these things? Was he so far behind the times?

"Sir, General Miles was indeed a brave man of his time, but his time was the nineteenth century, and this, 1901, is the dawn of the twentieth.

"Mr. President, General Miles was so out of date that, until recently, he wouldn't permit the army to acquire rifles with magazines like the Germans have. I was told he felt it would cause men to fire inaccurately and waste ammunition. Therefore, too many of our men did not have the new weapons with which to confront the Germans, which canceled our advantage in raw numbers."

"Lord." Roosevelt's voice was almost a cry.

"It does not get better, sir. Prior to the attacks there was no attempt to concentrate in overwhelming force at any point or points. The army simply surged forward in great, but not decisive, numbers all along the line. Had we concentrated our numbers at selected places, we might have achieved a breach in their lines, and additional forces could have moved into their rear and overwhelmed their reserves, who would then be out in the open. Even though the Germans in the forts could communicate with each other, they were still relatively immobile, so I think this could have been done."

"Did anyone try to tell this to General Miles?"

Patrick didn't know, as he had not been privy to all of the higher councils of war. He did remind the president that Miles did not accept criticism. "Sir, even so, he almost pulled it off. With no coordination, no artillery preparation or support, and no logic, we almost overran several of their strongpoints and did get in the rear of their lines in a couple of places, only to be driven off by their reserves. Those reserves were not numerous, but they were strong enough to take on our unsupported attackers. Thanks to the rain we were able to close on them without too many casualties. Unfortunately, our infantry tactics were out of date even before the Civil War. We have to do something better than mass formations moving slowly forward and firing as they go. The casualties would have been much, much higher if the weather hadn't been on our side."

"Patrick, you know General Shafter's dead, don't you?"

Patrick thought of the aging, overweight caricature of a general who'd been so sick in Cuba he'd had to leave for health reasons. Miles had given him command of the second corps and he'd died of a heart attack while viewing the retreat. "Yes, sir. And Pershing's wounded."

"Fortunately, not seriously. I have a feeling we're going to need a lot of strong, young fighters like him. Do you have any good news at all?"

Patrick sighed. "We did hurt them, sir, more than they anticipated. From a percentage standpoint, I wouldn't be surprised if they suffered almost as badly as we did. Looking at numbers only, our losses were staggering. Wheeler and Smith estimate at least seven thousand dead and twelve thousand wounded. Another thousand or so are missing. So much of the new equipment we'd been getting from the British was lost or damaged that virtually the entire army will have to be reequipped. But there were about five to eight thousand total German casualties. At least we know that the Germans will not be able to move on us either."

"You heard what they did to the prisoners."

"Only rumors."

"They shot the ones who were German-born, as if they could somehow tell. The kaiser says they are all traitors for fighting against him. He has also announced that American-born sons of German immigrants will be transported to Germany for induction in their army. If they refuse, they too will be murdered."

Patrick was shocked. He immediately thought of Heinz and so many others like him. What would be their reaction? What about other Americans not of German ancestry or several generations removed? His own reaction was revulsion. "The man is a savage."

Roosevelt smiled grimly. "He is an animal, a mad dog, and he will be stopped." Again he smiled, totally devoid of mirth. "And he may have given us the weapons we need to use against him. Certainly it will now be clear to those who pressured me to authorize the attack that victory will not be so easy. With these atrocities, it is evident that we cannot negotiate with a madman."

"With respect, sir, what pressures?"

Roosevelt stood and waved his arms. "Anyone in this beloved land of ours with an interest or an opinion. The financial world is strained because the Germans now occupy Wall Street and the banks. The stock exchanges, by the way, have moved their operations to Pittsburgh and hate it. The shipping people say they are near economic collapse because the harbor is closed. Two million refugees are crying out because they can't go home, and the millions of other people who have to help them find themselves grossly inconvenienced. Then, of course, we have the superpatriots—and, yes, Patrick, I know I am often among them—who think that one American is worth ten Germans, and just what on earth is the problem with beating them? Well, now they know. This latest battle was the reenactment of the Civil War slaughters at Fredericksburg or Cold Harbor, wasn't it?" Patrick nodded and Roosevelt continued. "Well, now they know the truth as do I. It will be a long and hard fight, but we will prevail."

Roosevelt walked around his desk and put his hand on Patrick's shoulder. "I will accept your resignation, but, as you stated, not until this crisis is over. You've done your best for me and your country, and I will not forget it. Nor," he said, laughing, this time genuinely, "your damned insubordinate candor. Should you be punished for it? Or rewarded?"

"Sir, I'd like a command. Later you can tell me whether it is reward or punishment."

Father Walter McCluskey shifted his ample bulk on the hard wooden bench in a vain attempt to ease the pain emanating from his tortured buttocks. He was proud that he didn't stoop to using a cushion like that prissy and skinny little dago fanatic, Father Rosselli. Besides, he sometimes needed a jolt of agony to keep him awake during the monotony of these Saturday confessions.

Only half his mind at best was paying attention to the verbal meanderings of the old woman who was so distressed because she had been ill and missed Mass last Sunday, and who was so tired at night that she often fell asleep during her evening prayers. Poor dear.

Gently, he told her it was all right to miss Mass if you are sick— as if, he thought but refrained from saying, God wanted her breathing her own unique brand of plague on the rest of the faithful. As to her nightly prayers, a merciful and benevolent god would surely understand that her daily exertions caused nightly fatigue and, besides, wasn't it more important to live like a Catholic than to pray like one? He doubted she accepted that piece of theology. She liked the routine of prayer, but not necessarily the substance.

He gave her a nominal penance, which seemed to please her, as it acknowledged she had sinned, however slightly, and she departed. She would be back in a week, as would dozens like her. It was frustrating some days. It would be so nice to actually assist someone truly in need of help to leave a sinful life. Unfortunately, he sighed, those were the ones least likely to come to confession.

Father McCluskey deftly closed one sliding panel and opened the other. The part of his brain that had been ignoring the old lady had decided that this next person, still invisible, was also female, although quite a bit younger. He had deciphered this from the fact that he heard the rustling of a dress, and the person had not wheezed or groaned upon kneeling. It was a game he sometimes played to keep himself interested.

He waited. Instead of the opening request to be acknowledged as a sinner who needs forgiving, there was silence. Through the screen he could see the shadow of the woman. The silence continued and his senses came alert. Finally, he took the initiative.

"My child, how can I help you?"

The response was a whisper. "I don't know."

He caught the accent. The girl was Irish. "Have you sinned?" he asked gently.

"Some say I have. I don't think so." The girl started sobbing quietly.

"Talk to me, my child."

Molly leaned forward so her head touched the screen and her words tumbled out. "I went to that other priest to ask him why I hated all Germans for what one had done to me, and when he asked what caused my hate and I told him how one had raped me, he told me it was my fault."

She related how she had told the other priest of her standing on the barricade and being chased down and attacked by the German. "He said it was my fault for tormenting the man and leading him on. He said that what I did proved I was a loose woman and that no good Catholic would have been on the streets like that. He said I had brought that man into an occasion of sin by my disgraceful behavior."

Father McCluskey put his head in his hands. Damn Rosselli.

The girl continued. "Did I sin, Father?"

Time to be tactful, McCluskey thought. "No, child, you did not sin. I think the other priest might have misunderstood you." He also thought Father Rosselli would make a good missionary to the Eskimos, and would soon be one if he could swing it with the bishop. "You did the right thing by standing there to proclaim your right to be free. That is why we came to this land, is it not?"

"Yes, Father."

"And as to your actions being responsible for the attack upon your body," he had a difficult time using the word "rape," "you are no more responsible for the events that occurred than a passenger on a boat would be if it sank because of the actions of a captain. The person responsible for your being raped," there, he said it, "was your attacker, not you. Do you understand?"

"I think so." Her voice was definitely more cheerful, and McCluskey felt relieved. This was going to be a good day after all.

"Now, let us talk about your hatred of all Germans. May I assume you have met a German you do not particularly wish to hate?"

Molly giggled. "That could be."

"Now child, let us be serious. Did the Germans invent the heinous crime of rape? Are there no Irish rapists about? Could you not be assaulted someday by an Irishman? Has it not happened to others of our faith and our race?"

He saw her head bob up and down. "Yes."

"And if your assailant had been Irish, would you hate all men of Irish descent?"

"Of course not."

"Then have you not answered your own question?"

There was silence while Molly digested this bit of logic. "Thank you, Father. I know now that I have not sinned and I know also that I will succeed in not hating." She asked for absolution and he gave it gladly, along with a personal blessing and a promise to pray for her.

"But only if you will pray for me as well," he said, and she agreed warmly.

As she started to rise, she added, "You've answered one other question as well, you know."

He caught the humor in her voice. "Oh?"

"Yes, now I know why that other priest never has anyone in line at his confessional."

                         *   *   *

If the kaiser had still been a child, he likely would have been skip-
ping. As it was, he waved his good hand in a display of exuberance
that annoyed Holstein, especially since it was largely directed at him.

"See, von Holstein, did I not tell you we would be victorious?"

Holstein bowed. "That you did, All Highest, that you certainly
did."

"And now the Americans will surely come to the negotiating table
and we will have our empire. I told you it would be a short war."

"Sire, my people have heard nothing to the effect that the Americans are ready to negotiate. Even the neutral countries are silent on
that topic." But not on others, he mused.

"No matter. If not today, then tomorrow. They're whipped, beaten.
I have the finest army in the history of man, and they have utterly
routed the American farmers. Isn't it wonderful?"

Holstein's informants told him that the battle, although it had certainly gone Germany's way, might not have been quite as one-sided
as the kaiser believed.

"Sire," said Holstein, "have you given any thought to canceling or
delaying the troop shipments?"

The kaiser paused and turned to Schlieffen, who shook his head.
"No. We have two corps there and two on the way. There is no reason to stop."

"And von Tirpitz will be able to supply them?" Holstein asked.

Tirpitz was not present and the kaiser was irritated. "Of course.
Why wouldn't he?"

Holstein continued. "Well, for one thing, the American navy has
not been brought to battle. Although we certainly defeated their
army, we have not touched their navy."

"It's just as well," the kaiser said laughing. "When they come to
the table, we will have their fleet undamaged for our very own.
Won't the British love that!"

Holstein was persistent. "Sire, I hear unsettling rumors that the
execution of prisoners—"

"Traitors!"

He bowed. "As you wish, sire. But the international community is
upset by those actions, and the Americans seem to be outraged. It
may just delay their willingness to bargain."

The kaiser was surprised, indignant. "But what I did is within the law. Even the British do it."

Holstein winced. What the British had done, nearly a century earlier, was, under duress of war, to refuse to acknowledge that a British citizen could ever become an American citizen. Thus they impressed seamen off American vessels and thereby precipitated the War of 1812. The British no longer impressed seamen.

"Yes, sire, they certainly did. I must point out, however, that they merely conscripted them. They did not execute anyone unless they could prove with an absolute degree of certainty that the person had actually deserted a Royal Navy ship."

"Really?"

"Yes, sire."

The kaiser paced the room. "Well, then, we will show mercy. Change the directive from execution to transportation to Germany and conscription, unless, as you say, we can prove they actually deserted." His brows knit in thought. "Of course, if they refuse to serve, we will have to shoot them."

"Certainly, sire."

The meeting ended and Holstein, by design, found himself with Schlieffen. "General, I understand your army in America is in no shape to fight."

Schlieffen started to bristle, then thought better. "Almost true. They can certainly fight. What they cannot do until we reinforce and reorganize is move out of our perimeter. You are correct that the actual fighting force, not the occupation and administrative types, did suffer heavy casualties while winning their battle."

"Ah. And in that perimeter you plan to have two hundred thousand men, if I understand your plans correctly?"

"Just a little under that number, yes."

"Astonishing. And von Tirpitz promises that his ships will be able to protect the transport ships that will feed and supply them?"

Schlieffen's eyes flickered and Holstein saw an instant's doubt. "It will be a mighty endeavor, but he assures me his ships are up to the task. When the Americans negotiate shortly, as the kaiser assures, the point will be moot anyhow."

"Ah, yes," Holstein said softly. "The negotiations will solve everything."

*   *   *

"Moving pictures?" asked Roosevelt. "Secretary Hay, with all that is occurring, do we have time for this?" Roosevelt waved in the general direction of the projector. A screen was set against a wall of the East Room. "I thought you had meaningful plans to discuss."

Hay did not take his president's objections seriously. He knew the president loved moving pictures. "I certainly do. However, these gentlemen just arrived from Mr. Edison's laboratory in New Jersey, and Mr. Root has been delayed. I thought we'd take this opportunity to show you what we have."

Roosevelt was intrigued and took a seat. Moving pictures were such a marvelous invention and so full of potential. Cleveland had been the first president filmed; now Roosevelt was the third.

The Edison man explained that Mr. Edison would have liked to be there himself, but he was busy with important projects. Roosevelt tried not to smile. It was more likely that the deaf Thomas Edison didn't want to be embarrassed by having to answer questions he couldn't hear regarding whatever it was they were going to see.

The lights were turned off and the screening began. At first there was a title that screamed "Invasion," in large, bold letters. Roosevelt tensed and leaned forward. A second title read "Long Island," and the picture showed people lying on the ground. No. They were dead. The camera mercilessly showed bloodied corpses of men, women, and children while workers wearing masks prepared them for burial.

"Dear God," said Roosevelt.

The next scene was of New York harbor. It showed German warships moving about with the city in the background. The view of German ships around the Statue of Liberty almost moved him to tears.

Abruptly, the scene changed and he could see puffs of smoke coming from the ships' guns as they bombarded Brooklyn. This was followed by scenes of the fire and its aftermath—blocks and blocks of charred and smoking buildings. Even there, the cameramen found bodies to film.

Another scene showed German infantry marching down the blackened streets from the waterfront. They marched in precise steps, as if on parade and without a care in the world. It was chilling.

This was followed by scenes of refugees, thousands of them, moving about and living in wretched conditions, their faces gaunt, eyes dimmed by fear and exhaustion. The worst part was the crying children. If only there were sound, Roosevelt thought, it would bring tears to the hardest of hearts.

The last scene also showed bodies. These were dead American soldiers lying facedown in a field. The caption was simply, "Murdered."

The lights went on. The entire viewing had taken less than ten minutes. Roosevelt's cheeks were wet. "Your camera operators are very brave."

The man grinned cheekily. "And very sneaky. At one point I hid in the second floor of a collapsing warehouse to get the shots of those soldiers marching by."

"Good for you! John Hay, thank you for showing me this. Now, how can we use it best?"

Hay was pleased. "Sir, Mr. Edison has agreed to make more than a hundred copies at his expense and distribute them throughout the United States. They will be shown in vaudeville houses and other theaters as motion pictures are shown now. We can anticipate a very emotional response from the American public. Even better than when Mr. Edison showed films of the Spanish war. We may also send copies to other sympathetic countries. But I am most anxious that all Americans see what has happened and just what we are fighting against and fighting for."

Roosevelt smiled thinly. "Bully!"

Chapter 13

MOLLY AWOKE SLOWLY from her deep and dream-filled sleep. She realized that something had disturbed her. The night was warm and sticky, and the windows were open in a vain attempt to catch a night breeze. She lay still and listened. Very quickly she was rewarded with the sound of what might have been a whimper. She continued to listen and it was repeated. A cat? Some other kind of animal? Carefully, so as to not disturb Katrina, who slept in the other bed, she arose and walked to the window. When she heard the sound again, she realized that it came from within the small house she and Katrina shared.

Padding softly on bare feet, she went to the bedroom door and opened it. There was a small squeak, but Katrina slept on, her breath coming in almost a soft snore. Molly smiled fondly. Damned Dutchies could sleep through an earthquake.

She entered the hallway and looked about. The sound, now more like an animal in pain, was coming from the bedroom across the hall where Heinz was sleeping. Heinz had arrived at Katrina's rented cottage late the evening before and had cheerfully informed them that both he and Patrick Mahan had survived the disaster unharmed, and the general had sent him ahead with that message. Patrick would come by as soon as he could.

When it had come time for Heinz to leave, Katrina would not hear of him trying to find quarters elsewhere. Lieutenants were the lowest form of life in a village filled to overflowing with refugees, lost troops, and the walking wounded. Heinz had protested that it would not be appropriate for him to stay with the two women, and Katrina had nearly exploded. "Who gives a damn what people think? Propriety? The hell with propriety! There's a war on, isn't there?"

Heinz had sheepishly given in and agreed to take the bedroom that had been Molly's, which accounted for her bunking with Katrina. In retrospect, it seemed that Heinz hadn't protested all that much.

Molly closed the door behind her, walked over to Heinz's room, and placed her ear to his door. While she did this, she hoped fervently that he would not suddenly open the door and confront her, barefoot as she was, clad only in a thin cotton nightgown, and with her ear pressed to his door. A person could get the wrong idea.

She hesitated, then opened the door. Heinz was in his bed, his large body contorted and his face twisted as his closed eyes saw something she could not. His mouth opened and a small wail of pain emerged. Molly closed the door and walked across the room to stand by him. He had kicked off his covers and was clad only in his underwear. Molly was, quite frankly, astonished by the size and bulk of the young man. When he was clothed it was apparent that he was tall and powerfully built, but now she realized just how muscular he was.

Heinz moaned again. Was this, she thought, so different from the dreams that poor dead Cormac sometimes had? She knelt beside Heinz and began to whisper his name, calling for him to awaken, to emerge from his nightmare, her voice a comforting purr.

He awoke and looked about, trying to register where he was. When he saw Molly his eyes widened in astonishment, making her smile as she stood up. He grabbed the bedclothes and covered himself, the futile gesture amusing her even more. A boy, she thought, a lieutenant in the army but still a large boy. How could she have chided him as a potential enemy?

"Molly," he whispered. "What're you doing here?"

"You were having a bad dream. I heard you crying out."

"Oh, God," he said and sagged farther back into the down pillow. "I keep seeing them. It's so awful."

Molly was puzzled. "Seeing what?"

"Them. The dead. The wounded. Oh, God, Molly, I never, ever

thought it could be like that. I never saw a battle before, never saw what could happen to a man when a bullet hit or, worse, a cannon exploded. The word 'horrible' doesn't even begin to cover the sights, the sounds, and the smells. I don't think there are any words in any language that can."

He looked at her and she saw how drawn his face was. No, this was not her brother Cormac coming back from a night of fighting and carousing; this was a confused young man trying to comprehend what had happened to him. She felt deeply moved by his genuine distress.

"I'd never seen battle. I missed that little ambush General Mahan and General Funston cooked up, so when this big one occurred, I was thrilled. I was all dressed up in a spiffy new uniform and had a sword and pistol and was going to be the brave hero, a twentieth-century knight-errant." He laughed harshly. "Fat lot of good that did! I saw the men go forward and wanted to be with them, so brave they looked, but I had to stay with General Mahan, and generals don't lead charges anymore. At the time I didn't know how lucky I was."

He sighed and looked up at the cracked ceiling. "Then I saw the troops come back, all bloody and filthy and torn. And whipped. They were crying and hurt. When the fighting finally stopped and they sent people out to help the wounded, I volunteered. By that time many of the wounded had died from bleeding or shock. Some of them may have drowned in shell holes that were filled with rain from the storm. Anyway, we gathered up as many as we could and took them back to the field hospitals. Some died on the trip. I tried to keep one boy from bleeding to death from where his arm had been torn off. I squeezed his exposed and bleeding veins with my fingers, but they were too slippery and he died anyhow and I got his blood on my uniform. I'm not sure he would have survived under any circumstances. The crowds of wounded waiting for care at the hospitals were so large."

Molly sat on the edge of the bed and drew his uncomplaining head to her shoulder. How could she have ever thought of this young man as her enemy? "You did what you could," she said soothingly, running her hand through his thick blond hair.

"It wasn't enough! You know, some of the worst wounded didn't even make a sound? Maybe they couldn't. When I was younger, I read of the Civil War where the operating tents were surrounded by piles of amputated limbs. I thought that was horrible and, stupid me, I thought those days were over. They're not, Molly, they're not. I saw mountains of arms and legs all covered with blood and flies and realized that they could have been mine."

Heinz was crying as he spoke, and Molly realized her own cheeks were wet with tears.

"When the ambulances went out again, I did too. This time we picked up only the dead. In some ways they were worse than the wounded. Some of them just looked at you with open eyes on their blank dead faces, as if they were accusing you of causing them to die. When we couldn't find any more bodies, we started picking up the bits and pieces. When the cart was full, we went back to the camp." His voice broke and his chest heaved with racking sobs that nearly tore her apart.

Molly held his head to her bosom and rocked him gently as the two of them cried together. After some time, Heinz disengaged himself. "You better get back to your room," he said gently, trying not to look at her.

Molly smiled and wiped both their tears with a corner of the covers. "When I'm ready." She shifted so that this time her head was on his shoulder. Almost instinctively he put his arm around her. They sat silently for a few moments.

"You shouldn't be here," he insisted.

"Do you really want me to leave?"

"No. I don't ever want you to leave," he said softly, his face now full of a youthful sincerity that charmed her. "Where will you go when this war is over?"

She shrugged. "Boston perhaps. I seem to recall we have cousins there. Of course," she giggled, "we Irish have cousins almost everywhere. Except Ireland, of course; everyone's over here."

"Any kin in Ohio? Cincinnati?"

"None I'm aware of. Why?"

"I want to take you home with me and I wouldn't want you to be lonely for your folk."

She sat up in the bed and turned so that she was kneeling, facing him. "Heinz, don't joke with me."

"No," he said with deep sincerity. "I've been wanting to tell you that for a long time."

A long time? They had known each other only a few weeks, but war has a way of making otherwise short periods of time seem eternal. Go with him to Ohio? Be the Irish wife of a German husband? No, she reminded herself, he is not a German. Heinz is an American and, as she'd been reminded several times, so is she. "If you really want me to, I'll go with you," she said softly.

They hugged and he kissed her. When was the last time a boy had kissed her? Billy McCaffrey, she recalled. It was about a year ago and the little pig was trying to run his hand up the inside of her thigh at the same time. She and Heinz kissed again and she felt her body meld into his as the kisses grew more eager, more intense, as they grew more familiar with each other.

Heinz was acutely aware that she wore nothing under the thin gown and that it had ridden well up her legs. He could feel her young breasts against him, and he was aroused as he'd never been in his life. "Now I think," he gasped, "you'd really better leave."

Molly sat up and smiled. "I think not," she said as she slipped the gown over her shoulders.

A few minutes later and a few feet away, a shocked and confused Katrina Schuyler lay in her bed and tried to sort out her feelings and thoughts. She had awakened and found Molly's bed empty. Assuming only that the girl had to answer a call of nature, she'd thought nothing of it. When, after a decent interval, Molly hadn't returned, a drowsy Katrina started to worry. She got up and peered into the hallway, where, to her surprise, she heard sounds coming from Heinz's room.

Unknowingly repeating Molly's actions, she placed her ear to the door and listened. For a moment she was puzzled, then astonished. Although she had never before heard two people making love, she knew exactly what the excited and passionate moans and murmurs meant. Her face flushing, she dashed back to her bed and pulled the covers up to her chin.

Oh, my lord, she thought. She had hoped they would become friends, but she had never anticipated or desired that they would become lovers. This was going to complicate things. Or would it? It likely meant that she and Molly would be seeing a lot more of both Heinz and his commanding officer, the strangely intellectual Patrick Mahan. Would that be so bad?

That there was an element of jealousy she cheerfully acknowledged. Like many young and wealthy women of her era, she had had no sexual experiences. Oh, she knew where babies came from and how they were made, but she had never participated in the exercise. Still a virgin, she had to acknowledge the fact that she was considered an old maid. Many of her younger friends were already married and had become mothers several times. A few had taken lovers, discreetly and within the limits that society permitted. As to herself, she had been kissed a few times, always chastely, by a handful of would-be swains, most of whom were more likely after her family's money than her own thin body. No one had ever suggested she go to bed with them, and no one had ever tried anything really sexual. Indeed, she realized ruefully, the only man who had ever intentionally touched her breast had been the thug who'd tried to kidnap her as they fled New York.

She imagined Molly and Heinz naked and entwined only a few feet away. They were naked, weren't they? People making love should be. Then her imagination replaced them with herself and Patrick Mahan. Again she flushed. Molly, so many years her junior, had a much fuller and more feminine figure. As to Patrick, she could only imagine. He was taller than she, well built and muscular looking. So what if his hair was receding a little. She found the thought of lying with him a pleasant one. But what if he didn't find her attractive? Well, he keeps coming around; that must mean he thinks something of her. God, she thought, what if he thinks of me as a sister? That had happened before and was something she could not bear. Was it her fault she came on so strong about women being educated and able to vote? Was it also her fault she had such small breasts when men expected much more?

She thought again of Patrick's body against hers and his hands caressing her gently and intimately. Damnit, she thought. Damn, damn, damn.

The handful of men in the president's office constituted his brain trust. They were his secretary of state, John Hay, and the secretaries of war and navy, Elihu Root and John Long. Long had arrived late and had been enduring some reasonably good-natured ribbing from Hay, who, as usual, was taking it on himself to make the situation less tense. Hay was also puffing on a long and smelly cigar. He glanced at Roosevelt and saw that the ruddiness and color were back in his cheeks. The man was amazing, he thought. Just a day or two ago he had looked as if the weight of the world had fallen on him. Now he looked as if he could take on the world alone.

Which, Hay thought, he might have to do.

"Gentlemen," Roosevelt said, smiling, "we are gathered here to embark on the journey we should have started back in June. It is, after all, never too late. Except, of course, for the poor dead who have already given their all for their country."

There were murmurs of polite assent and he continued. "Events tend to repeat themselves. Do any of you recall what happened to Winfield Scott at the beginning of the Civil War?"

Since Roosevelt was looking directly at Hay, the latter removed his cigar and responded. "Of course. Scott was an ancient of seventy-five, a hero of the Mexican war and the War of 1812, and the commanding general of the Union army at the time of Fort Sumter. He came up with a complex military creation called the Anaconda Plan by the press. It would have involved a blockade of the South, and a long series of campaigns to cut up and isolate the Confederacy, to win a war that he estimated might last three years."

"Precisely. And what happened?"

Hay took a long pull on his cigar. "The poor man was forcibly retired. No one wanted to even think of a war lasting any longer than a few weeks. Hell, 'On to Richmond' was the cry, and they meant right now and not next year. Of course we got our asses whipped at the first Bull Run and a few other spots until we settled on generals like Grant and Sherman to win the war." Hay smiled. "And, yes, they basically did so by implementing the Anaconda Plan and taking four and a half years to complete the task instead of three."

"Precisely, again. If the country had as its goal winning a war and not just a battle, the war would have been over many months earlier, and so many more lives would not have been lost."

"Is that your point, Mr. President," asked Root, "that we have been attempting to fight a battle and not a war?"

"That, gentlemen, is exactly what I mean. The recent debacle at Danbury showed that we are not yet capable of winning a climactic battle against the Germans, and we may never be ready enough. Instead, we must prepare for a war." He leaned forward. "A long war. And a war of attrition that may never be concluded by a decisive battle. The enemy is far too strong."

Hay nodded. "I think the major portion of the country realizes that now. The people who thought in terms of glorious victories have to confront reality. Now it is time for hard, hard work."

"Excellent," said Roosevelt. "And in order to win that war we must greatly enlarge our military. I propose increasing naval production to double our existing fleet." Long scribbled furiously on a pad, his face betraying nothing. "Further," Roosevelt continued, "I wish to develop an army of a million men to combat the Germans." To Root's shocked expression, he asked, "Does that create problems, Elihu?"

"More than I can enumerate here, sir. Not the least of them is the question of a command structure. Who shall lead?"

Roosevelt's face was expressionless. "Why, a new general, of course."

Root agreed. "And I must reiterate the need for a new structure for command. The concept of one general in charge is obsolete. We need something more like what the Germans do with their General Staff."

Roosevelt agreed. "Yes, but in time. First we have the immediate problem of winning the war, and, gentlemen, I believe the country needs a hero to lead it. Someone of stature and credibility to coordinate, if not lead in the traditional sense, our war efforts. Yes, a hero."

"Hero?" Hay snorted and almost dropped his cigar. "Theodore, who do you have in mind? Grant's dead and so's Sherman." Long and Root glanced at each other. Hay was the only one who would presume to call the president by his first name in any but the most private of settings.

"Why, John, what about Arthur MacArthur?" chided Roosevelt. "He's old enough and certainly vigorous, and he'll be here from the Philippines in a few weeks."

Root shook his head. "If we do that, who'll command in the field? Baldy Smith is good enough for right now, but we will need better men up there. If Mac is in the field, who will coordinate? Besides, most of the country doesn't even know who the hell he is, so he won't qualify as your hero."

"Yet you agree we must do something?"

There was no dissent. The newspapers and political opposition were adamant that Miles had to go and that other changes had to be made. Either the war had to be fought to its fullest or a negotiated peace had to be entered into. Since the latter would humiliate the United States and condemn her to second-class status in perpetuity, nobody in the current administration wanted any part of such a catastrophic settlement.

Hay relit his cigar. "A hero? Where the hell you gonna find one of them? They've been in short supply lately."

Roosevelt smiled. "If people had listened to Winfield Scott, he'd be revered, wouldn't he? An elder statesman whose wisdom led the country in its time of travail. I know we would prefer that our heroes be young, broad shouldered, and golden haired, but it does not always work out that way. Sometimes heroes are old and gray."

"Damnit, Theodore, what the hell have you got in mind?"

Roosevelt smiled. "Gentlemen, I propose a man who has served his country long and well. He graduated from West Point, distinguished himself in the Mexican war as a young officer, and then achieved high rank in the War Between the States. When that tragedy was over he served his country as ambassador to Turkey—"

"No!" said Hay, rising from his chair as realization dawned. "You must be joking."

"I assure you I am not joking."

Hay couldn't stifle a grin. "Good lord, I didn't even know the man was still alive."

While Long and Root exchanged puzzled glances, Roosevelt stood, recognizing that what he was doing was the equivalent of a political nominating speech. "Oh, he is alive. Alive and well, I assure you. Hale and hearty for a man of his years. A trifle hard of hearing, but no other problems."

"Ancient," Hay chortled. "The man is ancient. And he's not hard of hearing, he's damn near deaf."

Roosevelt chided him fondly. "John, just because a man is old doesn't mean he has to be one of the living dead."

"I assume you've spoken to him and he'll accept?"

"Certainly. It was a delightful conversation. And had you forgotten that he is currently serving as our commissioner of railroads?"

Long looked blank. A well-educated lawyer, he thought he knew just about everyone and certainly everything he needed to know about his beloved navy, but he had no idea who the commissioner of railroads was. Few navies, he reminded himself, traveled much by rail. "All right," he said, laughing, "I cannot stand the suspense. Who is this knight in shining armor?"

Roosevelt stood, his arms behind his back, and his chest and jaw outthrust in the pose that was so frequently caricatured. "Gentlemen, tomorrow I will go before Congress and propose that the rank of full general, four stars, be given to James Longstreet, lieutenant general (retired) of the Confederate States of America."

There was a moment of silence until Root broke it with a simple, "Jesus." As usual, Hay filled the void. "Well, Theodore, you are right, he is old."

"And vigorous, John. He did have ten children."

"Any recently?"

Roosevelt chuckled. "None that I'm aware of, but I wouldn't bet against it."

Root drummed his fingers on the arm of his chair. "I will grant you he is a hero to many, but there are those, both North and South, who hate him rather than think of him as a hero. Remember, after the war he committed the twin sins of returning to federal service and, worse, criticizing the South's patron saint, Robert E. Lee."

Roosevelt nodded. "As to the first part, I think that is behind us. A number of ex-Confederate officers served well in the Spanish war and others are serving now with our army in Connecticut. As to the second point, well, history has proven him right. Even Lee admitted that the defeat at Gettysburg was his own fault and not Longstreet's. Although there may be a few diehards who feel he is not deserving, I think his name and his reputation will carry the day. Especially," he said, smiling, "if his nomination is supported by a man of such stature as John Hay, who actually knew and worked with Abraham Lincoln."

"You bastard." Hay laughed. "Of course I'll do it. If nothing else, I want to see the look on certain people's faces. Just a quick question, Theodore, how old is he?"

Roosevelt smiled genially. "Eighty-two."

*   *   *

The kaiser laughed so hard his crippled hand came out of the pocket where it had been tucked, and dangled uselessly until he retrieved it. Chancellor Bulow tried not to notice. Once again the kaiser was alternating between high good humor and flaming rage in a display of inconsistency that had von Bulow concerned.

"Longstreet? James Longstreet? How bankrupt are the Americans if they must trust their efforts to an octogenarian? Bulow, tell me, are they jesting?"

"Apparently not, sire. They made the announcement officially, and Congress is very likely to accede to the wishes of Roosevelt. They don't have much choice."

The kaiser cackled, causing Bulow to blink. It was so unseemly. "I have a wonderful idea. Why don't we disinter Blücher and have the British dig up old, dead Wellington? Then we can have all three cadavers, one still breathing, in the field at the same time."

Bulow, who had been talking with others in the government, Holstein in particular, did not see the humor. "Sire, the appointment of Longstreet, coupled with their other announcements, seems to indicate a further unwillingness to negotiate a settlement."

The kaiser's good humor disappeared immediately. "They'll negotiate. They must. Their army is defeated and their navy is in hiding God knows where. They will talk because they have no other choice. As to this nonsense of an army of a million men, that is utter rot! Certainly they could put that many in the field, but they would be mowed down like wheat by a scythe. They would be a rabble in arms."

A rabble that could learn, thought Bulow, who remembered his history and knew how the Americans seemed to be able to create armies out of whole cloth when given enough time. He was about to mention that tactfully when the kaiser stood up and went to a large globe of the world.

"I have studied, von Bulow, the history of the many empires the world has known. In the early days, there were the Assyrians, the Egyptians, and the Persians. Athens called herself an empire, but a city-state and a handful of islands do not qualify for the title. Rome was an empire. God in heaven, and what an empire! Did you know that the word 'kaiser' comes from the Latin Caesar? So does 'tsar' for my dear cousin Nicky, who seems to be so upset by my American adventure. So I am the inheritor of the Caesars of Rome."

He spun the globe gently. "Now look at today's world, today's empires. Russia calls herself an empire, yet most of her empire is Siberia, which is 90 percent frozen tundra, unfit for human life. Of course," he said laughing, "the rest of Russia isn't so wonderful either."

"It certainly isn't, sire."

"Britain has a true empire. Just look at her possessions. Every continent, von Bulow, every continent! Magnificent. Spain once had an empire, and now it belongs to those fool Americans, who have no use for it and wish to give away many of their new lands to the little brown people who live in them. Idiots! That cannot be permitted to happen!"

"Certainly not, sire."

The kaiser smacked the globe with his good hand. "Now look at Germany's 'empire.' What do you see besides a slightly above average sized country virtually landlocked in the middle of Europe? Where are our colonies? A desert in southwest Africa? A handful of islands in the Pacific? Von Bulow, even the Dutch have a larger empire than we do. If the Americans do not wish to negotiate, then they will have to continue bleeding until they do!"

"Yes, sire."

Chapter 14

THE CROWD SURROUNDING the White House and lining both sides of Pennsylvania Avenue was large but surprisingly silent. Virtually the only noise to be heard was the hum of normal conversation, punctuated by the occasional sounds of vendors hawking balloons, ice cream, and souvenir pennants. The ice cream sales were far surpassing the rest as people purchased in a vain attempt to ward off the early August heat.

It was as if the crowd, although curious and respectful, did not know quite what to do, how to behave. Roosevelt, sweating profusely in a dark cutaway, had to agree. How were they supposed to react? For that matter, how was he?

The dignitaries assembled with him were equally silent. Congress had argued for two days over whether to give Longstreet the rank of four-star general and finally acquiesced. As Hay had predicted, the opposition came from three sources. First were the hard-core Unionist Northerners who objected to this authority going to someone who had fought against his country. These were a grizzled few, and they quickly gave in. The second group consisted of Southerners who felt that Longstreet had gone too far in being reconstructed, and had committed the heresy of criticizing Lee. These, some as old as Longstreet, were also talked down.

The third opposition group was the most disconcerting. These did not oppose Longstreet. In fact, they thought him a fine, heroic man.

What they opposed was the war itself. They saw the change in command as an exercise in futility. The United States had lost and should take its lumps and go on with life in peace and without Cuba, the Philippines, and those other islands. These people were a minority but an increasingly vocal one, and they would bear watching. Couldn't they see, Roosevelt thought, what would occur to their nation if America lost this war?

His thoughts were interrupted by the sounds of the Marine Band, led again for the day by its ex-conductor, John Philip Sousa, as it started to play from across the street in Lafayette Park. The crowd responded quickly to the sounds of the "Stars and Stripes Forever," and people started to clap hands in cadence. Better, Roosevelt thought, much better. A few minutes later, the crowd started to shift and people craned their necks to see down Pennsylvania Avenue. Longstreet was coming.

First in view were three rows of plume-helmeted cavalry, stretching across the avenue, their sabers drawn and carried in front of their chests. This brought polite cheers and applause. They were followed by two other troops of cavalry in column of fours trotting slowly down the street.

Behind them came a battalion of infantry, marching in precise steps, their polished bayonets gleaming in the sun. Someone near Roosevelt wondered aloud why the whole lot of them weren't up fighting the Germans.

There was a pause and the band ceased playing. Now people were truly stretching to see. What they saw was an automobile, an open-top Daimler, with two people in it. One was a uniformed driver and the other an old man beside him.

An automobile? The old rebel was arriving by horseless carriage? Stories of how Miles hated the things had circulated broadly, and the symbolism was not lost. Old Pete, the accepted nickname for Longstreet, was more up to date than Nelson Miles. Now the crowd cheered warmly.

The vehicle pulled up in front of Roosevelt, and a nervous lieutenant offered Longstreet an arm for assistance. Both he and the offer were ignored.

Longstreet stood erect, and those nearby gasped. Few knew that he was more than six feet tall and a powerfully built, handsome man. With his shock of white hair and his long white beard, he looked like a biblical patriarch come to call down divine wrath upon his enemies. The crowd cheered again as he confidently strode the few steps to his president. He was wearing blue—Union blue, federal blue—and four stars glistened on his shoulders. Longstreet stopped and saluted Roosevelt, winking quickly, and the crowd cheered even louder. He turned and saluted the flag waving high on its staff, and the roar from the multitude became tumultuous, causing the hair on men's necks to stand on end.

Longstreet spoke briefly. He said the United States would fight and that the United States would win. Only a few could hear him, but it didn't matter; the substance of his message was apparent and the crowd was thrilled.

Finally he turned and saluted the throngs. The cheering, frenetic before, became even louder as women wept and grown men pounded each other on the back. "Pete, Pete!" the chant came and Longstreet held the salute. Sousa's band was playing again, but no one heard.

Longstreet wheeled and shook hands with Roosevelt, who guided him into the White House along with the few dozen important people who would talk and dine with him at the president's table.

Inside, while the guests sorted themselves out, Theodore Roosevelt dashed to his private quarters on the second level and tried to compose himself. His face was red and his cheeks were streaked with tears. He could still hear the crowd, not wanting to disperse, singing and shouting while the Marine Band played on. Did he hear "Dixie"? What a triumph!

And to think, he smiled, the only reason he'd held the arrival at the White House instead of the Capitol was to save the old man from having to climb all those steps.

"Who's that tapping, tapping at my door?"

Patrick laughed, easily recognizing the drawling voice, however slurred it might be. "'Tis I," he answered, "and nothing more."

"Shit," came another voice from behind the wooden door. "Another goddamn Yankee." This voice, too, was slightly slurred.

"Enter at your peril," responded the first voice. Patrick walked into the room, which was on the second floor of a hotel in Hartford, Connecticut. Whatever view the room might have had was irrelevant, because the air was thick with cigar smoke and reeked of alcohol.

Seated about the room in varying states of disarray and disheveled comfort were three of the U.S. Army's most senior field commanders in the combat theater. Senior in rank was Maj. Gen. William "Baldy" Smith, who, for the time being at least, commanded the entire front. With him were Maj. Gens. Fitzhugh Lee and Joe Wheeler, who, despite the similarity in rank, were Smith's subordinate division commanders.

Grinning, Patrick presented himself to Smith and announced that he was prepared for duty.

"Well then," Smith said, pouring himself a drink, "you're likely the only one in this room who is. Quit being a smart-ass and get yourself a drink."

Patrick knew when to obey a direct order and poured a couple of inches of whiskey into a glass. "May I ask what the celebration is for, if this is indeed a celebration?"

The diminutive Joe Wheeler cackled. "Well, we sure ain't celebrating your arrival as our savior. For two months you been Roosevelt's suck-ass toady and now you're supposed to get a command! Gawd, there ain't no justice! What do you want? Miles's old job?"

Patrick simply smiled. He knew Wheeler's comments were without malice. "Gentlemen," he said, raising his glass, "to old Civil War generals."

"Call it right, goddamnit," snapped Wheeler. "Where I come from it's called the War of Northern Aggression."

"Aw, shit," groaned Smith. "Can't you people ever realize you lost the goddamn war?"

"Never." Lee smiled and shifted his hefty body. Unlike Wheeler, he had allowed himself to gain a great deal of weight and no longer resembled a cavalry leader. "And when will you realize why so many top positions are going to ex-Confederates?"

Patrick took another sip of the whiskey and let the warmth permeate his tired body. Yesterday he had been in Washington. Today, only thirty hours later, he was in Hartford, having bypassed all German activity.

The three old comrades facing Patrick were engaged in a bout of wet reminiscing. Smith had commanded a Union corps at Petersburg at the end of the Civil War; Wheeler and Lee had commanded divisions for the Confederate cause. Thirty-five years later they had found themselves on the same side against a new enemy, Spain. Three years after that they were at it again against Germany.

"To Longstreet," Patrick said cautiously and raised his glass. The three generals also drank. So much for the appointment being controversial to his new subordinates, he thought. "And why is James Longstreet called 'Old Pete'?"

Wheeler shrugged. "Beats the hell out of me. He doesn't have a middle name that I know of. Maybe it was the name of an old horse or a favorite hound."

The evening continued with the older generals talking and Patrick usually listening. It was a fascinating slice of history, and he desperately wanted to remember it all. They relived battles fought forty years prior and discussed a dozen times since. There had been tragedies as well as triumphs. The man with the biggest burden to bear seemed to be Baldy Smith, who remembered the day in 1864 when he and his corps had stood before a virtually empty Petersburg and balked. He had halted, waiting for reinforcements he didn't need, and let slip the opportunity to take Petersburg and Richmond. His mistake caused the war to drag on for another bloody year, and it saddened him every time he thought of it.

Finally the effects of Patrick's trip and the liquor started to take their toll and he became afraid he would fall asleep. He rose and excused himself. The old men bade him good night. They still had several more campaigns to refight.

"Don't worry, Patrick," said Smith. "Longstreet will do all right and so will we. We'll talk about your command tomorrow. If you like challenges, you'll love this one."

Wheeler jabbed the air with his hand. "We're getting Longstreet and a million men." He dropped his hand and looked confused. "What the hell will we do with a million men?"

Instead of going directly to bed, Patrick walked a bit to clear his head. If he was to report more formally to Smith the next day, he would prefer not be suffering from an agonizing hangover, although he might be the only senior officer without one.

After a while and feeling more sober, he went to his tent, stripped to his underclothes, and washed up out of a basin as well as he could. Then he lay down on an uncomfortable cot and looked at the stark top of the tent. It was, he decided, a damned hard way to make a living. Here he was, nearing forty and sleeping on a cot in a tent in the middle of an otherwise civilized and respectable city. Of course the war made certain there were no rooms available, and he might have gotten Smith or Wheeler to find him a place, but that would have been imposing. Worse, some poor soul might have gotten bumped, and he didn't consider that quite fair. What the hell, at least he'd pulled rank and gotten someone to put up the tent.

How long had he been in the army? Counting time at the academy, twenty years. That was enough, he decided. Twenty years and two wars and how many skirmishes against Indians? Was he eligible for a pension? Did it matter? It was time to leave.

He knew he had found his real calling when writing his German report at West Point and lecturing on it. The contacts he'd been making over the years would pay off with a teaching position at one of several universities if returning to West Point was not feasible. More and more he was starting to think that West Point was not the proper place. That left his other two major possibilities: the University of Michigan in Ann Arbor, and the University of Detroit, in the center of the city of that name. There was logic to this, since the area was his home and he and his family knew so many people. It also meant he wouldn't have to sleep on any more cots. Ever.

Yet what sort of life would he have? He was not poor, so there would be no trouble with money, but he was still single. With whom could he share his life? How would he meet a proper companion at his age?

He ran down the list of women he had known and found it depressingly short. Certainly he'd socialized with women, both before the academy and afterward, and enjoyed it. His nomadic military life had made such acquaintances brief, but some had been intense. There had been a particularly splendid relationship with a major's daughter during a two-week idyll in Southern California. He had considered proposing, but she had dumped him a few weeks later, leaving him with only memories of naked bodies frolicking in the moonlit surf.

But that was more than ten years ago. The woman was now married to some banker and had two children. Probably got fat, too. The thought depressed him.

The only woman he knew at all now was Katrina Schuyler, and despite what he had told her, she did frighten him. No, not because of her mind or her opinions, but because she was so rich and sophisticated that she must think him a barbarian bumpkin. Yes, she was attractive, interesting, and polite, and perhaps they really were friends, but how could it ever go farther than that?

He willed himself not to fantasize about life on a college campus with Katrina. She could likely buy her own college if she so wished.

Well, at least Heinz and Molly had hit it off. A short note from Trina had informed him, with equal degrees of shock and amusement, that the two young people had fallen in love. Her words also implied that they were sleeping together.

That, of course, partially explained why his young aide was not in Hartford and why he, as a brigadier general, had to sleep in a tent. Patrick vowed insincerely to teach the young pup a lesson when he finally did show up. What the hell, let them have their joy while they can. Only God knew what might happen to them tomorrow.

Patrick sat up in the cot. Of course. What the hell was he being such a fool for? If such an unlikely pair as Heinz and Molly could find themselves, why couldn't he and Katrina? The worst that could happen was that she would reject him, and he would be no worse off than he was right now.

Did he love her? He didn't know. He knew that he enjoyed her company and liked to see her smile, and loved to hear her talk. And hadn't she kissed him and urged him to return? Once again he could see her face and feel her slender body against his, even if it had been for only the briefest of moments. What had Admiral Nelson said about a good commander being able to do no wrong if he laid his ship alongside that of an enemy? He laughed. Katrina Schuyler was not his enemy, but he certainly wouldn't mind lying alongside her.

He lay back down and prepared for sleep. Tomorrow would be a long day, what with finding out about the type of unit he would be commanding, but he would try to make arrangements to see Katrina.

And just what did they mean about command being a challenge?

Chapter 15

THIS WOULD BE James Longstreet's first dealing with both his superiors and his immediate subordinates. Theodore Roosevelt sat quietly at one end of the table and was flanked by Elihu Root and John Hay. The only two military men besides Longstreet were Maj. Gen. Leonard Wood and the recently arrived Arthur MacArthur, who had immediately been promoted to the rank of lieutenant general. In some ways, this meeting was as much for MacArthur as it was an inauguration of Longstreet.

MacArthur had arrived from Manila the preceding day after an epic journey that began with a high-speed dash on a British cruiser. When the cruiser finally reached the western Canadian port of Vancouver, MacArthur and his two-man staff had been ensconced on a special, sealed train that sped them to the border at Buffalo. Another special train brought him to Washington, D.C.

Longstreet began with a brief announcement. "General Miles has submitted his resignation."

There was genuine sympathy in the room for the usually unpopular Nelson Miles. Despite a lifetime of good service, the world would forever remember him for the disaster that had transpired at Danbury.

"General Wood," prompted Longstreet, "why don't you begin your presentation?"

Wood recapped briefly. The Germans had not moved from their perimeter, which included Manhattan, part of Long Island, and the area north of Long Island Sound running from the Hudson east to a point just short of the Housatonic, near Danbury, where a virtually solid wall of fortifications ran southward to the sound.

Wood estimated the Germans at eighty thousand, with additional troops arriving almost weekly in heavily guarded convoys. They were deployed throughout the perimeter. A few battalions were stationed on Staten Island to protect the Narrows, where the entrance to the upper harbor was only a mile wide.

In numbers, the Americans had the larger force, with about 130,000 in the field. But this apparent superiority was an illusion, as only about half the Americans had modern weapons and few were well trained by any standards. The only problems fully resolved were those of food and shelter.

MacArthur leaned forward. "But what about fighting, General? Surely we are not being totally inert."

Wood flushed. "There are patrol actions and minor skirmishes almost daily, but nothing major is occurring. We have, of course, been utilizing spies and saboteurs behind their lines wherever possible. That includes New York City and Long Island as well as Connecticut."

Longstreet turned to Hay. "Can the Brits send more of their rifles?"

"No. Their explanation is that they cannot strip their own forces in order to arm ours. We are getting about five thousand rifles a week through Canada, and they feel that is enough. Further, they do not want to go too far in offending the Germans."

Longstreet nodded. MacArthur looked stunned at the scope of the problem.

Wood continued. "We also have serious deficiencies in machine guns and heavy artillery. Our local companies, like Winchester, Remington, and Colt, are expanding military production as quickly as they can, so these problems may be resolved reasonably soon, perhaps in a couple of months. As to the problem of rifles, we had been experimenting with the German Mauser prior to the war and were considering producing it at our Springfield, Massachusetts, facility. We already have the tooling, but we do have a minor hitch."

"Which is?" asked Longstreet.

Wood looked embarrassed. "General, this is almost beyond ridiculous. I've been informed by both our legal staff and our quartermasters that the design of the Mauser is patented and Germany owns the patent. They say it might be illegal for us to use it without their permission."

Longstreet turned an interesting shade of red. "Get their permission? That is the stupidest piece of shit I've ever heard. Inform those people that we are at war with Germany and are not required to say 'May I?' before shooting them. Tell anyone who objects to stay out of the way, or else. Jesus." He laughed. "God save us from our friends."

"Gentlemen," said Wood, continuing quickly. "We have also largely solved the problem of uniforms. We have enough mills either turning them out or just about to, so we will have a well-dressed army very shortly. Of course the million-man army the president plans will strain us, but we will solve that problem. We can also make enough shoes and boots."

"I want brown," snapped Longstreet.

"Sir?" said Wood. The others looked surprised.

"Brown. I want brown, not blue. Don't you Yankees know what splendid targets you made in blue? Hell, you couldn't hide at all until your boys got all dirty. My boys were dirty to begin with. Look, just like forty years ago, the enemy's got rifles and guns that can kill from a mile away. Bright colors may have made sense in the days of the crossbow, but not now. The British gave up red and are using khaki in Africa against the Boers and it seems to work. Hell, even the Germans' dark gray is better than blue! And, yes, I know the French are still wearing red and blue, but it's their concern if they wish to continue their stupid love affair with Napoleon."

Wood scribbled a note. "Brown it is."

"Now, what about officers?"

"General," answered Wood, "like the navy, we don't have enough qualified officers to staff the billets we currently have, much less the huge expansion planned by the president. We will also need more officers to train the new men when they arrive. We have stripped many of our regular regiments and sent numbers of their officers to stabilize guard and militia units. Although this has somewhat strengthened the guard and militia, it has also lowered the quality of the regulars."

True enough, Longstreet thought. "All right, get a list of all the officers who left the service for civilian life in the last ten to fifteen years, and find out how many there are. A lot of good men probably left because of the low pay and the need to feed their families. Telegraph them and offer them a return to at least their last rank for the duration of the war."

"And if they don't respond?"

"Then the hell with them. Who needs them? Don't forget we've also got at least two good military schools in addition to the academy: the Virginia Military Institute and The Citadel. They all just graduated classes, didn't they? Well, make sure their graduates are all commissioned too. Then commission the underclassmen. At this point they've all had at least a year of military life under their belts, which puts them well ahead of most other people. We can also promote enlisted men to officer rank—selectively and temporarily, of course."

While Wood took notes furiously, Longstreet glanced about the room. The others seemed to be in agreement. Good. "Now we are going to do something drastic and find enough officers to staff a complete new division." There, that got their attention. "We will take the officers, all of them, from the 9th and 10th Cavalry Regiments and form a division around them. In order to keep the 9th and 10th intact, we will commission all their sergeants and corporals as officers."

Wood was shocked. "You're joking," he said softly.

"No."

"Negro officers? As majors, colonels?"

"Temporary rank. For the duration only."

"Sir, I don't know if we can do it."

"General Wood, I ain't asking. That's an order." Longstreet laughed hugely. "Do you find it as ironic as I do that an old rebel is promoting Negroes?"

There was no opposition. Roosevelt again remembered how colored soldiers had charged up San Juan Hill, or Kettle Hill to be precise, during the last war. The colored troops had gotten mixed up with his own white Rough Riders during the assault, and he'd been impressed by their discipline and bravery. Their blood had stained the hill as well. How could he ever object?

"Now for commands," said Longstreet. "Lieutenant General MacArthur will command the entire theater of operations, which now consists of parts of New York, Connecticut, and New Jersey. If that changes, so will his area of authority. For the time being, he will have two corps of three divisions each. The first will continue to be commanded by Baldy Smith; the second will be given to Funston. We will replace no divisional commanders at this time. We will, however, keep looking for qualified people. God help us if we have to go to a third corps."

MacArthur shrugged. "I'd be comfortable giving it to Pershing. By the way, your act of commissioning academy underclassmen makes my son an officer."

Longstreet smiled. "Was gonna happen sooner or later. Just make sure his mama doesn't try to come with him." MacArthur flushed slightly. The entire army was amused at how young Douglas's mother had moved into a hotel in West Point just to be near her son.

"General Wood, you have a big problem. Your responsibilities will include the arming and supply of the army as well as the training and staffing of the new units the president has requested. You will, in effect, be my chief of staff and be responsible for ensuring that Mac has the tools necessary to do the job."

Wood gulped. "Yes, sir." Longstreet smiled to himself. Wood was a capable administrator who also happened to be a close friend of the president's. An unbeatable combination if Wood played his cards right, and Longstreet was confident he would.

Longstreet smiled benignly. "I've spoken with the president and Mr. Hay and we are in agreement about what the Germans are likely to do. In strictly European fashion, they've fought us for a particular goal. They do not want to conquer and occupy this country. They want exactly what they asked for, which is Cuba, Puerto Rico, and the rest of our possessions, as well as rights to the Isthmus of Panama and other intrusions into the New World. They've done this before and think this is the way to get what they want.

"Thus when they invaded New York and defeated us at Danbury, they fully expected us to cry uncle and wanted to talk about settling. Since we haven't, we understand they are a little confused and frustrated. They know they can't sustain their operation forever. It was not their intention to go to a full war of nations against us, and it still isn't. They do not want an extended stay in New York.

"On the other hand," he said with a grim smile, "we will do all in our power to make their adventure an uncomfortable and unpleasant one. Mac, I hate frontal assaults like what happened so tragically at Danbury. I have seen them fail everywhere. They cost too much in humanity and I will not have it. Some criticize me as a general who is overcautious. Well, I'll accept that if the alternative is to be reckless."

MacArthur nodded. "A siege then? Combined with irregular operations?"

"Exactly. And for however long it takes."

"And what if they decide to continue toward Hartford and Boston instead of staying in their forts? At the rate they are enlarging their force and piling up supplies, they could soon be strong enough to do it."

"If that happens," said Longstreet, "then we will fight them in open battle and God help us. And please, General MacArthur, no frontal assaults. Let them come to us."

The next day's meeting had a significantly different cast and approach. Longstreet and Roosevelt were there, but Hay was not. Secretary of the Navy John Long attended, and Adm. George Dewey, the hero of Manila Bay and ranking naval officer, was the primary guest.

And guest was the proper term. Longstreet as a four-star general reported directly to the secretary of war; Dewey, the senior admiral, reported directly to the secretary of the navy. Thus the rivalry between the two services was legitimized and institutionalized by a table of organization that emphasized their separateness. It was somewhat affected, too, by the fact that Theodore Roosevelt had served as assistant secretary of the navy and was sometimes accused of considering the fleet his personal toy.

Longstreet greeted Dewey cordially. It was the first time they'd ever met and they took stock of each other warily, like two dogs meeting on a street. Dewey was a trim and fit-looking man of average height and build but of impressive bearing and commanding presence. One could easily envision him on the bridge of the *Olym-*

pia, white mustache flaring, while directing the battle and daring fate
to get his white uniform dirty, much less harm him.

Dewey was sixty-four years old and smiled slightly behind his
bushy mustache. "I am honored to finally meet you, General."

"And I to meet you, sir."

"General, if you are the slightest bit concerned that I may be difficult to work with, let me assure you of my fullest cooperation.
Please recall that I serve in the same navy where Admiral Porter and
General Grant worked wonders in cooperation, and I have assured
both Secretary Long and the president that you will have that cooperation. Utterly and totally."

Longstreet responded with mild sarcasm. "I seem to recall some of
those wonders causing the fall of Forts Donaldson and Henry, as well
as enabling the successful siege of Vicksburg. Don't you wonder
whether we'd be having this conversation if they hadn't cooperated
so fully?"

Dewey joined in the mild laughter. Good, Longstreet thought.
Good. "Admiral, I know that you and Captain Mahan have been discussing possible actions. Would you be so kind as to share those
thoughts with us?"

"Of course. Have you read Mahan's books?" Dewey asked, and
Longstreet nodded. Alfred Thayer Mahan's texts were required reading for naval officers throughout the world, and it was rumored that
the kaiser had tried to memorize them.

Dewey continued. "Specifically, his theories hold that we should
take aggressive action with our main battle fleet as soon as possible.
Second, he has felt that a war against an enemy's commerce is a
waste of time. Needless to say, I do not totally agree with him. It is
now my goal and obligation to find ways in which the American
navy can help win a land war against the Germans, and those ways
include cutting off their supply lines and starving them to death."

Dewey walked briskly to the map. "We have right now about a
hundred ships in our navy that can be classified as warships. Most,
however, are small, and a disturbing group are old as well. Further,
not all are in the Atlantic. A significant number of smaller warships
are still on the West Coast or in the Philippines. Frankly, I see no
reason to bring them here. Some are so decrepit they might not make
the passage around Cape Horn.

"However, the key to our fleet is the existence of our eleven capital ships. These are nine true battleships, including the ancient *Texas,* and two armored cruisers. They have all successfully made their way to the Gulf of Saint Lawrence and are now protected by the British fleet under Admiral Fisher. We also have about two dozen other ships—monitors, cruisers, and gunboats—up there as well, and a few more are scheduled to arrive as soon as and as best they can. The way the British have defined the gulf and excluded the Germans from entering, we are safe in a fairly large body of water.

"Unfortunately, the German navy is larger than ours. They have sixteen capital ships in our waters. If we were to force a fleet action right now we would lose. If that were to happen, we would be opening our shores to bombardment again. It would even permit the Germans to simply take by force the lands they covet without fear of retribution. Without a navy, we could do nothing about it, either now or in the future. They also have about thirty smaller ships—cruisers and the like. One cruiser squadron is in Long Island Sound; the main portion of their fleet is either in New York harbor or just outside it. Quite frankly, I believe they are waiting for us. They know we will have to come to them sooner or later, and they would be able to fight close to their own base and not risk missing us in the Atlantic."

Dewey paused and took a sip of water. "Other than our fleet in Canada, we have a half dozen older cruisers, about a score of torpedo boat destroyers, and one submarine in various Atlantic ports. There are also some naval reserve ships available, but I would consider these obsolete and useless."

Longstreet raised an eyebrow. "A submarine?"

"Yes, we took possession about a year ago. A certain John Holland has been trying to build and sell us submarines for a few years now. Some of the European navies have them, so why not us?"

"Do the Germans have any of the things?"

"Not that I am aware of. I also have no idea how well a submarine might work under actual combat conditions."

"Ah."

Dewey continued. "Now, our fleet in Canada has not been idle. We have been working with the British under Admiral Fisher and practicing long-overdue fleet maneuvers. We have also been working hard to improve our gunnery techniques. I assume you are aware that a very small percent of our shells fired against the Spanish actually hit them, even though many of their ships were stationary targets." He sighed. "Despite the victory, it was not an inspiring performance. It seems the technology of the gun has outstripped our ability to use it effectively. Well, a young British officer named Percy Scott has been working with one of our naval officers, William Sims, and they have established both a friendship and a professional rapport. They have also developed a gun-firing technique that appears to improve matters. Evans used it against the German cruisers off Florida, and we are practicing it intensely."

"Excellent. Are the Germans using it?"

Dewey smiled. "Again, not that we are aware of."

Dewey returned to a map, this time one of the world. "Germany's naval ambitions puzzle me. I am a fighting man and not a military philosopher, but I do not understand the Germans. Naval theories say that the oceans can be either a moat or a highway, or, in special cases, both. England is such a special case. The waters around her are her protective moat, which is constantly patrolled by the Royal Navy. Thus any increase in the size of the German fleet is an imme- diate threat to England's moat and will be matched by England. Therefore, Germany will never be permitted to catch up to England. Obviously, too, the waters of the world are England's highway and enable that small island to carry on commerce with her far-flung empire and other lands, thereby making her rich and powerful.

"The situation is similar with us. We have long considered the oceans our moat, but they also function as our commercial highways. The fact that our moat has been breached, we hope temporarily, is a sobering lesson.

"Yet Germany is a land power, not a naval power. England is a naval power and not a land power." Dewey chuckled. "Until the re- cent war in Africa, England's army was about the size of ours; thus England's source of protection was its navy and not its army.

"But now the kaiser, under the prodding of von Tirpitz, is trying to make Germany a naval power as well. It is most puzzling."

Longstreet humphed. "Are you doubting their ability to succeed?"

Dewey nodded. "Most assuredly, yes. They do not have a great maritime tradition on which to draw. Germany herself is only forty years old, and her coastline, although densely populous and containing

key ports, cannot compare with either ours or Britain's. Further,
since they are a land power with arguably the best army in the world,
there is the nagging feeling that most of their better military talent
naturally gravitates to the army and not the navy." Dewey smiled
genially. "Unlike here, where the navy definitely gets the best."

Longstreet laughed. "Horseshit."

Dewey continued. "People like Diedrichs, who commands their
North Atlantic Fleet, and von Tirpitz are first rate. I nearly went to
battle with Diedrichs after Manila Bay when he and his fleet tried to
take control of the city. He and many others are, indeed, very good. Yet
I still have doubts as to the depth of that talent. I think this may have
manifested itself in their actions since losing those three cruisers.
Please recall that forty years ago there was no such thing as a German
navy, except as a minimal coastal defense force, and any expansions
have been very, very recent. Thus until the Florida battle, no German ship had ever fired a shot in anger against a major power."

Longstreet saw where Dewey was going. "And they lost badly.
Must've done wonders for their confidence."

"Exactly. Right after that, they pulled all their patrolling ships
back to Mother and the main fleet. They didn't even make any effort to interdict our ships on the way to Canada. So far we have
lost nothing!"

"Incredible."

"General," continued Dewey, "consider also how their ships were
built and for what purposes. The German warships are heavily
gunned brutes that were designed to take punishment while doing
battle against Britain in the rough confines of the Baltic. Unlike our
warships and those of England, which are designed for worldwide
travel, the German warships do not fare well over great distances.
They cannot carry much in the way of supplies and are incredibly
cramped. When in port, the luckier crews live in barracks and not on
ship in order to prevent disease and dissatisfaction. Our ships are
certainly cramped, but theirs are absolutely barbaric in comparison."

"No pun intended, Admiral," Longstreet injected, "but it sounds as
though you are saying their fleet is an imperfect vessel."

Dewey nodded. "But potentially a lethal one. It is up to us to de-
vise a way of defeating it while staying away from its claws. I have,
of course, the broad outlines of such a plan."

Dewey glanced around the room. He was relieved that his naval theory lecture had not yet put anyone to sleep. "First, I would like to know from Secretary Long whether our fleet can realistically be enlarged in a short period of time."

Long took a second to gather his thoughts before responding. "Prior to the Spanish war, we enquired of certain countries whether we might buy ships from them, and we did succeed in purchasing two cruisers from Brazil. One of these was already commissioned and the other was nearing completion in English yards. Although some lesser ships are currently available, as well as older and obsolete ships, there are no foreign capital ships or, for that matter, any modern major ships at all for sale to us."

"Why?" asked Roosevelt, obviously surprised.

"Sir, none of the European powers, other than England, wishes to risk offending Germany. The South Americans were delighted to help us against Spain, their hated colonial enemy, but they do not love us, have been intimidated by the Germans, and don't want to wind up on the losing side. Therefore, they will do nothing. Their fondest hope may well be that we destroy each other."

"Bastards," muttered Roosevelt.

Dewey ignored the comment. "Mr. Long, what about the *Illinois?*"

Long brightened. "Of course. She has her engines and her big guns, along with much of her crew, and is scheduled for commissioning in a few weeks. That can be expedited and she will be sent immediately to the Saint Lawrence."

"Sixteen to twelve," muttered Longstreet. "The ratio is getting better."

"Almost better," chided Dewey. "It will take a while to get her in fighting trim. Thus we will go for now with what we have. I will be dividing our fleet into unequal parts while still maintaining overall control. We will also be addressing the officer shortage problem in much the same manner as the army: by recalling ex-officers, promoting underclassmen at the academy, and, if necessary, promoting some enlisted men.

"First, our main battle fleet will stay where it is and continue to maneuver and gain skills. On occasion we will send all or part of it south to make the Germans react by sending their fleet out to intercept. For the time being at least, we will decline combat unless they

too divide their own fleet and offer a portion of it to us as a gift. All
we wish to do is wear out the Germans and make them complacent as
well as fatigued. Charles Clark, currently of the *Oregon,* will be promoted to command the battleships. You recall Clark, do you not? His
was the epic journey from the Pacific to Cuba in time for the battle.
Although we were afraid his lonely ship might run into Cervera's
squadron, he was actually hoping for it and had a plan to destroy
them single-handedly. He likely would have done it. He is a fighter!

"I also propose to develop two cruiser squadrons. Please recall the
analogy about the seas being highways. Well, right now those highways are running from Germany to the United States. I propose to
cut them. The cruisers will be able to locate and attack the German
transports. Here, look at the map. Ships leaving British or American
ports can do so from scores of places and arrive at hundreds—thousands—of destinations. But look at Germany. There is only a handful of ports, and all on the Baltic: Hamburg, Bremerhaven, Stettin,
and others as well as her main naval facilities at Kiel and Wilhelms-
haven. Their points of departure are limited even if they do utilize
the Kiel Canal to bypass sailing around Denmark."

Dewey looked and saw he had the men's rapt attention. "At that
point, they can either go through the English Channel or around
Scotland. Most will choose the shorter and safer Channel route.
When they do make the Atlantic, the highway widens but not impos-
sibly so. Unless a ship takes a huge, expensive, and time-consuming
detour, there are only so many ways to get from the English Channel
to New York. Even there, the highway narrows, like a funnel, down
to a predictable area outside the harbor. My first squadron, under
Robley Evans, who will leave the *Alabama,* will consist of a dozen
fast cruisers that will patrol the Channel and other areas off Europe.
The second squadron of six cruisers and an equal number of gunboats will be commanded by George Remey, and they will attack the
German convoys off New York. Evans was scheduled for such a
squadron against the Spanish, but the war ended so quickly he never
got it. Remey is a solid and progressive man who won't make mistakes so near the main German fleet and homeland."

Longstreet was puzzled. "What about Sampson? Schley?"

Dewey replied sadly. "Admiral Winfield Schley no longer has our
confidence. Although he considers himself the victor at Santiago, he

made key mistakes that could have been disastrous had the enemy been other than the incompetent Spanish. I am afraid he is our equivalent of the army's Nelson Miles. Far too many of our officers consider him old-fashioned, a laughingstock. We no longer find him fit for command."

"But what about Sampson? He is considered a great leader with a great mind."

Dewey shook his head, his face downcast. "Gentlemen, this should not leave this room. Admiral William Sampson is ill, very ill. You referred to a great mind. Well, he has an illness that is slowly depriving him of his ability to reason. He remembers little and does not even recognize friends. It saddens me deeply."

The group took in the reality that one of the great leaders to emerge from the recent war was nothing more than a living shell, senile before his time.

"A pity," said Longstreet.

"Indeed," added Dewey. "But, back to my stratagems, I do have one other small plan I wish to implement. I have directed Captain Hobson to assemble a number of torpedo boat destroyers and attack German shipping in New York harbor. Just how and when I leave to his fertile imagination."

This brought smiles all about. At age thirty, Richmond Hobson was the youngest captain in the navy. He had gained his rank by inspired, perhaps insane, daring against Spain. It was an intriguing selection.

"I have also given him our lone submarine, the *Holland,* and have directed him to use it."

Longstreet mulled over what he had heard from Dewey and liked it. He did, however, have some thoughts. "Admiral, may I assume that, with all the naval construction going on and the number of ships authorized but not yet built, you might have some big guns lying about without ships to put them on?"

"Yes. There are a number of 6- and 8-inch guns in the Washington Navy Yard, as well as some larger ones in Philadelphia. Not all are new, however; many were taken from older ships that have been decommissioned or scrapped. Sounds as though you may have some use for them and would like to borrow a few."

"I might." Longstreet grinned.

"Then be aware that, although the guns—both older and newer model—are perfectly serviceable, there are no turrets or gun carriages. Right now they are little more than long metal tubes lying on the ground."

Longstreet nodded. "Well, that's why the Good Lord invented engineers."

Dewey smiled. "Try not to break them. My guns, that is."

A little while later, the conference broke up. Teddy Roosevelt repaired to his office and shut the door. He was both delighted and sickened. He was even more confident that his selection of Longstreet, supported by MacArthur, was the right one and would ultimately bring victory. Yet that victory would take a great deal of time and would cost dearly.

Time.

He didn't have time. He saw the beginning of the dilemma with the Senate confirmation hearings on Longstreet. The country was starting to come out of its daze and question the value of continuing what had so far been a disastrous war. He now knew that his monstrous new army of a million men was a polite fiction. Men would be enlisted and trained, but they would not be available as a fighting force for at least a year, probably much longer. When they did become available, the physical constraints of the German salient would prevent most from finding a place to fight. No, the war, if it was to be won in a reasonable amount of time, would be won largely with the weapons and the army at hand.

The same was true for the navy. The completion of one battleship could be rushed, but the other ships under construction would not be available for many months, perhaps years.

How long would it be before the Germans saw through the fiction that permitted the American fleet sanctuary in the Saint Lawrence, and put pressure on Britain to stop it? Roosevelt had no illusions about Britain. She would be a true friend for as long as the United States stood a chance of winning. When that ceased to be likely, the good things flowing so freely from England would slowly disappear.

But his greatest concern was his fellow Americans. They were starting to realize they'd suffered nearly thirty thousand military casualties and tens of thousands of civilian casualties, with millions dislocated, and they saw no end to their privations. At least, he sighed, this was not an election year. Although he did not have to run for office until 1904, there would be congressional elections next year, and if the war was still raging with no victory in sight, they could result in a less supportive Congress than existed today.

Already there were cries from Capitol Hill that the disaster in New York was a result of expansionist policies gone awry. Many people were beginning to grumble that we had enough troubles at home without taking on the added burdens of brown people in far-off lands; thus we were getting only what we deserved. William Jennings Bryan, McKinley's Democratic opponent in the last election, was one such voice, and a very eloquent one indeed. Although the great orator had been supportive during the first weeks of the German war, the stalemate was giving him grist for comment. End the war, he was starting to say, testing the public waters; end it with a victory or end it with a settlement. We never did need the Philippines and Cuba. Get rid of them and good riddance.

Roosevelt nearly sobbed. What would a German victory do? First, there would be no American canal across the Isthmus of Panama. The Germans would build it and control it. There would be no great American navy. Why bother? There would be nothing to protect. The Germans would exert pressure on some of the less stable countries in South and Central America and gradually convert some of them to colonies. Within a few decades, this would result in German hegemony in the New World, and the Monroe Doctrine would be scrap.

Yet he could not urge his generals and admirals to do anything foolish. Another lost battle would likely lose the war and end the American dream of Manifest Destiny, which he and most Americans held so dearly. But he was pleased again with his choice of Longstreet.

Longstreet.

In a year, would old, deaf Longstreet still be available? Yes, he was relatively healthy, even rejuvenated, and seemed up to the challenges in front of him, but when would the rigors of command start to grind him down? He was eighty-two and his allotted biblical life span had long since passed. How much more could be expected of him? If he fell, then to whom would Roosevelt give command? MacArthur? Most likely. Then who would command at New York?

In another few weeks the weather around New York would start to turn. Truly cold weather would move in and the millions of refugees and tens of thousands of soldiers would start to suffer further privations. Longstreet said he would fight for as long as it took. Roosevelt wondered sadly if he and the United States would be permitted that luxury.

Brigadier General Patrick Mahan rode his brown gelding carefully in front of the dressed ranks of men, thousands of them uniformed mostly in the new brown, their rifles shouldered and pointing skyward. It was his command. He was aware of the many eyes that followed him despite the fact that men at attention were supposed to be looking straight ahead. They wondered about him, of course, and why shouldn't they? If he failed them, he could get them killed or, worse in many minds, maimed. They all knew crippled old men who'd lost limbs and sanity in the Civil War. Could that happen to them? Could they be blinded or lose their manhood? In the best of battles it was possible, but with a poor leader it was far more likely.

They were ordered to stand at ease as he read the orders creating the brigade and giving him command over it. Then he spoke briefly of his plans to work them hard so they would be ready for whatever their country had in mind for them. He did not try to inspire them with soaring rhetoric. That simply wasn't his style. Stating plain, blunt facts was more to his liking. Besides, the men knew why they were here. There were Germans on their soil.

When he finished, the men managed a reasonable cheer. He got a more rousing one when he told them that hard training would begin not tomorrow but the day after. Tomorrow they could rest and prepare.

After dismissing them, he sent Heinz out to gather his regimental and battalion commanders. Patrick had seen a lot he liked, but much more that was lacking. Well, he laughed to himself, I wanted a command, didn't I? I guess I got what I asked for. And yes, by God, it is going to be a challenge.

"Lieutenant Schmidt," said Patrick. "Don't forget enough glasses. We will inaugurate the brigade's creation in the traditional manner."

Chapter 16

ANY QUESTION EITHER Patrick or Trina might have had as to how they would greet each other after several weeks of separation was immediately dispelled when, seeing Patrick's arm in a sling, Trina pulled him to her.

"What happened?" Her voice was near a sob.

Patrick grinned and tried to make light of it. "I fell off my horse. I told you infantrymen can't ride worth a darn."

"Then you weren't wounded?"

"Hardly," he assured her.

She tilted her head upward and kissed him lightly on the cheek. "Thank you for trying to spare me worry, but I know exactly how you broke your arm. You were out on a patrol with some of your men and the Germans started shooting at you. That, sir, is how you hurt yourself."

Patrick shrugged. "I think I have to get a new aide, perhaps one who doesn't have such a big mouth. Yes, that's exactly what happened, only my arm isn't broken. I just have a strained shoulder and it was caused by my falling off my horse. I can use it a little and I'll be better in a few days."

Trina laughed. "Well, if you're staying for dinner, will I have to cut your food this time?"

"Do you want me to stay?"

For an answer, she moved into his arms and they were embracing before either realized it and despite Patrick's arm. "Am I hurting you?" she asked.

"The agony is overwhelming," he murmured, "but I shall try to endure."

She laughed again, the sound muffled by her mouth against his chest. Trina was both elated and confused. This was something that had never happened to her before. A quiet intimacy had developed between them almost without either of them noticing. What truly confused her, however, was what she should do now.

"I love your hair," he murmured teasingly, kissing the top of her head.

"At least it's long enough to see. Now I can go into town and not worry about frightening children, or having to wear a hairpiece that makes me look like some peasant woman from Poland or a refugee from a convent."

They stepped apart and he took her hand. "I cannot imagine you in a convent. Perhaps as a Polish peasant, but definitely not a nun."

Noises in the kitchen reminded them that they were not alone. Molly was preparing the promised meal. Heinz would not be there this evening. He was working on the myriad reports that an unfeeling higher command always required, war or not.

"I will stay for dinner, but I must get back to my men before it gets too late. I never realized I had so much to do."

They ate quietly and alone. A very tactful Molly excused herself from becoming a third party by pleading a headache and the need to write some letters. After dinner, as the late-August night started to darken, they sat side by side on a couch in the small living room.

"Patrick, I think I like having your brigade just a few miles down the road."

Patrick smiled. "Well, I like it too. I just don't think we'd better get too used to it. We could be moved at any time and for any reason."

"But you are—what was the term you used?—strategic reserve, aren't you?"

"Yep, but that's only because the higher-ups don't think my unit is quite ready for Broadway yet. My job is to whip them into shape and get them prepared for war. When that's done I think we'll be moved into the Housatonic line, probably on a rotating basis."

"Well, don't feel you have to hurry the process," she said grimly. "Now, tell me all about your command."

It was, he told her, officially called the 1st Provisional Brigade and it initially consisted of the two regiments of infantry that were originally intended to become the German Legion. That idea had flopped because neither Governor Nash of Ohio nor Governor La Follette of Wisconsin could agree on what American of German descent would command the Legion. Only the fact that both were Republicans prevented the argument from becoming more serious and permitted the compromise whereby Patrick Mahan, a decided non-German, was given command.

"I think Teddy Roosevelt might have beaten them up pretty badly if they hadn't gone along," he added.

His command gave him close to four thousand poorly trained and ill-equipped would-be soldiers. "The first thing I did was act on a hunch that there were immigrants from Germany who'd actually served in their army as well as men who'd served in ours. We searched and found more than a hundred. Although some of them were already in positions of command, most weren't, and valuable experience was being wasted. I've been reviewing their records and placing them where I think they belong. The big problem with that idea is that some of them don't speak English very well or not at all. It also means some people who were already in command positions, and who aren't qualified, are being displaced. And," he added ruefully, "most don't particularly like the idea. One of our good American *Bürgermeisters* got drunk a couple of days ago and took a punch at me."

"Goodness!"

"Fortunately he missed. Heinz hit him hard in his stomach and he spent the rest of the night in great pain trying to give up a week's worth of meals. He is also now a plain private and lucky he's not breaking rocks at some federal prison."

"It's almost funny."

"On the good side, the immigrants are so eager to learn. They are also going to be quite useful. I've suggested to General MacArthur that small units be sent into German lines to provide hard intelligence and spread a little mischief, such as inducing others to desert. Since virtually all of them read and speak the lingo fluently, I think they could be of great assistance."

Good God, she thought, don't send Heinz. Molly would be hysterical. As if reading her thoughts, he asked about the relationship between the two. "Well," she answered, "the fact that you are so close by means he slips over here as often as he can." She did not add that Heinz had no qualms about leaving his wonderful army to spend the night in the arms of his beloved. She was not sure how Patrick would take that. She whispered, almost embarrassed, "They are still cohabiting. I am terribly afraid she will become pregnant. In fact, I think she already is." There, maybe that small fib—was it a fib?—will keep him from permitting Heinz to do something reckless to satisfy his sense of manhood.

When she decided that Patrick had had enough time to mull this over, she asked, "But you now have other regiments, don't you?"

He rolled his eyes. "Yes, I just got the 9th and 10th Cavalry of the regular army—all colored troops and all dismounted except for one battalion of the 10th. Horses are in short supply." He laughed sharply. "Of course, everything seems to be in short supply for Negro regiments with Negro officers. You can make a man a major, but in the eyes of every supply sergeant in the army, he's still a nigger."

"Terrible. What are you doing about it?"

He smiled grimly. "Well, every now and then I have to go and assert my rank. I don't like to do it too often, because my officers, white or black, need the confidence to get things done on their own."

"Goodness, I never realized you were such a liberal in your attitude toward race."

"I'm not. I really don't know where I stand with Negroes and their problems. I just feel we should fight one war at a time, and right now the main enemy is the German army."

"And these two regiments aren't ready for combat either?"

"Actually, they're very ready. Stripping them of their white officers to help fill another division cost them some manpower, but what remained was a solid core of professional soldiers with a lot of experience. And that numerical loss is being made up by new enlistments of Negroes who are plain tickled to be in units commanded by men of their own color. It's just that the move created yet another bastard unit like the German Americans. Nobody knows what to do with them, so they're all mine. Just to complete the picture, there's a rumor I'll be getting a battalion of Poles from Chicago."

Her sarcasm was mild. "How wonderful for you."

He chuckled warmly and squeezed her hand. "They are now calling it Mahan's Bastard Brigade. When I'm done it will be the pride of the army. Well, at least the talk of it. Now, what have you been up to?"

In their few remaining moments together she told him that although her work with refugees was diminishing as the flow of those unfortunates appeared to have slowed, her work with the wounded and other soldiers was increasing. "We try to arrange transportation home for the wounded who have healed enough to travel. Then we try to arrange for visits from home for those who cannot yet make such journeys. Some," she added sadly, her eyes moistening, "will never leave hospitals. I am glad I didn't try nursing. I don't think I could ever do it. Although, I suppose one never knows, does one? I certainly never thought I could do the work I'm doing now."

True enough, he thought.

"Also I write letters for the soldiers and try to arrange for some wholesome recreation for them, like baseball. Football and basketball are too rough."

"War isn't?" he chided.

She admitted the point. "Well, as a general you surely don't want the men injured playing football when that would cause them to miss the next battle."

Finally he realized he had to leave. Once again it would be a night on a cot in a tent. Lucky Heinz. He took Trina's arm and stepped outside. Molly had brought his horse around and tethered it out front. Because of his sore shoulder, mounting it would be a little difficult, but he could manage.

In the cooler air of the outdoors, they paused for a moment, then embraced. Their lips met, this time parting in a deeper and more probing kiss as their tongues searched tantalizingly. They squeezed each other tightly and arched their bodies against each other. Patrick again felt Trina's lithe form as he pressed against her. Reluctantly, they parted. He kissed her on the forehead, mounted his horse awkwardly, and assured her he'd be back as soon as he could.

Trina walked about the yard, not quite willing to go inside and lose the moment. She also knew she was just a little disheveled and mussed and wasn't ready for Molly's grinning scrutiny.

If what she had just experienced was the beginning of passion, then she felt herself rewarded. It was indeed worth waiting for. He truly was very strong and secure. She also wanted to sort out her own astonishing reactions to the feel of his body growing against hers. Oh my, she thought. Oh my, my, my.

Corporal Ludwig Weber looked at the gruesome items on his plate with poorly concealed disgust. The bread was stale and hard, needing a solid soaking in what was referred to as beef stew in order to be chewed. He also had doubts about the stew. Beef? If he were any judge, those few chunks of stringy meat floating in the lukewarm liquid had once been graced by a saddle. Ah, well, at least it was food and it was somewhat warm.

Better, they were out of the damned mud fort and in a proper camp where they could clean up and rest. The probability of an inspection in a dress uniform meant they were in an area of relative safety where they were not subject to potshots by Yankee snipers.

The 4th Rifles had been pulled out of line a couple of days now and were starting to get back some of their snap and vigor. There was also talk of a possible bit of recreation time on Manhattan. Weber thought that would be interesting, strolling down Wall Street as a conqueror and not as the child tourist he'd once been.

Some conqueror. No matter how hard he tried, he could not rationalize what he and the army were doing here. It was an act of naked aggression, and for what purpose—to gain some stupid islands that most of the men in the 4th Rifles had never heard of? Even with his teaching background, he'd had a hard time locating the islands on a map of the world they'd found in a schoolhouse.

Finding the school, abandoned, derelict, and vandalized by unknown hands, had made him feel sick at heart. He was supposed to be teaching people, not carrying a rifle in order to kill them. What was the kaiser's purpose in this? Certainly Ludwig was proud of Germany, proud that the disparate collection of petty kingdoms and occasional tyrannies had been bound together in one nation. But did it have to be with the soulless Prussians in charge? Why not the Bavarians? Then, instead of war, they could have challenged the Yanks to a beer-drinking competition.

He smiled. There were others who felt as he did. He knew it even though such thoughts were rarely verbalized. Speaking with your eyes, or a gesture, or a tilt of the head could be equally as eloquent. The men were confused, and so was he.

He'd tried to sound out Captain Walter on the topic and had been politely rebuffed. The captain was obviously a different man from the one he'd been before seeing the murdered Americans lying face-down and bloody in the field. That the captain had his own thoughts was obvious also from his eyes and the manner in which he turned his words and phrases. He conveyed that the Germans were totally correct in their support of the kaiser and the empire. But was there a hint of something else?

Yet what to do? There were other indications all was not well. The food, for instance. America was a land of plenty, yet the army was, to a large extent, existing on rations shipped over from Germany. Oh, there was plenty of ammunition and weapons, and they expected heavier uniforms and other equipment to be shipped over soon, but food? If the quality of the slop on his plate was any indication, they were in for a long, lean, and nauseating winter.

Good God, could they be here all winter? With this swill for food? It was even difficult to obtain water. Just the other day they'd been refused the use of a well by an old woman at a farm. When Captain Walter politely offered to pay her, the woman had spat on the ground and told the captain to go to hell. He had flushed and done what was necessary: his men were thirsty so they took the water while the woman's angry eyes bored holes in them. When Sergeant Gunther offered her a few American coins, she'd hurled them at him. At that point, Kessel had threatened her and Sergeant Gunther had cuffed him on the side of the head, knocking him down and drawing blood. Welcome to America.

The 4th Rifles had received no replacements. Of the twelve hundred men who'd landed on Long Island only a few months ago, scarcely nine hundred remained fit for duty. Eighty had been killed and hundred or so wounded. Another fifty were listed as missing. What did that mean? Did they fly away? He snorted. They had deserted, and everyone and his brother knew it. The officers, in a not very subtle manner, used the murder of the Americans to discourage further desertions, saying the Yanks would kill anyone who tried to come over, but it hadn't stopped some of them from trying. A couple of would-be deserters had been captured, and the men of the 4th had been assembled to watch the hangings. What wonders that did for morale!

Weber heard the sound of mild cheering and wandered up to a group of men from his company.

"Ludwig, did you hear the great news?"

The speaker was Ulli Muller, a younger-than-average recruit from Saxony. A nice boy, he was generally considered to be not very bright. "No, Ulli, I haven't. Please enlighten me."

"It's finally come through. We get a week in New York. Isn't that wonderful?"

"Sure is," Weber replied jovially. He clapped Ulli on the shoulder and walked on. Sure it was wonderful. In a pig's eye. Despite Ludwig's earlier eagerness at the prospect, he was depressed. They'd get to see the ruins of Brooklyn and German cruisers blocking the view of the Statue of Liberty, the symbol of freedom. Rumors told him that Manhattan was a virtual ghost town. It would be difficult to square the current reality with his youthful memories of bustling crowds, colorful sounds, and marvelous smells. Perhaps someone would try to sell Ulli the Brooklyn Bridge.

The sound of laughter once again interrupted his thoughts. Ulli was bragging about how he was going to get laid once he got to New York. The humor of the situation overcame Weber's bad mood. Ulli was such an oaf. All he thought about was women. "Ulli, you are nothing but a penis with suspenders," Ludwig shouted. Ah, such innocence. Such depraved innocence.

Holstein and Schlieffen walked the garden slowly, as befitted men of their age. For Holstein in particular, walking was an unwelcome chore in which he indulged infrequently. He preferred instead to think, exercising his still-supple mind and not his aging body with its myriad aches and problems. This time, however, he had deferred to the chief of the Imperial General Staff's suggestion that a little fresh air might be in order. Besides, the flowers that surrounded them, whatever they were named, were truly lovely.

"I take it, General, that you were present when the All Highest found out about it."

"Certainly. It was delicious." Schlieffen smiled tightly at the memory. It caused his pointed mustache to tilt upward, an effect that Holstein found almost ludicrous.

"And the kaiser's reaction?"

"Apoplexy. Predictable apoplexy. He threw a tantrum."

Holstein nodded. The whole court was in an uproar. Half the courtiers were outraged; the rest, like himself, thought the development hilarious. The kaiser had just found out that, war or no war, emigration from Germany to the United States was still going on unabated. Ships still took on hundreds of people each week and departed for Boston, Philadelphia, and other American ports. Not, of course, New York. And also not on American- or German-flagged ships. The vessels flew the flags of France or Denmark or Britain, among others.

It was an insult almost too deadly to bear. The fact that the kaiser's people were still migrating to the land of his enemy during an actual conflict struck his pride like a lightning bolt. Too bad I wasn't there, Holstein thought. It would have been wonderful.

The problem was the German bureaucracy. Although fully aware of the war, they'd never been told to shut down the processing of applications to depart; thus they continued doing what they'd last been ordered to do. Holstein chuckled. They were mindless twits.

The kaiser was not mollified one bit when he was told that stopping people from leaving German ports would not halt the migrations. People were also going over the border to France and out the Channel ports, or even through Austria to Trieste on the Adriatic. The only way to stop it would be to seal the borders, and this would outrage those other countries. Whatever the kaiser said or did, the emigration would continue. It was a hopeless situation and the kaiser was furious.

Holstein chuckled at the thought of the red-faced kaiser. "Ah my, the crown is such a burdensome thing."

Schlieffen answered Holstein's comment with his own small laugh as he stopped to examine a vivid red rose. He knew better than to aggravate Holstein.

"But, dear general," Holstein continued, "I hear more rumors that your army is having unexpected problems."

Schlieffen sighed and straightened. Damn the man and his sources. Again it would do little good to deny or even obfuscate, but he would try. "All campaigns have unexpected problems. If we knew the future, there'd be no need for generals. Or for statesmen."

"I hear there are desertions."

"Some. It's to be expected. Virtually all our rankers are conscripts and believe America to be the land of milk and honey. It was nothing that overly surprised us."

Holstein was insistent. "But I understand the numbers are higher than pleasing."

Schlieffen paused. That fact was being withheld from the kaiser. Why risk another tantrum and fruitless orders to halt desertions? How did the old bastard find out these things? Was everyone in Germany a spy for him? "True enough, but we think it has stabilized."

"Even so, I understand that the number of missing is starting to equal the number of killed and wounded."

"Well, since we haven't fought a major battle in some time, I think that might be expected." His mouth puckered in a line of worry. "Even without battles, however, the war seems to be entering a particularly brutish phase. There have been murders, assaults, sabotage, and other small incidents behind the lines as well as numerous small-unit actions along the front line. As a student of military history, I find it evocative of Napoleon's problems with conquered Spain."

Holstein chose another topic and probed. "Now that your army is over the one hundred thousand mark, is the navy still up to supplying it?"

This time a visible cloud passed over the general's face. "Food," he answered promptly, "is becoming a problem. We are unable to acquire it from the countryside, and virtually all of it must be shipped over and prepared locally. Much of the meat is spoiled on arrival, and no army likes to live out of tin cans for very long. To be frank, dear von Holstein, the food issue does worry me. More than your deserters, by the way. In simple, round numbers, each man needs about ten pounds of food and supplies each day. No, he doesn't eat ten pounds; that figure takes into consideration such things as spoilage, theft, accidents, sabotage, and the like. Thus each day we require a million pounds, or five hundred tons, simply to sustain ourselves at the current level. As our numbers increase, so will our needs."

Holstein was surprised. "Five hundred tons? That is nothing. A good-sized freighter holds several times that amount."

"Of course, but as I said, our numbers are increasing. We are also required to feed much of the civil population that has remained behind, many of whom are working for us. They too have no other source of food. We did offer to let the Americans ship food to the city, but they quickly realized that our soldiers were helping themselves to the better selections and stopped the shipments. I do not condone looting, but the taking of food by a hungry soldier is something entirely different. There are, we estimate, yet a half million civilians within our lines. Some we have impressed into work gangs, repairing roads, bridges, and the like, and these we must also feed. And there are still women, children, and nonworking males to consider."

"Useless mouths. Have you a solution?"

"We are working on one. It will probably involve the forced expulsion of most of the useless ones."

"Excellent."

"And," Schlieffen sighed, "we still have several thousand of their prisoners to administer. They refuse parole, and the Americans aren't so stupid as to exchange one of our trained soldiers for one of their scum. Besides, we hold more than twice as many prisoners as they do. No, the actual daily tonnage of food needed to sustain the enterprise is well above the amount I mentioned. And as the war grinds on, we will commence shipment of winter uniforms and replacement equipment as well. I might add that some of our more enterprising soldiers are already liberating winter blankets and such from local houses. Again, I can hardly blame them for being prudent, however much it outrages the locals."

Schlieffen paused and cast an anxious look at the clouding sky. Rain was imminent. "There is another reality to confront regarding supplies. Simply put, the longer the Yanks refuse to negotiate, the more likely it becomes that we will have to continue with the part of the original plans that calls for us to march on toward Boston to teach them a further lesson. When we prove that we can march across their country at will, they will act more reasonably toward our demands. That march, of course, will require copious amounts of supplies of all sorts, not just food and ammunition. You must understand that an army on campaign and doing battle uses supplies at an enormous rate—much greater than an army in a static environment. Sadly, we seem to have underestimated the stubbornness of the Americans regarding the islands in question. A European power would have negotiated a long time ago. Neither I nor the kaiser can understand this reluctance on the part of the Yanks."

"Then I take it you cannot be pleased with the overall situation."

"Von Holstein, no man likes another to be master of his destiny. So far, the navy has done an excellent job shepherding ships to safety, but we are also hearing rumors that the American navy is, belatedly, going to start attacking our transports. If they are successful in causing a major interdiction of our supplies, we could have a crisis."

Holstein mulled over the comment. A crisis. What a polite way of saying that the German army, isolated in the land of plenty, could starve to death. Schlieffen had also confirmed the fact of the desertions. Although he might try to pooh-pooh them, the reality was that a few desertions could easily become a torrent, which would disable the army. And the man had inadvertently thrown him another piece of information by acknowledging that sabotage, however minimal, had occurred.

Holstein paused and politely sniffed a nameless flower. After a few trivial comments and amenities, "We must have these little chats more often, General," he said. Then they went their separate ways.

Chapter 17

JOHNNY TWO DOGS was happier than he had been in a long time. It had been five years since he'd last tracked a man, and that had been to help bring to ground his revered leader, Geronimo. Even though that final hunt had been successful and resulted in the capture of the southern Chiricahua leader, it had saddened Johnny to see the proud and grizzled old man surrender to the overwhelming might of General Miles's army. It had made him perversely proud to see that only a score or so of Apaches had kept such a mighty host at bay. Geronimo might have been bent in body, but not in spirit.

In years past, Johnny had ridden with Geronimo, but that had been back when he was young, full of pride and fire, and possessed by the hope that the white man could be driven off the sacred Apache lands. Then the toll of years and the deaths of his comrades mounted, and with them came the realization that the white man was too strong, too numerous, and too damned greedy to be deterred. The only way any Apache would survive would be to make peace with the conquering whites. It had even been the whites who had given him his name of Johnny Two Dogs, thinking his old and twisted body bore a hilarious resemblance to two dogs fucking. He had an Apache name, of course, but that was his alone and he did not share it with the whites. Let them call him what they wished.

Making peace with the whites did not come before he had exacted his price—his pound of flesh, literally. There were several blue bellies whose bones were bleaching in the sands of New Mexico as a result of his deadly shooting and his stealth in stalking the ultimate enemy—armed human game.

Johnny had resigned himself to spending the rest of his years with the remnants of his nation on the grounds of Fort Sill, Oklahoma, where, even though he had helped track Geronimo, he had been interned along with Geronimo and his band. All the Apache scouts had been treated thus. The white bastards were consistent, at least, in their treatment of the red man. Unfair, but consistent.

Geronimo had understood Johnny and forgiven him. Now—and the thought made Johnny's face crinkle in a rare grin—the old man was becoming a Christian and urging the Apache children to stay in school. He was also making a fair living selling autographed pictures of himself to the fat tourists who wandered onto the grounds and wanted to see the legendary warrior. Talk about adapting!

Until a couple of weeks ago, all Johnny could see coming down the road was age, not tourists. Who would want his autograph, even if he could write? He was nothing but a squat, unwashed little man in his middle fifties who dressed in rags, lived on the government dole, and would likely die on the handouts of rotten food and shabby blankets if the cheap liquor didn't get him first. But then came word that the Apache scout's particular talents might be needed again by the army. And, hallelujah, he would be paid for killing the goddamn whites.

The fact that two white nations were at war with each other, and that one set of whites was paying for the privilege, was mildly interesting but unimportant. He'd agreed promptly and, along with a score of other equally delighted Apaches, entrained for unknown lands back east.

On arrival in Connecticut, he saw that the whites lived in an astonishingly lush and crowded land. Johnny and his fellow Apaches had passed through countless towns and seen farms and dwellings more numerous than the stars in the sky. It was an awesome display of the white man's power, and Johnny again resolved never to challenge it, at least not head-on. He'd almost changed his mind and gone back to the dismal but predictable comforts of Fort Sill, but the twin urges of money and the satisfaction of killing his ancient enemy held him in this strange and verdant land. Here he was given instructions on how to tell good whites from bad whites by the way they dressed and talked. That amused his fellow Apaches, who were convinced that the only good white devil was a dead one. They knew that the statement was similar to what whites said and thought about red men, and they silently reveled in the irony. They were shown pictures of warriors from the German nation and told to kill them all anytime and anyplace. The Apaches were specifically told not to kill women or civilians and, especially, not to kill their new comrades—those same blue bellies who, until recently, had been trying to kill all the Apaches. There was some grumbling about the exclusions, but one of the blue soldiers explained that there were more than enough Germans to satisfy the Apaches. They doubted this but allowed the man to continue. Could these Germans have more soldiers than Generals Crook and Miles had used against the Apache? They thought not. Not, at least, until they realized the immensity of the camps of soldiers of the great white father in Washington.

Johnny sighed. It was an imperfect world, but it was his world and he was still alive in it. And he had permission to kill. He was told that he was a member of the 1st Scout Company, which reported directly to Gen. Arthur MacArthur. The scouts were pleased. This was a great honor, since General MacArthur's frontier skills and experiences were legendary. In actuality, however, the company reported to the general's young son, who had been born and raised on the frontier and who also respected the Apaches' unique fighting abilities. The dark-haired puppy was very young, but he seemed to know what he was doing.

It also amused Johnny that the blue bellies were becoming brown bellies, finally acknowledging the advantage those nice blue uniforms conveyed to a sniper. He was told the Germans wore a dark gray that was as difficult to see as brown.

Although Johnny would have preferred to wage war in the arid lands he knew so well, he had to admit that the ruined and abandoned buildings surrounded by woods and lush, uncropped fields and tall grasses might actually be better. Right now, for instance, he was only about a hundred yards away from a road down which horse-drawn wagons, German wagons, flowed at a steady but irregular rate.

He had been waiting hours for an opportunity. He would wait for weeks if he had to, but he knew from the insolent way the Germans traveled that his time would soon come. There were no pickets and no scouts or guards. The Germans must have thought they owned the land over which they traveled.

As the night shadows lengthened, the flow of wagons thinned almost to a halt. Finally, with the sun well below the horizon, Johnny's sharp eyes spied a single wagon, lightly loaded and pulled by two slow horses, moving in his direction. As it drew closer, he saw the shapes of two heavyset men sitting in the front. By their silhouettes he confirmed they were Germans, and he knew they probably carried weapons. But he also felt he recognized their type. They were not combat troops. These were the older and fatter men who worked in the warehouses and parceled out their treasures as if they belonged to them and not their government. He could understand and respect the soldiers who fought him, but the ones who insulted him, spat at him, and made him beg for a blanket to ward off the cold he had learned to hate. The approaching sound of loud guttural voices showed the men's indifference to their surroundings, which made them unlikely to be dangerous unless forewarned.

That would not happen.

Johnny carefully laid his rifle on some leaves. There would be no need for it. He left his shelter and began the stalk. On reaching the road, he stopped, checking first to ensure that no other wagons would disturb him as he closed in on his prey. As he did so, a change came over him. No longer was he a red-skinned, funny-looking little man who limped when he walked. Quietly, he had become the night in which he hid. Many of his people were still afraid of the ghosts of the dark, but Johnny had learned through bitter experience that the night was his protector. In a darkness of gentle breezes, he became the wind as well, any sound he made masked by the chatter of crickets and the caressing whisper of the grasses. In a few strides, he was within yards of the unsuspecting Germans. He was so close that he almost ran into the wagon when it unexpectedly stopped. He recovered quickly and froze in the weeds. The two men were discussing something in their own strange language, and one seemed a little angry while the other laughed.

Finally the one who had laughed stepped off the wagon and into the brush, only feet from where Johnny lay poised, ready to pounce.

A moment later Johnny heard the man grunting and fumbling with his clothes. This was followed by more grunting and a quick stench that told Johnny that the fool was defecating. He checked the man on the wagon and saw him looking stolidly in the other direction, his body indicating he was upset by the delay. Johnny snarled silently and was behind the defecating German in an instant. His left hand reached around and clamped his mouth in an iron grip while the razor-sharp knife in his right hand ripped the life out of the German, who flopped for a few seconds and then lay still.

Johnny spun and checked the other German, who was still gazing at the sky. Johnny left the body and moved noiselessly around to the driver's side of the wagon. He lunged upward like a panther and drove his knife into the second German's skull from under his chin. The man gave a gurgling whimper, then he too was still.

Now what? The young MacArthur had said the idea was not only to kill Germans but to make them afraid as well, afraid of the night and the creatures roaming in it. Johnny grinned and went back to the brush for the first German. He dragged him out and laid him in the back of the wagon with his excrement- and bloodstained pants around his ankles. He followed this with the corpse of the second German, all the while coping with the horses made skittish by the sweet smell of blood.

When the bodies were neatly arranged, Johnny checked the wagon to see if there was anything important in it. There were only some rifles and ammunition, which he decided to keep, and a couple of tents, which he nonchalantly slashed. He scalped the two men and disemboweled them. Then he urinated on them.

He slapped the horses on their rumps and started them clopping down the trail. With a little bit of luck, they'd be well away from the kill site before they were discovered. If so, he could use the area again. Perhaps the wagon with its grisly load would make it all the way to a German camp. Wouldn't that spoil their sleep!

Johnny slipped back into the night and the trees. His stomach growled a little, reminding him he hadn't eaten in a while. He pulled a piece of jerky from his pouch and commenced chewing with gums that had lost most of their teeth. He hummed a happy tune. The two corpses in the wagon made for a total of six kills. Not bad for the first day.

*   *   *

Ian Gordon was resplendent in his red tunic. He snapped a quick salute. "My heartiest congratulations, General. To think I knew you when you were nothing—a mere, total, and useless nobody."

Patrick smiled warmly. "Thanks, Ian. I knew you'd help me keep things in perspective." He rose and grasped the other man's hand. "Now, what are you doing here? How can our leadership in Washington spare you?"

"As a matter of fact they can do so rather easily. I am now one of several British officers assigned as observers to General MacArthur. There are others from several nations watching this wonderful war unfold. If you would spend more time at headquarters you would see other Imperial types like me: garishly uniformed Frenchmen, even more garish Italians, and—are you ready for this?—little yellow men all the way from Japan. All of them are here to see how the mighty Imperial German Army wages war against your brave little army. None, save us, gives a fig who wins. They just want to see what might happen if they go up against Germany."

Patrick caught on quickly, recalling Gordon's background in military intelligence. "Certainly. And as an 'observer' from an ostensibly neutral nation, you would be in a position to pass on information that you might receive through your private channels, wouldn't you?"

Gordon rolled his eyes in mock despair. "Patrick, that would be horrid. Unfair. How can you think so ill of me?"

"All right, have it your way. What brings you to my humble tent?"

"An overwhelming urge to see Mahan's Bastard Brigade. My goodness, Germans and Negroes. Why haven't they given you the Apaches as well?"

Patrick shuddered. "Little Mac can keep them. My God, have you heard some of the stories?"

"Yes. Wonderful, aren't they? Still, the Apaches are not quite as clever as the Pathans or the Zulus when it comes to making death even more horrid than it usually is. Remind me to tell you how the Zulus impale live prisoners with a stake up their arse, and how long the Pathans take to skin a man alive."

"No, thanks. Now, what's your real reason for being here? And unless that's some of your family's ancient Scotch whiskey in that container, I may be forced to ask you to leave."

Gordon laughed and pulled a bottle from the container. They opened it and poured generous amounts in the glasses Ian had also thought to bring. They toasted each other's promotions, Patrick to general and Ian's much more recent one to lieutenant colonel.

Gordon lolled back in a camp chair that came dangerously close to falling over. "Yes, as in your case, the powers that be decided that nobody pays any attention to mere majors, and they promoted me. I wish they'd had the foresight to make me a general instead."

"Wait for your own war. You're only an observer, remember?"

"Ah, and what a wonderful assignment. I get to gaze worshipfully at MacArthur if I wish, or talk to that lovable barbarian Wheeler, or even come slumming down here."

Patrick refilled his glass. "Insults can be damned expensive. Did you get a chance to meet Longstreet? I haven't yet."

Gordon nodded. "Indeed. And almost made a proper fool of myself. That's what happens when you meet a historical character who actually participated in ancient events of legend." Gordon flushed slightly at the memory. For both professional and personal reasons, the American Civil War had been a source of great interest to him, and he'd wangled an introduction to Longstreet just after receiving his orders to go north as an observer. In dress red, he'd introduced himself to Longstreet in the other's office at the War Department. Gordon had started to stammer like a schoolboy meeting the headmaster for the first time until the old general rose and put a hand on his shoulder to calm him down. "Finally, we had a decent conversation. I asked him some things about your Civil War I'd always wanted to know, and I told him what my duties were going to be up here."

"As an intelligence source?"

Gordon ignored him. "Longstreet was quite impressive. For an old man he has his wits about him and seems bent on surrounding himself with skilled helpers like Leonard Wood. He seems to know his own limitations, both physical and as a general. I left with the impression that there is no way on earth he would attempt to lead an army in the field, but that he will work diligently to see his policies implemented. His reputation is that of a cautious general who accomplishes what he is told to accomplish if he is given a specific task. He is not reputed to be a great thinker. Of course, the people who say that are always comparing him with the mythical Robert E. Lee. It might not be fair to judge him so harshly."

"Ian, is it so bad for someone to know his own limitations? We just lost a battle because of someone who didn't."

Gordon took a couple of thin cigars from his tunic and offered one to Patrick, who cheerfully accepted. Gordon lit them and they drew deeply. "Longstreet understands that he has just one task. It is to drive out the Germans. He fully understands that task and his role in it. For an old warhorse he seems to thoroughly comprehend modern warfare, how it has recently changed as a result of technology, and how he can be a noble figurehead for your nation. After meeting him and talking to others, I can see why Roosevelt tapped him instead of simply reinstating John Schofield, General Miles's predecessor. Schofield was a good and solid general as well, and is a decade younger than Longstreet, but although he's a solid professional, he's not an inspirational leader. Schofield, by the way, has offered himself as an adviser to Longstreet, who graciously accepted the offer."

Ian tactfully did not voice the British concern that the country was so ill prepared it was necessary to bring back someone like Old Pete Longstreet in the first place.

It was getting late, and Patrick was tired. "Will you be dropping by again, or are you going to stay with the exalted ones?"

Gordon buckled his tunic and made to leave. Patrick noticed he made no effort to take the half-filled bottle. "With your permission, my general, I will be by rather often. Being an observer means I can go and do my observing wherever and whenever I wish. I understand you are sending your tame Germans and your Negroes out on scouting and information-gathering patrols. I would be honored to accompany them sometime."

Patrick nodded. Now dressed in brown and at MacArthur's urging, the brigade was sending small daily patrols of German-speaking soldiers up to and sometimes behind the German defenses to either observe their activities or grab a stray prisoner. At night, his Negro troops moved like panthers through the territory separating the two armies. The Germans also patrolled the areas, and sometimes the groups would meet and savage little battles would ensue. Although there was little glamour in war in the first place, there was even less in this type of killing.

"Ian, it's a dirty war out there. You are certainly welcome to go.
Just promise me you won't wear red."

Blake Morris surveyed the small pile of rubble that had once been
his home. It had been the first house he'd ever owned and he had
loved it, almost as much as he'd loved the wife who had made it a
place of joy and the child who had made it a source of delight.

Now they and it were gone. Somewhere in the debris were his
clothes, his valuables, and his history as a being in this world. There
was a catch in his throat and he fought back the sobs that, once
started, might never end and might unman him at a time when he
needed to be strong. He did not have to make this journey right at
this time, but he knew it was something he had to do sooner or later.
It helped remind him that what had occurred was true and not some
nightmare. Seeing the ghost town brought back the sounds of the
guns and the screams of the dead and dying as if it were yesterday.
Good. He needed to be focused.

The small ship had sneaked him and his heavily armed companions across Long Island Sound and deposited them a few miles west
of Roosevelt's home at Sagamore Hill. From there it had been easy
to cross the island and find Ardmore, or what was left of it. The summer had been kind and the surge of undisciplined grassy growth hid
many of the scars from that morning in June. Was it only three
months ago?

Morris had to look hard to find some of the other buildings, but
they were there, or at least some of the ripped wood and charred
stones. He did find some bones, but he knew they did not belong to
his life. Perhaps they weren't even human. Never would he forget the
sight of the awful explosion that obliterated the two persons who
gave him reason for existing. Perhaps if he'd had something to bury,
it would have made it easier to go on living the remainder of his
bleak life. He had hoped working in the camps and aiding others
would help him as well. It had not.

He walked a bit farther and stopped short. There before him was a
neatly laid-out cemetery with several score of white wooden crosses
in a well-cared-for lawn. He looked more closely and saw names on
the crosses. Slowly, half hoping for and half dreading what he would
find, he walked down the rows of crosses, reading the names and

connecting them to half-forgotten faces of those who had been his friends. Entire families had been wiped out by the onslaught. The names of a few people he had known were missing, which, he hoped, meant they'd survived.

Blake stopped suddenly and sucked in his breath. About halfway in were two crosses, and neatly lettered on them were the names of his wife and daughter. Had someone found their bodies, or was this simply a memorial? It didn't matter. Someone had remembered and cared, and it touched him deeply. The hatred for the Germans was not displaced, but for a moment the kindness made living a bit less unendurable, and he found his vision obscured by the sudden rush of tears.

A shadow moved from behind a shrub. Blake and the others swung their rifles toward it.

"Don't shoot, Chief, it's just me."

Morris relaxed and lowered his weapon, and the others followed his lead. It was nothing more than Willy Talmadge. And nothing less, either. "You nearly got your empty head blown off, you idiot."

"Hey, Blake, is that the thanks I get for taking care of this?"

The astonishment on Morris's face was evident. Willy had never before called him by his first name. "Well," Willy continued, "maybe I didn't dig all the graves, but I did identify the bodies and help with the crosses." He felt he had done well and wanted to be told so.

Morris wanted to ask about his family's marked graves but decided not to. He didn't want to know. "Then I guess I should thank you, Willy, and I do. Now, what have you been up to since then?"

Willy informed him that he had returned to the site after the Germans had marched off. A few days later, some local people arrived, buried the bodies, and made the cemetery. "Some people were here with cameras, too." He seemed proud that his dead town had been the scene of such activity. From that time on he'd lived off what he could scrounge in the area, either eating fruits and vegetables out of gardens or raiding abandoned root cellars. "I knew you'd be back. Never doubted for a minute. Now you're gonna take me with you, aren't you?"

There was a plaintive note to Willy's voice. Gone was the insolent drunkard and thief. This was a man who'd been scared by forces he'd never known existed, and now he desperately craved a level of security. He also knew he had to find more food than he had been able to before now in order to survive the coming winter. Willy was almost gaunt. Blake Morris sighed and looked at the longing eyes of the man. "All right, Willy. You can tag along, but you're gonna have to work for your keep. If I catch your worthless ass drunk or stealing one time, you're gone and on your own to starve. You understand me? I got a job to do and I won't have you in the way."

Willy nodded eagerly, like a puppy. Morris slung his rifle over his shoulder and started to walk inland, away from Ardmore. The dozen hard-eyed men with him fell into a column. One man sprinted ahead to take up a point position, a second pushed Willy into the middle of the column, and a third took up position as rear guard.

Blake surveyed them quickly. Dressed as farmers and mechanics, they were as natural to the countryside as the trees. The well-intentioned officers on the mainland had made him promise they'd wear uniforms in case they got captured. In that case they'd stand a chance of not being executed as spies and terrorists. He had laughed bitterly. Wear uniforms? Why advertise their presence? No, there wasn't a man in the group who wasn't a volunteer and who was afraid of death. There was a job to do and they would do it.

Chapter 18

PATRICK MAHAN LOUNGED comfortably on a folding
chair in front of his command tent—a larger structure than
a regular tent that combined sleeping quarters and office—
and tried to enjoy the relative cool of the morning. The
camp was just beginning to stir, and he felt it appropriate that his
brigade see their commanding officer up and ready well before they
were. It also gave him some quiet time to enjoy a cup of coffee, read,
and think. His staff understood this need and worked to ensure it.
That growing staff was now headed by Lt. Col. Jonathan Harris, late
of the Connecticut Militia, who had recently been invited by Patrick
to be his chief of staff. Patrick had run into him at MacArthur's
headquarters and remembered the diligent way the then major had
led his men after the disaster under Colonel Blaney. Or was it
Haney? It seemed so long ago. When his own militia unit disbanded,
Harris was left without a position. An owner of a prosperous shoe
factory, Harris knew how to organize and manage.

One of the first instructions Harris issued was that the general was
not to be disturbed during this time of day unless a large portion of
the German army was directly behind the general's tent.

Handing the general a fresh cup of coffee did not constitute an
interruption, and Patrick took the new cup of steaming brew from a
grinning mess attendant, then went back to his newspaper. With the
military situation relatively stable, it was possible to get the news in
a surprisingly up-to-date fashion. What he was reading this fine

morning was the *New York Herald,* although the edition was printed in Boston and contained a lot of news local to that town. With New York City occupied, no local news was emanating from there.

A major story bemoaned the fact that food rationing might be imposed as a result of the war and warned people not to hoard. Great, thought Patrick, there is nothing like warning people not to do something as a certain means to motivate them to do it.

Another story referred to the growing number of sailors getting into fights and being generally disruptive. The story implied that there were many more sailors in town than before. Patrick shook his head. An intelligence agent with even a minimal intellect could infer that something was afoot and that ships were being stationed in Boston Harbor. The same article stated that certain areas of the coast were out-of-bounds to civilians because of military construction. Why not just send the Germans a letter stating that coastal forts were being built?

Yet another article hinted at an army training camp being built outside Springfield, Massachusetts, about eighty miles from Boston. Construction jobs, it said, might be available. Well, people have to eat, and there were enough refugees available to provide a labor force. Patrick knew that most wars resulted in economic prosperity for many of those not actually being shot at, but this war was not normal. For one thing, the refugees had overwhelmed the charitable resources of many locales and were unable to find work. Worse, some were underbidding the local labor force, which was causing bad feelings and some violent confrontations. An article in an earlier paper noted an upsurge in militant unionism as a result. Also, the closure of New York harbor was causing transportation problems, although other ports were trying to take up the slack and at a profit. Yes, he thought, there were many areas of the country and industries that were making a killing, but not too many in the immediate vicinity. Unless, of course, you counted the liquor merchants and the whores.

Baseball was still being played. Boston had beaten Hartford by one run. Hartford? Games were going on under the shadow of the German guns. Well, thank God, he thought, someone has a firm grip on what's important and what's not. It would be nice to get home to Detroit and see a game. He wondered whether Trina liked baseball.

He flipped to the editorial page and read a column exhorting the

State Department to get more aid from foreign governments. The writer clearly had no idea what aid the British and, to a lesser extent, the French had been providing to the large but awkward American army.

Another impassioned writer wondered where the navy was. It was inconceivable, the writer said, that the same navy that had humbled the British in 1812 and whipped the Spanish in 1898 would hide and act cowardly in 1901 against the Germans. Patrick wondered where the writer had learned his history. We hadn't humbled the British in 1812, merely sunk a handful of the ships in their vast navy; as to the Spanish, well, they were so totally inept and poorly led, it was no contest. No, the German navy would be something else entirely.

The letters to the editor were interesting. One writer groused that the entire theater season would be lost if this war wasn't over soon. The *Herald* staff must have had fun printing that one. Another complained about the number of beggars and refugees in the streets. He offered no solution, just complaints.

More seriously, several writers decried what they perceived as inaction by the army. Why didn't the army drive out the invader and restore things to normal? Good question. One particularly poignant letter concerned a son who'd been killed at Danbury and questioned whether it was all worth it.

Another writer said that this was God's punishment upon us for being so greedy. We had no need or right to lands beyond our shores. Give them up, he said. People should not have to die for Puerto Rico. He alluded to a speech given just a few days prior by William Jennings Bryan in which the orator had said much the same thing.

A woman writer opined that there would have been no war if women had been able to vote. Patrick grinned and determined to clip the letter for Trina.

The letters and articles, taken in aggregate, showed frustration and pride. There was pride that the United States had not been humbled further by a great European power, but there was frustration that the war had not been decided, one way or the other. It was almost as if it would be better to take action and lose than to wait and win. When he read letters like these, he understood the pressure on the political leaders to move before they were ready. It was hard to sympathize with Theodore Roosevelt or the late McKinley, but he did understand a little better.

The first clue that something was wrong was the sound of distant angry shouting. Patrick rose quickly from his chair and looked for the source. One of the many patrols was likely returning and there must have been trouble. Lieutenant Colonel Harris, his face flushed, ran over.

"General, a patrol got cut up."

Patrick nodded. It was always tragic, but it happened. The war between the lines was a deadly one. "Continue, Colonel."

Harris wiped his sweaty brow. "Damnit, it was the one with the British officer and Heinz. Somebody said Heinz is dead."

To Ludwig Weber, New York City evoked thoughts of what ancient Rome must have looked like in the Dark Ages. Although being in the city was immensely depressing, he felt himself privileged to have seen what could only be described as living ruins. In normal times, several million people lived in New York, but now the population was probably less than a tenth of that. No one knew precisely, of course; any figure was someone's guess.

The streets of Manhattan were virtually deserted. Almost anyone moving about was either a German or one of the relatively few Americans who'd chosen to stay and collaborate with them. These people were very suspect and were trusted little by the occupying army. There were very few locals about in this area of town. Weber had been warned that the slums and tenements of the Lower East Side of Manhattan, where so many of the immigrants had once lived, were still occupied and potentially dangerous because of the large number of criminals and social deviants who lurked there. Stay away was the warning. Virtually all of the immigrant Germans had fled, but there were still some Jews, and everyone said they were thieves. Some Italians remained in the Bowery, and other nationalities were scattered about. Most of them had no reason to love Germans.

What a joyous leave. The 4th Rifles had marched from their encampment and headed toward the city, all the while watching every brush and shrub in case some red savages were lurking there. Fear of the Indians had kept all but the bravest and most foolish in their tents at night. Guards were doubled and latrines moved closer to the living quarters. This made it safer to relieve oneself, but it also made camp life a more noxious experience.

It was sweetly ironic that Kessel had been required to stay behind with a few others and protect the camp. Apparently Captain Walter feared a repeat of Kessel's earlier looting escapade if he were turned loose in New York. Kessel said nothing. His eyes said everything. They were filled with hate.

Fortunately, no one in the 4th had been murdered by the savages, but everyone knew of others who had. Sometimes Ludwig felt that the stories of the Indians were like the stories old people told about bogeymen in order to scare children out of their wits. Only these bogeymen were real. The Indians scalped, mutilated, skinned, and sometimes left men dying and castrated with their penises in their mouths. Germans could stand up to an enemy in the field, but not as well to shadows in the night. Morale was dipping. There were other problems as well. Horses were being lamed and supplies burned by American irregular troops. Just a few days ago one of the bridges over the Harlem River had been blown up. No one had been caught, but there was agreement that this act of sabotage was not the work of Indians.

Even more interesting than the sabotage was the sudden proliferation of pamphlets and signs offering help and amnesty to any German soldiers who deserted their units and surrendered. They would not, the documents said, be repatriated against their will. America was the land of opportunity, and they would be helped, even given money, to begin a new life somewhere, anywhere, in this huge land. It was very seductive. All the notices were in fluent German.

This was the second of their three days in the great city, or what had once been a great city. Ludwig, as befitted a schoolteacher, took his friends on a tour of the many places he'd seen as a boy. The Statue of Liberty was off-limits and Ellis Island was being used as a naval barracks, but that left many others such as Grant's Tomb, Madison Square Garden, Wall Street, Broadway, and the Brooklyn Bridge, which everyone cheerfully tried to sell to Ulli, who laughed hugely at himself. How could anyone dislike the clod? It was, Ludwig thought, one of the few truly pleasurable moments of the trip.

Ludwig had wanted to take in the Metropolitan Museum of Art, but it was closed. When he pursued the matter, he was informed that the treasures were being shipped back to Germany as advance reparations for the war. He could only shake his head in puzzlement.

Perhaps the biggest disappointment, aside from the desolation in the city and the ruins plainly visible across the river in Brooklyn, was Central Park. Once it had been a wonderful place for a child to romp. Then came the war and it had housed thousands of American prisoners until they'd been moved to more secure quarters in warehouses. The park had been thoroughly ruined. The fact that the Germans were not at all interested in landscaping and maintaining it didn't help either. It looked like a jungle in the making, and too much like the overgrown fields in Connecticut and on Long Island.

Madison Square Garden and Carnegie Hall were empty, although a concert for officers only was scheduled for Carnegie. Would Captain Walter be there? Music by Wagner and Beethoven was to be played by the army band. Probably better than nothing. Of the churches, Saint Patrick's Cathedral was surprisingly small in comparison with the great churches of Europe. Ludwig felt that it paled in comparison with the cathedral in Köln. Besides, it was Catholic. Only the unfinished Saint John the Divine showed potential.

The most intriguing sight was the view of Jersey City across the Hudson. There was an unofficial truce between the Germans and Americans in which neither fired across the river at the other. As a result of this live-and-let-live approach, Ludwig was able to borrow a telescope and watch Americans at work and play. Some of them had telescopes and were doubtless looking at him. He did not give in to the childish urge to wave. Sandbagged fortifications and people in uniform were a grim reminder that there was a war on, unofficial truce or not.

Worse, no one had obtained sex yet. The army operated some beer halls, in which cold and virtually free brew was available, but no brothels. Someone at the top must have gotten religion. Ludwig had heard it was the kaiser's wife, the Kaiserine Dona, who was known as a prude, who'd stopped the idea of official whorehouses. Or else they were all afraid of the clap. Ludwig had never been to a whore and had no intention of starting, but others, like poor Ulli, bemoaned their fate as celibates. In a burst of insight, Ludwig realized that, far from being sexually active as he liked to brag, Ulli had probably never had a woman.

Ludwig glanced at the sky. It was early evening and their instructions were to be back in their quarters by dark. Although the army controlled the town, it was still considered dangerous.

The sound of loud laughter and running footsteps brought him back to reality. It was two of the younger men, the brothers Klaus and Hans Schuler, all giggling and red faced. A few moments before, Ludwig had seen them with Ulli. Now where the hell was poor, dumb Ulli?

"He's getting fucked," said one, laughing. The other nodded, giggling too much to speak.

Ludwig, as corporal, was their leader. The Schuler brothers were the intellectual equal of Ulli. Sergeant Major Gunther had once commented acidly that they didn't have one full brain among the three of them. They were, however, cheerful and friendly, fit companions for each other. "He's getting what? Where the hell did he find someone who'd screw him in this forlorn place?"

They waved. "A couple of blocks back. This woman, young and not too bad if you like them scrawny, came up and asked if we wanted to fuck her. She was white, too," he added, as if that gave her greater status.

"Just like that?"

They nodded. "Just that simple. She said she'd do it for one American dollar each. None of us had any dollars, but Ulli got her to agree for some of our money. She offered to take us all on, but Ulli said he was gonna keep her busy and we should come back in about an hour."

Ludwig laughed. "My God, she's probably giving him six different kinds of clap."

"Nah, she's clean. Ulli made her lift her dress and show him her crotch before he'd go with her." Hans snickered. "He got so close I thought he was gonna put his nose right up her pussy."

They all doubled over in laughter. Ulli was so horny, yet so naive and particular. "Well," Ludwig chuckled, "we better go back and wait for him. We can't have him wandering off alone in this town. The poor fool'll get lost and we'll get blamed."

The small group of German soldiers walked casually to where they'd last seen Ulli. The area was empty. Where the hell had he gone?

"Ulli!" Ludwig yelled. Nothing. He hollered again, as did the others.

It created a din, and one of the German military police walked over and asked what the matter was. Upon being told, he asked where the woman had come from, and one of the Schulers pointed to an alley. Grimly, the soldier pulled his revolver and moved slowly into the grimy passageway, littered with refuse of all kinds. Ludwig and the others followed, all suddenly aware that they were unarmed in a hostile land and that the shadows of the alley conveyed a sense of menace.

The alley turned a corner and, now thoroughly frightened, they followed. The policeman gasped, then paused and pointed. A pair of bare feet jutted from behind a barrel. Not wanting to see but knowing they had to, they moved closer. It was Ulli. He was naked and his crotch was a bloody mess. His throat had been cut. His penis was in his mouth.

Richmond Hobson watched as the train rolled slowly into the huge warehouse and dock complex on Newark Bay. When it finally stopped, the guards dropped nimbly to the ground. They were all wearing civilian clothes instead of their customary uniforms. Hobson had wanted no uniforms to attract attention to the unidentifiable, canvas-draped shapes on the flatcars.

As he walked along the train, the guards acknowledged him and moved away. Richmond Pearson Hobson had a reputation as a very different and difficult man. At thirty-one, Hobson was the youngest officer in the U.S. Navy to achieve the rank of captain. It was the result of an incredibly brave action in which he had tried to sink a coal ship, the *Merrimac,* in Santiago harbor during the war with Spain. If he had been successful, the Spanish fleet would have been unable to sortie. But he hadn't been successful. Although the *Merrimac* had indeed sunk, he failed to block the channel and, worse, wound up as a prisoner.

It was more than ironic that he had been promoted and lionized in the press for achieving nothing. The attempt was a failure and it galled him.

Undeniably brave, Hobson was also highly intelligent, some said brilliant. He had graduated at the head of his class at Annapolis and was thought to have a magnificent future ahead of him. His specialty was naval architecture. Of course, no one could yet give him command of the fleet, but now he had been given responsibility for hurting the Germans in some manner, and that was good.

A righteous man, Hobson neither drank nor swore. He had a stern
and handsome look that made women turn and stare. He was not a
womanizer and scarcely noticed their existence.

A small, bearded man in a dark suit and a derby hat walked up to
him. "Satisfied, Captain?" Unlike the guards, who were military men
in civilian clothes, this man was very much a civilian and unawed by
Hobson's rank.

"Not until the Germans are gone, Mr. Holland. One more trainload
and my men will be ready for action. They are getting nervous. Idleness does not suit them with the enemy in sight. How about your
crew?" he asked, thinking of the strange vessel that bobbed helplessly alongside the dock.

"They will be ready, Captain, and they will perform well, as will
my little creation."

"Good," Hobson said. "Just what I expected." The two men strode
outside and stood in the soft rain staring at the covered shapes in the
water. To a casual observer, they looked like small craft that were out
of service. There were many such covered craft in the harbor and
these went totally unnoticed among them.

"Mr. Holland, do you know what I did today?"

"Can't imagine."

Hobson chuckled, an act that surprised the other man, since
Hobson rarely smiled, much less laughed. "I took a carriage over to
the East River near Hoboken and looked at the enemy through my
telescope. And do you know what I saw?"

"No."

"John, I saw German officers looking through their own telescopes at me! Their presence on American soil made me ill. They
must be driven off and made to pay."

Hobson glanced down into the water at the small boats that were
his command and smiled grimly, which caused the other man to
shudder. "And very soon, Mr. Holland, we shall come to collect."

The scene at the field hospital was one of organized confusion.
Several of the colored soldiers from the 10th Cavalry loitered around
the tents, wondering fearfully about their comrades. Patrick pulled

back the tent flap and entered. Ian Gordon, dirty and bloodied, tried
to rise from his chair. Patrick pushed him down. "Ian, how badly are
you hurt?"

"Mainly my pride. Except for some bruises and minor cuts, the
bulk of this blood belongs to others."

"Heinz?"

Gordon nodded grimly. "Sad to say, yes. He's badly wounded.
Possibly dying. Damnit, we did all we could to bring him and the
others back."

"I know." At least the boy was still alive. Better this was a skirmish, not a great battle. Thus the doctors could give Heinz proper
attention, and not be overwhelmed by the numbers of hurt and
maimed, as had happened in the past.

Gordon continued. "He got shot in both the arm and the leg. The
leg wound seems fairly simple, but his arm is all ripped up. We just
stuffed a rag into the leg hole, but we had to use a tourniquet on the
arm to stop the bleeding. There were bones sticking out too. Thank
God he was unconscious most of the time. I just hope he hasn't lost
too much blood. Tourniquet or not, he just wouldn't stop bleeding.
The doctors have him now and are operating on him. They say it
might be hours before they know whether he will make it."

Patrick forced himself to think beyond Heinz. "How many others?"

"One of the 10th dead, and two wounded. The wounded were able
to walk back under their own power."

One dead and three wounded out of a patrol that normally consisted of ten men and had been augmented to twelve by the addition
of Heinz and Ian. Not good numbers. "Okay, what happened?"

Bad luck, Ian explained, just poor, dumb, bad luck. It had been organized as a two-day, two-night patrol by the 10th Cavalry, entirely
on foot. They'd made it to within sight of the German defenses in
one day and settled in to observe. They spent that night and the next
day in safety, but discomfort. "Damn mosquitoes were bigger than
some birds we have in England. It rained, of course. It was impossible to brew tea."

They were on their way back the second night when they'd blun-
dered into a German patrol. "One minute we were moving along in the
dark, trying not to step on each other, and the next we were clawing
and stabbing at shapes in the night. It was so sudden, so awful."

Ian added that there had been little time for gunplay, and few shots had been fired. The accident of fate had brought both patrols within arm's length of each other before bullets could be chambered and safeties removed. For what seemed an eternity, they fought with hands, clubbed with rifles, and stabbed with hunting knives. Finally the Germans fled, leaving several dead comrades. As they distanced themselves from the Americans, a few got their weapons ready and fired. It was then that Heinz had been hit.

"If it's any consolation, we killed three of the bastards, and others must be wounded. We almost got a prisoner, but he slipped away in the confusion. I guess we had too much on our minds to keep proper track of him."

Patrick sighed. No, it was not really much consolation, although it would have been interesting to have a fresh prisoner. "Well, at least you saw the German lines. What are your thoughts?"

"Of Byzantium." He smiled slightly at Patrick's puzzlement. "Surely you remember Byzantium and its fabled triple walls. Didn't you get to Istanbul during your European trip?"

"No, Ian, I managed to miss Istanbul. But I do understand your analogy." Byzantium had been the capital of the Eastern Roman Empire for about a thousand years until its fall in 1453. During that long time, its triple walls were the stuff of fable and legend. Huge and high, incredible works of man, they encompassed the city and protected it from barbarian invaders, many of whom could only stand in awe at the massive constructions. It was not until the advent of gunpowder and the siege guns brought by the attacking Turks that the walls were finally breached and the city was conquered. The result was the end of the Eastern Roman Empire and the city of Byzantium. After a period of looting, it was renamed Istanbul. The walls, even in ruin, are impressive to this day. If Ian was comparing the German fortifications to Byzantium, then he had truly been impressed. "Are they that good, Ian?"

"Yes, I'm afraid they are. They have spent a huge amount of effort building fortifications that run solidly from the Sound to the boggy ground about twenty miles north. Unless you have some secret advantage like the Turkish artillery, the American army I've seen will not be able to penetrate them. Sorry."

Patrick shrugged. "I'm not too surprised. The near miss at Danbury must have put the fear of God into them."

"So why haven't you built as sturdily as well? The American lines

are nothing in comparison with theirs—just some trenches and some
barbed wire."

"Good point. The fact of the matter is we don't want them to fear
our forts so much that they won't come out. You're right, we can't
take them. Their forts are not really impregnable—nothing ever is—
but the price we'd pay to take them would be just too horrible. The
Germans must come out of their defenses and fight us. MacArthur's
plan is to tempt them with several lines of defenses, but not any one
as formidable as theirs. He hopes to entice them to come out. Then,
pray God, we can defeat them, no matter how good they are."

Patrick stood. "If you can, stay here and let me know about Heinz.
I'd like to stay, but there is the rest of the brigade to take care of."

Ian nodded sadly. "I know. There's a war on."

To Patrick's relief, Trina was not nearly as upset as he had feared
she would be when he finally summoned the nerve to confront her at
her cottage. "Then Heinz will live?" she asked, her face pale. Once
again the war had struck someone she knew.

"Yes, he should live. As Ian suspected, the leg wound was minor,
although he will limp for a long while. It was the arm and the loss
of blood that were the major problems. The arm was disinfected and
the bones were set. He will probably lose some use of it because of
the way the bones were broken and the muscles were shredded, but,
barring infection, he will keep it. We will know for certain in a couple
of days."

"What about the blood loss?"

"He's getting transfusions."

She paled. "But those are so dangerous. I've heard that many
people die from them, and for no apparent reason."

Patrick smiled. "Well, you learn something every day. The doctor
treating Heinz is a civilian and a correspondent of another doctor, a
Karl Landsteiner, who recently discovered that several different
blood types exist and a person can receive a transfusion only from
others with a compatible type. He checked and found people with the
same blood type as Heinz—type O, I believe—and started providing
him with blood."

"Fascinating. And invented by a German?"

"No. Landsteiner's an Austrian living in the United States."

Trina folded her hands on her lap and nodded her head. "Good. Much better an Austrian than a German."

He thought of saying that she sounded more like Molly than Katrina Schuyler, but he deferred to discretion. The thought of moving blood safely from one person to another was intriguing. What if blood could be taken in advance and stored until needed, not only for military purposes but for other problems and disasters as well? The army doctor—what the hell was his name?—said they were working on it. He also reiterated how lucky Heinz had been that he'd been wounded during a period of low activity. Along with the time to treat him, there was the matter of sanitation. Both the doctor and the operating room were clean. Although the idea of doctors and attendants washing up before operating was widely popular, it was not universally held to be advantageous. And after a battle, the press of numbers often precluded sanitation, good intentions or not.

Patrick left Trina with the burden of informing Molly about Heinz. Thus he was not surprised when Trina showed up at his command tent a few hours later.

"How's Molly taking it?" he asked.

"Badly at first. She screamed like the day we first saw her. It took a while, but I finally got her somewhat calmed down. I left her at the hospital on the way over here. Heinz is out of surgery but still unconscious. It helped to know that he will make it." Patrick nodded. Ian had kept him informed.

"He will likely make it, Trina," he corrected gently. "Nothing's certain with these things." He remembered so many who'd died from wounds and infection long after receiving medical treatment.

"I know. That's why we're starting to make arrangements to get him back home so we can care for him properly. I'm sure you know a hospital's no place for a man to get well. You will help us get him out as soon as possible, won't you?"

"Can you handle his care?"

"I could not. But I'm confident Molly can. She had to help both her brother and her father through convalescences, and she has some experience treating infections. Her father died from gangrene after cutting himself in his meat shop." She shuddered. "Yet another awful experience for the child, but what she learned then will be useful now. Please don't forget that a battle could occur at any moment and result in a flood of patients to the hospital, and that could be tragic for Heinz's recovery. No, I think Heinz will be all right with us. Agreed?"

Patrick remembered his stay in various places as the result of wounds and malaria. "Yes."

"And, of course, we don't want Molly to risk losing the baby."

"Then it's true? She is pregnant? Funny, but I kind of thought you weren't certain the last time we spoke of it. Might've even been teasing me."

"Yes," she sighed, "the girl is truly pregnant. Soon to be great with child. The eager youngsters have gone and created themselves a family. We shall have to get them married before anything else happens. Then we can ship them to Ohio where they'll be safe."

Patrick agreed, although with the caveat that it might be a while before Heinz could be sent back to Cincinnati. He reminded her that Heinz had volunteered for the duration of the war and might not want to go home just yet. If the wound healed properly, he could be returned to some duty. The decision would be Heinz's, not theirs. He would certainly be able to serve. Even with a bad left arm—was he right- or left-handed?—there was a place for his mind, if not his body. Thank God he wanted to be a lawyer and not a doctor.

"Now, brave General Mahan, please tell me—just what on earth was he doing out near the Germans in the first place? Aren't staff people supposed to perform their assignments in the rear of these armies? And please don't insult me by saying he was only doing his duty. I know that. I have kept from being angry with the thought that you probably didn't even know he was out on that patrol."

It was true; he hadn't known. "When Colonel Gordon said he wished to go as an observer with an upcoming patrol, I had no objections. Since Heinz was impressed with the British colonel, he'd volunteered to 'see him off.' When they got to the jump-off point, Heinz said it wasn't right for the only officer in the patrol to be a Brit, and he suggested that he should go along to 'help out as liaison.' Colonel Harris thought this was a good idea and agreed. Although I take full responsibility, I have to admit I knew nothing about it."

"What would you have done if you had?"

"I honestly don't know."

They had been sitting in chairs facing each other. Trina arose and stood over him for a moment, studying his upturned face. Then she settled quietly and easily onto his lap. "Just hold me for a moment," she said as his arms went around her. "It was so easy to forget that you were preparing for war. Without casualties I could block out the fact that you and others, like Heinz and Colonel Harris, could be killed at any time." A shudder ran through her body. "Imagine, I was starting to think of you as a vast collection of overgrown schoolboys on a camping trip."

He held her, stroking her back with a gentleness he didn't know he had, and hoping no one would walk in on them. "Sometimes I forget too."

"Just hold me for a few more minutes. Then go back to commanding your precious damned army and leave me to figure out how I'm going to care for a pregnant sixteen-year-old and a huge lout with a broken arm."

Chapter 19

AS THEODORE ROOSEVELT glanced about the room, he could not help but feel fortunate that he truly was well served. Whether that good service would suffice to win the war was another question, but the talent pool from which he drew counsel was, in his opinion, top-notch.

Today, he had the services of the civilian secretaries of state, war, and navy, along with the military minds of Longstreet, Schofield, Wood, and the naval genius Alfred Mahan. Dewey was up with the fleet. This afternoon in September, the civilians would listen gravely and try to look wise while the military reported on what had transpired since they last met a week ago.

Roosevelt smiled eagerly. "General Longstreet, would you please begin?" Longstreet gestured in the direction of General Wood, who took his now-accustomed place at the podium.

"Sir," began General Wood, "although the press and the public seem to think that the war has slowed down, I would like to remind everyone that a great deal of armed contact is going on between the two sides. General MacArthur reports that our army casualties are running more than a hundred a week, and we assume the Germans are suffering about the same. The contact consists mainly of patrols meeting and fighting in the areas between the two armies—no-man's-land."

Roosevelt shook his head. "What an ominous name. Is such patrolling necessary? What is the purpose of it?"

231

"Sir, although we do use the patrols to give the army the experience of actually fighting and being in danger, the primary purpose is to gather information. We have other means of getting some information, like observation balloons and airships that patrol the skies above our lines. These are good for spotting large masses of men moving about in fair weather, but they cannot see at night or during bad weather. In addition, the airships have to stay over our lines so they do not get shot down. So we need the patrols to give us specific information about what units are confronting us, what they are eating, how their morale is, and many other things. In some areas we have been sending Americanized Germans during the day and Negroes at night to keep tabs on the enemy. There's very little truth to the theory that Negroes' darker skin makes them invisible at night. They smear their faces with dirt to keep the shine of sweat from giving them away. Regarding our Germans, they sneak up and listen in on enemy conversations. Very rewarding."

"How so?"

"Well," injected Longstreet, "we just found out that two of the divisions on line are reservists."

Roosevelt was surprised. "You're joking. Reservists? Why?"

Longstreet nodded in the direction of John Hay, who smiled affably and responded. "General Longstreet and I believe they have made a conscious and calculated decision not to invest more of their frontline regulars, because it would weaken their military forces in Europe. As a result of this war, they are confronting an angry France and a very unhappy England and Russia. Since their reservists are almost as good as their regulars, I think they feel they can afford it. From a military standpoint they may be right, but it may damage them politically. We have been informed that the German public was not too happy about the war in the first place, and the fact that older reservists with families and jobs have been called up and sent over pleases them even less. The radical German press has been scathing in its criticism, and there has been some unrest in the cities, particularly the university towns with large student populations."

Roosevelt leaned forward. "This is something we can use to our advantage, isn't it?"

Hay and Longstreet both agreed. Hay said his sources in Germany were trying to gauge the mood of the German public. Longstreet said that however good the reserve divisions were, they were not quite as good as the regulars. The result was a small benefit to the United States, but hardly enough to confer a decisive advantage.

Wood went on. "As we continue to modernize weapons, we are also upgrading other areas of our military technology, and we feel we are finally gaining some solid advantages." He knew that this was a slap at the previous military administration and regretted the necessity of saying it. "Our battle lines are now fully connected by telephone and telegraph, as well as semaphore and light signals. We are getting heavily involved in wireless telegraph as well. Some of our clandestine units on Long Island are using wireless to communicate, as well as a telephone line we managed to lay from New Haven to the Island."

Roosevelt chuckled. "Just how did you accomplish that? I thought the Krauts had the place sealed off."

"Not entirely, sir. We worked hard and, with the outstanding cooperation of the navy, it paid off." Wood did not add that much of the work of laying the line had been done by the submarine *Holland*. What Roosevelt didn't know, he couldn't inadvertently tell. Wood and others felt very strongly that the ability of the underwater craft to penetrate Germany's naval defenses should not be divulged, not even to the president. The secret would be theirs and the navy's.

Roosevelt seemed satisfied. Airships and radios appealed to his sense of newness. "Bully. Now what about my army? How does it grow?"

General Wood grinned. "Slowly, sir. As we explained in the past, we have neither the resources nor the leaders to create an immense army overnight. We have built camps and are filling them with recruits as quickly as we can, but it will not be as fast as we had hoped. The training sites in Georgia, Indiana, and Missouri are starting to fill."

A brief cloud passed over Roosevelt's face. He had wanted to hear a different report. "You know, the German press is having a field day with the empty camps. They are saying we cannot get enough recruits because no one wants to fight their invincible army. I hope you can do something to change that perception, and soon."

"Well, sir, it is not an entirely false perception. A number of states have indeed declined to send their guard and militia. They say they

are required to defend their home shores and cities. Georgia, for instance, has declined to release its militia for our use. Ironically, they
did the same thing in the Civil War, refusing to help the Confederacy
despite Jeff Davis's pleas.

Roosevelt nodded. The problem of who controlled the state units
had arisen during the Spanish-American War as well. It represented
another item that needed to be corrected. Presidents should be able to
control state militias during a time of national emergency. "I'm sure
it's only a coincidence that Governor Candler is a Democrat,"
Roosevelt said drily.

"I also presume you are aware that recruiting in the war zone has
dropped dramatically," continued Wood. "Although we are building
a camp outside Boston in hopes that enlistments will pick up, we are
getting virtually no volunteers from that area. One can understand,"
he added, "that the heavy casualties taken already have dampened
local ardor. Although, to be fair, sir, we have many thousands of local residents under arms at this time."

"Humph," sniffed the president. "Well, then, what good news from
the navy, Captain Mahan?"

Alfred Thayer Mahan was a small man with a trim white beard.
Basically an academic with little command experience, he seemed
uncomfortable in this setting. "I can only say, sir, that events are
progressing largely as we expected. Admiral Dewey continues to
train the main battle fleet while Admiral Evans is working his cruisers off England and Spain. You know we have received initial reports
of successes, but the impact is not yet what we wish. Admiral Remey
has his smaller ships operating off our East Coast, and he has sunk
some transports and taken some prizes."

"Excellent. Anything we can use?"

Mahan demurred. "Nothing significant, I'm afraid. The really
important cargoes are sent by armed convoy. The prizes we've taken
consist mainly of foodstuffs and other basic supplies. Sometimes the
ships are taken because they, not the cargoes, can be useful. To add
to what General Wood has said about wireless, I should inform you
that we have sets installed on many of our more important ships and
are using them for ship-to-ship communications. How it will work in
battle remains to be seen, but it does appear to be effective. We are
also communicating with our ships from Canada by wireless." He

looked at Roosevelt. Once again the man appeared to be entranced by the development of technology. "The British have built huge antennae in both England and Canada that we are using to broadcast information to our ships. Although the ships cannot send messages to us, they can receive using their masts as antennae. In order to make certain a message is not missed, the ships have at least two sets, and they must be manned around the clock. Regarding the limitations of antennae, someone had the brilliant idea of using the balloons and airships as antennae to broadcast signals, and it appears to work."

Roosevelt grinned, pleased. "Amazing! I had no idea anything like that was afoot."

"Sir, the British have been trying to develop such capabilities for some time. A test was scheduled for later this year. We simply urged them to accelerate the process, and it has succeeded."

"Excellent."

"I should also add on behalf of Admiral Dewey that we have been sending the big guns that General Longstreet requested."

Roosevelt turned to Longstreet. "What are you doing with them, General?"

Schofield responded for Longstreet. "Sir, a number of them have been sent to reinforce coastal defenses at key points such as Boston, Norfolk, and Charleston. No German naval attacks are anticipated, but it is certainly good for civilian morale. Others are dug in along the Housatonic defense line as an unpleasant surprise for the Germans should they come by. We solved the problem of carriages, temporarily at least, through the use of heavy wooden sledges that look like they were last considered modern during the Middle Ages and are about as mobile as a dead elephant." A grin split Schofield's round face. "Like my good friend General Longstreet, they are old and ugly but they work."

Longstreet laughed at the jibe and Roosevelt watched in delight. How wonderful, he thought. Two of the keenest surviving minds from a war in which they fought against each other were now harnessed in tandem against a common enemy. Better, cooperation between the army and the navy was a reality.

As the meeting broke up, Longstreet glanced quickly at Admiral Mahan, who nodded briefly. It was enough. They both understood the necessity of not telling the president everything. His outgoing and ebullient personality sometimes led him to blurt out things that were better kept secret. That would not do, thought Longstreet; the war was difficult enough without telling everything to the president and seeing it printed the next day in the papers.

Ahead of him Longstreet saw the short, round form of General Schofield, another old warhorse recalled from retirement. After the Civil War, Schofield had served as secretary of war and then until 1895 as the army's commanding general. He was considered to be an outstanding administrator, and Longstreet was pleased to have his support. Longstreet was also aware that, immediately after the Civil War, Schofield had been sent on a secret mission to France and the court of Napoleon III. There, he had informed the emperor in no uncertain terms that the French army in Mexico would have to leave or it would be kicked out by the Union army. Napoleon had backed down and abandoned his Mexican venture, not wanting to face Phil Sheridan and the force arrayed on the Rio Grande. Yes, Schofield's pudgy, soft-looking facade hid a measure of steel. Longstreet decided he would be forgiving about the reference to his being ugly. Schofield would pay, of course, and a dinner at the Willard seemed an appropriate price. Who the hell said the Civil War was over? Longstreet hurried his pace to gain on Schofield.

"Count von Holstein, I am honored to make your acquaintance."

Holstein nodded and tried to measure the man before him. Middle-aged, stocky, with dark, thinning hair, he gave off an aura of confidence and middle-class wealth.

"Herr Becker, how kind of you to come." He gestured Becker to a chair and watched the man place himself with surprising confidence and calmness. Becker was a merchant, the type of man who would not normally meet with the aristocratic Holstein, especially not in the latter's private office. But times were not normal, and Becker was a member of the Reichstag, an elected delegate in what was Imperial Germany's highly tentative step toward democracy. Becker had always been a supporter of the kaiser's policies, but he had begun to speak out against the war. More to the point, Becker was a leader who was listened to by many other moderates. It was important to Holstein that he find out more about both the man and his motives.

"May I get you anything? Tea?" asked Holstein. Becker declined and Holstein saw a line of sweat on the man's forehead. Perhaps he was a little nervous after all.

"I'm afraid I must begin with a tired old phrase and ask if you are wondering why I invited you here today."

Becker managed to summon a small, tight smile. "It had crossed my mind, Count."

"You are a merchant, are you not?" It was almost a rhetorical question. Holstein was well aware that Becker was a merchant, a sausage manufacturer from a small town north of Munich, in Bavaria. "And most important, you represent your lovely home area in the Reichstag."

"Correct, sir."

"And as a member of the Reichstag, you have recently made comments and speeches that appeared to be critical of our kaiser and the war effort in America."

Becker stiffened. "Critical would be far too strong a word. I have questions and, frankly, some doubts. I revere our beloved kaiser and wish only to have my doubts resolved." He lowered his voice, as if someone else were in the room and he didn't want them to hear the comment. "I, and members like me, am beginning to wonder if the All Highest is getting the advice and good counsel he deserves. From others besides yourself," he hastened to add.

Holstein smiled and changed the subject. "Do you not export your sausages?"

"Some."

"To America?"

Becker blinked and his eyes flashed anger. "If you are insinuating that I wish this war to end so I may make a greater profit, sir, you are sadly mistaken. I am a loyal and proud German. In the early days of my youth, this country of mine, of ours, did not even exist. I would die to defend Germany." He took a deep breath, calmed. "Let me clarify something about my business, just to make certain you understand me, sir. Before the war, less than 2 percent of my income was represented by exports to America. That 2 percent has been more than made up by sales to the army. No, sir, if I wished to get greater profits and be even wealthier than I am, I would pray each night that the war might continue for a great long time!"

Holstein took the rebuke in silence. He was not used to speaking to people who were cruelly termed commoners, regardless of their wealth. It was also apparent that the outburst had purged Becker of any remaining traces of discomfort or apprehension. A usually predatory Holstein now saw a strong and intelligent man who could be a serious adversary. Of course, Holstein would not let him become one.

"I am glad you clarified the point, Herr Becker," he said smoothly. "Yet it had to be mentioned. There are others, and I am not one of them, who might impute your motives to something base, like money. We—I should say those of the kaiser's closest circle—are used to being criticized by the anarchists and Socialists or the followers of that fool Marx, but not by someone with credentials like yours. You, and those like you, are considered the bedrock of the German nation." He forced himself to smile warmly. "Yet you speak of doubts and questions, all the while saying you would defend Germany. Is there a paradox?"

"Hardly, Count von Holstein. As I said, I would die to defend Germany, but this act of aggression has no purpose and can do no good for Germany. We are a European community. We should be working to develop our strength on this continent, not on any other one. We do not need foreign possessions that sap our strength. Sir, in the course of developing my business, I have traveled and observed extensively throughout both Europe and the United States, and I strongly feel that our real adversaries are nearby or next to us in the form of France, England, Russia, Turkey, and Austria-Hungary." To Holstein's raised eyebrows, he continued. "Yes, Austria. That empire is corrupt and failing. There are millions of Germans who would be harmed by the chaos that would result if Austria were to fail. The country should be united with us and quickly, before the empire collapses and civil war results."

"But, Herr Becker, Austria and Italy are our allies."

Becker snorted. "Austria is not an asset and the Italians are worse. They are the Negroes of Europe."

Holstein was quite frankly amazed, not by the harshness of the appraisal, since it so closely mirrored his own; rather, that such prescience came from someone outside the government. If a presumed nonentity like Becker understood this, how many others did as well? Perhaps there was more depth to the Reichstag than Holstein thought.

Becker had additional things on his mind. "There is a more personal reason for my objections. The kaiser has our army and our reserves fighting the Americans, many of whom are of German descent. I—we—are truly upset that we might be fighting and killing our own blood relatives for no good reason. Sir, I have a brother in America and he has three sons. I have another brother still in Germany, and his son is in our army. My wife, my family, and I are distraught at the thought of them possibly fighting and killing each other. It would be different if the United States had attacked us, sir, but this is totally the opposite. Again, I swear to you that I and mine would die to defend this Reich. The kaiser refers to it as the Second Reich, and it has been almost a thousand years since the first. Should this German nation fail as a result of this foolishness, I fear I will never live to see a Third Reich."

There was little further meaningful conversation. Holstein implied his support while Becker again asserted his loyalty to the kaiser and the Reich. Finally Holstein hinted that the conversation should be concluded, and Becker departed after yet a further protestation of loyalty.

Alone, Holstein brooded upon the conversation. Becker was the intelligent voice of modern and moderate Germany. He was intensely loyal and proud of his new nation, yet very unhappy with the current state of affairs. If such a man as Becker was so distressed, then what of the others? Certainly, Becker was not a radical, not one of the students rioting in the university cities like Heidelberg. Becker had only a nephew or two serving in the armies. What of those who had sons and brothers? Or husbands and fathers, what with the reserves now being sent over. With more than a hundred thousand soldiers and many thousands more naval personnel involved, how many angry and dissatisfied families were there? The kaiser, he thought sadly, would never understand.

The meal was over and Patrick was stuffed. Trina had come up with a tender beefsteak covered with an elegant wine sauce and mushrooms, delicate mashed potatoes, fresh vegetables, and an apple pie dessert that was light and sinfully good. Washed down with a decent Bordeaux, it was, he decided, about as good as dinner gets.

"Some more pie, Patrick?"

With sincere regrets he declined. "I suppose I should have stopped eating at some point to tell you how delicious everything was."

She smiled, delighted. "I cooked it all myself."

"Really?"

"Of course not. I did help and could cook if it were the only way to avert starvation, but Molly did most of it, and I bought the pie from a neighbor."

"And I'll bet you didn't stomp the grapes for the wine, either," he added, wiping what he hoped were the last crumbs from his chin.

"'Fraid not." They both smiled at the vision of the elegant and very patrician Katrina Schuyler jumping up and down in a grape-filled vat.

Cautiously, so as not to disturb his meal, he rose, and the two of them walked through the house and out to the yard. It was getting measurably darker as the days neared the start of fall, and, although it was still quite warm, there was the barest hint of the coming winter in the air. They sat side by side on a high-backed bench.

"Katrina, do you like baseball?"

She turned, her eyes wide. "Why Patrick, I do believe that's the most romantic question anyone's ever asked. Was it the meal or the wine?"

He chuckled. "Both. So, do you?"

"I've seen a few games. They're rather slow but pleasant enough. Why?"

"Well, I read the papers every day and see the scores. It reminds me there's a life going on without me. There's a major-league team now in Detroit and I've never seen them. Frankly, and for no logical reason, it left me a little depressed."

"I think I know the feeling." Life, she sometimes thought, was passing her by as well.

"Do you like football? Basketball?"

She laughed. "I hate football. I've seen games at Princeton, but it's just a bunch of thugs trying to push each other down a field. I have no opinion on basketball since I have only heard of it and never seen it played. I understand the purpose of it and that it can be quite rough."

"It's a new game meant to be played indoors. Teams of men try to put a large ball in a basket."

"Sounds rather foolish."

"So does any game when you try to analyze it, I guess."

They were silent for a few moments, each taking in the presence of the other. Finally Trina broke the spell. "Patrick, Heinz will be coming home to us in a few days and I will again be forced to look at what war does. When will this end?"

"Honestly? I don't know. I can tell you that my role in it has apparently changed. MacArthur has told me my brigade will not be going into the line."

"Wonderful!"

"Hah! Beware of generals bearing gifts. We have been ordered to practice maneuvering on the attack. Apparently we will be used as assault troops if the Germans breach our lines."

"You're right. That's awful."

"So we've been out learning how to operate as a whole brigade. It hasn't been easy. Even the 9th and 10th have rarely operated as whole entities. They've usually been broken up into small frontier garrisons. The men are willing and they're learning quickly. I just have no idea how much good my little brigade will be if the German army comes through. I've also been working on different tactics to minimize the awful losses now possible thanks to repeating rifles and machine guns."

Trina shuddered at the thought. Enough of war. "Patrick, I do like sports. I've golfed, played tennis, swum, hiked, and ridden. You should be well aware there are few opportunities for women to play anything. Men have concocted a fiction that we are frail little creatures, incapable of honest physical effort. Worse," she sneered, "there are many foolish female creatures who like to live that way and they simperingly conform to the myth, thereby perpetuating it."

Patrick put his arm around her shoulders and she moved slightly toward him. She was slender but hardly frail. "Patrick," she continued, "when this is over, where do we go? You and I."

It was a question he almost dreaded finding the answer to. "I don't know. I've come to depend on you so much. I want the war to end, but not us."

She moved a little closer. "Why, Patrick, that actually was almost romantic."

He smiled. She hadn't rejected him. "I mean it," he said, his voice barely a whisper.

She put her arm around his chest and squeezed. "I don't want you to go away either." She disengaged herself and sat up straight. "Brave general, can you get some time off, say about a week?"

"I think so. Why?"

"I forgot to mention, but my father is in Albany. We have a small house there." Katrina smiled pleasantly. "Most people would call it a castle, but we rich folk call it a house. I would like to take you there to meet my father. We could eat like little pigs, and hike and swim off all the food. Father could watch." If he hasn't brought along a girlfriend, she thought. If he had, they both could watch. Oh dear. That was something she would never have thought before.

Patrick could see her eyes shining brightly in the clear night, and he made the easy decision. "I will inform MacArthur that he will have to continue the war without me. Give me a few days to arrange things and we can go." He paused. "Uh, what about Heinz and Molly?"

"Molly can handle him. She already informed me of that and in no uncertain terms. If she does need any help, there are people around, like Annabelle Harris, and I'll arrange for them to look in. Somehow I think they'll revel in the privacy, broken arm or no broken arm."

They leaned toward each other and kissed deeply. Both were aware that a new threshold in their relationship had been crossed. Patrick had never been to Albany, never wanted to go. Now he wanted more than anything to go there and be with Trina. And he knew she wanted him there as well.

Chapter 20

THE BRIDGE ACROSS the small stream was a fairly solid-looking stone structure that easily supported the weight of a wagon loaded with materials or the marching feet of fifty or so armed men. Until recently, the bridge hadn't even been necessary. Generations of Long Islanders had simply eased themselves down the gentle banks on each side and walked across the stream, sometimes barely getting their feet wet. Even in flood, the stream was rarely more than a few feet deep, and today it was quite shallow.

But a bridge was meant to be crossed and that meant traffic took advantage of its existence all day long and sometimes into the night. Blake Morris sat comfortably in the shade of a shrub and watched the quaint little bridge, barely two hundred yards away. The three men with him were all of his little band that he'd allotted to this task. The rest were in the warehouse area of Brooklyn, or what was left of that lovely city, and had their own assignments. There had been some discussion as to the wisdom of dividing up their small force, but the men in charge of the Brooklyn operation were more than qualified. They would hurt the Germans in the area of materials; he would hurt their souls. As the Apaches on the mainland made the Germans fear the night, he, Blake Morris, would make them fear the day and cause what had been familiar and friendly to suddenly seem sinister and hostile.

Which was why the bridge, so quaint and charming, gently span-
ning a stream whose name he didn't know, was such an appropriate
choice.

"What time is it?" Blake hissed, unnecessarily quiet. The response
came that it was a little past two in the afternoon. Blake sighed and
continued to wait. If all had gone well in Brooklyn, that event was
already over. Perhaps he should have gone there with his men. No,
he reminded himself, this would strike at the enemy's soul, if the
Germans had souls.

A tremble, a murmur, passed through the air. He looked and the
others had heard it too. There was the soft exhalation of their own
breath. The wondrously punctual Germans were arriving.

Shortly, the sounds took on definition. The bastards were actually
singing! A few minutes later he could see them as they approached
the bridge, his bridge. His cute little bridge. First came a lead group
of ten, a squad. These were followed by a handful of mounted officers and then the remainder of the battalion, hundreds of men in column of fours. They were in step, he noticed. Despite the fact that
they were in the country, their commander had evidently continued
to insist they march in step rather than walk at a natural pace. What
a fool! Did he think the creatures in the meadow were watching his
parade? He must be loved by his troops.

Blake's three men checked for outriders and saw none. It wasn't a
surprise. There had been no outriders yet when the battalions
changed positions, as they did every Tuesday at this time. When this
battalion reached the encampment a few miles up the road, the one
currently out there would return down the same road to the dubious
comforts of Brooklyn.

The head of the column reached the bridge and crossed without
breaking stride. It didn't take long. It was such a little bridge.

Blake waited until the officers and the first company of infantry
were completely across. The lead squad was near the red-leaved bush
he'd arbitrarily designated as the end of the target area. "Now," he
ordered himself aloud and pushed down on the plunger. For the barest second nothing happened. There was the inevitable momentary
fear that the device had failed, then the bridge lifted into the air and
seemed to come apart, stone by stone, soldier by soldier. Before the
Germans had a moment to even blink, lines of additional explosions

walked down the dirt road in both directions from the now-atomized bridge structure. Almost immediately, the sound of the explosions and the shock waves engulfed them. Then there was silence.

It was several seconds before the screaming started. Because of the slow-settling clouds of dust, Blake couldn't actually see what he'd done, but he was fairly certain the battalion no longer existed.

Later, he would meet up with the crew sent to Brooklyn. If all had gone according to plan, a score of the German warehouses had gone up in smoke and flame. His only regret was that they were not ammunition warehouses. Those were kept under tight guard within the inner German perimeter. What he had been able to gain access to were the stores of food and uniforms; thanks to his other crew, these had doubtless been dynamited as well.

The fucking Krauts wouldn't starve or go cold any more than they would stop coming down the road and crossing the stream. But it would make them think every time they took a step or opened a door.

Tonight when he slept, maybe his wife would come to him and nod her approval. He smiled.

If there was anything more boring than guard duty, Ludwig Weber couldn't think of it. Even peeling potatoes was more rewarding. Unless, of course, he had to work with Kessel. However, as a corporal and the captain's aide, he really didn't have to perform kitchen police and usually got out of pulling guard duty as well.

But this, as Sergeant Gunther calmly explained over Ludwig's mild protests, really wasn't guard duty. It was a roadblock and, because of the recent incidents of sabotage and worse, the idea was to check on who was coming up and down the road. So it was that he and a handful of others watched a dusty and largely untraveled route behind the German lines in Connecticut. At least, thanks to his exalted rank of corporal, he was in charge of the little group. Better, Kessel was not with them. Thank you, Sergeant Gunther, for that small favor.

Although not all of the men at the roadblock had been with him during that fateful stay in New York, they all had been touched by it. As far as he and his men were concerned, the whore who had murdered Ulli had not been found. Of that he was certain, even though a woman had been executed for the crime. Perhaps even worse than

Ulli's murder and castration was the fact that some poor woman who fit the general description of the prostitute had been arrested, shown to them, and, over their protestations, shot.

Ludwig shuddered. He hadn't seen the woman who seduced Ulli, but the Schuler boys had, and they had tearfully insisted that the retarded-looking slattern with the greasy dark hair whom the military police had picked up wasn't her. The German police simply insisted that she had to be because she had been found in the area and fit the general description. They had the company watch as a firing squad pulverized her with bullets. The poor thing had been wide-eyed and slobbering with terror. Her mouth was deformed and she wasn't even able to speak, only grunt. It was then that Ludwig realized with a chill that the police were more concerned with closing the case than with solving the crime. Bastards. The event had seared them all. The death of dumb Ulli was such a waste, such a shame. What bothered him more than anything, except the attitude of the police, was the fact that some of his men, speaking in whispers, blamed the German military for having them here where they could be killed and not the slut who'd cut off Ulli's cock.

And Ludwig had a hard time disagreeing with them.

"Hey, Ludwig, wagon coming."

Ludwig shaded his eyes with his hand. Yes, it was a wagon. One lone wagon with two German soldiers in it, and it was pulled by one slow, old horse. Yes, it was a real threat. He rose slowly and started to walk the score or so strides from the shade to where the sun shone on the hastily improvised roadblock. This consisted of a length of wood on a stone stretched across the road, and a hand-painted sign that read "Halt."

One of the Schuler boys offered to go with him, but Ludwig told him to go back to sleep. He could handle this massive threat to their security all by himself. It was only the third or fourth time anyone had come down the road all day. Ludwig stood in front of the sign and held his hand palm outward, and the wagon stopped. He could see that the two men were a little older and their uniforms didn't fit that well, which made him fairly certain that they were reservists. Ludwig may have hated the army, but he took pride in the way they looked. This pair looked like slobs in comparison with the regulars. Perhaps he was being too harsh. Ludwig also didn't recognize their unit, but that wasn't surprising either. With all the reservists about, he hadn't heard of half their regiments. After all, he thought, stifling a yawn, he was a teacher, not a soldier.

One of the men in the wagon was a sergeant; the driver was a private. Well, Ludwig thought, reserves or not, the sergeant has more stripes than I do and that makes him God if he wants to be. The sergeant didn't want to push it, however. He smiled amiably and asked what the matter was.

"Nothing much." Ludwig grinned back. "This is the most important road in America and we're watching it for the Reich."

The two men laughed and agreed. They knew make-work when they saw it. Funny, Ludwig thought, he didn't quite recognize their accents, and he thought he knew all the regional nuances. "Where to?" he asked.

"Just going in to the supply center," the sergeant replied. "We got a shopping list and specific directions from our captain. Jesus, what an old lady."

Ludwig grinned and looked around. It wasn't proper to criticize an officer that harshly. He and his friends did it privately, but not to a perfect stranger. He asked them what unit they were from and was told they were with the 141st Infantry, a reserve regiment. Well, that confirmed his guess and was probably why they were so critical of their commander. Rumor had it the reserves were not overwhelmed with joy at being here. For that matter, neither was he.

As he looked in the back of the wagon, Ludwig idly asked the sergeant where his hometown was and was given the name of a village he didn't recall. It didn't matter. He was getting bored again. The only things in the back of the wagon were a steamer trunk and the soldiers' rifles, which lay flat on the floor. He noticed that the trunk was unlocked and the hasp had worked its way open. A piece of paper was protruding. He decided to do them a favor, so he pulled out the piece of paper and opened the trunk to reclose it properly.

He gasped. It was full of sheets of paper. Thousands of them. And they all had similar messages. "Surrender," they read, or "Stay in America," "Live Free," or "Americans Are Your Friends—Not the Kaiser."

His knees weakened and he had to grab the side of the wagon for support. He looked at the two men, who were staring at him, their faces suddenly pale and their expressions frozen. In his mind, he started to cry out for help, call for the others, but no sound came.

Dear God, these are Americans, not Germans. No wonder their accents are so strange. Either they never lived in Germany or had lived there so long ago their accent had changed. Oh, God. Help.

Instead, a hand—it was a stranger's, although he knew it was connected to his arm—closed the trunk and fixed it tight. Then a voice—it sounded like his—told them in a hoarse whisper to leave. Leave now. Get the fuck away from here! Now, now, now!

With forced slowness, the driver eased the wagon around the slight barricade and trotted on down the road. The sergeant turned and looked incredulously on the source of his good fortune, his survival. Had they been caught in German uniforms they would have hanged. Ludwig stood there, his body drenched in sweat, and tried to regain control of himself. He felt himself quivering. Finally he gathered the strength to return to his squad. He was certain they knew what had happened. He had let the Americans go, and the fact of his treason had to be emblazoned on his face. Instead, no one was even looking at him. One of the Schulers had found a toad and they were trying to make it jump by sticking it with a penknife. Ludwig leaned against a tree and tried to breathe.

"Hey, Ludwig, you look like hell."

Ludwig forced a thin smile. "I made a big mistake. I ate that sausage crap you cooked for lunch, and now I gotta take a shit. You people watch the road for me. Let me know if you see the kaiser."

They laughed and returned to their mindless game, and Ludwig walked into some bushes where he knew he would be left alone. Then he pulled the piece of paper from his pocket and started to read.

"General von Schlieffen," Holstein began, practically purring, "I understand that you concur with the actions recommended by General von Waldersee. Quite frankly, I am surprised."

"Dear count, I had no choice but to support the commander of our forces in the field. He is a continent away and in daily contact with local hostiles. His position, although hardly untenable, requires drastic action to prevent it from becoming so."

Holstein nodded sagely. "I have no doubts as to the military necessity of the action, but the political implications will be enormous."

"Are you concerned," Schlieffen asked bitterly, "that we might find ourselves with yet another enemy? Who is left? Ecuador? No, dear count, I find myself in broad agreement with both the kaiser and von Waldersee that the war must be won first and the politics cleaned up later. I think you will agree with me when I say that a victor is forgiven many transgressions, even crimes against humanity. After all, is what we are doing to the Americans so different from what the British are doing to the Boers? Or what the Spanish did to the Cubans? No, I think the idea of expelling useless and dangerous mouths from the zone of occupation and requiring the remaining Americans to be incarcerated in concentration camps is now a necessity. We have lost too many men and too much equipment to their depredations."

Holstein arched an eyebrow quizzically. "And supplies are now a problem?"

"Not for the military, and certainly not yet. The destruction of so many of our supplies simply means that we cannot afford to feed the Americans within our lines unless their presence outside would be dangerous to us, or if they have skills useful to our effort."

"They will resist."

It was Schlieffen's turn to shrug. "Then they will be shot. We have given them one week to register with us. We will then determine whether they will be expelled or imprisoned. Anyone we find roaming loose after that who is not working for us as a collaborator will be executed as a spy and saboteur. I have given responsibility for the task to General Lothar von Trotha. Do you recall him?"

Holstein shuddered. "Yes. He did some of the kaiser's best work in China. General von Schlieffen, the man is a butcher. Why not Hindenburg or von Moltke?"

"They declined."

"General, there will be mistakes," stated Holstein. "Surely you do not hope to reach every small child or old woman hiding in a slum basement. Would you kill them?"

"And why not?" answered Schlieffen. "The women in America are quite cunning with knives and very supportive of the men. As to children, sir, they are being used as messengers and deliverers of weapons and ammunition. Please do not scold me with prattle about innocent children."

Holstein did not respond. He was surprised at the kaiser's actions in expelling all Americans, but he was not shocked. American irregulars behind German lines were causing terrible losses. Schlieffen might try to downgrade the loss of the warehouses in Brooklyn, but they represented two weeks' worth of food for the German army. It was getting more and more difficult to resupply them, since part of the American navy was now sitting in a rough arc running from Brest in France to Penzance in England; a second group sat off Dover, where the Channel was only a score of miles wide. Every German ship now had to travel by convoy, and each convoy had to fight its way through the American cruiser lines. The result of this had been the slowing down of supplies reaching the army as well as the siphoning off of warships from their coastal defense and fleet duties in order to protect the convoys.

Most of the ships got through, but a surprising percentage did not. The Americans tried to attack with a force larger than the warships shielding the convoy. Thus, although the convoy guards tried to protect themselves and their charges, American ships were almost always available to slip into the convoy and cause damage before being driven off. The Americans seemed to not want a major battle. Rather, they preferred to nip and snap, like a wild dog after a large prey, causing a multitude of small wounds rather a single large one. Holstein recalled that the Chinese had a name for such a torture. They called it something like the death of a thousand cuts. Well, he sighed, Germany was being sliced and bled by very sharp American scalpels.

"Yet, General, the battles have not all been one-sided," said Holstein.

"Certainly not. On several occasions, von Tirpitz's new navy has given a good account of itself. The Yanks are without at least one cruiser, and a couple of others are temporarily out of action. Sadly, we have lost a little bit more heavily than they. The score or so of merchant vessels sunk by them is a matter for concern. So too, by the way, is the question of how they find out about the force and composition of the convoys. It almost seems as though someone is telling them."

Holstein laughed. "Who would have to? By the time the convoys form off our coast, a thousand eyes have seen them and reported. When they try the Channel off Dover and Cherbourg, they might as well be on display. Better we should eliminate any confusion or mistakes by sending the Yanks our sailing schedules. No, by the time our ships reach Plymouth, the Americans know exactly what is coming at them. I'm surprised we aren't sending more around Scotland."

"According to von Tirpitz, it wouldn't accomplish that much," explained Schlieffen, "and it would extend the trip at least a week in what are quickly becoming cold and dangerous waters."

Holstein shuddered. He had seen the North Sea in anger once. It was not a place for any but the strongest sailors. "There is another rumor that you are pulling your soldiers back to a small perimeter in Brooklyn and effectively conceding the rest of Long Island to the Americans."

"With regrets, that is true," acknowledged Schlieffen. "With the need to keep so many in the trenches against the Americans, we found ourselves unable to protect our facilities scattered about the area. We are not afraid they will suddenly land an army on Long Island and attack us. Our navy is in complete control of Long Island Sound. I think of it as a consolidation, not a retreat."

Call it what you will, Holstein thought, but it looks, smells, and sounds like a retreat. Were these fairly innocuous acts the first indication that a crisis was approaching?

Holstein thanked the chief of the Imperial General Staff for his time. Then he sat in his office and brooded.

Johnny Two Dogs watched intently from where he hid in the shrubs as the long line of people walked slowly eastward down the road in the general direction of the American lines in Connecticut. They were still behind the German defenses and had many miles to go. A shame, he thought; so many of these people looked either too old or too young to be out in the open, even though the weather mercifully continued to be mild.

The column, although broken here and there, seemed virtually endless. Only a handful of Germans guarded the forlorn civilians as they shuffled along, their slumped bodies exuding despair. Johnny was puzzled. These people were not a threat. How could this be? Were these the same white tribes that spawned the soldiers who finally took Geronimo? These people were weak and thin, often dressed in tatters, and they carried what they could of their belongings in bags and sacks. He saw few suitcases and no carts or wagons. Reason told him the Germans had confiscated anything that looked like a horse or a cow. He had no way of knowing that these sad-looking people were largely recent immigrants for whom this trek was yet another march away from a tyranny they'd left Europe to escape.

It was hard for Johnny to feel any mercy or regret for the white people parading dismally before him. How many of his people had died when shipped from Arizona and New Mexico to the stinks of Florida and then to Oklahoma? How many of the Cherokee had died in their long march from the white man's land to Oklahoma in years past? He spat on the ground. The Cherokee dead were no great loss to him. The Cherokee were women. They had sold their souls to the white devils and had adopted many of the white man's ways, so many they were called the civilized tribes. It didn't help to be civilized when the whites wanted their land. Later, he knew that many of the Cherokees, Chippewa, and others had picked the losing side when the North fought the South. He wondered if he'd picked the right side in this war and decided he didn't care. When it was over, he and many of the others had decided they would not return to the hellish conditions on the reservation. They would go elsewhere, somewhere.

One of the Germans grabbed a bundle from an old man and spilled it on the ground. Then he used his booted feet to stir the man's possessions in a search for valuables. Johnny knew that the soldier was wasting his time. These refugees had already had to surrender much of what they owned at earlier roadblocks set up to ensure that nothing taken from the city could be used against the Germans. He had crept close to one and watched while the Germans stole watches, jewelry, and anything else that took their fancy. That included some of the women, who were taken into tents and raped while their families were held at gunpoint.

The German said something to the old man, who wailed and raised his arms. The soldier reacted quickly and smashed a fist into the man's face. The old man fell to his knees and the German kicked him in the head. Finally the old man lay still. No one, Johnny mused, had come to help him.

Hell, let them all die. It's their turn.

*   *   *

In Washington, Theodore Roosevelt was livid with rage. He paced his war room and cursed under his breath. John Hay, who ordinarily felt comfortable dealing with the temperamental man when he was in a foul mood, knew better than to interrupt now.

When Roosevelt finally gathered himself to speak, his voice was high, almost squeaky, with barely contained anger. He was trying mightily not to take it out on the people close to him. His friends were not the ones at fault. "They will pay for this outrage. They will pay dearly. They will not expel our people from their homes as though they were the Israelites being taken into captivity. No, sir, they will not. What a tragedy our country is enduring."

He sat down in a chair so hard that his feet came off the floor. "They will pay," he repeated. "This merely strengthens my resolve to defeat them. The devil with Bryan and his peace-loving sheep! How can we ever deal with a country that commits such atrocities?" he asked, his voice now nearly a roar.

John Hay, the presenter of the news that the rumored expulsions were actually taking place, was far more relaxed. "Theodore, it is indeed an awful thing, but let us look at how we can use it to our advantage, and legitimately so. First, although not very many have died en route, some have. We will certainly play up each death as the tragedy it is. The dead all have names and families, and we will remind the press that either they or their forebears came from other lands in search of liberty. Instead, they found this mad kaiser and his army chasing them, hounding them, expelling them from hearth and home, and dooming them to live as refugees. The recently arrived we will describe as being chased from their homelands to the ends of the earth by that madman." He smiled. "And the best thing is, it's all true."

"Humph. That's not exactly what I had in mind. I want that kaiser bastard in chains."

Which is not very likely to happen, thought Hay. "A worthy goal; however, not a particularly realistic one under the circumstances. The brave kaiser is quite safe in Germany, and he will not leave that land while they are at war. His only real danger lies in being burned by the flames of outrage sweeping Europe. The English and French papers are calling him a despot and comparing him to Attila the Hun.

One French paper said Attila was preferable to the kaiser. Even Russia has called for a cessation of the expulsions, and Austria has hinted broadly that they should stop. The kaiser's reaction, unfortunately, has been to withdraw into a shell. He feels that time will pass and all this will be forgotten. Sadly, he is probably correct."

"Damn people and their short memories."

"It also means we are hurting him. The Germans cannot feed and control that large a local population. Our saboteurs are becoming extremely effective. They are denying the Germans a safe haven anywhere on this continent."

"Sabotage. It all sounds so unsporting."

"Theodore, this isn't a baseball game. We are at a serious disadvantage and must use every means at our disposal to win."

Roosevelt nodded agreement. "You're right, John, you're always right."

"I certainly try to be. Unfortunately, Theodore, that is not the end of the bad news."

"Spare me; I've heard enough for today."

Hay ignored his request. "As the Germans contracted their perimeter on Long Island and, in effect, gave the Island back to us, they burned or destroyed just about everything they could not use in order to deny it to us. The land is a ruin."

"Dear Jesus."

Hay looked at him sadly. "I am truly sorry to report that one of the places destroyed by fire was your home at Sagamore Hill."

There was a stunned silence for a moment, then Theodore Roosevelt began to weep tears of pain and impotent fury.

Chapter 21

THE SCHUYLER ESTATE was located about twenty miles south of Albany on the east side of the Hudson. Upon first seeing it, Patrick could readily understand Trina's description of it as a castle. There was a barbaric splendor about the multistoried stone and brick structure. As he came closer, he saw it was basically a three-level building with a stone turret that carried another two levels into the sky. Using his soldier's background, he reviewed the place as a fortress and decided it would hold out quite well against light opposition. As he eyed the construction more closely, it became apparent that some of it was quite old and perhaps had been built with defense against Indians in mind.

Trina greeted him at the massive oak door and showed him his quarters, a three-room suite with a view of the forest. He was honored, she assured him; less-favored guests had views, and smells, of the barn and stables in the back.

Later, when he had changed and refreshed himself from the one-day trip, he met her outside for a tour of the grounds. She wanted to show him around while it was still light. The interior of the house could wait until later.

Her choice of clothing shocked him at first, then pleased him. She wore a man's flannel shirt and denim pants. It was the first time he'd ever seen a woman in pants, and it was a little disconcerting. Because the pants fit quite well, he decided two things: first, she had a delightful figure and, second, the pants had been made especially for her. She confirmed the latter by saying they had been custom tailored for her by Levi Strauss & Company.

Trina took his hand and showed him the buildings around the main house. In addition to the house and a large barn with storage and animals that made the estate almost self-sustaining, there was a stable with a number of horses.

The house, she explained, had been started by an early ancestor in the eighteenth century and added to by succeeding generations of Schuylers. Along with quarters for a half-dozen servants, there were ten bedrooms, living and entertainment areas, kitchens, baths, a ballroom, and a pool. There was also indoor plumbing, electricity run by a generator, and a telephone.

It was impressive and Patrick was a little awed. "Eighteenth century? Does that mean you're actually related to the Schuylers who fought in the Revolution?"

"You mean the one who lost Ticonderoga to Burgoyne? No. We are a different branch of that family. Any relationship is now quite distant."

As the afternoon shadows lengthened and dinnertime approached, they walked a little through the woods. Trina was quite agile as she navigated the narrow trails. The terrain was a very good reason not to wear a dress.

"When I was a little girl I liked to walk through the woods and think of fairy tales and trolls and things like that. It can be a scary place. Delightfully frightening when you're small."

"How much of this is your family's?"

"From here to Oregon," she replied with a straight face. "Are you really so concerned about how much my family owns?"

He flushed, confused. "Concerned? No," he finally stammered. "But I confess to being intimidated. I've met people before whom I considered rich, but you are far beyond that."

She took his arm and squeezed. "Well, don't worry about it. Actually it's rather pleasant being rich, and I'm not in the slightest ashamed of it. Some of my friends feel guilty that they have so much while others do not. I look on it as an advantage that gives me the opportunity to do things that might prove useful. I hope most of them will be for the right causes and reasons. At any rate," she said merrily, "I have no intentions of giving it all away just so you can have more money than I do."

A look at the sky told her they'd stayed outdoors later than they should have. "We have to get back for dinner. Wear your uniform and all the stars. It'll impress my father more than you know."

The largest dining room could seat fifty. With only four people present, they used the library and seated themselves about a mahogany table in front of a small but sparkling fire in a large brick fireplace that took up almost all of one wall.

Staying at the castle with Katrina's father was a buxom, dark-haired woman in her early thirties who was introduced as Sylvia Redding. She was, the elder Schuyler explained, a widow and a companion. Katrina was slightly nonplussed at her presence, but she was polite. Patrick was also courteous. The woman appeared to be her father's mistress, and she turned out to be quite charming. Jacob Schuyler, Patrick decided, had taste.

Whereas Sylvia Redding was charming, Jacob Schuyler was fascinating. About the same height as Trina, he was a powerfully built man with a full beard and mustache that were almost totally white. His equally full head of hair was also long and white and made Patrick conscious of his own darker, but thinning, top.

But it was the eyes that held Patrick. Deep blue and penetrating, like Trina's, they radiated intellect and force. Jacob Schuyler was someone to be reckoned with. The foursome started the meal as "General" and "Mr.," but the relationship quickly evolved to a first-name basis.

"Trina has written me of you, Patrick. She is impressed by you, which is very interesting, as there is not much in this world that impresses her." Trina flushed slightly at the comment; Sylvia smiled wisely.

"Well, I am impressed by her as well," Patrick responded. "Perhaps more than impressed." That earned him a gently placed foot against his leg under the table. "It seems as though we have known each other a very long time, even years, but it has been only a few short months."

"Yes, war has a way of contracting and expanding time. Fortunately,

I've managed to avoid war all my life. I'm sure Trina told you that I received a guard commission during the Spanish war but spent it entirely in New York. Probably for the better. You were in Cuba, I take it?"

With that, Jacob Schuyler began a gentle interrogation that resulted in a complete telling of Patrick's life up to the time he met Trina. Schuyler seemed to be well versed in what Patrick was doing now, which led Patrick to realize that father and daughter were a little closer than he had at first thought.

"Most impressive," Jacob said. "And when this is over, you are going to write?"

"I hope to. As well as teach."

Jacob Schuyler nodded approval, took out a couple of cigars, and offered one to him. Patrick glanced quickly at Trina, who nodded a yes. Smoking in the presence of women was unusual. He lighted his cigar with a candle and drew in deeply. Again he was impressed. Jacob Schuyler liked very good cigars.

The rest of the evening was spent in congenial small talk, and they retired well before eleven. The next day Patrick was awakened early by a servant and informed that breakfast would be ready shortly. He dressed in hiking clothes and devoured a plate of eggs and bacon while Trina and Sylvia watched amused at his appetite. "Army food," he explained between mouthfuls, "gives you an appreciation for real food."

They walked again through the woods, this time with a small hamper containing sandwiches and cold tea. The surroundings were beautiful, and Trina finally confessed that her family owned a couple of thousand acres. "This is such a wonderful place. Almost my own little country."

"Between here and New York, you must feel you have a perfect existence."

Trina made a face. "New York? No, Patrick, that is not my home—this is. New York is where I went to school, bought my clothes, and enjoyed the theater; but this is where I return when I need some peace. New York is far too huge to call home. Do you know it now stretches almost sixteen miles up the Hudson? What'll it be in the future? Besides," she added sadly, "I wonder if the New York of old will ever return. Certainly not for a very long time. First we have to get rid of the damned Germans."

Feeling slightly guilty, she asked how the soldiers under Patrick took to the idea of his going on leave.

"I don't think they care, Trina," said Patrick. "Since the situation seems to be fairly stable, commanders are allowing leave to the men on a rotating basis. Men who can't make it home and back in the allotted time—we're giving each man ten days—often meet loved ones halfway. In too damn many cases, those loved ones are trooping into the camp and taking my innocent soldiers away to the local hotels. God only knows what they're doing," he grinned evilly. "But I'm afraid we're in for a tremendous population explosion in a little less than a year."

Trina smiled in agreement. "I should be shocked, but I suspect they're doing just what Heinz and Molly are."

"With his arm in that huge cast? My, my."

She covered her face with her hands to hide her embarrassment. "I asked her about that and she assured me there would be no problem. All he would have to do was lie there and she'd handle the rest." Her face turned red as he roared with laughter.

He took her hand. "I think our world of innocence has ended forever as a result of this war, hasn't it?"

She agreed. "Perhaps for the better. I've learned more about myself and about life and what I want out of it in the last few months than I did in the previous three decades."

The remaining few days were spent in a pleasant round of talking, eating, hiking, and horseback riding. With Trina's assistance, Patrick showed signs of becoming a passable horseman.

In the evening, the conversation included Jacob. Sylvia generally smiled and listened. Far from being stupid, she simply knew when not to intrude. Talking with Schuyler gave Patrick an insight into his fertile mind.

"Jacob, I understand you are going into the business of producing oil."

"Producing oil? Certainly not. Messy, beastly stuff. Besides, there's no real demand for it as yet."

Patrick was perplexed. "But I understood you were out west establishing an oil base for the time when automobiles become popular. Aren't you a believer in what Henry Ford has been trying to sell you?"

"Him? A narrow-minded pain in the ass." Trina giggled and Sylvia smiled tolerantly. "The sad part about Henry Ford is that he's right. Someday there will be a huge demand for an inexpensive and well-built automobile, and the first person who produces one will become rich. Filthy and disgustingly rich. If that obstinate man is the first to do it, I shall have to reconsider my belief in God."

Patrick had not met Ford, but he knew others who had. They all agreed that he could be difficult. "Now I am puzzled. If I'm not being too curious, just what were you doing in the West if not getting into the oil business?"

"Ah, General, I prefer to think in terms of strategy, not tactics. I am in the business of producing money, not oil. What I have done is bought up drilling rights on land that is likely to contain oil. I will own those rights for twenty-five years with an option to renew for another quarter century. The current owners get some money from me with which they can buy additional cattle or goats or whatever the hell they think can live down there. While they do that, I wait patiently for the time when the oil can be removed for a profit." He grinned happily at himself. "And that profit, I assure you, will be a huge one. I will not rush into the market."

He puffed on the inevitable cigar and watched the smoke work its way about the beamed ceiling. "Let others pull the sticky, gooey stuff from the bowels of the earth. I will let them pay me dearly for the privilege."

"And what if those nice Texas ranchers decide to cheat on you?"

"Doesn't a good general send out scouts? Seriously, Patrick, I've retained people to keep a distant eye on things." His face turned grim. "Some have indeed tried to cheat me in the past. They do not do it a second time."

The next morning, Trina reminded Patrick that the current day would be their last full one together. He would have to commence his return journey the following morning. "We have done so many things together, and I've enjoyed it so much, I hate for it to end."

Patrick agreed. The preceding days had been a wonderful and soothing experience. "I don't want it to end either. Not ever."

They had been walking toward an area near the house, but one he had not visited before. Thus it was with a small shock that he realized she'd brought him to a cemetery. "This is where a great many

of the Schuylers are buried." He walked through the score or more
of graves and found a number from more than two centuries past. It
was a fascinating history lesson. He turned to say something to Trina
and saw her standing, head bowed and deep in thought, by a com-
paratively recent grave. He walked over and gently slid his arm
through hers.

"My mother," she said simply. "She died when I was twelve. Had
she and the baby lived, I would have had a little sister. I wanted one
for the longest time to help me aggravate my brother, and I felt
guilty that my wanting a sister had caused her to die. Stupid, isn't it?
Now I come here when I need to clear my brain and pretend she's
giving me advice."

"Maybe she is," he said gently.

"Perhaps you're right. She hasn't failed me yet."

"Did you get an answer today?"

Her smile was wide and her eyes twinkled. "Yes, I did." She took
his hand and began to lead him to the house. "Well," she said
brightly, "let's do something different this evening after dinner.
We've hiked and ridden, and even tried to fish, but you've never
swum in our pool. Have you been avoiding that?"

"Trina, I swim like a rock."

"I'll teach you. I taught you to ride, didn't I?"

"I don't have a suit."

"Not a problem, dear general. You can wear my brother's. He's
just about your size."

"What if I said I hated swimming and didn't want to?"

"Wouldn't matter. I've outvoted you. It's my house and you're my
guest and courtesy says you must humor me."

Later that evening, as he walked barefoot down the basement hallway toward the pool with a robe over his arm, he hoped he did not
look as foolish as he felt. As a boy and later as a soldier, going
swimming meant a bunch of boys or men peeling off their clothes
and leaping naked into a pond or stream. Only rarely had he gone
swimming in mixed company and in a proper setting, and right now
he wasn't comfortable. For one thing, the suit he'd borrowed reached
below his knees and covered his arms. He might as well be going in
the water in a full uniform. Worse, it appeared to be wool, and he
wondered how it would feel when wet.

"Patrick, you look magnificent." Trina was similarly attired, although in at least one more layer of clothing. Except for being barefoot, she was dressed demurely enough to be seen in public. For that matter he was barefoot as well.

"Is your suit wool?" he asked her.

"Yes."

"How's it feel wet?"

"You'll live. Now let's get going." With that she pushed him toward the door to the heated pool room. There was a small glass window in the door and they paused when they saw motion behind it.

Trina gasped. "Oh, lord." Emerging like Venus from the pool was a totally naked Sylvia Redding. Water flowed down her voluptuous body and cascaded off her large, full breasts. Patrick, conscious of Trina's embarrassment, grinned but tried not to stare. At least not too much.

"There's father," said Trina. "Oh, thank God he's wearing a robe." They stepped back from the door. "We can't let them see us."

"Well, we better go back down the hallway then. Your dad's coming this way and Sylvia now has her robe on and is right behind him."

Like children caught in a prank, they scampered back, turned around, and pretended to be just arriving. As they passed the other couple, Sylvia smiled warmly; Jacob Schuyler looked puzzled. Patrick, who had days ago decided he liked the man, decided to further confuse him by winking.

Inside, they set their robes on chairs and climbed into the warm water, which was heated by steam. The pool was tiled, and large enough for them to take several strokes before reaching the far side. Patrick found the water quite pleasant and the suit not too uncomfortable.

"Well, sir, you do not swim like a rock."

"Thank you."

"But not much better. Your dog paddle is not very stylish. Here, reach out your arms and pull the water back toward you like this."

He watched as her slender arms, white where the suit rode up, pulled her through the water with surprising speed and strength. After a few tries, he got the timing down and found that he was swimming much faster than he thought possible, and with much less likelihood of drowning.

After a while they stood facing each other in the shallow end of the pool. The water came just a little over Patrick's waist, and he was very conscious of the way Trina's suit clung to her body. He began to hope he wouldn't embarrass himself.

"Kiss me, Patrick." She slid her arms around his neck and their lips found each other's. "Do you love me, Patrick?"

Surprised, he managed only to gasp a yes. Then he asked his own question, and his voice was weak with what he could only describe as fear. "Do you love me?"

"Certainly," she responded gently. "Why do you think I brought you here?" She smiled. "I don't bring just anyone to meet father and his latest mistress. Now pick me up."

Facing her, he put his arms on her sides and lifted her easily, aided by the buoyancy of the water. Thus supported, she wrapped her legs tightly around his waist with a strength that astonished him. Then they stood there and kissed even more deeply. "Now touch me," she said, her voice hoarse. He moaned and ran his hands down from her shoulders and over her breasts and from there around her back to her firm buttocks. They swayed in the water as his hands repeated the journey again and again, daring also to slide beneath the overblouse she wore and be as close to her bare skin as he could without removing her suit. He felt her nipples harden. Between kisses she stared at him in wonder, her upper teeth biting down on her lower lip.

She took her legs from around his waist. He casily slid the loose pants of her suit over her knees and begin to caress her silken hair–covered thighs, moving his hands up to her waist. It was only when he touched her belly and below that she stopped him and then only with the utmost reluctance. She was awash with feelings she had never before experienced. The long and intimate conversations with Molly had been her only source of specific information on how to arouse a man and be aroused herself without losing total control. In a way, she had thought wryly at the time, it was a sad commentary on her life that an immigrant girl more than a decade younger than she would be her instructor. But lord, how right she was.

Finally, Trina took his hands and held them on her bosom. "Do you truly want me?"

Patrick no longer cared if she felt his penis against her. He wanted her to. She had slid lower on him and he was pressed against her abdomen. "Great God, yes."

"Then you'll have to marry me."

"Marry?"

"Yes, dear Patrick, marry. As in living together for decades and having children. You said you loved me, didn't you?"

"Of course I love you, and I want very much to marry you, but how can I compete with this castle, with everything else you have?"

She separated from him and moved a step away. "You don't have to, you ninny. When we marry, this'll be as much yours as it is mine. We can live in your precious Michigan and visit here whenever we wish. Now, are you going to propose to me or not?"

Patrick thought she had just done that for both of them, but obediently he complied and she accepted. "Well," she said, "it may be very unladylike, but I think I want you as much as you want me. However, I am afraid you might get a case of misplaced honor or something equally foolish regarding my family's wealth, and change your mind about marrying me if we make love before the wedding. I want it perfectly understood, mighty general: you are not marrying me for my money. I am marrying you because I love you and you are marrying me because you love me.

"So we are now going to call it an evening. We shall try to sleep soundly, if that is possible considering how I feel, but we will sleep separately." With that she left the pool and began to towel herself off. He followed a moment later. "Patrick, they do have forests in Michigan, don't they?" Many, he assured her, and close by, along with boats and trains to take them farther north—as far as Mackinac and beyond if she desired. Fully robed and fairly dry, they walked down the hallway from the pool. "Trina, just what problem did you share with your mother today? What question did she answer?"

"I told her what I planned to do to you tonight."

"And?"

"She approved wholeheartedly."

When Lt. Micah Walsh, U.S. Navy, told his family and friends that his first command was a converted yacht, they naturally assumed that his craft was a sleek and racy wooden vessel that looked like a clipper ship when all sails were rigged, or one of those marvelous vessels that raced for the America's Cup. What they didn't realize was that the *Chesapeake,* previously *Anna's Favor,* had been built for a Pittsburgh steel magnate who preferred comfort with his speed, and had opted for steam as the basic means of propulsion. Sails were a secondary consideration, although very useful to conserve precious coal.

When configured for comfort, the *Chesapeake* could make an impressive eighteen knots. Now, however, she would be lucky to make fifteen under steam and half that under sail. The difference was the result of the additional weight required for her to become a warship. First, there was the unturreted 3-inch gun located just in front of the bridge, and the additional deck supports needed to ensure that the gun didn't fly off the deck when fired. Some further weight was added with the two 1-pound pom-pom guns located fore and aft and the two machine guns located amidships. What really slowed her, however, was the crew of fifty men, the ammunition for the guns, and the supplies for the crew.

It didn't matter to Walsh that the yacht was such an irregular type of warship. For that matter, he was an irregular naval officer. After ten years of serving his country in quiet poverty, he had opted for civilian life and resigned his commission. For the past five years he had been a rising manager in a Boston-based import company while still retaining a reserve commission. He had responded to the query regarding his temporary return to service with delight and trepidation, and the *Chesapeake* had been his reward for saying yes. His country and his navy needed officers, and he would help fill those needs.

Lieutenant Walsh was presently chasing and gaining on his prey, the heavily rusted freighter *Astrid* out of Hamburg. At the same time he was keeping an eye out for the telltale signs of other ships in the area. If spotted by a German cruiser, he would flee immediately, and he had already decided to throw everything overboard, including the guns and ammunition, in order to regain some of that lost speed. He would not even think of fighting a real warship. First flight, then surrender, if it came to that.

It wouldn't be long now, he thought. They had gained rapidly on their target and were within hailing range of the *Astrid.* He guessed her at about two thousand tons. From the fact that her Plimsoll line was well out of the water, it was evident she was running home empty. Although some German transports were returning with plunder, such as bullion from the banks and artworks from the museums—these sailed in convoys and were protected by warships—the majority, such as the *Astrid,* were empty. The Germans had decided that the *Astrid* and others like her could travel alone in safety.

Bad idea.

In a burst of logic and cunning, Admiral Remey, who commanded the American navy's efforts off the East Coast, had decided that a ship sunk on the way back to Germany would be unable to return again with another cargo. It wasn't as effective or desirable as sinking one with a full load of supplies or ammunition, but it would work. And that was why the *Chesapeake* and other small craft like her had started prowling the sea-lanes off New York looking for strays like the *Astrid,* whereas the larger warships tried to interdict the incoming convoys.

"Signal her to heave to and that her crew has ten minutes to leave."

It was done and there was no response. Perhaps no one understood Morse. They were closing rapidly on her, and Walsh was concerned that she might be armed. Although sturdily built, the *Chesapeake* was a wooden ship, and even one machine gun could cause substantial damage.

"Forward pom-pom, fire one round in front of her bridge."

The order was repeated and the front gun barked angrily. That brought a burst of activity from the *Astrid* as her crew exploded onto the deck and started lowering lifeboats. Midshipman William Halsey laughed. He was nineteen and had just completed his second year at Annapolis. The war had given him a temporary commission. "I think they'll all be gone well within your ten minutes, Captain. Are you going to send over a boarding party? They could open the sea cocks and we wouldn't have to expend any more ammunition."

It was tempting. The *Chesapeake* simply didn't have room for many shells, and each round of ammunition was precious. "No, Halsey, not this time. It would take more than an hour to get there, do the job, and get back. Remember, we scoot if we see something we can't handle coming over the horizon. I wouldn't want to have to run and leave you there to explain to the German navy just what you're doing trying to sink one of their ships."

As soon as the lifeboats were clear, Walsh ordered the pom-poms to each fire three rounds into her hull below the waterline. When Halsey asked if such a small weapon would penetrate, Walsh said the ship was so rusted that a pair of scissors would probably work. The guns fired in rapid succession and raised small splashes by her hull.

"Sir, the 3-inch crew wants to fire."

"William, how many 3-inch rounds do we have?"

"Thirty, sir."

"Well, then, we shouldn't waste them when the pom-poms can do the job, now should we?"

"Just a reminder, sir, the men in that crew have trained on the gun, but they've only had dry runs; they've never fired it. It might be good experience for them."

Walsh saw the logic and reluctantly gave permission for one round. He heard the gun crew whoop; seconds later, the larger gun fired with a racket that made the pom-poms sound like dogs yipping. Walsh was gratified that the deck supports held. The *Astrid* was little more than a hundred yards away, so missing was almost impossible, and the ship was nicely holed, with a secondary explosion following quickly. They must have hit a boiler.

"Sir, the machine gunners would like a chance to fire as well."

Walsh rubbed his eyes. "Oh, what the hell. One short burst each. Then check and see if the cook would like to throw some garbage at her before she sinks." Warriors all, he thought, but maybe the experience of actually shooting at another ship might be helpful someday.

As he continued to watch, the *Astrid* started to settle lower in the water. A shouted voice from one of the lifeboats attracted his attention.

"Captain, will you not take us aboard?" The caller, an older man with a short white beard, appeared to be the captain of the *Astrid*. There were almost a score of men in two boats, and not all were German, as some very dark and swarthy faces attested. Not all were men, either; many were scarcely boys. But could Walsh take them on board? If he did, how would he keep them secure while he sought out other ships? What about his mission? If he took them, he would have to feed them out of his meager stores. And what about crews from future ships? It was certainly not intended that he should return to Norfolk every time he sank a rusting freighter.

The voice from the lifeboat continued, a small note of fear evident. "Captain, we have taken what food and water we could, but it cannot sustain us for very long. We are three hundred miles from shore, and the prevailing currents will take us in the wrong direction. You must help us."

A gurgling, rumbling sound emanated from the stricken *Astrid*. She was sinking much faster than Walsh would have thought.

"Engines, one-third ahead."

Halsey was pale. "Aren't you going to help them?"

"No."

The voice from the lifeboat was desperate and fading slightly as the *Chesapeake* pulled away. "Captain, if you leave us, you are condemning us to die."

Walsh leaned over the railing and yelled back angrily. "I believe your kaiser shares at least some of the blame for your predicament, and I find it likely you came to a war zone voluntarily and in search of profit." He turned and confronted Halsey and others in the crew. The stunned expressions on their young and eager faces told him that what had been a lark had just turned deadly. Most were only students with some knowledge of sailing who'd enlisted for the duration.

"War is hell, Mr. Halsey. I'll be in my cabin. Let me know if anything important happens."

Ian Gordon had recovered from the minor wounds he'd suffered in the raid with Heinz. He looked fit and sounded ebullient as he relaxed in a folding chair in Patrick's headquarters tent. "Patrick, my lad, how was your love tryst with the fair maiden Katrina?"

"We both survived. I met her father. A very interesting man."

"The truly wealthy often are."

"Trina and I will be getting married." In response to that announcement, the dark-haired Scot jumped up and began pounding him on the back.

"Wonderful, or as your beloved president says, bully!" He allowed Patrick to recover his breath. "When will the sacred event take place?"

"Soon. Very soon. She'll be back here in a couple of days with her father, and it'll take place as quickly after that as possible."

"Such a hurry," he teased. "Either you want her in the sack real bad, or you're afraid she'll awaken from whatever trance she's in and see you for what you really are."

"A little of both," Patrick responded, whacking Ian on the back with enough force to drive his breath out. "Now, what vile things have you been up to while I was gone?"

"Been to Ottawa."

"Oh?"

"To see the king. Well, almost the king. The prime minister, Lord Salisbury, who, as you doubtless are not aware, is also serving as foreign secretary, along with the colonial secretary, Joseph Chamberlain."

Patrick was impressed. "That is exalted company."

"Indeed, although they also brought Joseph's son Neville and that fatuous, stammering ninny Winston Churchill. The reason for the meetings with me and others is not a total secret, although I would appreciate not seeing it in the newspapers. Britain is very concerned that Germany might prevail over here and win the war."

"Concerned enough to get involved, say, with your marvelous navy?"

Gordon coughed. The Royal Navy could sweep the seas clean of the Germans without breaking a sweat.

"No, we are not quite ready to do that, although the entire war is causing changes in how we do business. For starters, every German convoy that steams through the Channel is now shadowed by elements of our Home Fleet as well as your nasty cruisers. Having seen how suddenly they fell upon your shores, we have no intention of inviting one of their convoys to make a sudden right turn and disembark an army at Portsmouth or Dover."

"You really think they'd do that?"

He shrugged. "Anything's possible. Their intelligence services are not as inept as we would like. They are now well aware of what aid you are receiving from us, and of the fact that your fleet is in our waters and under our protection. They are angry and potentially capable of almost anything. We are also returning a large portion of our army from South Africa in order to further discourage any sudden thrusts on their part. That, sad to say, is resulting in an armistice with the Boers and terms for them that are far better than they deserve or could otherwise have hoped for."

His face flushed and he became uncharacteristically angry.
"Damnit, Patrick, we fought the Boers for more than three years, and
we finally had those dirty farmers on the run. We were on the verge
of wrapping up that war on our terms. Now the Boers get almost
everything they wanted in the first place, just so we can pull our
army out and protect the United Kingdom. All the deaths we suffered
are in vain."

"How do you think we feel about the deaths we are suffering?"

"Touché," Ian said sadly. "It isn't fair and it isn't just. Of course,
it never is." He took a deep breath and recovered his poise. "Well,
some good might come from it. The prime minister told me there
would be more money for the military. More new ships and some
bright new regiments, with modern weapons for all. All to ensure
that the mad Hun doesn't do unto us what he'll do unto you if you
lose. Should you win, wisdom says he will be so disgraced that he
won't try anything like this for a very long time." He paused
thoughtfully. "However, I believe he is perfectly capable of doing
something truly evil just for vengeance and the sheer devil of it."

"And you lack confidence in our ability to win?"

"Until you actually do win, there will always be the possibility of
loss. To be frank, I am not convinced you can win on the ground.
When the Germans decide to come out, I do not think you can stop
them. Right now you have a wonderful stalemate, and that's all. One
side or the other will soon grow tired of it and attempt something
precipitous. If you attack them, you will surely lose. If they attack
you, you stand only a slightly better chance of not losing. No, you
cannot hope to defeat a fully equipped and supplied German army in
the field. If they explode from their fortifications, defeat your army,
and move on to take Hartford and Boston, you will have to sue for
terms. You will have no other choice unless you wish to have them
remain on your soil until you can construct a new army and try
again. In the meantime, they will be in control of several of your
ports and a large number of your citizens. Your papers indicate that
a growing number of Americans are already tired of the war, and that
number will certainly increase if the Germans defeat you and take
more cities."

Patrick had to agree. If the Germans did win and began a rampage
as Ian described, there would be no recourse. Another army could not

be formed, and there would be the new possibility that all American land east of the Hudson would fall under German control. If that were to happen, what terms would they want then? With such an important prize, would they want to give it back at all? Perhaps greedy minds in Berlin were right now envisioning the possibility of New England as a German colony.

As he sat in his office in the War Department, Longstreet, for the first time since taking on the responsibility of command, felt every one of his eighty-two years. The hours had been too long and the challenges far greater than he had imagined. How naive he'd been. When he'd first become a Confederate general, he was opposed by another army that knew both as much and as little as he. Both sides had learned of war together; ultimately, as the skills of the North increased to match their abundant resources, the Confederacy had been worn down.

But this was now no even match. In excess of a hundred thousand Germans were entrenched in their salient and more were on the way. They were opposed by an army that was months—years—removed from being their equivalent. Yet how could it be otherwise? The Germans had half a million of the best soldiers in the world and many others in reserve. The American army was less than one-fifth that size, and much of it had begun the war isolated in Cuba and the Philippines. No, the war would not be won by the army alone, regardless of the numbers involved. At least, Longstreet thought, both the press and the president would soon be off his back regarding the Springfield, Massachusetts, training site. That would start to fill up soon, although not with the expected recruits from the New England area. No, not that camp.

"Penny for your thoughts, James."

Longstreet's head jerked up. John Long, secretary of the navy, stood in his doorway. "John," he said, rising, "what are you doing here?"

"I believe you requested that someone give you a new perspective on the naval situation."

Longstreet laughed. "Indeed I did, but I expected some aging, redundant captain or admiral, not you."

Long found a chair and settled himself comfortably. "Well, nobody's redundant anymore, and everybody else is busy. I seem to have done a wonderful job of delegating responsibility, and now I am the only one available to come and review matters with you."

"I'm truly honored."

If Long was giving himself a compliment, it was doubtless deserved. The man's reputation as a skilled organizer and selector of talent had not diminished one whit since the commencement of the war.

"John, I am compelled to admit that the situation with the army remains much the same. We will need the efforts of the navy even more than I had realized."

"Well, I can give you some new information, and not all of it is bad. Evans's attempts to attack German transports were quite successful in the beginning. The Germans were slow to respond, and we gobbled up a number of single ships and small convoys. By small I mean six or seven transports protected by one or two escorts, usually small cruisers. These Evans simply overwhelmed. Then the Germans got smart and began forming larger convoys with stronger escorts. When that occurred, Evans changed his tactics. He would try to attack the escorts and, when they formed to meet him, send one of his fast ships into the convoy, like a wolf into the sheep herd, to cause some damage and run out. If the Germans split their force to chase that ship, then Evans would try to overwhelm the remaining escorts."

Longstreet found the vision exhilarating. "And has he continued to be successful?"

"Yes, but at a price. While he has sunk or damaged up to fifty transports and several warships, he too has suffered casualties. What began as an even dozen cruisers is now only seven. Two have been sunk and three are in English ports too badly damaged to sortie. It may be months before they are repaired. Although we seem to be winning this phase of the war, the victor may well be the fleet with the last remaining ship."

The war at sea, Longstreet realized, had quietly escalated to an intensity that startled him.

Long continued. "The war on this side of the ocean has had similar successes and failures. When a German convoy makes it to open waters, we usually lose sight of it until it is very near our coast.

We've gotten lucky on occasion, but we cannot count on luck. Admiral Remey, therefore, has been using his squadrons to seek out those convoys and any single German warships. Again, we have had successes and failures although our successes to date outweigh our failures. I believe we simply have a better navy, ship for ship, than they do. Remey has also commissioned a number of small yachts and such and instructed them where to seek out and destroy German transports on the return trip, which they usually make alone. In this, the converted yachts were very successful, and more than a score of those transports never made it back to the kaiser's land. Now, the return ships are also required to form convoys and be escorted. This requires additional German warships to perform escort duties, and puts a greater strain on their resources."

Longstreet gave him a tired smile. "Bully."

"On the other hand, we have not made up the difference in the size of our respective main fleets. They still have sixteen battleships and we have twelve. While we may be better on a ship to ship basis, Admiral Dewey still believes, and I concur, that we cannot hazard a major fleet action at this time."

And, Longstreet thought, until that fleet action is somehow won, the Germans will still be able to supply their army. As if reading his mind, Long again continued.

"A large convoy is now approaching New York. When it left Germany, it consisted of about sixty transports and at least ten escorts. Both Evans and Remey have attacked it. They damaged it but were unable to stop it. The original sixty is now more like fifty. Some of them were hurt, and several of the escorts had to turn back for repairs. None of those were sunk. The convoy has met up with additional protection from Diedrichs's fleet and will begin unloading in New York in a few days."

"Damn."

"James, we hurt them and we whittle them down, but they have so far managed to bull their way through. I'm afraid it may be a long time before we begin to make a material difference in their ability to wage war on us."

Chapter 22

BLAKE MORRIS STEADIED himself before stepping into the small ship that bobbed in the dark, choppy waters by the half-ruined dock. The vessel had come to take him and the others back to the mainland. He wondered if his efforts on Long Island had been entirely too successful.

The Germans had withdrawn to a small perimeter in Brooklyn and relinquished de facto control over the Island. But they were at least as strong as ever. Their perimeter now bristled with weaponry and was virtually impervious to assault or penetration. Blake's spectacular successes of past weeks were not likely to be repeated soon, if ever. The German army, its warehouses, its men, were out of reach.

Thus the withdrawal of Blake and his few remaining men, with the ever present and totally useless Willy Talmadge, back to Connecticut meant the end of his exacting revenge on his home ground. Whatever he could do now would have to take place elsewhere. The schooner would deposit them once again behind enemy lines, but now their efforts would have to be different, more circumspect. Whereas Long Island was a large piece of land with relatively few Germans, the mainland salient was only about twenty miles by seventy and it absolutely crawled with Krauts.

Unsteadily, Blake made his way to the hold of the little ship. He and the others would travel as cargo. If they were spotted, they hoped their small size would convince any German warships they were of no consequence. Despite the so-called German blockade, Long Island Sound still swarmed with small craft of all sorts as people managed to eke out an existence in spite of the war.

Blake settled himself against the dank hull of the ship and tried to make himself comfortable. They still had enough dynamite remaining to do considerable damage if they could only find some good targets. Just where and how to use it he would have to decide.

As they cast off, the ship tossed a little more than he expected. He opened a hatch and sniffed the air, ignoring the angry looks of the crew, who much preferred that he stay out of sight. He was right, there was a storm brewing. Maybe, he chuckled, his dynamite could provide some thunder and lightning.

A few feet away, the skipper of the craft struggled with the rudder. "Gonna be a bad one?" Blake asked.

The skipper, a weather-burned old man whose name he didn't know, spat over the side. "No such thing as a good storm. If anything good comes of it, 'twill be to make us a little less visible to the Heinies."

Blake eyed the sky and sensed the direction of the swirling clouds. They appeared to be coming from the south. That made it likely that the storm was the remnant of a hurricane and not an isolated squall. Although Blake was not a seaman, he had seen the devastation wrought by such storms along the New York and New Jersey coasts as well as farther south, and he asked about the intensity of this one.

"This fucker's about shot its wad," said the old sailor. "It'll be a nasty one, but we have these all the time. Nothing to write home about—that is, if you can write."

"It won't hurt the Germans?"

"Aw, it'll make 'em puke a lot, but it shouldn't really hurt them. Most of 'em will just make for the harbor and wait it out. Those that have to stand duty out in the ocean will simply endure it. Hell, my boat'll make it, so why should a battleship have a problem?"

A wave hit the sailboat and engulfed them both in spray, silencing any further comment Blake might have made. He was aware of a couple of other figures scampering around doing whatever sailors do in choppy seas. He realized that the Sound was somewhat protected by the existence of Long Island and that the open ocean would be even more turbulent. Give me solid ground anytime, he thought.

"Hey, soldier, enough talking. Get your ass down in there and keep that hatch closed so the water don't pour in. I'll tell you when it's time to come up," the skipper cackled. "Speakin' of puking, if you ate anything in the last day or two, you'll probably be seein' it again real soon."

Ludwig Weber shivered. Not only was his uniform soaked by the rain, but the blanket he'd used to cover his shoulders when he went out to the latrine was also drenched. Nice move asshole, he told himself, remembering too late that he had to sleep under that same blanket.

The storm, now in its second day, had caused a breakdown in the delivery of supplies. Food was even more miserable than usual; tonight it had consisted of a congealed, tasteless, soggy mess that he barely managed to keep down. Worse, several of the men were ill, and not just with colds and sniffles. The weather was causing fevers and hacking coughs, and there was worry that some illnesses would deteriorate into pneumonia. Keep the men warm and dry, he was told. How the hell do you do that when the entire world is a sea of rain and mud? He wanted to ask the question, but prudence deterred him.

Now it appeared that the rain was getting colder; some of the men were saying they could see half-frozen flecks of ice in the drops. Could sleet and snow be far behind? Ludwig had no idea how severe winters could be in this part of North America, but if this were any indication, chances were the soldiers would be even more miserable, and very soon.

Rumor had it that their issue of winter uniforms had been held up because of sabotage in Brooklyn and the fact that shipping was having a harder time than expected getting through. The nights now had a distinct chill to them and he hoped the delay would not be too long. He also wanted a dry blanket.

His feet were wet as well, and some of the men were complaining about rashes between their toes. Again, the advice was to keep dry. But now the men of the 4th Rifles were back in the trenches, occupying one of the northernmost forts on the line facing the main American army. As a result of the rains, the trenches were ankle deep in mud, and in some places water rose up to the knees. Some of the trench walls had collapsed, which required working in the storm to repair them in case the damned Yanks used the cover of weather to attack. Fat chance. They'd drown before they got close.

Ludwig put his hands in his pockets in a feeble search for warmth and found the tightly crumpled flyer he'd taken off the Americans. His fingers caressed it and his mind recalled virtually every word on it. There was no reason for him to keep it; it was probably foolish for him to do so. But he could not yet convince himself to dispose of it. For one thing, it said that possession of it guaranteed the bearer safe passage through the American lines. He knew that it also guaranteed the bearer a prompt hanging if he were found with it by the Germans. *The* Germans? Wasn't he a German? Yes, he realized with sudden clarity, but not one of *those* Germans. He made up his mind that, should the time and opportunity ever arise, he would make it through to the Americans and begin a new life here. He did not want to return to the kaiser's Germany. Let fools like Kessel return to serve the Reich; he would become an American.

The piece of paper, one of tens of thousands like it, had become his talisman, his reminder that he had made a choice and had to fulfill it. Somehow, he had to get to the Americans, and the paper served as a reminder that there just might be a better life out in the great land beyond the trench lines.

Ludwig looked around at the men in the tent. Kessel was staring at him with a glowing hate burning in his one good eye. Did the man know about his intentions? It had long become obvious that Kessel was keeping tabs on him and doubtless hoped to exact some measure of revenge. The man was sick as well as evil, of that there was no doubt.

So why didn't he just slip over the trench wall and out into the woods? The Americans were only about ten miles away and the rain would provide a degree of cover. He could be there by dawn.

He could, he realized with a chill that was caused by fear and not the weather, also be caught by one of the many German patrols that watched over the no-man's-land. It was said they looked for deserters as much as they watched for the Americans. No, the straight way was not the best way. He would have to wait for an opportunity. He'd seen enough executions recently to keep him satisfied for a lifetime.

*   *   *

From where he sat, alone and disconsolate, Capt. Richmond Hobson could barely see a hundred yards of New York harbor, much less the familiar outlines of Manhattan and Brooklyn. It was so frustrating. Somewhere, only a scant mile or so away, were scores of German ships, mainly transports, but a number of warships as well, and he could not even see them, much less do anything about them. There were always several German ships in the harbor, but this situation was unique and, therefore, tempting. First, a large convoy had recently arrived and was still unloading and reorganizing for the return journey when the storm struck. Then a number of warships, including, he was told, a couple of capital ships, had sought shelter from the storm in the harbor. Somewhere in the mess there might be as many as a hundred German ships of all shapes and sizes.

The storm, they said, was starting to abate. If so, Captain Hobson could not detect it. The winds were a stinging fury and the rains came down not in sheets but in virtual clouds that rendered everything invisible. He looked upward to see the sky and found it a foot above his head.

What was most frustrating was that he was ready. All the weeks, all the plans, and all the work, and he was ready. His tiny force was assembled and ready to strike. It didn't matter that many of his men were sure they wouldn't live for more than a few minutes after he gave the signal to get on with it. He was confident they'd persevere. He'd had enough glorious failures. Now was the time for a glorious success.

A fervent and devout man, Hobson prayed for the storm to end soon. He also prayed that it would end at night, and he did that for several reasons. First, his tiny force needed every advantage it could get, and the darkness would help mask its actions. Second, the Germans could be counted on to remain in the harbor until daylight. With no sense of urgency to make them leave the harbor, they, or most of them, would logically wait until dawn in order to make the passage to the open seas a little safer.

Third, and perhaps most important, the darkness would reduce the likelihood of some traitorous New Jerseyite seeing what Hobson was up to and somehow warning the Germans. During the weeks he'd been assembling his little force, it had been kept as great a secret as if he were in a hostile land. Too many of the people of New Jersey were petrified that they might get involved in the war and have their comfortable lives disturbed. He knew this was an overharsh assessment. New Jersey had provided a number of men and units for the army, and many others wanted, like him, to destroy the Germans as soon as possible. But he had to contend with the reality that a small but significant percentage wanted peace at any price, and that price would include sacrificing him and his men. His handsome face wrinkled in a scowl. He would kill them first.

Rains, Trina informed one and all, do not stop weddings. They might stop armies and close businesses, but weddings will go on. Particularly hers. Damnit, hadn't she waited long enough?

Upon arriving back at the cottage, she and Molly, assisted by Lieutenant Colonel Harris's wife, had worked hard to arrange an early ceremony. First, a clergyman had to be found. Since neither she nor Patrick had any strong religious affiliation—she was Dutch Reformed and he wore his Anglican faith lightly—almost any minister would be suitable. Father McCluskey, a portly Catholic chaplain who had been discussing marriage plans with Molly and Heinz, was approached. He had demurred and seemed worried that the Pope might find out what he was doing, but he was mollified when Trina's father promised to build him a new church in his home parish. It was in Kansas and far away from the Pope.

Getting food for a reception and a place to hold it were no problem. As Patrick reminded everyone, generals do have some power. Whereas clothing for the men simply meant dress uniforms, getting gowns was complicated. But the Schuyler money produced a small army of nimble-fingered seamstresses and dressmakers, seemingly from nowhere.

Thus, even though the weather was an utter ruin, the wedding went off without a hitch. Jacob Schuyler gave away his daughter, who, dressed in a simple white gown, was radiant. Molly—in a better dress than she'd even seen before, much less worn and owned—was the maid of honor. Her pregnancy was not evident, as it was still in its early stages. Patrick wore dress blues, and Ian Gordon, as best man, was resplendent in Imperial regimental scarlet. Along with a handful of staff and other friends, the fifty or so guests included Funston, Wheeler, and MacArthur. MacArthur stayed only a little while.

Pershing and Lee sent regrets. There was, after all, a war on. Funston and Wheeler, however, made up for the others' absence and raucously tried to outdrink each other. They didn't even notice when Ian left with a woman guest, a recent friend of Trina's who'd also been working in the refugee camps. She was a little overweight and rather plain, but Gordon treated her as though she were the Queen of England. Patrick whispered to Trina that he would soon be her king, at least for that night. Molly and Heinz left early as well. Unable to walk or stand for long because of the still-healing leg wound, and with his arm heavily wrapped and suspended, Heinz was forced to spend much of the day in a wheelchair and was clearly uncomfortable and a little embarrassed.

Both the ceremony and the reception were held in a school, and a handful of musicians from the brigade provided a fairly high level of musical talent. Harris had found them. They'd gotten together to help alleviate the boredom of an army camp and were really quite talented.

It was not very late when Patrick and Trina made it back to the cottage. Tonight it would be theirs alone. Molly had made other arrangements for Heinz and herself. Patrick and Trina would have only the night and the next day. Work for Patrick was piling up, and Trina was starting to feel guilty about the latest wave of refugees she'd missed helping.

A little before dawn, Trina slid naked from their bed and padded softly to the window. There wasn't much to see of the world as the rivers of water coursed down the panes. They might as well be on the bottom of the ocean, she thought, and wondered whether she'd be surprised if a fish swam by. On the other hand, the rain did appear to be slackening ever so slightly. Well, it couldn't rain forever, could it?

Behind her, she heard the deep breathing of the sleeping Patrick Mahan. She sat on a trunk by the window and drew her knees up to her chin. So this was marriage. No, this was just the beginning. She smiled. A very interesting beginning. She stood and stretched catlike by the window.

The motion awakened Patrick and he lay still, looking at her. How exquisite she is, he thought, and how lucky I am. She was as lithe as a dancer, a picture of sinuous grace, with small but exquisitely pointed breasts and a flat belly with a tuft of light hair at its base.

Her legs were slender and lean, not chunky as he'd been told Dutch and German girls' legs often were. And to think she thought so little of herself. Once, she had described herself as plain and thought others considered her homely. What utter nonsense. He would have the rest of their lives to convince her what a remarkable person she was.

"You're beautiful."

She smiled softly. "I thought you were asleep."

"Who me?" he teased. "I'd never fall asleep on our wedding night." At least not now, he thought, as he watched, enthralled. She was so slender and lovely as the soft light of the stormy dawn danced across her body. A flash of lightning illuminated her like fire, and he saw she was smiling at him.

"Can I convince you to come back to bed before you catch cold?"

"Possibly," she responded and returned. She knelt on the bed beside him and looked at his body. Not bad at all, she thought. Not a Greek statue, but a good, solid, live man. She ran her hands down his chest, found his manhood, and felt it harden under her touch. "Oh my."

A malicious thought entered her head and she responded by lying beside him and then on top of him, straddling his chest. "What are you doing?" he asked, his eyes fixed on the way her breasts swayed above him.

Trina slid farther down until she was directly above him. "Molly explained to me just how she and Heinz have to make love because of his wounds. Now lie still." He groaned as she maneuvered herself so he slid easily into her.

"Are you going to dominate me like this all the time?"

She giggled. "Only when you deserve it. Or when I want to."

Much later and in the light of full morning they sat in their kitchen, primly dressed in gowns and robes, and sipped some hot coffee while they debated how to spend the rest of their day. Their conversation was interrupted by a sharp and insistent pounding on the front door.

"Who the heck is that?" Patrick asked.

"Probably not Paul Revere, since he's been dead awhile," Trina remarked. "You better go answer it." Patrick, muttering half angrily, opened the door to find Lieutenant Colonel Harris. It was on the tip of Patrick's tongue to rip the colonel hard for daring to interrupt his commanding officer on the morning after his wedding, but he recognized that Harris was visibly upset.

"What's wrong, Jon?"

Harris took a deep breath. "A general alarm just came over the telegraph. We don't know whether the Krauts are coming out or not, but we think something awful has happened in New York."

Chapter 23

CAPTAIN RICHMOND HOBSON felt that at least some of his prayers had been answered. The awful rain had slackened and his instincts told him it was likely to cease altogether in a little while. Visibility had improved dramatically and he could now see the running lights of scores of ships anchored in close formation in the upper bay of New York harbor. Although the wind continued to be strong and the waves choppier than he would have thought optimal, both were well within acceptable limits. The only problem was that it was already midnight and his plans had to be executed in the darkest part of the night. If he did not rush, it would be dawn before he and his men could make their way out and back, and there would be a slaughter.

Of course, he could wait one more day and start earlier in the night, when better weather would make their attempts that much easier. If he did that, however, then many of the dozens of ships would have made their way out the Narrows and into the lower bay anchorage or, worse, started back to Germany.

It was a real Hobson's choice. He smiled ruefully and silently condemned the English stable owner of the same name who had created the statement.

There was no choice. It would be tonight. "Mr. Holland!"

John Holland had been gazing at the Germans as well, and the summons startled him. A small, bearded man in his sixties, he looked like an innocuous college professor, not an inventor of military devices.

"Yes, Captain Hobson?"

"Can you get your boat ready to depart in one hour? And in position to attack no later than four the morning?"

Holland thought a moment. "I believe so. I might have to settle for a long shot, but perhaps I can run on the surface a little longer than I first planned. The Germans shouldn't be too concerned about what might look to them like bobbing debris after such a great storm."

"Then get started." Holland nodded and turned away. "And don't forget which fleet you're shooting at." Holland looked back and flashed a quick grin. John Holland's personal sympathies lay in a desire for Irish independence, which resulted in an almost pathological hatred of things British. He had openly proclaimed a willingness to use America's only submarine against the Royal Navy.

A part of Hobson's mind was intrigued by the possibility of using a submarine as a part of his plans, but the poor little boat had so many limitations. First, it had only one torpedo tube; thus, although it carried three torpedoes, it could only fire one at a time and then the tubes had to be torturously reloaded. Second, the vessel was very slow. Holland said it could do seven knots on the surface and four submerged, but Hobson had doubts whether the choppy seas would permit such speeds to be achieved. Worse, the half-dozen or so crewmen lived, if that was the proper word, in a stifling environment and breathed chemical-filled air. The submarine called the *Holland,* also known as the A-1, used diesel engines for surface travel and acid batteries for underwater propulsion. Hobson was surprised that anyone survived a cruise, however brief. It was no wonder that submarines were referred to as floating coffins. Had he not been ordered to do so by the secretary of the navy, he would have left Holland and his odd craft behind. But the powers that be wanted a little return for their investment.

Under normal circumstances, Hobson would not have permitted a civilian like Holland to participate, but the man was the inventor, designer, and builder of the boat, had been working with the crew, and knew more about his revolutionary craft than any man alive. The *Holland,* which he had so humbly named after himself, was the sixth submarine John Holland had built and the first accepted by the navy. John Holland was determined that this one would succeed and that others would follow. It would doubtless make him a rich man, and he would use the money to help free Ireland.

A soft, chugging sound disturbed Hobson, and he turned to see the *Holland* departing its anchorage. This brought a genuine smile to Hobson. Holland and his crew had indeed been ready. Well, they had better be. They had only a few hours to make it out of the Kill Van Kull channel, which connected Newark Bay with the upper bay. Judging by the way the submarine was having to bull its way through the chop, she would need every minute of it. At four in the morning they had to be ready.

God, what an ugly duckling the submarine was, Hobson thought as he waved at the little man whose derbied head projected incongruously from the conning tower. It was time for Hobson to charge up the real weapons at his disposal.

Passage through the channel and out into the bay was a wretched endeavor. Even though the *Holland* was able to run on the surface through the channel, the hatches had to be kept closed to prevent the sub from being swamped by the waves. This made the already miserable air worse, and the men began to sicken.

Upon reaching the bay, they submerged and started to fight the currents that were trying to push them out to the ocean. All the men, Holland included, were nauseous and drenched with sweat. Holland checked his watch to estimate the distance they'd traveled, then he ordered them back to the surface, where he gazed through the small windows of the conning tower and tried to fathom where he was. If his calculations were even remotely correct, he had at least two more miles to go before he would be among the German ships and within firing range.

The submarine had one advantage that Holland hadn't told Hobson about. The Whitehead torpedo was the standard torpedo in use in most navies. It had been invented about thirty years previously. The current version carried a 220-pound warhead at a speed of twenty-eight knots and had a range of half a mile. The *Holland* carried two of them. But the one in the single torpedo tube—and this was John Holland's secret—was an experimental model, developed by two gentlemen named Bliss and Leavitt. It sacrificed warhead for range and could cruise for more than two miles. That is, if it worked.

After a while, John Holland decided he had closed the distance enough and ordered the submarine to submerge. Periodically, the sub raised itself enough for him to get a rough bearing by looking through the small, heavy glass windows of the conning tower. It was frustrating, and it defeated the purpose of being submerged. Holland thought there had to be a way to view the surface from underwater. A periscope would work if only he could figure out a way to retract it so it wouldn't be destroyed by waves and current.

The tiny sub—it was only fifty-three feet long and displaced seventy-four tons—continued its up-and-down journey until Holland again looked at his watch and saw it was only a few minutes until four. Wherever he actually was would have to do.

"Please surface, Lieutenant."

The actual crew consisted of one officer and six enlisted men. Technically, John Holland was a supernumerary, but the regular commander had recently been transferred and another young graduate of the naval academy was temporarily assigned as her captain. Although the lieutenant was eager enough and surprisingly experienced for his age—he had actually seen action during the Spanish war—he knew nothing about the sub. There was no other option; Holland had to command the vessel.

The ship bobbed to the surface. Holland opened the hatch and stuck his head and shoulders out to behold an incredible sight. To his left was the Statue of Liberty and, behind it, the squat bulk of Ellis Island. To his right lay Governors Island and the borough of Brooklyn; immediately to his front was the tip of Manhattan. Lovely though these sights were, the most exciting scene was the rows of brightly lighted German ships. All he had to do was pick one.

Holland was like a child turned loose in a toy store. Which should he choose?

"Mr. Holland, what do you see?" asked the ship's officer.

"An absolute abundance of targets, Lieutenant King. Please come and help me."

The young officer squeezed through the hatch and stood on the bobbing deck of the sub. "Absolutely amazing, sir. Not at all like Ohio." Ernest King had been born in Lorain, Ohio, twenty-three years prior and, until a few hours ago, deeply regretted the impulse that made

him volunteer for duty in the navy's first and only submarine, despite
the promotion from ensign. Now his dull world promised to be wonderfully exciting. He selected what appeared to be a large cruiser or
even a battleship about a mile away. As he understood the orders
given to Holland, the submarine was to attack warships. If they were
successful, the rest of Hobson's command could concentrate on the
vulnerable transports. "Even if we miss her, we ought to be able to
hit one of those big freighters anchored behind her."

Holland peered at the target ships and agreed. The cruiser was a generous side shot, and the freighters were anchored together in a curious cluster behind her. Although he would certainly prefer a warship,
the freighters were large, rode low in the water—which told him they
were fully loaded—and, judging by the way they were secured away
from the others, quite important.

The sub's position was adjusted for aiming. King gave the order
and the torpedo surged from the tube with a splash that Holland
feared would attract the attention of the entire German navy. It was
not so. Quiet returned and the only sounds were the grunts and cursing of the men laboring below to load a second torpedo.

Holland squinted at his stopwatch and counted down the seconds.
With only a mile to travel, the torpedo should take about two minutes
to reach its target, perhaps less. As the count neared the two-minute
mark, Holland's anxiety grew. As it reached two, he began to worry.
When the seconds continued past two minutes, he had to accept the
fact that he'd missed. He asked how soon the second torpedo would
be ready and was told a couple of minutes more. Then he realized
that he was out of range for a normal Whitehead torpedo and would
have to get much closer to a target.

He was just about to order Lieutenant King below and the sub to
get under way when a flash of light by one of the clustered freighters caught his attention.

As he watched spellbound, the flash grew into an explosion that
fed itself into a monster, turning night into day as it started to roar to
the heavens. Seconds later, the shock wave hit the submarine and
hurled John Holland into the rear of the hatch, crushing his skull and
snapping his spine into a dozen pieces. Lieutenant King, who had
been on the deck, was hurled into the sky and down into the foaming

black water. Then the *Holland,* its plates ruptured everywhere, settled into the muck of the Upper Bay.

In the Kill Van Kull, Capt. Richmond Hobson looked on incredulously. It was a few minutes past four and his little flotilla was barely under way. Ammunition ships, he realized. Holland has blown up ammunition ships. "Brace yourselves," he hollered and heard it repeated down the line of ships.

By the time the shock wave reached him, its force had dissipated substantially. Even so, it rocked him and he heard cries as several of the crew were flung to the deck. When the roar and the shock had ended, he looked toward Manhattan and beheld a sight he never could have imagined. Ships were on fire everywhere, and some of those not burning had been capsized. Exploding ammunition from a multitude of sources popped off like giant firecrackers and sent shells in all directions. It was glorious! He had no idea how the *Holland* had managed it, but what a wonderful event!

"Mr. Blaine, signal the boats forward. Nothing has changed. We will attack according to plan."

Behind him, the eleven other torpedo boat destroyers began to surge forward. They would attack in pairs, each married to a ship with corresponding speed and size. As the engines roared, Hobson allowed himself a moment of pride. These torpedo boats, often called destroyers, were considered obsolete, since they had virtually no oceangoing capability and little range. Already there were designs about for ships that were many times the size of his, which would also be called destroyers. Until the larger ships were built, however, the smaller torpedo boats would continue to be used as they were being used tonight.

As Hobson's flagship, the *Alvin,* accelerated to its maximum speed of nearly thirty knots, and its mate, the *Farragut,* ranged alongside, he thought of how difficult it had been to have all these boats shipped by rail and still retain secrecy.

The *Alvin* was one of the largest destroyers, at just over two hundred feet, and it displaced 280 tons. It had a crew of three officers and fifty-three enlisted men but only two precious torpedoes. Hobson thought she was overlarge for this small a payload. The smallest destroyer was the *Talbot,* which was only ninety-nine feet long, had a crew of fifteen, and chugged along at a mere twenty-one knots, although she too had a pair of torpedoes. The disparity in sizes reflected the confusion in the Navy Department as to exactly what the so-called destroyers were supposed to do. Tonight, their task was quite simple. They were to sink Germans ships.

With their greater speeds, the destroyers needed only a few moments to come into clear view of the carnage wrought by the *Holland*. As they roared past a burning cruiser, they chose to ignore the mortally wounded ship. It would likely sink without their assistance. Hobson looked around and saw his well-trained and meticulously instructed crews peel their ships off and begin to make attacking runs. His orders had been quite simple: one torpedo for one ship. If the first missed, or the target didn't sink, crews could use another, but they were not to intentionally fire two at one ship. He had also instructed them to ignore empty transports unless there were no other targets available. Let Remey's vultures pick them off.

It was then that Hobson realized his further good fortune. Although the fires had illuminated the harbor and deprived him of the cover of darkness, the Germans were in such shock that they hadn't even noticed his boats. Or perhaps they thought their own ships were coming to their aid. After all, who would have expected a dozen American destroyers in the midst of the German convoy? He could only hope that they could make their attack and get away before the Germans recognized their mistake.

The rattle of machine-gun fire and pop of 1-pound cannon firing told him that he would not get his wish. He lurched and grabbed a railing as the boat righted itself after launching a torpedo. There was no time to watch for results as the *Alvin*'s skipper turned sharply to avoid machine-gun fire and find another ship. The *Alvin*'s gunners added to the din by shooting at anything within range. All around him were the explosions of other torpedoes striking home. It occurred to him that there was a real danger of crossing one of their own torpedoes' paths in the chaos of the swirling attack.

The *Alvin*'s second torpedo was launched only moments later, and then it was time to depart. Signaling the *Farragut* to return to base without him, Hobson ordered the *Alvin* to stand off in the harbor and wait for his boats to race by. When the count stopped at eight, he knew that three of his small craft would not be returning.

He looked about and realized that the harbor was a circle of flaming buildings and ships. All about him the sky was turning red, not from a false dawn but from the multitude of fires burning on Manhattan and in Jersey City and Brooklyn. He gasped when he realized the Statue of Liberty was headless and without her outstretched torch and arm.

Hobson ordered the *Alvin*'s captain to circle while he assessed the damage on the land. Most of the German warehouses on the Brooklyn side were giant torches and continued to be racked by explosions. As he watched, the wall of one burning building collapsed on another, creating a huge shower of sparks that fell on running figures. He thought he could hear their screams.

On Manhattan, he could see numbers of people running about in panic, some even jumping into the water to escape the fires that had burst in on their sleep. Where had all the people come from? Hadn't the island been evacuated by the Germans? Or were these Germans he was seeing? Not likely. He knew that part of town was populated by immigrants, and it appeared that many had remained regardless of the kaiser's orders. On the New Jersey side, the damage seemed to be substantially less, as a result of the greater distance from the explosions. Already, people were starting to work on the fires, and there seemed to be a little less chaos as well. As he watched, fingers of water began lifting from horse-drawn pumpers and onto burning buildings.

He had intended to hurt the Germans and had accomplished his task. But had he hurt his own country worse? Totally confused and disoriented, he ordered a return to Newark Bay. What had he done?

Roosevelt's face was red. He was upset and distraught. "Would someone please tell me why it was necessary to destroy several of our largest cities in the course of that action? Is this our definition of victory? My lord, spare us from future victories if that is the case!"

Hay tried to soothe him. "Now Theodore, buildings can be rebuilt and, frankly, I don't think the damage or loss of life to civilians is as great as the rumormongers say."

Longstreet agreed. "Sir, I think you'll find that the damage to Jersey City and Newark was confined to the dock and warehouse areas, and the local population was able to put out the fires in a few hours.

As to Brooklyn, well, virtually the only buildings left undamaged from the earlier fires were the ones being used by the Krauts for storage, and that makes them legitimate targets. I don't think we care how many Germans or collaborators were killed."

"But what about Manhattan?" Roosevelt wailed, reminding all that it had been his home.

"Regrettable, sir," said Hay, "but let's put the blame where it belongs. The Germans made it an armed camp, and it was the Germans who moved out the civilians and the city organization that might have stopped the fires. To be blunt, the bulk of the damage from the exploding ammunition was largely confined to the slums and tenements of the Lower East Side, and those buildings are no great loss, if you ask me. Again, we will rebuild. As to the numbers of American civilians dead on Manhattan, it is tragic, but, hell, we may never know."

Roosevelt sank back in his chair. "All right. But Governor Voorhees has been on the phone several times in the last two days and wants blood."

"German blood, I trust," said Longstreet dryly. "Mr. President, some of the people of New Jersey were living in a fool's paradise. How could they expect to get through a war and not be involved in it with the enemy only a mile away? Why not tell Voorhees to go to hell?"

Roosevelt smiled at last. "I can't. He's a Republican." He rose and began to pace. "All right, you tell me it was a victory, but what did we win?"

John Long cleared his throat. "Well, now that the rains have come back and helped drown most of the fires, and we have been able to reestablish our lookout posts on Manhattan and in Jersey City, we can tell you that an undetermined number of transports were sunk and at least twenty-five badly damaged. We can logically assume their cargoes have been largely destroyed. As to warships"—he paused and allowed a catlike smile—"we believe two heavy cruisers, one light cruiser, and two gunboats were sunk, and that two heavies and four lights were damaged. By damaged I mean it will be some time, months, before they will be back in service."

"Good," said Roosevelt, then he saw the smile on Long's face widen. "What else do you have for me, John?"

"Three capital ships were in the harbor. They were not sunk but they were badly damaged. They are no longer a factor and will not be available for the kaiser's use for quite some time. They can probably be repaired, but not in the short run."

Longstreet whistled. "Thirteen to twelve."

Secretary Long laughed. "Yes, their advantage is now but one battleship, and we are confident our twelve are at least equivalent to their thirteen."

Roosevelt leaned forward. "Does that mean Dewey will do battle?"

"It does. The information has been cabled to him, and he is now trying to determine a proper time and place to do battle."

"Capital!" said Roosevelt, who chuckled at his own bad joke.

"It gets better," added Longstreet. "The warehouses destroyed in Brooklyn along with the ships in the harbor, particularly those ammo ships that started all the ruckus, made up the greater part of the Germans' strategic reserve. About half their ammunition, most of their food, and virtually all of their winter uniforms are now gone. Those German boys are gonna get hungry and freeze their tails off pretty soon." He turned to Long. "You might not have known this, but those warehouses also contained a lot of naval supplies, including their coal reserves, which they'd been piling up on Governors Island. Those piles are now glowing a bright cherry red. They have a real problem on their hands."

Elihu Root finally spoke. "James, are you suggesting they won't be able to fight?"

"Oh, hell no. They can fight and fight hard. They just can't fight for very damn long. One or two major battles and what they have on hand in their units, as well as their tactical reserves, will be used up. Then they will be in real big trouble."

"What a lovely picture." Roosevelt laughed. "So what will they do about it? Resupply?"

"Yes," said Root. "It will have to be quick and massive. That is just about their only option. When that occurs, we feel they will then try to end this war as quickly and as savagely as possible. Sir, we have won a battle, but we may have set some terrible forces in motion, forces we are not yet ready to control."

Roosevelt pondered. "So be it," he said solemnly. "Now, what about our casualties?"

Long cleared his throat. "In the initial phase of the attack, we lost three destroyers sunk and most others damaged. There were about 150 men killed and wounded. In the second phase, when the Germans sent some cruisers through the Kill Van Kull and attacked the remainder at anchor, we lost the surviving nine destroyers and another hundred men. That should not have happened, but no one thought the Germans would counterattack. The New Jersey Militia on guard simply ran as the cruisers entered the harbor and started pounding the docks. The destroyers had not yet been rearmed with torpedoes and were sitting ducks. Hobson and the rest of his men ran down the streets and tried to make themselves scarce in the city. It was a rather inglorious end to a glorious beginning. On the plus side, we did find a survivor from that submarine we experimented with, the *Holland*. One of the departing destroyers found him floating in the harbor. The man is badly hurt but he did confirm that it was the sub's torpedo that hit an ammunition ship and started the whole shebang."

Roosevelt snarled. "Well, thank God for that. Now, what was wrong with the militia? Didn't they fire at all?"

"No, sir. Either they were too terrified or their orders were to not do anything to further upset the Germans."

"Damn them!" In frustration, Roosevelt turned to the issue of the torpedo boats. "There are a lot of docks and wharves in that area. How did the Germans know where our little ships were?"

"Sir," said Long, "it could have been spies, but I think they saw where the crowds were." He grimaced. "Some well-meaning supporters had festooned the area with flags."

Longstreet chuckled. "Well, at least your idea went off a whole lot better than I had planned. I was just going to put some of those big guns we borrowed from the navy on Staten Island and try to close the Narrows."

Roosevelt's jaw dropped. "You could close the Narrows?"

"Probably not entirely," he admitted, "but we could make entering the upper bay a real adventure for them. I'm thinking we'll still do it. They may have to land some troops to push us off Staten Island, and then we'll get a chance to fight them in the open."

Roosevelt thought it was a good idea. "Now, what about Hobson? A medal or a court-martial followed by a public hanging?"

"A medal," said Long. The others agreed, with the exception of Longstreet, who said he hadn't seen a hanging in a number of years.

The kaiser was pale and drawn. "How could this have happened? A submarine? Torpedo boats? And at just the moment when we had so much to lose? How did the Americans find out? There must be traitors in our midst. There is no other answer. We will find them and exterminate them, whoever they are."

Holstein took a deep breath and turned to Tirpitz. "Were our losses in New York that severe?"

Tirpitz, normally serene in his confidence and powerful in his bearing, looked uncomfortable. "Of the smaller ships, a few cruisers were indeed sunk or damaged, as were a number of transports. Two of our capital ships, the *Brandenburg* and the *Odin,* were also damaged. They will have to return to Germany for repairs."

Holstein nodded. And that cannot possibly happen until the war is over. They might as well have been sunk, too. He also had it on good authority that a third capital ship had been damaged as well. Tirpitz must have been hoping it could be repaired before his kaiser determined the true extent of the disaster. "And all this from a submarine and some little torpedo boats?"

Tirpitz was agitated. "The use of a ship that can go underwater is unmanly. As the kaiser says, a stab in the back."

"Do we have any of those strange little ships?" Schlieffen asked.

"No," answered Tirpitz.

"And we won't," snapped the kaiser. "Those are coward ships. Let the Americans and the French have them. We will never stoop to that kind of warfare. Battleships," he said, smiling at Tirpitz, "will win this war for us."

Schlieffen rose. Clearly concerned, his face was flushed with uncharacteristic anger. "Battleships? Have you forgotten, All Highest, that an army moves on its stomach? Our food, clothing, and ammunition reserves are gone and with them much of our ability to wage war." He wheeled and confronted Tirpitz. "I want to know if those supplies will be replaced and just how soon! If they do not arrive within the next few weeks, we will be forced to take drastic action to end this war before the onset of winter makes resupply via the North Atlantic an even more chancy affair than it is now!"

Tirpitz's face was pale. He was not used to being scolded. "We have already started the resupply effort," he countered. "Transports from all sources are being gathered and loaded with equipment and supplies. Soon there will be a massive convoy, an armada of more than a hundred transports with everything your army and my navy will need. Furthermore, the kaiser has given me directions that another corps of reserve soldiers will be shipped over with them. I will provide that convoy with the strongest possible escort, and it will get through."

Now it was Schlieffen's turn to be startled. He had not been informed that more of his army was being sent to America. A reserve corps would likely be another twenty-five thousand men. Twenty-five thousand additional stomachs to feed and backs to clothe. He recovered quickly and turned to Tirpitz. "You guarantee their arrival?" His voice was a sneer, and even the kaiser looked uncomfortable.

"Yes."

"You will be using the High Seas Fleet to protect it?"

Tirpitz shook his head vehemently. "No, of course not. We cannot entirely denude Germany of naval protection with the French still so angry at us and the English and Americans off our coasts. No, we will use our existing resources. They will be more than sufficient." They will have to be, Holstein thought. "The convoy will get through!" Tirpitz slammed his beefy fist on the table. "On my honor!"

Holstein had often wondered about Tirpitz's honor, and he wondered, therefore, about the worth of the oath. He remained silent, and the meeting was adjourned. While leaving, he managed to walk beside Chancellor von Bulow.

"Von Bulow, you look pale. Do you perhaps have stock in Hamburg-America?"

Bulow barked a laugh. The Hamburg-America Line was the largest shipping company in Germany and one of the largest in the world. When a transport was sunk or captured, it was often one of theirs. "Don't we all? No, that is not the problem. When von Tirpitz said we were gathering ships from all over, he didn't say how that was being accomplished. Very simply, the German navy is now commandeering anything that floats and damn the owners, regardless of nationality."

Even Holstein was astonished. "We are seizing foreign flag vessels?"

"Only from small countries. But there are many of them and they include some of our neighbors, like Holland, Belgium, Norway, and Sweden."

"Not England, dear God, not England."

"No, nor any of the lands of the British Empire. Nor are we taking ships on the high seas. But I feel we are courting disaster. Those foreign countries will demand compensation, and will probably not permit other ships to enter our waters until we agree. They may close their ports to our ships as well. Can you imagine the effect on our economy? We will be devastated before long."

Holstein could indeed imagine. It was becoming increasingly apparent that the war must be won soon if it were to be won at all.

"Von Bulow, have you considered what might happen if we did not win?"

Bulow paled. "It would be a catastrophe, von Holstein, a catastrophe."

When Ian Gordon returned to his quarters in the pleasant cottage rented for him by His Majesty's government, he was surprised by the carriage waiting in front of it. His first thought was that it was Mrs. Adams, the woman he'd taken home from the wedding. She was getting to be a bore. He'd had no idea just how much pale fat her clothing obscured. Worse, she was obsessed with him, and he could think of nothing less appealing than someone who continuously craved sex with him and then performed poorly. If it were only his physical needs that required fulfilling, he could accomplish that by himself, as he had as a youth.

He entered his home and his valet informed him of a gentleman waiting for him in the parlor. Did Mrs. Adams have a husband? She had said she was a widow. He entered the parlor and laughed in relief.

"Captain Sigsbee, how are you?"

Sigsbee rose and assured him he was fine. Sigsbee was dressed in a civilian suit and not his naval uniform. It did not surprise Ian, since Sigsbee was the recently appointed director of the Office of Naval Intelligence (ONI). "Ian, I see you've managed to land comfortably again."

"Certainly. After all I am an observer and not a participant. Let the common soldiers live in tents and trenches; I prefer a solid roof and greater comforts." He poured each of them a brandy and offered cigars, which Sigsbee declined.

"How is the Office of Naval Intelligence? Have you finally gotten into the spying game?" Ian asked. It was a sore point. The ONI and its army equivalent were solely charged with gathering factual data from open sources about other countries' militaries. They did not spy.

"No," Sigsbee said, "not yet. We'll leave spying to you British. You're so much better at it than we naive Americans."

"Had you been less naive, Charles, you might not have gone to war with Spain. Did you really believe that saboteurs blew up the *Maine?*"

Sigsbee hid his grimace behind the snifter. He had been the captain of the *Maine* when it blew up in Havana harbor and had endorsed the theory of sabotage. He had never been quite comfortable with that conclusion. "I had doubts."

"Like a lingering fire in a coal bunker being the actual cause? I know. But enough of old times. You obviously have a reason for being here."

"Indeed. Although we do not spy, sometimes we find things out about our supposed friends that we don't particularly like."

Ian put down his glass. Sigsbee's eyes were cold. "Through informal but reliable sources we have reason to believe that His Majesty's government is providing Germany with information about our navy, such as its location and disposition. Since you are the senior British officer about, and since you also met recently with your prime minister, I thought you might wish to comment."

Ian thought for a moment, then he spoke softly. "Someone once said that England is interested only in England, and will go to any lengths to protect England. That, of course, is quite true."

"You admit it?"

"I admit nothing. It is very much in England's best interest that Germany not win this war. Notice, I did not say that Germany had to lose, just not win. To assist in this, we have been providing you with both materiel and information. Yet we live in an imperfect world and must confront the fact that a German victory is still very probable. Should that occur, we shall have to continue living with them. Thus all our efforts against them must be indirect so that Germany will not become so irrationally angry as to go to war against us."

"Surely the navy could stop them."

"Certainly. But our very real fear is that the Germans will attempt an invasion and that it will, even if unsuccessful, result in a massive bloodletting for very little gain. It is a situation best avoided."

"What are you saying? Is Britain providing them with information or not?"

"Charles, German military intelligence is not an oxymoron. They are quite clever. Even though we never announced it publicly, they've known where the American fleet was gathering since the earliest days of the war. As to the status of particular ships, well really. Just a few weeks ago the *Texas* had to put in to Halifax because of a boiler problem. Some secret! Germany has a consulate in Halifax; even if it didn't, are you so sure that all the German immigrants are honest citizens? If you were the kaiser, wouldn't you plant some spies among them, both in the civilian sector and on your own ships?"

Sigsbee looked uncomfortable. "The matter of immigrants is one of grave concern. There are many Germans in our army and our navy and I am indeed worried about them. Others tell me not to be concerned because so many of them fought so well against Spain or in the Civil War, but those wars were not against their homeland."

Gordon laughed. "Fighting your so-called homeland is not a unique experience. I seem to recall a recent war in which Americans killed hundreds of thousands of other Americans. Previously, those who called themselves British fought those who no longer wished to be British. I do not think the vast majority of Germans will disappoint you with their patriotic zeal."

Sigsbee was unconvinced. "I have ordered a complete check of all Germans in our navy and will be demanding proof of their loyalty. I have no idea why Longstreet and Root aren't concerned about the army."

"Captain, I seem to recall that many of those immigrants, although they may have been proud of some aspects of their old land, left it because of oppression and tyranny. Germany today is more a prison for some than it is a nation." He thought of the workers' revolutions that had enflamed Europe in the middle of the previous century and the brutal manner in which they were put down, even in England. In Germany, pleas for a more democratic form of government were ignored by Bismarck and the kaisers. Wilhelm II was reaping what others had sown. "Please recall, sir, that your army now has several regiments made up of German volunteers."

Sigsbee nodded thoughtfully. "I also seem to recall they haven't been permitted to fight yet." When Ian informed him of their numerous small-unit actions in the no-man's-land, he expressed surprise. "Well then, I guess those boys are all right. Must be descended from the ones who left because of the kaiser, eh? But that's another tale, and you're trying to distract me from my purpose. Let's get back to what the German command knows. Is England providing them with information, other than what you think is obvious?"

"Of course."

"But why?"

"Charles, by providing them with information, we are ensuring our status with them in the unhappy event you lose."

"Perfidious Albion again."

"If you wish. However, we are providing them only with data that would have been theirs sooner or later anyhow. Such as confirming the presence of your fleet, which they have known for some time. Their diplomats were even chartering pleasure craft for 'fishing expeditions' and scouring the Gulf of Saint Lawrence looking for the fleet. As to other matters, much of what they have learned they also would have found out sooner rather than later. For instance, the names of commanding officers are no secret. When Captain Brownson replaced Evans on the *Alabama,* it was reported in his hometown newspapers. Similarly, the technical data on your ships is also available in *Jane's Fighting Ships* and other places. No, what we are doing is establishing ourselves as a source with impeccable credentials. The fact that we have, to date at least, given them largely irrelevant data is itself unimportant."

Sigsbee's eyes widened. "Ian, are you perfidious people setting them up for a fall?"

Gordon grinned and offered a freshened drink. "Charles, would we do that? Are you staying for dinner?"

Chapter 24

AT THIRTY-EIGHT, Rear Adm. Franz von Hipper was one of the youngest admirals in the German navy. He felt the weight of his responsibilities as he paced the bridge of his flagship, the *Furst Bismarck*. She was a heavy cruiser of almost eleven thousand tons capable of nineteen knots. She carried four 9.4-inch guns in her main battery and twelve 6-inch guns in her secondary, along with a host of smaller weapons. The *Furst Bismarck* was new and impressive. Hipper almost dared the American cruisers to attack.

Yet, he chided himself, battle with the damned Yanks was not his mission. His duty was to ensure the safe arrival of the awesome panoply of ships that steamed in seemingly endless ranks behind him. It was the largest convoy in modern military history and it had to get safely to New York. Behind him in ten rows were almost 150 steamers and freighters of all shapes and sizes, and from a dozen disparate nations. Not all had come willingly. It was too bad that Germany had to seize so many foreign ships by force, but the needs of the Reich came before the conveniences of Brazil and Holland. Many of the captains had screamed and cursed and not been willing to comply, until detachments of armed sailors were added to their ships to ensure their cooperation. That a few of the damned foreigners had continued to resist and died was of no consequence. The German flagships had, of course, come willingly.

Hipper's eyes took in the magnificent view. To his right were the chalky cliffs of England. To his left were the beaches of France. The Channel was gray and choppy and there was a bite in the air that hinted of an early and cold winter. All the more reason to get the convoy to New York as quickly as possible. Along with the additional three divisions of sullen reserves, the ships were crammed with uniforms, blankets, tents, food, and, of course, ammunition. Included also were a number of colliers stuffed with coal for the North Atlantic Fleet. To his amazement, there were ships loaded with forage for the army's many horses. Couldn't the land of plenty provide anything?

Far to his front he could barely see the screen of light cruisers. He ordered the *Furst Bismarck* to signal them to stay in sight, and signal lamps quickly flashed the message. He and his heavy-cruiser squadron, along with the three battleships of the High Seas Fleet, led the convoy. Smaller cruisers and gunboats of all sizes and ages flanked it and brought up the rear. The presence of the battleships was reassuring. Hipper was thankful that reason had prevailed and a compromise had been reached regarding the use of the fleet. Specifically, it had been publicly announced that the battleships and a number of cruisers would escort the convoy until it was met off New York by the main battle fleet under Admiral Diedrichs. It was also stated that such a force would be more than adequate to prevent the Yanks from trying something stupid.

Unfortunately, it was not entirely true. Although the capital ships of the High Seas Fleet would sail quite a ways out into the Atlantic and ensure that the American cruisers under that devil Evans did not attack, they would turn back well before New York and make a surprise return to European waters. It was somehow hoped that this would both protect Germany and possibly trap Evans's cruisers in confined waters. Hipper didn't understand the first reason and seriously doubted the second, since Evans had proven himself quite capable of avoiding traps. But such is the nature of compromises. Still, he was happy that Evans's six remaining cruisers were now well behind the convoy and not likely to cause trouble.

A lookout announced the presence of British warships hugging the shadow of the English landscape. Hipper was puzzled. Did the British really think Germany would invade England? He laughed. Who would want the damp and dreary place? It would not be long before they were out of the Channel and into the North Atlantic. Already reports told of cold weather and high, stormy seas. He would have the devil's own time keeping so many ships together in tidy ranks when each captain had his own mind and each ship had its own sea-keeping capabilities. Worse, regardless of the weather, the convoy was limited to the speed of its slowest members. Because the convoy had been thrown together in haste, there were some real tubs gurgling along at turtle speed. Hipper was young now, but he might be much older by the time they reached New York. But make it they would.

Young Admiral von Hipper announced he was going to his cabin. All was well.

The kaiser squeezed a glove in his right hand. It was a poor substitute for wringing both hands together, but it was all he could accomplish considering the withered condition of his left hand.

"Von Tirpitz, how soon?"

Tirpitz's voice was deep and strong. "Only a few days, All Highest, then our ships will turn back and the Reich will be safe."

"But what if the American cruisers arrive here first and attack our ports?"

Tirpitz shook his head. The kaiser loved his warships and had read all he could find on naval theory, but his fears still needed to be allayed. "If they come, All Highest, our coastal fortifications will destroy them. We have spent enormous amounts of time and money on those coastal batteries. I wish the Americans would attack so we could see how well we spent our resources."

The kaiser acknowledged the point. It was also one of the longest statements the normally taciturn admiral had made. It was said that Tirpitz could be genial and friendly under the right circumstances, but when the topic was his beloved navy, the man was all formality and business.

"Then Diedrichs's forces meet the convoy. How wonderful." The kaiser chuckled. "And then we spring the trap on the Americans."

Tirpitz smiled, itself an unusual occurrence under the circumstances. "They will be trapped and defeated. With the reinforcements in the convoy, we will be able to put an end to this nonsense."

Uncertain for a moment precisely what Tirpitz meant by nonsense, the kaiser turned and gazed at a large map of the eastern United States. "But do we want it to end?" he said softly. "I have been thinking. If we defeat the American navy, we can have what we first wanted in the way of islands and coaling stations and rights to dig canals. But we can also have much more."

"And what might that be?" Holstein asked.

"New England," the kaiser responded eagerly. "If we cannot conquer old England, then let us take the new one. With the forces that will be at our disposal and with the American military in ruins, why can't we lay claim to all American lands east of the Hudson River? The Hudson would present a nice, defensible boundary, and we would own several of the richest states in America."

"Interesting," said Tirpitz. Only Bulow and Schlieffen looked even a little dismayed. Holstein hid his personal feelings behind a mask of imperturbability. Why did the kaiser continue to think the Yanks would trade states the way European powers traded provinces? Clearly the kaiser had forgotten that the United States had, in his own lifetime, fought a war so bloody that it had cost many hundreds of thousands dead just to preserve its union. Certainly it would not accede to such demands, and if Germany did attempt to force such a measure, the Reich would have to govern millions of angry and hostile people who were poorly disposed to obey orders.

"I agree with our admiral," Holstein said finally. "Your proposal is indeed quite interesting and contains many possibilities. But first things first. The convoy must make it to New York. Admiral, I sincerely hope the young men you have chosen for these coming tasks possess the wisdom and talent to prevail."

Tirpitz bowed slightly, acknowledging the fact that his and his navy's futures were on the line. "I have every confidence in their abilities."

In the spacious stateroom aboard his flagship, Admiral Diedrichs stared at the orders in his hand. He was confused but dared not show it. The orders were quite specific: he was to send a strong part of his fleet to escort the convoy as it neared the American coast, while maintaining the greater portion of it in New York harbor. The order, which came from Tirpitz and had been concurred with by the kaiser, was detailed. It specifically named the ships to be used for each purpose. Not for the first time, he cursed the transatlantic cable that sped messages from Berlin to him. He handed the sheet of paper to his aide, Captain Paschwitz, who read the orders and was equally puzzled.

"Admiral, it would be folly to split our forces. We could be defeated in detail by the American fleet."

"I agree," said Diedrichs. He dropped his voice even though he and Paschwitz were alone. "However, there was a second and private message. Berlin has information that Yankee spies will falsely say that the Americans are going to attack the convoy with their entire fleet. They will not. It will be a feint. The Americans want us to rush out with our entire fleet, which will give them the opportunity to attack the harbor and close it off. It would not take too many ships in the harbor to seal the Narrows and turn it into a gauntlet we would have to run. Without the harbor, the convoy would have no place to land. We could retake it, but that would be both time-consuming and costly, since the Americans would reinforce their batteries on Staten Island and move in army units to help them.

"However, we are ordered to do just the reverse. Much of our fleet will remain here while a strong force steams to the convoy to help it beat off the feint. After defeating the American feint, it is hoped that the reinforced convoy escort can join with us in smashing the American fleet as it does battle with us."

Paschwitz retrieved the order and read it a second time. "But what if they are wrong, Admiral? This seems too incredible."

Admiral Diedrichs walked to the window of his stateroom. He could see the ruins of Manhattan in the distance. "We have our orders, Captain Paschwitz, and we will obey them."

Several days after the departure of the High Seas Fleet, Hipper and others had cheered lustily when the picket ships announced the arrival of the reinforcement squadron from New York. He'd exulted when he'd first spied the masts of the line of mighty ships as they came across the horizon. But his exultation had turned to dismay when the ships came close enough to be counted and identified. Where was the North Atlantic Fleet and its capital ships? Certainly a portion of it was coming to meet him, six battleships to be exact—

and under the command of his friend and rival Maximilian von Spee. But where was the remainder? Instead, he had another six cruisers, and light ones at that, to flesh out his escort. Where the hell was the rest of the fleet?

The trip across the Atlantic had been the epitome of misery. Squalls and high seas continually threatened to scatter Hipper's ships as they plowed with exquisite slowness in the general direction of North America. The escort crews were exhausted and the machinery was fatigued by the need to chase down strays and return them to the dubious bosom of the convoy, and too damn much coal had been burned while they steamed at such inefficiently slow speeds.

Of the 146 ships in the original convoy, 7 had turned back because of mechanical failures and 4 had simply disappeared. Although they might have sunk unnoticed in a night squall, there were more sinister possibilities. Perhaps the sailors sent as guards had been overpowered and killed, and the ships had escaped. If Hipper ever found them, he would hang their crews.

Now, with the battleship squadron ahead and Spee, as senior admiral, clearly in charge, Hipper thought about the surprising change in the military situation of which Spee had managed to advise him via signal lamp. Both ships had wireless, but the *Furst Bismarck*'s had quit working the day before.

How fortunate that German intelligence had found out about the American plans. What a wonderful opportunity! The Yanks were going to send only a small force of four capital ships as a decoy against the convoy while the remainder attacked New York harbor and tried to retake it. How diabolical. If they succeeded, the convoy would be rendered useless because it would have no place to go, and the army would be trapped. But now Diedrichs, with the rest of the battle fleet and the cruisers, lay in ambush for the Americans at New York. Hipper wished that he and Admiral Spee would arrive so they could crush the arrogant Yanks between their two forces—after, of course, defeating the token Yank force sent to distract them.

"How far to New York now?" Hipper asked.

"Just over two hundred miles, sir," the navigator answered quickly. Hipper knew that it was an estimate but it would do. A couple of days and they would be safe.

Distant signals from a ship in the advance screen caught his eye:

"enemy ships in sight." He sucked in his breath and heard others on the bridge gasp as well. It was time. They had sailed long and far for this moment. He would not fail Tirpitz, his kaiser, or the Reich.

High in his perch on the *Alabama,* Ens. Terry Schuyler contemplated several things. First, it was his birthday and there was a good possibility that it would be his last. Second, he was going to be a witness to history.

The lookout post was jammed with Schuyler, another named Lt. James Sloan, and four seamen. All were constantly yelling information into the phones and speaking tubes, trying desperately to keep the men on the bridge informed of what they saw.

And what they could see was stunning. The *Alabama* was fourth in the long line of battleships steaming in a basically southerly direction. First was the *Iowa,* which was serving as Dewey's flagship. It was followed by the *Oregon* and *Indiana* and then the *Alabama.* Behind the *Alabama* in a stately line came the *Illinois, Kentucky, Massachusetts, Wisconsin, Kearsarge,* and *Texas.* They were followed by the armored cruisers *New York* and *Brooklyn* and the protected cruiser *Olympia* of Manila Bay fame. The American navy considered all of these capital ships.

In a separate squadron slightly behind the main battle line came three monitors. Slow and unseaworthy, they had been designed for coastal defense and took the waves poorly. But they did have heavy guns and could be a force in the coming battle.

To either side were scores of smaller ships—cruisers and gunboats primarily, although there was a handful of torpedo boat destroyers. These latter had been towed by the monitors to conserve fuel. There was even a score or so of armed yachts. If it could float and carry a gun, it was out there.

"Schuyler, did you say something?" asked Lieutenant Sloan.

Terry realized he must have been thinking out loud. "No, sir."

"Captain wants a confirmed count on the German big ships."

Terry nodded and took a telescope from one of the seamen. Many of the German ships were not yet in view, but, as happened so often, their presence was given away by the feather of smoke caused by their coal-burning engines. In this case, the number of such smoky feathers was almost beyond count. If they were all warships, then the

American navy, signaling its presence with its own smoke, was in deep trouble.

Terry tried to focus on the line of dark shapes that seemed to be coming directly at them. He could almost imagine them to be giant beetles. What were they, battleships or cruisers? The answer could bear directly on whether he saw another birthday.

Lieutenant Sloan was new to the *Alabama*. He had been serving on the steam tug *Triton* at Norfolk and had been transferred to the battleship as the navy made frantic attempts to make up the officer shortage on the all-important capital ships. Terry had spent many long nights memorizing the shapes of German ships, and he knew that Lieutenant Sloan would defer to his expertise. He also knew that the captain must have already received some information regarding the advancing enemy from Dewey, who was much closer to the Germans in the *Oregon,* and doubtless wanted a second opinion.

"Lieutenant," Terry said, trying to be formal and also to keep the quiver from his voice. Off duty, Sloan was a very good guy and insisted Terry call him Jim, but this was for history. "I count nine in a line. They're all over the horizon now and, if there are others, they're not in this battle line."

He heard Sloan relay the information into the phone and then into the speaking tube. Already Terry felt better. If that was all there were, they might be in good shape. He squinted and tried to make specific identifications.

"Who are they?" asked Sloan, his voice almost a yell. Terry waved him off and held the ships in focus. He was trying to remember. He smiled and put down the telescope.

"Six battleships and three heavies."

"Jesus," said Sloan and repeated the figures. Even through the tinny and scratchy phone, they could hear the shouts from the bridge. Terry slumped against the railing of the tower. Ten American battleships, three heavy cruisers, and three monitors against six battleships and three cruisers. They just might pull it off.

As the *Furst Bismarck* took its place in line behind the last of Spee's battleships, Admiral von Hipper knew a moment of deep dread. He looked at the faces of the others on the bridge and realized they felt it as well. This was no token force. This was the entire American navy! Diedrichs, Tirpitz, and the kaiser had all been fooled. Hipper could only trust that the remainder of the German fleet had realized the error, was now steaming to their rescue, and would come up behind the Americans and crush them in the vise he had hoped to see off New York. He also knew he was clutching at the proverbial straw. It was the German fleet and not the American fleet that was caught in the vise. The smaller warships guarding the convoy would have to be on their own until the American battleships were defeated—if they were defeated. There was no other choice.

Admiral von Hipper's lookouts continued to provide him with information about the swarms of light cruisers, gunboats, and small ships now streaking toward the convoy like wolves toward fat sheep. Wolves, he thought. The smaller Yank ships were wolves and were attacking as wolf packs. They would overwhelm the flank escorts and the rear guard in detail and chew up the convoy, and there was nothing he could do about it.

The precious convoy he had sworn to protect was as good as lost. Even if relief came immediately, the American wolf packs would have sunk or damaged so many of the transports that the effort would be useless. It was already useless! Now his only alternative was to fight for survival. His survival and that of his ship and the Imperial Navy were at stake. The future of the Reich's navy was going to be decided this day in the North Atlantic.

He and his ships had been betrayed and were outnumbered, he thought bitterly. It would take a heroic effort, hard and desperate fighting, to drive off the Americans. Could they do it?

"The Americans have opened fire!"

He nodded, having caught the winking of lights from the distant lead ships. Too far away. They were just barely in range. They were wasting ammunition. Automatically, he counted off the seconds and waited for the fall of shot. When it came, he was stunned to see how close the opening salvos were to the leading German ships.

"They've fired again."

"Impossible!" he snapped, trying to refute the evidence of his eyes that beheld the line of lights again flashing from the still-distant but rapidly closing shapes. Experience told him ships cannot fire that fast. Yet they were. This time the first two German battleships were straddled by giant splashes that lifted dirty, wet towers into the sky. Bracketed, he moaned, bracketed already and we haven't yet fired.

On board the *Alabama,* the opening salvos shook the ship and deafened Terry and the others despite the wads of cotton in their ears.

"My God," said Sloan. "Look for splashes."

Terry nodded and held the binoculars tightly against his face. The ships ahead had fired first and, as he looked, let off a quick second salvo. There were splashes ahead of the German line taller than the ships themselves. Soon, as the enemy steamed on, hits were scored on the lead ships. Within moments, all the American ships were firing away with their main batteries while the secondary batteries, with their shorter range, waited their turn. Terry could not believe the noise and vibration. It was beyond anything he had ever thought possible.

The Germans began returning fire with a vengeance as they found the range and scored repeated hits of their own on their tormentors. For salvo after salvo the ships closed the range and hurled tons of hot and angry metal at each other. Terry was buffeted and thrown to the deck of the tower several times by the impact of shells striking the *Alabama,* and once he was almost thrown over the side. He wondered if the ship would sink as clouds of smoke engulfed him.

As the battle reached full fury, the Germans continued to press closer while the Americans maneuvered to maintain more distance, trusting in their better long-range firing skills. As the two lines of ships passed starboard side to each other, the three monitors, armed with 10- and 12-inch guns, broke out of line and turned sharply starboard. The effect was to execute a crossing of the German T while still keeping the line of battle essentially intact. Caught between two fires, the lead German battleships were literally blown to pieces. One of the monitors exploded under return fire and sank quickly. Terry thought it was the *Puritan*. The monitors' sudden maneuver broke the German line, and the remainder of the battle became a swirling melee as ships sought and battled each other, sometimes as pairs, sometimes as clusters of three or four.

Terry nearly screamed when it appeared that the *Alabama* was actually going to ram a badly damaged German cruiser, but the *Alabama* veered and missed the German vessel by only about a hundred yards. With something to do at last, the smaller guns on the *Alabama* raked the burning and distorted German cruiser, the *Furst Bismarck*. Terry watched in horror as unprotected sailors were blown to bits, some tumbling into the cold water. Wherever Terry looked, battles like this were taking place.

A German shell landed in the water beside the *Alabama* and lifted a huge column of black water filled with metal high over Terry's head. When it came down, the crow's nest was drenched in heavy foam and raked with steel splinters, slamming Terry to the floor of his post. He started to say something when he realized he was lying on his side and couldn't move. His vision blurred and then blackened.

Terry screamed as a heavy foot came down on his injured shoulder. As consciousness returned, he thought the shoulder was either broken or dislocated; it felt as though knives were ripping into his bones as he lay on the floor of the tower. "Watch out," he moaned.

The response was the sound of an animal in agony. Terry forced himself to look up at the man who'd stepped on him, and he recoiled in horror. It was one of the enlisted men, and there was nothing but raw meat where his eyes and nose had been. Terry used his good arm to pull the man down to him and tried to wrap a cloth about his head to protect the wound. The sailor screamed once, tried to say something, then collapsed unconscious across Terry's waist.

Terry managed to wriggle out and pull himself upright. He was covered with blood, but apparently not much of it was his. Was he the only one left alive? No. Thank God, no. Others in that cramped space were moving as well, but a couple were ominously still. He heard sounds and picked up the phone. Dead. He tried the voice tube and heard the distant plea of the executive officer yelling for someone, anyone.

"I'm here, sir, Ensign Schuyler." He immediately thought it was a banal thing to say.

"Where's Sloan?"

Terry looked at one of the bodies and recognized Jim Sloan. A piece of metal protruded from the top of his skull. "He's dead, sir. I think I'm the only officer left."

There was a pause, then the executive officer continued, his voice firm. "All right, Schuyler, can you handle your duties?"

Terry looked about the ship. The two guns of the stern turret were pointing in different directions, and smoke was pouring from several holes in the turret around them. Everyone in there, he realized, had been reduced to ashes. There were other fires on the ship, and flames were pouring from one part of the bridge below him. It looked as though the ship had big problems. "I can handle it, sir." He glanced down and saw that someone had started pulling bodies from the bridge.

"Good, Schuyler. Now, tell me what you can see from up there. We're blind down here."

Blind? thought Terry. What about the sailor without eyes?

Terry had wanted to see history, and now his wish had come true. How much time had elapsed since the great guns first roared? An hour? Two? Eternity? He tried to sort out his memories and put them into some sort of context so he could develop his report.

He looked about at the American ships. The water was covered with debris, both human and material. He was appalled by the number of corpses bobbing like toys in some giant tub. Where were the other ships? The *Texas* was settling by the bow, and a score of lifeboats were already in the water around her. The *Kearsarge* had simply disappeared. There was some burning debris approximately where he had last seen her before blacking out. Was the debris all that was left? Other ships like the *Iowa* and the *Indiana* were still under power while flames consumed portions of them. Was it possible they weren't as badly hurt as they looked? Then he realized the *Alabama* was still plowing strongly through the seas, her engines evidently undamaged.

The horizon in every direction was dotted with ships of all shapes and sizes. Mostly they were the transports. The once-neat lines of the convoy were in total disarray as the American cruisers, gunboats, and other ships knifed in among them, firing and creating their own horrors. It appeared that many of the transports were unharmed and dead in the water. It then dawned on Terry that they were surrendering. Of course. Where could they go? Back to Germany? Even if they could outrun the American ships, what would they use for coal?

Now there was relative silence, and Schuyler counted ships. Of the Americans, he saw eleven of the original thirteen capital ships, including his own, and two of the three monitors. The *Texas* and *Kearsarge* were indeed gone. He counted the German ships and blinked. Five. Only five, and they were all dead in the water and burning furiously. The others were not in sight, and he could only conclude they had sunk. One of the remaining five—he thought it might have been the cruiser that had passed so close—rolled over and began to sink as he watched.

"Schuyler! Your report!"

"Sorry, sir, it's just taking a little longer to sort this out. I know the captain likes things precise."

There was another pause. "The captain's dead, Ensign. You're making your report to me." For some reason the fact of Brownson's death struck him, and he started to cry. It was stupid. He barely knew the man who had replaced Evans. "Schuyler, give me your report as you see it and do it now!"

Terry composed himself and began to rattle off the ships and their apparent conditions. When he was done, there was silence again. Then he heard the distant voice talking to someone else on the bridge. "Well, we really did it to them. We really cleaned them," he thought he heard the voice say. Terry looked about him again. Death was near and death was far.

"Sir, can you get some help up here? We got some wounded who need medical attention."

"On its way, Ensign. Just hang on."

Terry sagged to the floor and tried not to touch the blind sailor who had stomped on him. He let the pain and the tears overwhelm him. He would need a lot of help climbing down the ladder with his lame arm. Even the blind man would do better. Happy birthday.

The armed yacht *Chesapeake* slid into the convoy proper while the cruisers and gunboats dueled each other on the perimeter. Along with the smaller ships, it darted in among the transports, sowing confusion and panic. Some of the transports tried to run away but quickly realized there was no place to run. Their way to New York was blocked by the titanic and thunderous battle to their front, and the gray Atlantic stretched for more than two thousand miles to their rear. They could never make it back to Germany.

The majority of the transports stopped and traded their German flags for the white ones of surrender. Some—those that looked to be of non-German registry—seemed almost eager to give up. However, a few had chosen to fight. Lieutenant Walsh, the *Chesapeake*'s commanding officer, could hear the sound of smaller guns, pom-poms, and machine guns as they raked the transports. The *Chesapeake*'s luck held and she quickly gathered up a covey of surrendered transports without firing a shot.

Then Walsh spied a large passenger liner that had not yet dipped its flag. He approached and fired a pom-pom round across her bow. As they drew closer, within a couple of hundred yards, the liner's rails suddenly erupted with a wall of armed men who opened fire with rifles and machine guns at the tiny *Chesapeake*. Micah screamed orders swiftly as his men started to fall at their stations. The pom-poms and the 3-incher fired back, and the two machine guns raked the thick line of helmeted Germans.

The fire from the liner stopped almost immediately. The railings meant for passengers to lean on provided no protection for the German soldiers, who simply disappeared. Walsh wondered if the captain or commander of the infantry unit on board had felt his honor required an attempt at resistance before surrendering. If so, the stupid bastard should be hanged. The battle was over, yet someone had demanded that honor be satisfied, and young people on both sides had died because of it. Fucking Krauts.

The white flag was raised quickly on the liner and the *Chesapeake* ceased firing. Walsh could see blood running from the liner's deck and could only visualize the carnage his guns had wrought. Using Morse, he signaled the liner that the German soldiers would have to pitch their weapons overboard. He watched grimly as they complied. He was realistic enough to know they probably still kept some, but at least he wouldn't be bringing a thousand armed and pissed-off Krauts into Norfolk.

Walsh ordered his captured charges to follow him while he threaded his way through and out of the battle area. Many other little convoys were doing the same thing, he noted. He set a course to Norfolk. It would take a few days, but they'd make it. He felt like a sheepdog with an especially motley flock. Along with the now-docile-liner, he had four other merchant ships, all having surrendered and been taken without incident. It was quite a sight and quite a haul. Too bad they didn't allow ships to share in the wealth of the ones they captured, like they did in the good old days.

Micah Walsh checked the condition of the *Chesapeake*. He knew she was sound and not taking any water, but that bastard liner had hurt her. Bullet holes riddled her once-pristine hull, and her stately funnel had been shredded by a passing hunk of metal.

Lieutenant Micah Walsh looked sadly on the row of dead, and could only thank God that there weren't more. His young friend Halsey and four others were dead out of the crew of fifty, and another eleven wounded were being treated below. Many others nursed bruises and lacerations that would have incapacitated them under normal circumstances, but there would have been no one to run the little ship without them. And it had taken only a second for the needless destruction to occur.

Walsh choked and tried not to sob as he looked at the five men tightly sewn in their white mattress covers. The still-sticky blood had stained through a couple of them. In a while there would be a brief service, which he would hold and remember forever, and then the five would be consigned to the sea. Poor Halsey. Which one was he? Third from the left or second?

By all rights, Adm. Otto von Diedrichs should have been worried at the sight of so much of his fleet disappearing to the east. But he had obeyed his orders and his conscience was clear. It would take a little more than one day to make the rendezvous and about two days to complete the return journey with the slower convoy. Although he knew he had cut it very fine, he still didn't like the idea of being without nearly half of his force for three minutes, much less three days. But he took comfort in the fact that he had fulfilled his responsibility and obeyed his kaiser.

So he commenced to wait. As the hours stretched into days, his concern became doubt and the doubt grew into worry as the allotted three days stretched into four and no convoy hove into view.

Had the timing been off? Had they missed the rendezvous point? To the latter question the answer was easy: no, they could not have missed the point of meeting because the convoy had been directed to sail a specific route and course. Even if the convoy had not been on time, the battleships would have found the meeting point without much ado. No, there had to be something wrong with the timing. Perhaps the battle he had hoped would give the Yanks a bloody nose had caused more confusion than he anticipated. Of course, that must be it. That and the question of timing.

Hipper had been given a set of specifics that included more than just the course his ships would take. He had been mandated a speed that would result in Diedrichs's being able to send his ships at a precise time to a precise place. Any ship that could not keep up with the speed, and it was a slow one, would be left behind.

However, Diedrichs knew that Imperial edicts couldn't command the wind and the tide, and he had taken other steps. The needle-thin wireless tower on Long Island had commenced broadcasting a week before the convoy was expected, and he had been rewarded by the receipt of a weak response from Hipper saying all was well.

So where the hell were they? And where was the American main fleet? Were they planning to pounce when the convoy got closer? As yet his thin line of picket ships had seen nothing. German intelligence sources had reported the departure of the American fleet from Canadian and American waters, and other sources had reported it off the coast of Maine. Could Dewey have decided not to attack? That would have been the logical thing. Perhaps the American fleet was simply heading for Boston. Regardless, Diedrichs and the remaining fleet were ready, armed, and with steam up, to sail out at almost literally a moment's notice.

His thoughts were interrupted by a commotion in the passageway outside his cabin, and he spun his chair to face the door. "What is it?" he snapped.

Paschwitz entered with a piece of paper. Other men were clustered behind him and none looked happy. "Sir, we just intercepted a message that the entire relief convoy and our escort force have been destroyed, with all ships either sunk or captured. The Americans are calling it the greatest naval victory in their history."

Diedrichs rose to speak but could not find his voice. There was something else in his throat that prevented it, and he recognized the acid taste of his own vomit. He moaned and clutched his chest as he fell back into his chair. Paschwitz and the others rushed in to help him as he collapsed.

*   *   *

The kaiser's voice was a high-pitched scream and his face was beet red. "My ships, von Tirpitz, where are my ships? As Caesar Augustus cried for Varus to return his three legions, I now cry for my ships. Where are they? Where is my navy?"

Even though Holstein detested the arrogance of Tirpitz, he could not help but feel a little sorry for the man. Only moments before, he had exuded power and confidence. Brutally direct and often bullying and confrontational with those who disagreed with him, Tirpitz had appeared to many as the current personification of German power, a reincarnation of the mighty Bismarck. But not now. The transformation had been sudden and shocking. When the information began to flow in, he crumbled as they watched. His eyes glazed over and he was having trouble breathing. The grayness of his skin made Holstein wonder if perhaps the man was having a heart attack. It would not surprise him.

The arrival of the American announcement had been a devastating surprise. Funny how no one doubted it, Holstein thought. Somehow they all knew that the Americans were telling the truth. Corroboration from other sources would follow, but it was not needed. The Imperial German Navy had been defeated utterly and totally, and the frantically gathered convoy was destroyed. There would be no relief for the army from that quarter.

The kaiser continued to scream. "Even my namesake ship, *the Kaiser Wilhelm II,* was in that relief force!" He continued to read the names of the missing warships and paused only to wipe spittle from his mouth with his good hand. The kaiser was in a dangerous mood.

Bulow, too, looked chastened. "All Highest, will you now permit the remainder of the High Seas Fleet to reinforce Diedrichs?"

"So that incompetent can lose the rest of our navy? Don't be a fool." Bulow recoiled from the vehemence of the rebuke. Holstein recalled that the orders to divide the fleet had come from Tirpitz and the kaiser, but prudently said nothing about that. Diedrichs was as good as dead.

Instead, Holstein said, "The move by the Americans on Staten Island has rendered our position in New York highly unstable as well, has it not, General von Schlieffen?"

Schlieffen was in a high state of agitation. Normally composed to the point of arrogance, his eyes were wide and there was a twitch in his cheek. "The fact that the Americans have begun bombarding the Narrows and other portions of the harbor with their long-range guns is a more immediate problem to the navy than to the army. Should von Waldersee wish, we could land a division or two and drive them off. Of course," he added, "that is doubtless what the Yanks want—for us to waste our now-limited resources responding to pinpricks like their highly inaccurate cannonades. Let the navy run again if it wishes."

"Unfair," Tirpitz hissed, his voice a hoarse whisper. "We have done our best."

"And failed," snarled Schlieffen.

For the kaiser, the argument was the last straw, and he lunged, screaming at Tirpitz. "Get out! Get out of my sight. Get out of Berlin and get out of my navy. Goddamn you, you destroyed my navy!"

Tirpitz lurched to his feet and shuffled in a half run out of the room. With his departure, there was a sudden and not unwelcome silence. Well, Holstein thought, who will be next to feel the Imperial wrath and the Imperial need for someone to take the blame?

Kaiser Wilhelm had passed that point. He seated himself at the head of the table and wrapped his cape about himself as if in mourning. "What to do now, gentlemen, what to do?"

Schlieffen jumped to his feet, his face reddened with scarcely repressed anger. "All Highest, what we will now do is what we should have done all along. Depend on your army, not your navy. The army has always been successful and can still be successful now. We waited too long in our forts for the Yanks to see reason, and we are paying for our delay. Now we must fulfill the original plan as best we can: first by attacking, defeating, and destroying their army, and then by taking Hartford and Boston while we still have the resources. The alternative, All Highest, is to surrender."

The kaiser was stunned by the outburst from the normally tightly controlled Schlieffen. He was also appalled at the thought of losing an army; he would be shamed before the world. "You can retrieve success from this fiasco?"

"Yes, All Highest."

"When?"

"The moment you give the word. We have planned and prepared for this contingency from the moment we landed. With regrets, sire, we did not fully share von Tirpitz's confidence that he could control matters so vital to us. We have sufficient resources for at least one toss of the dice. It will be enough for us to win. And, I must hasten to add, we must do so while we are confronted by only one American army. The others that are being trained, some as near as Boston, must not be permitted to develop to the point where they can do damage to our cause. We must strike now and with everything we have in our North American arsenal!"

The kaiser nodded. It would be now.

Blake Morris and Willy Talmadge eyed the large farmhouse and made an unavoidable decision. Despite the presence of Germans in the vicinity and the likelihood that the house had been spared for use by the Germans, they would enter it and take refuge. It was getting just too damned cold out. Blake had no idea where the remaining few others in his group were, or if they were even alive. Now it was just he and Willy and a sack of dynamite. What a helluva note.

They made it to the house unnoticed and climbed through a basement window into the packed-earth cellar. It was still colder than Blake would have liked, but it was fairly dry and the walls of the house blocked the wind. The cellar was a honeycomb of small rooms for storage and work, and there was no problem finding a place to be comfortable. They dug a hole for latrine purposes and prepared to spend the next few days in relative comfort until they could decide their next move. Perhaps, Blake thought, it was time to go back through the American lines. He had a feeling that his effectiveness here was about over and he should call it quits. Then the images of his wife and daughter appeared and scolded him. No, dearest loves, he told them, I will not let you down. I will find a way.

Concentrating on their own needs, they did not sense or feel the presence of Johnny Two Dogs in another portion of the cellar. He, however, was well aware of them, smelled them, heard them. He did not have any idea what to do about their presence and was beginning to doubt his choice of a shelter from the early winter cold. It was getting just too damned crowded.

*   *   *

"Ludwig."

"Yes, Captain," Corporal Weber responded and snapped to attention. Captain Walter looked saddened.

"Draft an order to all my platoons. I want the men fed immediately and then they are to load as much ammunition and food as they can carry. Blankets and water as well. They are to be ready to move out in two hours."

Ludwig paled. "It's time, then." It was a statement, not a question.

"Yes, Ludwig, it is. As a result of that damnable defeat of our navy, we must win the war by ourselves, and do it right now if we are not to starve and freeze here this winter. We are going to move out early tonight when there is still a hint of light and attack them in the morning. I'm afraid we will not have an easy time of it."

Ludwig remembered the American dead piled up in front of his trench last summer. Now the shoe would be on the other foot. The captain read his thoughts. "No, we will not do it like the Americans. There will be a tremendous artillery barrage to soften them up, and then we will attack in great strength. Our generals have planned well. Not," he laughed sharply, "like the fools who led our navy to defeat."

Ludwig saluted and departed to carry out his orders. The captain had confirmed the rumor that was running rampant through the 4th Rifles. The navy had lost badly. Now the army could be stranded here in this strange land and be forced into captivity. He had mixed emotions. Although part of him did indeed want to stay, another part didn't find the thought of becoming a prisoner very attractive. All he really wanted to do was find those nice people who wrote the pamphlet and who would give him sanctuary. Instead, he was going to have to fight the Yanks again and probably kill some more of them. It wasn't fair. All he had ever wanted to do was teach school.

Chapter 25

THEODORE ROOSEVELT LOOKED anxiously at the report and the handful of men who were his key advisers. "You believe we are now going to reap the whirlwind?" Longstreet and the army men nodded. "You are certain the actions of the Germans in the no-man's-land presage a general assault?"

"Confident," Longstreet corrected, "but not totally certain. Their patrols have become larger and much more aggressive. It is as if they wanted us out of that area to mask their actions."

"And our balloons and airships?"

"Those same patrols have brought down several with machine guns and small cannon. The airships are stationary targets and prone to either collapse or blow up when hit. We are not totally blind, but the Germans are seriously impeding our efforts at determining their true intentions."

"I see. And you think they will now attack?"

"Yes," said Longstreet. "There really isn't much else they can do. I believe it will be an all-out assault to push us off the river line and destroy us out in the open field."

"Can we stop them?"

"We can only try. We have six divisions and they have seven. Our divisions are slightly larger than theirs, so the numbers, unless they bring in additional soldiers by stripping other areas, will be approximately equal. If we can stay on the defensive, we may wear them down. On the other hand, if we are forced into a battle of significant maneuver, we may be crushed. I have no idea just how the untried men in our army will react in a battle as major as the Germans are likely to attempt."

"And our navy? It can do nothing?"

Secretary of the Navy Long answered. "While we could force our way into Long Island Sound and bombard the German lines, I think the German assault will take place well away from the shore and out of range of the navy's guns. Dewey will do what he can, but the navy will not be a major factor in this battle." Long looked at Longstreet, who agreed. "Even though we won a great victory, we did suffer grave losses in men, ships, and equipment, and the greater portion of our navy is now undergoing emergency refits and resupply. Some ships can steam now, but the remainder of the navy won't be ready for a week to ten days."

Roosevelt thought about the irony. The greatest naval battle in American history had just been fought and won decisively. The United States had lost 2 battleships, the *Texas* and the *Kearsarge,* the monitor *Puritan,* and the cruisers *Boston* and *Minneapolis,* in return for the sinking of 6 German battleships, 3 heavy cruisers, and a host of light cruisers. There had been American losses in gunboats and yachts as well, but these had been offset by the capture of almost 130 transports, which now rested in the harbors of Boston and Norfolk. The balance of power on water had shifted, and America had the decisive advantage. But that success was going to precipitate the largest land battle in American history, the largest ever fought in North America, bigger even than Gettysburg.

"So this will be an army show," said Longstreet. "But we must think of the terrible weapons of destruction available to both sides. What we were able to do with muzzle-loaders can now be done tenfold by rapid-firing, breech-loading rifles and machine guns, not to mention the artillery."

"Is this why you sent Schofield up north? To be with MacArthur?" asked Roosevelt. Longstreet said it was. The battle would be fought in Connecticut, not Washington, and Schofield's years of experience might prove helpful. That he would coordinate events in support of the army was also understood. Roosevelt could not argue the point.

Why not have a man of Schofield's experience where the fighting would occur? "Then it is out of our hands. I think I should like to go someplace quiet and meditate."

The tension of Mahan's brigade headquarters could be cut with the proverbial knife. What had been a relatively quiet area would turn into a cauldron of war in a short period of time. The Germans were coming, the Germans were coming. It sounded to Patrick like the story of the sky falling. Only now the sky might actually be falling and there was little they could do to prevent it.

When he'd left Trina in the morning they had held each other even more closely than people usually do on their honeymoon. The idea that they might not see each other for a long time, perhaps forever, was foremost in their minds. It wasn't fair, he wanted to shout, but who would listen? Trina would, he knew that. He had told her he had six thousand and some men to command and, hopefully, bring back alive through whatever ordeal the future held in store. She said she was proud of him for that responsibility but hated the thought of it. Throughout the United States there were millions of people who were not going into battle, so why, she asked him, did Patrick Mahan and so many people she was fond of have to go to war? For that he had no answer.

"Anything?" Patrick asked Lieutenant Colonel Harris, who slipped quietly into the tent.

"Not a damn thing. Headquarters says there may have been movement into no-man's-land during the night, but they can't confirm it yet." Patrick checked his watch. It was 7:30 in the morning of November 17, 1901. It was a Monday and he always hated Mondays.

Patrick rose and looked at the situation map on the wall of the tent. His brigade was north and slightly east of the main defensive line on the Housatonic. Why were his men there and not directly behind the defenses along the river where they could be used to plug a gap? Instead, they were almost due north of Waterbury. When he'd asked about it, he'd been politely but firmly reminded that his was a strategic reserve and it would act as a blocking force if the Germans crossed the river to the north. It was not a comforting thought. There was the more nagging feeling that his brigade had been hung out to dry because nobody trusted the Germans and nobody wanted to associate with the Negro regiments. He thought MacArthur and Smith were bigger than that. He also hoped they knew what they were doing.

Patrick caught a noise—a distant, rumbling sound—deep and menacing. He and Harris looked at each other and each saw his own sense of horror reflected in the other's face.

"That's not thunder," Harris whispered.

They stepped outside and looked to the south, toward the river line. They knew there would be nothing to see, but they had to make the effort. As they stood, others emerged from their tents, stopped, and turned in the same direction, until thousands of men were simply staring toward the sound of the distant rumbles that presaged agony instead of rain. The volume of sound increased until it was a steady roar, and they knew they were hearing an artillery barrage of truly epic proportions. God help the men on the river line.

For Ludwig and the men of the 4th Rifles, the night march had been an uncomfortable but not a dangerous experience. German planners had done well, and their way was marked by white ribbons and human guides to direct them. When they reached a point about a mile from the first American defenses without any response from the Yanks, the men of the 4th started to feel better about their prospects for surviving the day. They fed themselves, checked their weapons for the hundredth time, and tried to rest, even sleep.

The shock and roar of the cannons jolted them and they thanked God that the shells were coming from their guns and landing on the Americans. They had all heard cannon fire before, but nothing like this! It was almost deafening, and the earth seemed to vibrate.

About midmorning, they were ordered into ranks and sent out toward the Americans. There were cheerful jokes that no Yanks would be left.

As they swept forward it was with a feeling of supreme strength and confidence. Even though Ludwig could see only a few dozen yards in either direction and sometimes not even all the men in his own company, he sensed enormous numbers all about him. Sometimes when fewer trees blocked his view, or the men moved to a slightly higher point of ground, he saw glimpses of the other companies, battalions, and regiments all sweeping forward with him. He also sensed that the huge numbers he could sometimes observe were only a fraction of what was going on out of his range of vision.

Another small comfort was the presence of other German soldiers in front of them. He wished them well. Even though there was a tendency to deride American efforts, he knew from experience what could be done from behind a good defensive position.

As they advanced, the barrage seemed to advance with them, and the sounds of impact and explosion caused the ground to vibrate under Ludwig's feet. He looked for Captain Walter and saw him striding erect, once again apparently without fear, urging his men on, and Ludwig wished he could be like that. He also wished that the captain would not get shot, as the battle was not that one sided. He could hear the rattle of small-arms fire and the bark of smaller artillery pieces and knew they were coming from the American lines. Every so often he would hear someone scream or cry out in pain and fear. More often than he would have liked, they passed German dead and wounded.

Ludwig had started the advance cold and wet as a result of the November mist. Now he could no longer feel the weather or his own discomfort. His heart was pumping as though it would go through his chest, and he was aware of sounds coming from his own throat.

Finally they broke into a clearing and he could see both the American earthworks and the river to their rear. How foolish, he thought; they could be trapped. However, he quickly realized that would not be so. As the advancing waves of Germans before him moved over and into the American lines, the brown-uniformed Yanks retreated over pontoon bridges to the other side of the river. He watched spellbound as German guns raked the last Americans crossing to the relative safety of the east bank of the river and saw men fall into the cold water, where they drifted toward the distant ocean.

A series of small explosions lifted the bridges off their temporary moorings and sent them floating down the Housatonic along with the bodies. Amazing, Ludwig thought; the Yanks had pulled off the retreat across the river and had done so while still being pounded by the crushing might of German artillery.

As they passed through the American outer earthworks, Ludwig was dismayed to find many more German than American dead. They had succeeded but paid a heavy price. There were other problems as well.

"Ludwig," Hans Schuler asked, bleeding from a cut on his arm, "what the hell is this shit?"

"Barbed wire."

"Yes, but so much of it?"

"I know," Ludwig grunted as he tried to finesse his way through a barricade made of coils of the stuff. "Be careful. This is really nasty shit." How many other surprises did the Americans have in store for them?

Captain Walter ordered them to pause and dig in about fifty yards from the river. "What else can we do?" sneered Kessel when the captain left. "We can't swim it."

Ludwig thought the river looked shallow and could possibly be forded at some spots, but he held his tongue. He didn't like the idea of crossing it either. It was much more satisfying to watch German artillery make the Yank fortifications bounce and lift into the air. They were less than half a mile away and it was an impressive show of sound, light, and fury.

After a while, the battered unit that had preceded them through the American earthworks was withdrawn. Ludwig realized with some discomfort that there was no one else between his 4th Rifles and the Yanks.

Captain Walter slid into the shallow trench beside him. "Got new orders, Ludwig. Go out there and tell the platoon leaders that we will be crossing the river in an hour."

Ludwig was dismayed. "I thought we won the battle."

"No, Ludwig, we only pushed them back to where they wanted to be in the first place. Now we have to move them to some other place where they don't want to be. Then maybe we will be able to say we won."

Ludwig looked at the river and the still-impressive American earthworks. "How will we cross, sir?"

"It has all been planned quite well. Typical German efficiency. Engineers will be along shortly to lay a pontoon bridge. We will cover them with heavy fire and then cross and establish a bridge-head. When we are strong enough over there, we will assault their main works. This, I'm afraid, will be a most difficult day."

Ludwig swallowed what he wanted to say, and the captain moved away, leaving him to carry out his orders. As he did so, he saw men

laying telephone and telegraph lines up to the river line. The captain
was right about German efficiency. A particularly large explosion
from the American side caught his eye. Something important had
exploded. Good. Whatever his sympathies and future plans, his most
significant efforts would be directed toward surviving this awful day.
As he looked across again, he saw the thin lines that told him there
was even more barbed wire to cross. Damned devils.

The war room in the chancellery was crowded with generals and
staff aides when the kaiser strode in, with Holstein and Bulow in
tow. Everyone rose. The kaiser acknowledged their deference and sat
down in his special chair.

"Well, Field Marshal von Schlieffen, what can you tell us about
the battle?"

Schlieffen drew his slight frame to an erect pose. "I can state with
confidence that we have achieved great success."

The kaiser exhaled noisily and sagged in relief. "Then we have destroyed them?"

"Not yet, sire, but that will happen shortly. Perhaps I should start
at the beginning?"

The kaiser laughed softly. It surprised those who had not heard
him laugh in some time. "Do that. Every time I asked for information earlier, I was told the battle was in progress. Good lord, I knew
that!"

Schlieffen chuckled and others joined in. Being on the winning
side was always a good feeling.

"Sire, at first light this morning, we commenced an enormous artillery barrage utilizing more than four hundred pieces that we had
gathered for that purpose. They consisted of weapons from 90 to
160mm. A very impressive display of firepower was then utilized to
batter a small section of their defenses west of the river while the
units we'd advanced to the jump-off point awaited the order to attack. For your information, we moved them all last night. At approximately midmorning, the attack began. We used one division on a
very narrow front corresponding roughly to the area of bombardment.
That one division was backed by three others ranked directly behind
it. There was little finesse involved. We simply overpowered the Americans at a specific point and swept through before they could react."

"And where was that point?" Bulow inquired.

Schlieffen indicated a spot on the map. "We chose what appeared to be the northernmost point of the American river lines. It is near the little town of Sandy Hook, Connecticut, and south of where the river is met by a minor tributary that would confuse and hamper our efforts. It is approximately thirty miles from Long Island Sound and the city of Bridgeport. It is," he said, smiling, "a point where the river is not all that deep and there are numerous places to cross. Even though it has been raining, the river is well below flood stage, perhaps even below normal for this time of year."

"God smiled on us," said Kaiser Wilhelm.

Schlieffen nodded. He preferred to think it was good staff work rather than divine inspiration or intervention.

"We pushed them across the river, bombarded them some more, and then successfully crossed." Schlieffen checked a clock and tried to recall the time differential. It was the middle of the night in America. "When dark fell, we had at least four divisions on the other side, and we will commence advancing eastward when the morning comes."

"Why not now?" asked Bulow, and the kaiser nodded.

"There are many reasons. First, the men are exhausted. They marched all night and fought all day. There are many men who have lost their units and many units that have lost their way. What Clausewitz referred to as the fog of war has arrived and must be blown away. Further, we must get ammunition to the men. Many frontline units have used up most or even all of what they carried. If we can get them some food as well, that too would be most beneficial. Our priorities are ammunition and food. As a result of the American bombings, we have been forced to decentralize our supply depots for safety, which will slow down the resupply efforts."

Bulow was puzzled. "What about medical care for the wounded?"

Schlieffen looked at him sadly. "That is a secondary concern." The response appeared to shock Bulow, and Schlieffen continued. "War, as they say, is hell. My first duty is to see that the living and unhurt continue to live and fight again. Although it is brutal, I must assume that many of the wounded will die anyhow. I might also say that we now have to reposition all those cannon we used so marvelously in the assault. They will be returned to their units so they can fight in a more normal manner. If it is deemed necessary, the Grand Battery will be reconstituted later."

Bulow appeared shaken and turned away. Holstein asked about casualties.

"Right now, we estimate we have suffered between five and seven thousand killed and wounded, the Americans somewhat fewer," said Schlieffen. "They have the immediate advantage of defending fortified positions, and, despite the barrage, we paid a heavy price to assault them. Now that we have pushed many of them out of those lines, we will begin to harvest them more heavily. We also lost about fifty of our artillery pieces in duels with the Americans. They were not totally helpless, not for one minute. They also used what appear to be large naval guns to good effect. Fortunately, there were only a few of them."

Schlieffen turned again to the map. "We are going to continue pushing almost due east and search for the end of their right flank. Of necessity, they will try to deny us that by stretching their lines farther east as well, and then by curving back toward the Sound. When they do that, we will have them trapped in a perimeter with their backs to the ocean."

"But what about Hartford and Boston?" Holstein asked. "I thought those were our objectives."

"They certainly are," Schlieffen said. "But not until we have destroyed their army. Right now we are between them and Hartford and are slowly pushing them toward the water. You are right about those two cities, and, yes, we could take them at any time we wish, but we cannot prudently do so and leave such a large American army in our rear. They managed to retreat in surprisingly good order and are still a very large and potentially viable force. They cannot be ignored. First we destroy them, then we will move on to Boston."

Holstein persisted. "And how long will it take to entrap them?"

"Two, three days at the most. Then we squeeze them, bombard them, and crush them."

It was Holstein's turn to go to the map, and he moved his bulk slowly. "Yet by doing so, you are ignoring any American forces to your north."

"Count, there are no Americans to our north. Other than a few thousand raw militia and untrained recruits at Springfield, there are no significant American forces in a position to help. Even so, we have not left that area totally unprotected. One of the divisions that led the attack has been sent there to act as a blocking force and for some rest. They lost heavily and will be of no further use in this campaign." Schlieffen turned to the kaiser and bowed. "By this time next week, the war will be over."

Bemused by Morris's and Willy's attempts at furtiveness, Johnny Two Dogs made it a point to follow them whenever they went outside. He was greatly surprised when they managed to steal some German uniforms, which enabled them to move about openly. He was further amazed that they did so without being able to speak any of that throat-clearing noise the Germans used as a language.

Morris and Willy remained invisible in plain sight because of the chaos resulting from the huge German offensive. They stole a wagon, loaded it with tools and such, and set about working on the telephone lines. Johnny had always hated the wires that sent messages faster than the wind, betraying the presence of his people to the vengeance of the goddamn blue bellies.

Johnny noticed that Willy and Morris were discreet and worked on lines only when no other German engineers were around. Then it dawned on him and he laughed aloud for one of the few times in his harsh life. The crazy bastards weren't fixing the lines, they were wrecking them! And they were doing it without actually breaking the wire, which would have made the damage easy to find. Pretty clever, those white dogs.

Well, Johnny thought cheerfully, he could play that game as well. Only he would have to actually cut the wires. The Germans would rush out and see the break, fix it, and, if Morris and Willy had done their jobs, go crazy when the damn phones and telegraphs still wouldn't work. Maybe some dumb German would wander into the woods to take a piss and Johnny would get a chance to cut another throat. And to think that young MacArthur actually said he would be paid to have such fun.

Roosevelt looked again at the map on the wall of the war room. For the first time in a long time, the red and blue flag pins representing the German and American forces had moved. What they showed was a hint of German victory. The U.S. Army was in retreat. It had been shoved back to the Housatonic and then over it. The German force had crossed and was between the American army and Hartford. North of Hartford was Boston, and the only blue pin in the Germans' path represented the brigade commanded by his friend Patrick Mahan. Fortunately for Mahan, only a small German force seemed to be opposing him. The bulk of the German army flowed over the river and toward the east, bending the American army back toward the ocean.

Roosevelt turned to Maj. Gen. Leonard Wood. "Is it as bad as it looks?"

"It could be worse, sir. We have only withdrawn, not been defeated."

Roosevelt shuddered. He had spent all day in the room listening to the reports of the bombardment, which had been followed by an assault in overwhelming strength against a single point in their defenses. It was the same strategy that Patrick Mahan had said General Miles should have used against the Germans in July. The president wondered if Patrick felt any satisfaction for being correct. Probably not.

"Where's Longstreet?"

"He went north to be with MacArthur in Hartford, sir," Wood replied. "He left last night. I don't want to put words in his mouth, but I don't think he could stand being here while the battle was being fought elsewhere."

Roosevelt couldn't blame the man. It was not as if he had abandoned his post, far from it. He had done well, and if he wanted to be present at what would undoubtedly be his last battle, then God bless him. For a moment Roosevelt toyed with the thought of going up there as well, but reluctantly abandoned it. Right now the worst that could happen was that the United States could lose the battle and its army and have to sue for peace. If he went up north and managed to get captured, it would be an additional disgrace for his young nation. Perhaps they wouldn't want him back after this.

It came to him, as it had several times in the last few weeks, that he was very likely going to be the first U.S. president to lose a war. If so, the territorial ambitions of the United States would be on hold until she managed to loosen whatever shackles a treaty with the Germans would demand. Also, it would doom him to the saddest of all places in American history. His name would be a mark of shame. What would become of his family?

He looked at the map again and saw that the trainees near Springfield were on the move. He knew about it and had given reluctant approval. They would be slaughtered, but it had to be done. Perhaps they could pull off a miracle.

And how many old Civil War generals could MacArthur possibly use? He now had Longstreet, whose career had been clouded by controversy; Schofield, who had retired six years ago; Smith, who'd failed outside Richmond; Wheeler, who'd lost to Sherman while serving under Hood; and Lee, whose only real claim to fame was being nephew to his illustrious uncle. Merritt had also been recalled from retirement.

These relics of bygone days were paired with younger generals like Pershing, Funston, Kent, and Chaffee. It was a real passing of the torch. He hoped it wasn't too late.

Trina made sure the carriage was packed with everything that could be useful on the trip. She had only a vague idea which way she would head with Heinz and Molly, although she thought it likely that they would try to head north and west toward her family's estate outside of Albany—if the Germans didn't get that far.

All about her were signs of evacuation. Carts, wagons, and people on horseback were heading anywhere but south, where the throbbing sounds of battle were ominously discernible. The people with vehicles were the lucky ones. There were long lines of men, women, and children walking along the trails and paths.

As Trina finished loading her carriage, she wondered how many of them would survive. The weather was getting colder with each day, and the thought of sleeping on the unprotected ground made her shiver. At least they had enough blankets to keep warm, and fodder for the horses. If they had to, they could nap in the carriage.

This time they were well armed. Trina had a revolver in her belt and a shotgun on the floor of the carriage. Molly had another shotgun that a local blacksmith had made more compact by cutting off most of the barrel. It was Molly's idea. She swore to Trina that she'd seen such weapons in New York and said it would be devastating at short range. Trina could only shake her head at the things the young one knew and she did not. How many different worlds could there have been in one city?

Also, they were not traveling alone. In the wagon ahead were Mrs. Harris and a lady friend. There were men in the group as well, so she felt secure, albeit distressed at the need to run. This would be the second time she had been expelled from her home. It was an extremely unsettling experience for someone who had always lived a life of privilege and comfort. But she had strong mental as well as physical resources and would endure.

Heinz had been a problem. "I should be there with them, with General Mahan and the others. I shouldn't be running away like this."

Before Trina could answer, Molly snapped at him. "Sure, you big ass, like you would be such a great help! You got one arm broken and can't walk right yet because of a hole in your leg. Would you want them to carry you to the battle? Christ, love, you fought your fight. You're wounded. Now, if you don't want to get hurt worse than you are, shut up and get in that carriage! I want the father of our child to be with me when the kid grows up, not in some fucking government cemetery!"

Finally Trina got things sorted out and started on the road north. She hated the thought of leaving Patrick, but they had talked about it and decided it would be more of a comfort to both of them if she left. God willing, they would meet later.

It was so inconceivable. The Germans had attacked and won. It was as if all the work put into making a defensive effort had been for naught.

The carriage rocked as Trina eased it over a set of railroad tracks. That was another thing: why weren't trains being used to evacuate people? she wondered. She and others had checked and been told that the trains were reserved for military purposes. What military purposes? It was common knowledge that the bulk of the army was cut off to the south. Where could the trains be sent? Trina was certain it was just another military foul-up. Or, as Molly would have said, a fuckup.

*   *   *

Ludwig and the rest of the 4th plunged into the icy water and began wading as the American bullets whizzed about them. The engineers had tried to build a bridge for them to cross on, but the return fire from the Americans caused too many casualties, and it was decided that the assault waves would ford the river. Men screamed and fell, and now the American dead were joined by Germans floating down to the same impartial Long Island Sound.

After what seemed an eternity, they made the other side and started up a slight rise to the American trenches. Since they were so close, the artillery barrage had to let up. The Yanks reappeared and commenced a withering fire. The only way through was to rush as quickly as possible, firing all the time to keep the Americans' heads down.

Then came more barbed wire, much worse than it had been before. It stuck them, cut them, entangled them in its sharp claws, and finally forced them to halt until they found a way past it. All the while, American rifles and machine guns blazed away, ripping holes in their ranks. The stench of battle almost overwhelmed Ludwig as both the dead and the living lost control of their bowels and the smell of bloody flesh filled the air.

When enough men were finally across the river, some units laid down covering fire while others tried to make their way through the wire barrier. At last the sheer weight of German numbers prevailed, and the American fire slowed, then stopped. Germans found ways through the wire where the artillery had blasted paths, or decided that cheap cuts were a small price for pay to saving their own lives.

Exhausted and stunned, the remnants of the 4th finally made the American lines, only to see the Yanks trotting away, occasionally turning to fire. As before, they were in good order, and Ludwig knew they would have to be fought again. He gasped and took a swallow from his canteen. The rush of excitement caused by the intensity of the battle ebbed fast, and the feelings of cold, wet, and hunger returned. Only now there was fatigue and pure fear.

Captain Walter came by, his arm wrapped in a dirty bandage. His face was pale and his eyes looked haunted. They would rest, he said; their battle was over.

But it didn't turn out that way. Just as darkness fell, they were ordered to march north. When the captain protested that the men were hungry and tired, and that some of them were nursing minor wounds and cuts, he was verbally savaged by an exquisitely clean staff major for being a slacker. It was sickening, although Kessel had grinned.

The captain gathered his shrunken company and they started to march.

Chapter 26

AS THE NEW day dawned, Ludwig lay stiffly in the shallow depression made by a dirt road and confronted a wall of trees about a quarter-mile away. His body was a mass of aches and he dreamed of a hot bath. He also prayed that no one would ever shoot at him again.

The captain had told the company they were part of a screening force in place to make sure the Yanks did not attack the now-vulnerable German rear. The main force was driving south to surround and destroy the Americans, who were being pushed into the sea. Ludwig had to agree that it sounded good. But he recalled that the Yanks had pulled out of their untenable trenches in a manner that showed they were a long way from being destroyed or pushed into the Sound.

Ludwig took another swallow from his canteen and tried to wash the taste of filth from his mouth. At least there was something to drink. No one had seen any food since yesterday morning, and his stomach was growling. He looked around at the others in the company, also on the dirt road. No one had dug in yet; they were just too tired. Some were sleeping while others watched the wide stand of trees. Later, when they'd rested, they'd start to dig in. There was no urgency; the American army was miles away and surrounded.

Captain Walter crouched beside Ludwig. "How much ammunition do you have?" Ludwig checked and counted only seven rounds. Had he used up that much? He barely remembered firing. "Well," Walter smiled, "I hope you hit something with all that shooting." Then, more seriously, he said, "Nobody has much ammo left. I've tried to get more, but the depots are all supplying the troops for the big assault. They say we are to rest and watch the leaves change."

Ludwig thought his stomach was more important and asked about food. "Same story," said the captain. "They are sending everything for the troops south of us." He took out his binoculars and scanned the forest. "Seen any Yanks in there?"

"A couple, sir. I think they're just keeping an eye on us. Not much else they can do, with their entire army trapped." Even with most of the leaves gone from the trees, the woods were dark and impenetrable; the shadows and limbs broke up any line of sight.

Captain Walter put his field glasses back in their case. "Oh, they'll try something. Latest rumor is that an untrained militia will be sent against us in a few days." He chuckled. "If that's all they have, the fact that they outnumber us won't mean a thing. On the other hand, it would be nice to have ammunition by then. I trust we'll have some before long."

"And food too, sir."

Walter slapped him on the shoulder. "Good German soldiers never admit to being hungry."

The corporal managed a small smile as the captain walked away on tired, unsteady legs. Ludwig was still hungry, and he decided he wasn't a very good soldier. Hell, he knew that already. In a little while it would be his turn to sleep. He prayed he would not dream of the barbed wire and see the dead lying across it like flies entrapped in a spiderweb.

He watched as the captain walked from man to man, checking each. Sadly, it didn't take long. Of the 120 who'd landed on Long Island in June, only 38 were present for duty this morning. More than 30 men were dead, wounded, or missing from yesterday alone. Maybe one or two would show up as the day wore on, but somehow Ludwig didn't think that very likely. The Yank fire had been just too deadly.

He tried not to think of the friends who now lay dead or bloody and mangled. There were too many. One of the Schuler boys was dead, killed in the crossing, and the remaining brother was inconsolable. Ludwig could hear the sound of his sobbing from farther down the widely spaced defensive line.

Battle had changed Ludwig, hardened him both physically and mentally. Once he had been an innocent and very naive itinerant schoolteacher. Now he had killed, and others had tried to kill him. His comrades respected him and he could lead them. Even Kessel no longer caused him fear. The scarred bully and thief was indeed a damned coward. A few weeks earlier, Kessel had finally cornered him in a supply tent and tried to fondle his buttocks. "C'mon, pussy boy, let me show you a real man." Ludwig had whirled and locked an iron grip around his throat. "Even think of touching me again, you fucking prick, and I'll kill you." Kessel had recoiled in shock and fled from the tent. Ludwig had surprised himself; it felt wonderful.

He would never be an officer in what he felt was the obscene German military machine, but he would be a force in whatever endeavors he took up. Teaching was still a real possibility, but he would now be a different sort of teacher. First, he reminded himself, he had to make sure he survived this battle.

He glanced upward. Funny, but he almost thought he heard the sound of a train whistle.

Theodore Roosevelt left the war room and tried to relieve his stresses by pacing up and down the second-floor corridor of the White House. Major General Leonard Wood poked his head out and watched his friend the president. Finally, Roosevelt paused.

"Leonard, now I finally and truly do understand what Lincoln went through during those awful battles. How maddening it is to do nothing but sit by a telephone and wait for it to ring, or by a telegraph in hopes it might start chattering. How utterly useless I feel!"

Wood glanced about to see who else could hear. "Theodore," he said, taking in private the liberty of using his first name. "I would a hundred times rather be actually doing something than waiting, waiting, waiting. You mention Lincoln, but what about McKinley while you and I were tramping through the Cuban swamps?"

Roosevelt laughed. "Damn, those were good days." His face clouded quickly. "But waiting for news of the battle is driving me crazy. The newspapers are pillorying me because the Germans are driving us back, and they predict an awful defeat that will end the war on very unsatisfactory terms. They blame me for the failure of the country to be ready. In a way, I guess they're right. After all, I was the vice president. Mr. Bryan and his friends are calling this the culmination of a policy of failure. In the Spanish war, Bryan had the decency to put on a uniform, but not this time."

"Well, at least the fleet has sailed," commented Wood.

"But to what avail? The German army will be well out of range, and the German navy can stay safely where it is. Oh, I suppose Dewey had to do something. Perhaps he can force his way into Long Island Sound and prevent the Germans from bombarding our perimeter."

Wood was no longer listening. He had gone to a window and was looking out at Lafayette Park. "Theodore, come here."

The president came and peered over his shoulder. "Goodness, what do they want?" Outside, in the park, were thousands of men, women, and children. They were staring at the White House in almost total silence. Even from a distance he could see the grim, sad looks on their faces.

"Sir," said Wood, formality returning. "I believe they want to see you."

Roosevelt looked again at the somber faces. "I should go speak to them. No," he said, smiling slightly, "I will go and ask them to pray with me."

The journey north had been a hard one for a man as old as James Longstreet, and he felt it in every bone in his body. Yet could he be elsewhere? He allowed his aide to help him down from his carriage and walked the few steps to where MacArthur and Schofield waited. Schofield looked a little more rested than Longstreet, but he had arrived a day earlier. Longstreet returned their salutes. "How is it within the perimeter?"

MacArthur answered. "Still holding. We have just about reached the water on our eastward swing and are digging in like mad. So are the Germans."

Longstreet nodded. He did not ask how long they could hold out. "With you up here, Mac, what's the command structure?"

"I'm still in overall command, of course, and keeping in touch via wireless and telegraph. We buried a number of lines between here, Bridgeport, and New Haven, and the Krauts haven't thought to dig them up yet. Baldy Smith is in tactical command within the perimeter and Joe Wheeler has taken over his corps. Chaffee commands the second corps. Division commanders are Funston, Pershing, Lee,

Kent, Merritt, and Scott. Bates commands north along the Hudson, and Ludlow commands the Jersey shore. Both might as well be on the moon for all the good they'll do us in this fight."

Longstreet realized that these were the cream of the American army command. If they were lost, then the army was effectively beheaded as a fighting force. What had he done? By answering his country's call, James Longstreet had put himself in position to preside over the greatest defeat in the young nation's history. Hell, a man in his eighties should be home watching his favorite hound sleep. But here he was, ancient and hard of hearing, trying for one last battle. He must be a fool.

The distant sound of a train whistle brought him out of his reverie. He took his watch from his pocket and checked the time. "Schofield, is it true the trains run on time in Germany?"

Schofield kept a straight face. "Everything runs on time in Germany. Everything is done precisely and to the numbers, and that includes the pious act of copulation for the betterment of the fatherland."

Longstreet was about to ask him what a man of his age recalled of the pious act of copulation when the train whistle sounded again, this time closer. Longstreet looked at the others and saw the expectant expressions on their faces. Working with Stonewall had taught him something about trains, and a stint as commissioner of railroads, a largely ceremonial position, had taught him even more. Yes, the German trains always ran on time; by comparison, exact scheduling in the United States was often a joke. But sometimes, just sometimes, they got it right.

The kaiser looked at his map and watched as staffers again moved the pins denoting a further surge eastward by his army. "Von Schlieffen, I am still concerned about that mob they have up north in their training camp. Although it might not be much, there is little to stop it from bursting into our rear and doing a great deal of mischief."

Schlieffen responded confidently. "We will not permit that to happen, sire. First, it will take the Americans several days to organize and move that force to the battle area. When they do that, our blocking force will intercept and delay them until reinforcements arrive." He pointed to another spot on the map. "We have generated enough additional troops to form a reserve corps of two divisions under

General von Trotha. He is simply awaiting orders as to which direction to send his troops—south against the perimeter or north against any relief force."

The kaiser was impressed. "And where did you find this reserve army?"

"Sire, we stripped forces away from Manhattan, the northern flank of the salient, and, of course, from the defensive fortifications along the river. We decided, and rather logically, that the battle was being fought here"—Schlieffen pointed at the American perimeter—"and that any troops retained elsewhere were useless. It was all planned some time ago," he added smugly.

"But what about the risk?"

Schlieffen shrugged. "In all things there is an element of risk. In this case it is minimal. The Hudson protects Manhattan, and numerous other water barriers protect the northern flank. As to the fortifications, well, if we keep pushing the Yanks back, the forts will be so far in the rear as to be moot. Besides, the moves were completely secret."

Johnny Two Dogs arrived back at the farmhouse from a pleasant day of cutting wires and throats to find the place crawling with German soldiers. He didn't know how the Germans designated rank, but he did know the American system, and his experience with the latter told him that some very important people were now in that building.

So too, he realized, were Blake and Willy. He laughed and wondered if they were hiding in that huge and labyrinthine basement. If they were, at least they were dry and out of the wind. There was no safe way they could emerge with so many guards and sentries, who would immediately stop any strange-looking line repairmen coming out of the basement. They would have to endure until the Germans left. Well, he didn't. He decided if he was going to be cold and uncomfortable, then others would pay for it. He had already killed once today—a messenger who had dismounted because his horse was going lame—and he would look for other opportunities. Then he would return to see what Blake and Willy thought of their new neighbors. And he decided it might be time to let them know he was around.

*   *   *

Patrick Mahan pored over the piece of paper on his field desk and didn't look up when Ian Gordon and Lieutenant Colonel Harris entered.

"You called, beloved general?" Ian asked.

"I did. Look at this." Patrick handed them the paper. "Just about the strangest orders I have yet received. According to what I read, I am to pull in my troops from their extended screening formation and stay within new brigade boundaries. The boundaries are very small and I am supposed to be ready to attack the Germans from the confines of those strange boundaries. All of this is to be accomplished within one hour."

Gordon handed back the paper. "That is indeed what it says."

"Gentlemen, does it make sense?"

"Not really," said Harris. "If we attacked the local Germans in a tight formation, I'm confident we could easily punch a hole in their lines. However, they could hurt our flanks and rear while we were pushing on to hit the main German force."

Ian added, "Even if we were then to make contact with that main force, it would outnumber us perhaps ten to one overall and would chew up our little brigade and spit out the pieces without much difficulty. I think I agree with you, Patrick—an attack would be suicidal. Our brigade is much too small to cause any significant damage. So, what are you going to do?"

Patrick shook his head sadly. "I am going to obey orders. The concentration of force is already under way, and we will indeed be ready to move out within an hour. But I do not think of myself as suicidal. I will attack if I must, but if it looks as though we are going to be overwhelmed, I will order a retreat as quickly as I can and the hell with what the history books might say." Getting home to Trina was another motivation. He didn't like the thought of her in widow's weeds after such a short marriage.

Ian agreed. "Good plan. I always did want to live to a ripe old age."

Patrick was about to remind Ian that he really didn't have to be there in the first place when a sentry opened the tent flap and stuck his head in. "Sir, General Schofield is arriving."

Patrick reached for his hat. "Shit. What the hell is the old man doing here?"

Ian Gordon sighed. "Probably wants to make sure you obey your orders."

When Schofield arrived he went directly into Patrick's command tent. He plucked the orders from where Patrick had laid them. "What do you think?"

"General Schofield, I am completely at a loss. If I didn't respect both you and General MacArthur, I would consider the mission suicidal."

Schofield smiled. "So you've doubtless been planning a way of not quite disobeying them, haven't you?"

When all else fails, why not tell the truth? Patrick reasoned. "Absolutely, sir. The thought of my brigade attacking all those Germans alone is not a pleasant one. It's not that any one of us wishes to shirk our duty, but this attack is doomed to fail. My brigade would not be able to do anything much against the Germans. We will attack as ordered, General, but I am planning on being able to beat a hasty and prudent retreat when the time comes."

Schofield took off his campaign hat and sat in Patrick's chair, a look of feigned puzzlement on his round face. "Why Patrick, whoever said you'd be alone?"

Trina saw the tracks and heard the train at the same time. It would beat her to the crossing, so she eased up on the reins and let the horses slow to a stop. Racing trains to a crossing was not her idea of a morning's fun.

"How is everyone? Isn't this a jolly trip?" she asked. Molly stuck out her tongue and Heinz moaned in mock agony. He was uncomfortable and in some pain but was really bearing up well. Molly, on the other hand, had thrown up her breakfast.

Trina checked and saw the people in other wagons and carriages in her group taking advantage of the enforced break to get out and stretch, and a few walked discreetly into the trees to relieve themselves. Stretching, she thought, was a splendid idea. She nodded and smiled at Mrs. Harris, and the two women walked toward the tracks. About time someone sent a train, she thought, but who was left to evacuate? She watched the thick, low column of smoke as it neared. It was, she realized, a very large train. Intrigued, she walked closer to the tracks.

The train rounded the final bend and came straight at her, moving at a good rate of speed. As it roared past, she realized there were three engines. Why? she wondered. The answer came as the flatcars rolled into view. At first she did not believe her eyes, did not trust herself to think. Then she realized what she was indeed seeing and, equally important, hearing as the sound of additional trains echoed in the distance. Along with talks of love and their future together, Patrick had confided in her and told her everything about the army— its strengths, its weaknesses, and its potential. Thus she understood quickly and totally the significance of the spectacle unfolding before her. Each of the many flatcars was jammed with hard and confident-looking armed men in American uniforms. Unlike the pasty- and flabby-looking recruits she'd seen, these men were tanned and fit, and there were some Asian faces mixed among the white. They had come. The American army was back from the Philippines.

Involuntarily her body convulsed. Uncontrollable tears poured down her cheeks and she clutched her chest as the train rolled by, causing unbearable waves of emotion that overwhelmed her. Annabelle Harris understood as well, and ran up to her. They held each other and sank to the ground. Trina grabbed a chunk of dirt and flung it skyward. Both their faces were wet with tears and they tried to yell over the sound of the rushing train. On board, only a few pair of eyes noticed the two crazy-looking ladies sitting on the grass and crying hysterically.

Chapter 27

ADMIRAL DIEDRICHS SAT up slowly in his bed. His head ached horribly and he was only beginning to keep food down. He kept his left hand under the covers to hide the fact that it had begun to quiver. He was reminded of how the kaiser pretended his left arm wasn't withered. Diedrichs was on board his flagship, the battleship *Barbarossa,* in the lower bay of New York harbor. The remainder of the German main battle fleet had been deployed to deny access to the harbor should the Americans foolishly try to force entry.

An aide handed him a message, which he read quickly. "Damn."

He signaled to his senior staff officers, who entered his stateroom and approached his bed. They looked dispirited, whipped. Diedrichs held up the message. "According to the kaiser's supposedly infallible intelligence services, the American fleet is believed to have departed Boston Harbor, probably yesterday. Proper emphasis should be placed on the word 'believed.'"

"What should we do?"

Diedrichs sank back on the pillow. His headache was returning. Perhaps he should have some broth. What he really wanted was an end to this humiliating war.

"Gentlemen," he answered in a near whisper, "it is only believed that the Americans have sailed. Until we can confirm that, and then confirm their destination, we will do nothing."

A young aide was aghast. "But sir, if they enter the Sound, they can support the American perimeter."

Diedrichs rubbed his head with his right hand. "Then let them. The German army has long bragged of its ability to whip the Yanks without us; well, now they will have the chance. When we know the Americans' destination, we will take action. Not before. Would you have me leave this anchorage and let them sneak in behind us? I think not." As he spoke, the distant crump of a shore gun sounded as yet another shell was lobbed at long range into the Narrows. "On the other hand," he sighed, "perhaps we should sail away and let them have this awful place." He waved them out. "Please turn off the lights when you leave."

Since no replacements had come aboard the *Alabama,* the lookout tower was far less crowded than usual. It was a common situation throughout both the ship and the rest of the fleet. There had barely been time to take off the wounded and bring on some badly needed ammunition and food before the order had come to get up steam and depart immediately. Now!

As a result, Ens. Terry Schuyler was again the senior man in the lookout post. His arm still ached awfully and there were many other bruises to remind him of that climactic day of battle, but he could still function as a junior officer. His mother, whom he barely remembered, would have referred to it as the resilience of youth. Resilience, hell. He hurt. But he had sworn an oath to his nation and he had a duty to fulfill. Too many of his friends were dead or wounded for him to let his injuries impede him. Besides, after what he had seen and done, he no longer considered himself a youth.

Charley Ackerman, the other officer in the tower, was an ensign like Terry, but slightly junior to him in time in grade. "What a magnificent view!" young Ackerman exclaimed.

Terry agreed. Ackerman had spent the last battle on the navigating bridge and had seen very little of the action. Too many senior officers had clogged up all the good viewing spots.

They looked ahead at the line of battleships in front of them. This time they were not fourth. Instead they were much farther back, second from the last of the battleships and ahead of the armored cruisers, because of their reduced firepower; the damaged stern turret had not been repaired. They had gotten the bodies out, and the sight had sickened him. Those blackened pieces of meat had once been men, friends.

Since none of the other big ships had lost any of their main armament, they went ahead. Behind the *Alabama* came the ungainly bulk of the *Maine*. The presence of the successor to the second-class battleship that had been blown up in Havana by the Spaniards was a tribute to the desperation that drove the U.S. Navy and the willingness of people to work around the clock and take chances with their lives. The ship had been launched in July, and completion should have taken more than a year. However, she had taken her place in the line of battle with only half her main gun turrets and none of her secondary guns. Her superstructure was incomplete, and Terry had no idea how she was commanded and controlled. But she had her engines, armor, two big guns, and a crew that had demanded the right to accompany the other battleships as replacements for the sailors of the sunken *Texas* and the *Kearsarge*.

It was said that Dewey nearly wept when he was confronted with their belligerent insistence. The presence of the clumsy and incomplete ship buoyed the spirits of all who saw her. Ahead and on both flanks, as well as to the rear, were the cruiser squadrons of Remey and Evans. It was a magnificent sight. Terry picked up his Kodak box camera and took a few pictures. The last time he had been unable to take photographs because of the press of people and the uncertainties caused by his junior position.

"Terry, you know where we're going?" asked Ackerman.

"To sink more Germans." He winced as he recalled that Ackerman's parents were born in Germany. "Sorry."

"It's okay. Y'know, I got a letter from my pa just before the big battle. He told me he had given it a lot of thought and that I shouldn't feel bad about fighting people I might even be related to. Basically, he said if they were so stupid that they stayed and fought for their fool kaiser, then fuck 'em."

Terry laughed. "Is that a direct quote?"

"Not quite, but close enough." Ackerman squinted at the bulk of a distant land mass off their starboard. "Hey, is that Long Island?"

*   *   *

Ludwig Weber continued to think dire thoughts. Even though the deep rumblings of the battle were miles to the rear, he had a nagging feeling that this current period of silence couldn't last forever. He and the others had been keeping a sharp eye on the woods in front of them. The treeline was only a quarter of a mile away. A good marksman could hide in the shadows and start picking them off. If Ludwig knew they were going to stay awhile, he would dig in. At least he might consider it after he got something to eat.

A rabbit burst from the woods. The men watched entranced as it darted first one way, then another in panic and confusion. "Lunch," someone yelled, and there was laughter. A second rabbit, then a third sprinted into the open. Ludwig heard Sergeant Gunther loudly assigning rabbits to specific riflemen as they came closer. One of the soldiers fired and the first rabbit tumbled over to raucous cheers. Let's see, Ludwig thought, three rabbits divided by thirty-eight wouldn't go far.

A long line of flashes from the woods, followed almost immediately by the bark of guns, stunned him. Ludwig first thought was that the rabbits were shooting back. Then he realized there was a large number of men in the woods, and they were firing rapidly, creating a hailstorm of bullets. A whistle pierced the air, followed by the thud of an artillery shell landing nearby. He quickly identified it as a 75mm field gun. A light gun. The goddamn Yanks were in the woods!

As he hugged the ground, Ludwig heard shouts and screams. Bullets whistled about him and kicked up clouds of dirt. He looked up to see a horde of brown-uniformed Americans emerging from the woods. They formed up and advanced rapidly, firing all the while. More shells pounded the ground and a machine gun added its voice to the insane din.

Ludwig could not believe his eyes. He had never seen so many Americans. Worse, they did not look like raw militia. They were advancing very quickly and in good order; some were firing as others darted forward under the cover thus provided. Ludwig was getting the shock of his life. He rose and ran in a crouch to where Captain Walter was looking at the advancing enemy.

"Captain, those aren't militia or recruits. Those are regulars."

"I know." The Americans had covered about a third of the way and were not going to be stopped. "Everybody pull back!"

There was no need to repeat the order. The men of the company commenced retreating immediately at a quick trot. As they did, they instinctively drew together in their fear, which made them an even better target for the American guns.

"Ludwig," yelled the captain. "Run like hell to the rear and tell battalion we're being overwhelmed."

Ludwig turned to go and stopped short. Wordlessly he pointed to his right. A column of horsemen had emerged from the woods and was already passing them on their way to the German rear. Ludwig was about to say something when a shell landed nearby and lifted him off the ground, sucking the air from his chest.

Maybe he lost consciousness for a moment. He lurched to his knees and gagged. Then he saw Captain Walter crumpled on the ground a few yards away and slithered over to him. He checked for a pulse and found it. Kessel ran by.

"Otto, come over here and help me move the captain."

Kessel turned his savage face to the Americans, who were now only a hundred yards away and coming on at a trot. "Fuck you, pussy boy! Save him yourself, if the Yanks don't kill you first," he cackled. Kessel swung his rifle, and the butt crunched against the meat of Ludwig's shoulder, causing him to scream and fall. The last Ludwig saw of Kessel was his back as he ran away.

Ludwig became aware that the firing had almost stopped. It occurred to him that the Yanks had run out of targets. He looked at the captain and saw his eyes blinking. Ludwig took the piece of paper he had kept from the American spies so long ago, raised his good arm, and began to wave it. Please God, let them not kill me, he prayed.

American shapes surrounded them and grabbed their weapons. Ludwig screamed when someone spun him around looking for a hidden knife. His shoulder was hurt and so was his chest. Maybe a rib or two was broken; at least there were some bad bruises. He started to say something when a large, red-faced American sergeant with squinty eyes told him in excellent German that he should stay where he was and a guard would take care of him and the others. It was then Ludwig noticed that he was not alone. Perhaps a score of his company had also been captured, and there were still more Americans pouring from the woods. Where the hell had they come from?

"Ludwig?"

"Yes, Captain?" Walter waved his arms as if trying to find something to grab. Ludwig pushed him back to the ground. "Don't try to move just yet."

"What has happened?"

Ludwig sat on the cold ground and picked up a chunk of dirt. American dirt. "Captain, I think our part of the war is over."

Major Esau Jones pulled out of the column and watched as the first company of his mounted battalion trotted past. They were on point and had the responsibility for scouting ahead. The job of Jones's battalion, more mounted infantry than true cavalry, was to ride on ahead and try to find the exact location of the main German force. With some reluctance, Jones had suggested to General Mahan that it might be better to split his unit into small groups to cover more ground, but the general had said no, keep the cavalry together. They would need all the men they had when they found the Germans. Major Jones had agreed with pleasure. His secondary orders were to destroy anything that might look useful to the Krauts.

He chucked his horse in behind the lead company's last platoon, and his messenger followed. At last they were going to war. The quick ride through the thin German lines had been an incredible tonic. For the first time he'd seen Germans running, Germans surrendering. And his Buffalo Soldiers had helped. He knew from bitter experience that many of the white soldiers despised the black troops, whether they had white officers or not. Having black officers had only made matters worse; white soldiers ignored them. The tabs on Jones's shoulder said he was a major, albeit temporary rank, and therefore an officer and a gentleman to be respected and obeyed. But the color of his skin told too many whites that he was nothing but a dressed-up nigger. He had long since decided that his world was not yet ready for colored gentlemen.

A rider galloped up beside him. He recognized a studious, young private the men teasingly called the Professor. "Sir, the captain's compliments, and would you stop the column and join him at the point immediately?"

Major Jones couldn't help but grin. "Now, son, that does not sound like my friend Captain Tyree. What exactly did he say?"

The Professor gulped. "He said you should stop this fucking circus train and get your ugly black ass up with his as soon as possible. And quietlike."

Esau Jones guffawed, gave the order, and spurred his horse forward into yet more woods. He had gone only a little way when a soldier emerged from behind a tree and stopped him, urging silence and caution. Jones dismounted and, following the soldier, went cautiously to the crest of a low hill where Tyree lay on his stomach, field glasses to his eyes.

"What's out there, Tyree?" He could easily see several score of men, horses, and wagons on a hill a half mile away.

"God and his angels, I think, Esau." He handed Jones the binoculars. When he brought the scene into focus, he whistled. His assignment had been to find the German army. Although this group of people was not the whole army, its importance was obvious. Was he justified in exposing his presence? It was apparent that the people on the hill had not heard the sounds of the battle behind them. They were all looking away from him and at something that was causing much smoke in the distance. Jones made up his mind.

"Tyree, tell the Professor to bring all the company commanders here, and pronto. Also damned quietly." He grinned at temporary-Captain Tyree. "We're gonna deliver some paybacks for all the shit we been takin' the last few months." He also recalled some of his men being skewered on German bayonets that awful day in early June. "Damn fine binoculars," he said as he handed them back to Tyree, who put them in a case bearing the insignia of the Imperial German Army. "Someday you gotta tell me how you got those."

Lieutenant Sigmond von Hoff hated every moment of his present existence. He was a Prussian and a Uhlan, an elite cavalryman, by God, not a damned baby-sitter. Or a nanny! Perhaps there were those who would consider his current position as guard to the high command both an honor and a safe place to be, but he was not one of them. All about him were the sounds and smells of battle, glorious battle, but he and his fellow Uhlans were not part of it. There was

some feeling at headquarters that this was not the right war for cavalry armed with lances.

It infuriated him. Why had the Imperial General Staff shipped
them over if not to use them? Some pea brains in headquarters had
stripped them of their lances and given them carbines, which they
barely knew how to operate. Now they were considered useless soldiers fit only for ornamental guard duties like this.

Hoff was personally considered much worse than useless. He was
a pariah. What had he done wrong? His orders had been to execute
American prisoners, and all he had done was to follow those orders.
And, by God, those orders had come from the kaiser himself. When
Hoff's actions caused such a stink, everyone had conveniently forgotten the fact that he hadn't acted alone. Now no one wanted to
even talk to him. Still more galling was the fact that others had
achieved promotion in this war, whereas he was still a lieutenant at
the ripe old age of twenty-four.

Disgusted, he lay down on the grass and stared at the sky. Let the
mighty ones he was protecting gaze at the smoke towers and try to
figure out where they were. He almost giggled at the thought of
some stupid Bavarian staff officer having to admit they were, while
not quite lost, not quite certain just where they were. They could
only assume that much of their army was in action a few miles away.

"Lieutenant!" Hoff sat up and looked where a soldier was pointing. A row of horsemen had emerged from the woods and a second
was forming behind it. Columns of cavalry commenced to gallop
both to his left and to his right. As he watched in astonishment, the
double line began to move forward. Toward him.

He jumped to his feet and yelled for his men to mount up, which
they did with alacrity. He had only one troop. It appeared that several hundred of what he now easily identified as Americans were
about to envelop his position. His actions had attracted the attention of the senior officers, and he saw them scrambling for their horses
and carriages.

In dismay, Hoff saw that the rapidly moving flanking columns
would easily cut off most, if not all, of the fleeing Germans on
horseback and certainly all of the slower carriages. Even if he managed to survive this debacle, his career was ruined.

"Open fire!" he shrieked, and his men let loose a ragged volley that appeared to accomplish little. Suddenly, he realized that the enemy cavalry all had dark skins. "Blacks!" he screamed. It was too much. In a blind rage he spurred his horse forward. He pulled a revolver and emptied it as the black horsemen swirled passed him. His horse stumbled, and Hoff fell heavily to the ground. As he attempted to pull his saber from its scabbard, a careening horse ran over him and he felt his legs snap. Before the waves of agony could reach his brain, he looked up at his assailant and saw an iron-shod hoof descending on his head.

On the hill, the fight deteriorated into a short-lived melee. At arm's length, carbines and revolvers emptied into living flesh. The Germans fought hard to protect their charges, but they were soon overwhelmed. As Hoff had guessed, none of the carriages escaped. In one, an old man flailed about with a saber in one hand and a pistol in the other. As a young black trooper reached for him, the old man shot him in the face. On the other side of the carriage, Maj. Esau Jones saw this and emptied his revolver at point-blank range into the back of the old man, who crumpled onto the floor of the carriage.

Then Jones looked about. His men had taken a number of prisoners, and virtually all of them appeared to be officers. "Who speaks English?" asked Jones.

A little man with a bad cut on his cheek, which had drained blood onto an immaculate light blue uniform, responded that he did. The man approached cautiously and looked into the carriage. "God help us," he said. Then he looked up into the stern face of Jones. "Do you know what you have done?"

"You tell me."

"You have just killed Field Marshal Count Alfred von Waldersee, commander of the Imperial German Army."

News of the counterattack brought Roosevelt rushing back to the war room. "About time. The papers are beginning to run extras about our total incompetence and what they think has happened. Hearst says I have sent dumb recruits to be slaughtered. Goddamn him!"

Roosevelt looked at the changes on the map. "Leonard, it happened, didn't it?"

"Yes, sir. At least so far. The four brigades brought over from the Philippines were successfully carried by train from Springfield and joined the one brigade in line. They pushed aside the German screening force rather easily and are now in the German rear."

Roosevelt fought the urge to chortle. When MacArthur had first proposed bringing his regiments back from the Philippines, he had said no. The trip was too dangerous. With no American ships in the Pacific to protect them, the German Asiatic squadron could attack and slaughter them. And there was the danger that the Filipinos would revolt and kill the troops and administrators left behind. No, he had said, too great a risk.

But then came word through the British that the Germans had pulled their ships as well. John Hay proposed a treaty of understanding with the Philippine leader Aguinaldo, which had been hammered out quickly by the American governor in the Philippines, William Howard Taft. Specifically, the Philippines would be independent one year after the end of the war with Germany, and the United States would guarantee independence from other predatory countries in return for a naval base at Subic Bay and coaling rights at Cavite. A similar agreement was quickly reached with the Cuban insurgents, who were scheduled for independence in a few years anyhow. The Democrats would crow and some of the more radical Manifest Destiny types would scream betrayal, but twenty-five thousand good American troops had been freed for use against the Germans.

Getting them home had proven less difficult than he had thought. Ships were chartered and the men brought to Vancouver, where they were put on trains and shipped across Canada and down through Maine to the camp at Springfield. By traveling through sparsely populated Canada, they managed to move in relative secrecy. Those who did see and wonder were told they were American recruits, nothing more.

Bringing them home had been MacArthur's idea. Coordinating the move from Springfield to the battle area had been the task of Longstreet and Schofield. One after another and only moments apart, the great trains had run down, their flatcars jammed with men and equipment. After weeks of practice, it took only minutes to get each train unloaded and the men on their way. The empty trains had then gone on a long, looping journey in the general direction of Boston and out of the way. "For all I care, they can run them into the ocean once they're unloaded," had been Longstreet's comment.

Roosevelt stared at the map. The blue pennants representing American units were encroaching on the red ones representing Germans. He exulted; we have thirty thousand soldiers in their rear! An aide moved a blue pennant across the Hudson and onto Manhattan. Roosevelt smiled. A brigade of marines in barges and longboats was landing on Manhattan. The marines were beginning to enjoy amphibious assaults.

Kaiser Wilhelm's voice was a screech. "What is happening? Why hasn't von Waldersee kept in touch?"

Schlieffen tried to mask his anxiety. "Perhaps he is too busy." The news of the American counterattack had shaken them. It was too soon, and too strong. Something had gone horribly wrong. The German army had been attacked in the rear by a large force and could easily be crumbling. Worse, Waldersee was not in control of the battlefield and did not appear to be doing anything about it. No one knew where Waldersee was. Probably moving from one place on the field to another, but the fact of his being out of contact at this critical time made Schlieffen extremely nervous.

"Then where is Hindenburg? Why haven't we heard from the younger von Moltke?" he asked, referring to the two corps commanders involved in the main attack. "Von Schlieffen, we have been betrayed. The Americans knew that we were going to attack, and they were prepared. How else could they have moved their army so quickly?"

How else indeed? thought Schlieffen. Although, in hindsight, should they not have presumed the Americans would do exactly what they have done? Had he and Waldersee been too arrogant and assured of success? If so, they would pay a high price for it. Schlieffen was, however, more concerned by the quickness with which the attack had punched through and destroyed the screening force. This indicated to him that they were not dealing with simple militia. He had a nagging thought and rejected it. They could not have done it. Impossible.

A junior officer at the telegraph gestured and Schlieffen approached. "What?" asked the kaiser.

Schlieffen paled. "In the continued absence of von Waldersee, young von Moltke has assumed command. He is going to order von Trotha's reserves to attack the new American force. Several of our divisions have been badly mauled and a number of supply depots and artillery sites overrun. Von Moltke is urging a retreat back to our original defenses; he says that many of our regiments will be cut off no matter what we do." The message ran onto another page. "He also says the Americans have launched attacks across the Hudson onto Manhattan as well as across the Harlem River." Schlieffen handed the papers to the disbelieving kaiser. "Sire, you said we'd been betrayed, and this proves it. Along with knowing when and where we would attack, the Americans knew we had stripped our defenses elsewhere. That was a closely held secret, just like the decision to divide our navy. There must be a traitor."

Wilhelm looked at the papers that told him of defeat. He had to salvage something from this travesty. The problem of locating the traitor would have to wait. "Von Moltke—can he save the army?"

"Sire, he will do his utmost." Schlieffen's calm words belied his inner turmoil. Moltke was the nephew of the great leader of the army against the French. But young Moltke was a lightweight in comparison with his famous uncle. So much so that, although he thought of himself as von Moltke the Younger, others talked of him as von Moltke the Lesser. Schlieffen would have much preferred that the older and more stable Hindenburg had taken command.

The kaiser became aware that Bulow and Holstein had also arrived in the chancellery office. Bulow looked terrified and Holstein angry.

"Dear kaiser," said Holstein solemnly, "I have further bad news for you. The Reichstag has heard about the impending defeat and has voted to demand that you end the war."

Wilhelm surged to his feet. "They have not that right. Disband them! I will rule by decree!"

"It may be too late," Bulow stammered. "People are gathering in the streets, and I do not believe they will accept the Reichstag's being sent home without great violence." He did not add that a number of army units, largely reservists, had begun to join the growing mob.

"What other misfortunes can befall me today?"

Holstein provided the answer. "Von Tirpitz is dead, sire. He committed suicide."

*   *   *

Admiral Diedrichs received word of the sudden assault across the Hudson only after it was over. Motor launches and tugs had pulled barges and lines of longboats linked like sausages across the river in a matter of moments. The boats, filled with American marines, had landed virtually without incident or opposition. Again, it was Diedrichs's fault. The few ships patrolling the Hudson and East Rivers were out scouting for the American fleet, while the remainder of his battle fleet waited outside the Narrows in the lower bay.

As Diedrichs contemplated this new disaster, he received a report that the Americans were attacking and rolling up the Harlem River defenses, easily defeating the small force the army had left behind. That would open the way for the Americans in the north to pour onto the island and across into Brooklyn. It didn't take much imagination to realize that his port was about to be taken from him.

A line of tall splashes rose from the Narrows. The Americans had moved their damned big guns closer and had now bracketed the slender channel. Any attempt to reestablish control over the area would be costly.

And, Diedrichs realized, futile. Without infantry to control the area, his ships could do little but steam up and down outside the harbor. There was no decision to make; the pitiless fates had made it for him.

"We will depart in one hour."

"Where to, sir?"

His skull throbbed. "Back to Germany."

Major General Joe Wheeler virtually bounced into Baldy Smith's headquarters. Despite Wheeler's diminutive size, his presence was immediate and dramatic.

"Baldy, we got them by the balls," Wheeler said gleefully.

Smith had always liked that expression. "It is beginning to look that way," he said. His forces had begun attacking northward in an attempt to link up with Schofield's brigades, which were pressing south. Reports had German units starting to stream in some disarray toward the west and the presumed safety of their old lines.

Wheeler stood directly in front of Smith and put his hands on the taller man's shoulders. "Now, old rival, we got to finish the job."

"What do you mean?"

"Baldy, I got Pershing here in Bridgeport with an entire division that ain't done shit yet. They're ready, primed, and pissed. I want to turn them loose."

"Where?" Smith asked. The map showed that any movement northward by Pershing's division could entangle it with other American units that had been pushed south by the Germans. Smith was also suspicious of a German force reported to be gathering west of the Housatonic for its own counterattack.

"Baldy, I want to move Pershing west and into those German defensive positions before the Germans can reoccupy them and keep us from pushing on to New York. We do that and the Krauts won't have a place to retreat to. In effect we'll be in their rear, and those great defensive works they spent so much time building will be just so many piles of dirt."

Weeks earlier, Smith had ridden out to observe the defense lines the Germans had constructed; he considered them better than anything he'd ever seen. "Joe, they'll be murdered."

Wheeler shook his head vehemently. "Those lines are empty. You can count peckers as well as I can, and all their troops are north of us, not in those lines. Maybe skeleton forces, but nothing of consequence. Look, Pershing cheated a little and kept two battalions on the west side of the Housatonic, so he can cross without opposition. From there they can dash up and rush those lines while there's still time."

Smith paused. He thought of another time and another war. He had been granted the opportunity to end the Civil War, but he had procrastinated, thinking the lines about Petersburg were full when they were empty. The rebels had fooled him, and it was a shame he had borne for decades.

But he still had to question. "And if their defenses are full of soldiers and not empty?"

"Then Pershing gets his nose bloodied and pulls back. Look, we don't have to take all the old German line; just taking some of it will make the rest irrelevant, and Pershing can do that. Baldy, just think of the lives that'll be saved if we don't have to root them out like you Yanks had to at Petersburg."

Smith remembered the ten-month agony of that siege. And all because of his error. He would not make the same mistake again. He had been given the opportunity to purge himself. "All right. Send them. How soon will we know?"

Wheeler turned to depart, a satisfied grin on his face. "A couple of hours."

Smith looked at the map and his watch. An expression of disbelief crossed his face. "You goddamn little shit reb son of a bitch! You sent him already, didn't you!"

Wheeler spat on the dirt floor and laughed while junior officers ran for cover. "Shit, Baldy, I trusted you. I knew you wouldn't make the same dumb fucking mistake twice in your life."

Johnny Two Dogs was cold, but he was almost used to that. The comings and goings at the farmhouse fascinated him. He never worried overmuch about white people, but he did wonder how Blake and Willy were faring.

Thus he was surprised when the door to the storm cellar opened and Willy emerged with some wires looped across his shoulder. He could see that Willy's face was pale; the man looked terrified.

Suddenly, there was the sound of gunfire and a rush of soldiers running toward the house. Willy dropped the wires and ran almost directly at Johnny. Willy hunched visibly at the sound of further shots, but they were directed at someone inside the house, and he continued his mad dash. As he passed, Johnny reached out and tripped the frightened man.

At that moment, there was a flash of light and a loud bang that blew out the insides of the brick house in sheets of flame. Johnny grabbed Willy and they ran until they reached the safety of a nearby grove of apple trees. When Willy finally stopped gasping for breath, he gazed in disbelief. "You, you're the injun who's been trailing us."

So much for being hidden, Johnny thought. I must be getting old. "What the hell happened in there?"

"The other guy, Blake, decided he was gonna do something really big to the Germans to get back for what they did to his family. He took some dynamite sticks and some caps and stuck them in his shirt. Then he told me to get the hell out of there. I didn't want to, so he pushed me." Not likely, thought Johnny. The little thief had doubtless run at the first opportunity. "Jesus, he killed himself."

Johnny looked to where the house was burning. Although the brick walls had held, the roof had collapsed and the structure had become an inferno. Anyone inside was dead. "So what did Blake do that was so big?" Johnny framed the words carefully. His English was not the best, even after all these years. "Who did he kill?"

"Some guy he thought was a big German general. Name was something like Trotha."

The battle was only a few hundred yards below and in front of them as Patrick, Ian, and Harris looked on from the crest of the hill. They watched in silence as the immense tableau unfolded. Before them, they could see thousands of men moving and swirling, fighting and dying. Somehow they knew such a scene would never occur again in their lifetimes. Nor would they ever wish it to happen again.

Ian was the first to break the spell. "Your General Sherman once said that war is hell. This has to be what he meant. I have never seen anything like this in my life."

Patrick's thoughts ran the same way. The sight was both astonishing and horrifying. "Ian, this must have been what it was like at Waterloo or Gettysburg."

"Of course." Ian watched as Patrick's brigade surged forward, almost into the densely packed German river of men trying to flee to the safety of the west. Beyond them and plainly visible was the American force advancing north. The Germans were being squeezed, and soon the two American forces would converge and the Germans would be surrounded. "Perhaps even Agincourt."

Patrick watched appalled as American gunfire scythed through the German mob, piling up bodies three and four deep. In most cases German discipline still held, and the return fire was almost as devastating. There seemed to be as many brown- as gray-clad bodies.

A new and hideous clatter joined in the torrent of sounds. The northward-approaching Americans had brought together a number of machine guns and were using them as massed weapons. The effect was devastating. German soldiers fell like wheat before a diabolical mechanical reaper.

"I'm sorry," said Ian. "What I saw previously was no hell. This is. Patrick, I believe we are seeing the future. Machines of mass destruction and using rows of machine guns are only the beginning."

The result was a parting of the German human sea, and the Americans joined forces. As the afternoon droned on, many of the trapped Germans attempted to break out, but their attacks were disorganized and fragmented and easily beaten back. Sometimes a few would make it through and run on, but they were the exception. Even more telling was the fact that no attempts were made by the Germans to link up from the west. The German command seemed to have written off its trapped soldiers.

"Behind you," hissed Ian. Schofield and MacArthur were approaching. They were prudently alone and on foot. Two more men joining the three on the hill would not attract undue attention from maddened German gunners.

Schofield spoke. "Well done, Patrick. It would appear we've bagged a large number of them."

Patrick mumbled appreciation and watched as MacArthur moved away from the little group. His face seemed tight and strained. Schofield explained. "He just got word that his son was badly wounded. He hasn't gotten a chance to confirm anything." Patrick nodded and gave the other man room for his silent grief.

There was an awareness that the sound level had decreased markedly, and the men turned again to what they could see of the battlefield, now strangely silent.

MacArthur stirred himself and came over. He shielded his eyes with his hand and stared into the distance, as did the others. "Thank God," he said softly. "They're surrendering."

As they watched, German soldiers started throwing down their weapons and holding their arms up in the air.

Chapter 28

THEODORE ROOSEVELT SIPPED his tea and looked out at the now-empty Lafayette Park. Was it only a few weeks ago that it had been the scene of riotous celebrations? He watched as a January wind took a whipped piece of newspaper about. He hoped it was from a Hearst publication.

"John, I have made some plans."

John Hay placed his cup on its saucer with a gentle clink. "I'm not surprised."

"This is a wonderful opportunity for the United States. I aim to see that we do not waste it. I will ask Congress for a constitutional amendment that will enable me, with their consent, to nominate someone as vice president."

"Excellent idea."

"Assuming it passes, I wish that person to be you."

"Theodore, I am honored, but I am also rather old."

Roosevelt flashed a toothy grin. "You are too old and I am too young. It averages out. John, let me be realistic. I need your experience and wisdom, and the country knows it. I am the youngest man ever to hold this office, and when I run on my own, many will still consider me too young. John, I need you."

Hay thought briefly of others, like Root, who openly wished higher office. It would be a problem. But he could deal with it. "I'm honored."

"Good. That's settled. Now to the rest of it. What happened last summer may never happen again."

"Agreed."

"Therefore, I am going to propose, along with accelerating the navy expansion, that our standing army be set at 250,000 men. That will be nearly a threefold increase over what we have now. We will need more warships, and that means submarines, not just battleships."

"The Democratic opposition will not like it."

Roosevelt rose and commenced to pace. "Damnit, John, we are a world power whether we wish to be or not. In the space of three short years we have defeated both Spain and Germany, and now the British wish us to join with them in an alliance of English-speaking peoples that would span the globe."

"Some are afraid the British will dominate us in any such alliance," Hay pointed out.

"Let them try. Their empire is on the decline, only they haven't yet figured it out, whereas ours is ascending. No, we will start out as equals and commence to dominate them. Especially when we dig a canal across the Isthmus of Panama." He clapped his hands in glee. "We have a navy; we will have an army and, very soon, a canal. We are a power!"

Hay sipped his tea. He would rather have had a whiskey. The idea of a canal was just about at the implementation stage. It would go forward whether the Colombians wanted it or not. He also felt that the American mood would permit Roosevelt's military expansions, and would do so for a number of years until some parsimonious future Congress again decided that years of peace meant no future of war. The shock of the attack on New York was far from having worn off. The Germans had been defeated, at least for now, but there were other potential threats. Japan, for instance, and Russia. Or perhaps the Ottomans. America would never again stand alone in this world.

Hay raised his cup. "To the future, Theodore, to the future."

Holstein's new office was in a building a few blocks away from where the construction crews were trying to repair the damage to the chancellery. It was of no import to him. He had always considered the chancellery a singularly ugly building. However, it had been a shame that the kaiser had been unwilling to leave. So many had died because of the man's stubbornness. Holstein shuddered as he recalled the mobs, interspersed with army reserve units, as they stormed the building, sacked it, and burned it. Imprinted forever, too, was the sight of the dead and dying on the street and the lynched victims dangling from the ornate lampposts. That must not happen again.

"Herr Becker, I must offer you my congratulations." Holstein held out his hand to the other man who had just entered. Becker smiled tightly.

"Thank you, Count von Holstein. I understand I had your support. In the background, of course."

"It was the only way, dear Becker. The old regime is in such disrepute that any public support of you by anyone with a 'von' in front of their name would have been a kiss of death. But now you are the prime minister of a new Germany."

"A temporary title, I'm afraid. When the new constitution is drawn and ratified, it may only be a memory."

"Then we must not permit that to happen." Becker's face reflected surprise.

"Have you decided what to do with the royal family?" Holstein asked.

"Wilhelm II is banished, of course, and I believe headed for Denmark with his insufferable wife. His first war, I'm afraid, will also be his last. But there is sentiment for the crown prince as a figurehead. He would become, of course, Kaiser Wilhelm III. The boy is only eighteen and seems to be more stable than his father. He could easily be controlled if it came to that. But what did you mean, we must not let my title become a memory?"

"Becker, men like you are the future of Germany. We Junkers have had our day in the German sun and wasted it. The Prussians will be useful in the army but not as a government. I hope that you will draw a constitution that permits the facade of democracy while keeping the real power in the hands of qualified people like yourself and away from the Socialists like August Bebel and those readers of Marx and Engels."

Becker grinned. "And in your hands as well?"

Holstein lowered his head in mock humility. "If called upon, I feel qualified to serve."

This time Becker laughed out loud. Power had fallen to him and he was finding it pleasurable. "I remember our earlier conversation. Are you dismayed at what has happened to our army and navy?"

"Not really." Diedrichs had been court-martialed for cowardice and executed; Schlieffen and Moltke had been permitted to retire in disgrace. As yet there was no head of the smaller navy, while two men, Hindenburg and Mackensen, were jockeying for command of the army. Others, like Kluck, Falkenhayn, and Ludendorff, also awaited their opportunity. Holstein's money was on Hindenburg, who, despite playing a key role in America, was strangely untouched personally by the disaster. "Becker, do you still believe what you said about opportunities for Germany within Europe?"

"Certainly. The idea of a two-ocean German navy and a colonial empire was absurd in the first place, and the North American disaster proved it. We are unable to project sufficient power against offshore enemies while surrounded by real and potential enemies on European soil. European matters must be settled before any overseas expansion can be undertaken. We are Europeans first, last, and foremost. We should be thinking in terms of first dominating, then absorbing the Austrians before their polyglot empire collapses of its own weight. Then we should take Holland and Denmark, even if the latter includes our departed kaiser." Becker laughed sharply. "Someday soon, the czar's Russia will suffer an upheaval from which it will not recover, and that will create further opportunities, perhaps along the Baltic. The Ottomans are on the verge of collapse, and the straits to the Black Sea could easily be ours. The opportunities for Germany's growth are endless. We should leave the New World to England and the United States, while we control Europe. We have a destiny to fulfill as a master race over these lower orders that surround us. Holstein, the Second Reich is finished. What we are going to build is a Third Reich." He laughed again. "And to think I was once afraid I wouldn't live long enough to see it."

Holstein beamed. "Wonderful."

Becker stood. His waistcoat was open. He stuck his thumbs in his suspenders and smiled confidently. It was an act of casual insolence that would have been unthinkable a few weeks earlier. Now it indicated that a shift in power had taken place. "I am almost inclined to forget the kaiser's rantings about treachery in our midst."

"Oh?" Holstein thought briefly of the sudden and unlamented death of the Italian cultural attaché who had proven so useful as a conduit to the British. "Almost?"

"Yes. I am inclined to blame the Jews. I see no reason why we cannot continue to accuse them. It will help shift blame for the defeat from the government. Who knows, a few executions might calm the population."

Becker put his hands on his hips and laughed. "God, I wish I had a drink. I would toast the future."

Holstein smiled and raised an imaginary glass. "To the future. To the Third Reich."

Trina finished buttoning her blouse and checked the time. It would be about an hour before the train arrived in downtown Detroit. The privacy of the Pullman sleeping compartment had been a pleasure, enabling them to make love slowly while the swaying of the train did virtually all the work, but it would be good to spend some time on firm ground.

"Shouldn't you be getting ready?" she asked Patrick, looking out the window at the thin layer of January snow that lay hard on the Michigan ground. "And you should wear your uniform."

"It really doesn't make sense. Technically, I am now a civilian."

"But you are a war hero and there will be a celebration." She knew he was very proud and was looking forward to having his family see him in his uniform. His mild protest meant nothing.

Patrick put on his blue uniform jacket and looked at the two stars on his shoulders. The promotion to major general had been an unexpected bonus. "A wedding gift," Roosevelt had chortled. Since Patrick had immediately resigned his commission, the promotion had been largely ceremonial.

"Patrick, have you given any further thought to Roosevelt's suggestions?"

"Yes," he said as he slipped the jacket on. Roosevelt had suggested that he return home, quickly write his history of the war, and then run for Congress in the 1902 elections. Since it was already early 1902, it would mean a lot of hard work. Roosevelt had given him further instructions: "Leave your answer with Governor Bliss when you arrive in Detroit. Aaron's a good Republican and will let

me know. We need people with your knowledge and world experience in Congress to convince others that the United States isn't a
hick farm country anymore. You know the German beast and he will
be back. Some faces at the top have changed, but Germany is still the
same. Mark my words."

Yes, Patrick felt that he knew both Germany and modern warfare,
and liked neither. The casualties from the war had been horrendous:
more than twenty-five thousand American dead and wounded, and
nearly forty thousand German dead. An additional twenty thousand
Germans had surrendered that day; the remainder formally negotiated an end to the war a few days later. They might have held out far
longer but for the fact that Brooklyn had been recaptured and
Pershing had stormed a two-mile length of mighty defenses. Moltke
had then given in to the inevitable. Had Pershing not made his assault, the Germans would have dug in behind their forts and used
their untapped reserve divisions to sweep the Americans back from
New York City and Brooklyn. There had been speculation that the
Germans would have withdrawn to Long Island and set up for a long
siege. Without supplies and low on ammunition, the German army
would have faced certain defeat. It would have been a protracted and
bloody affair with many lives needlessly lost on both sides. Patrick
shuddered at the potential cost of taking that island. Thank God for
Wheeler and Pershing.

"Well?" Katrina kissed him gently on the cheek, interrupting his
thoughts.

"Sounds very interesting. Would you mind being a congressman's
wife?"

"I would enjoy it immensely. Imagine what damage I could do on
behalf of women while at the seat of power. Besides, Washington
would be a fine place to raise a child."

"What?"

"Not yet, dear general. But soon, perhaps, the way we are going."

He laughed and told her he wanted to stretch his legs and see if
the porter had somehow gotten a current newspaper. He buttoned his
uniform jacket and stepped into the narrow passageway. So much
had changed in the past few weeks. Ian had returned to England,
and Harris to his factory. Heinz and Molly had finally gotten married and were in Cincinnati. Longstreet was back in Gainesville, Geor-

gia, and Schofield and MacArthur were organizing a new army. Dewey and the navy were in their glory and there was talk of additional submarines.

But MacArthur's boy was crippled, and most of his Apaches had apparently disappeared into thin air, reluctant to return to reservation life. The Negro cavalry had their white officers back, although some of the blacks, like Esau Jones, who was once again a sergeant, had their own medals. No one knew what to do about Blake Morris. His suicide had helped to further decapitate the German command, but no one was certain whether or not he had actually been in the army at the time. Roosevelt said they'd probably name some schools after him.

A glint of metal on Patrick's chest distracted him. Full uniform meant medals as well. He had been a little embarrassed on being given the Medal of Honor. He didn't feel he had done anything to deserve it.

"Of course you did." Roosevelt had been insistent. "I know there were many heroes out there; perhaps, if it will make you feel better, think of it as being for all of them. But damnit, Patrick, you did a splendid job of attacking the Germans and pinching off their retreat. That won the day for us. You're a hero and you'd better get used to that fact. You won't be permitted to forget it."

So be it, Patrick thought. As he walked through the coach car, two thin and pale young men in ill-fitting clothes immediately jumped to their feet on seeing his rank and stood at attention. "Relax, boys," Patrick said, assuming they had just left the army. They hadn't. His stars and medals were just too intimidating. "You *were* in the army?" asked Patrick. One, slightly younger and with his arm in a sling, nodded and mumbled an accented yes. "Which unit?" Patrick asked.

They looked at each other, and finally the younger of the two answered. "Imperial 4th Rifles."

Patrick blinked back his surprise. He had heard that many prisoners had chosen not to return to Germany, much to that country's chagrin. He told them who he was and that he knew of their unit. After all, his brigade had overrun it.

"General Mahan, was your command a mixed unit of blacks and Germans?"

Patrick laughed. During the rush of battle, many smaller units from the different regiments had gotten mixed up, with interesting socio-logical results. "Yes, it was."

The younger man smiled shyly. "Then I think your people made us prisoners. I am Ludwig Weber and this is my ex-captain, Hans Walter. His English is not as good as mine, but he does understand well."

"So you decided to stay?"

"I decided a long time ago. My captain only recently. We are on our way to Milwaukee, where we both have relatives."

"Well," Patrick said, holding out his hand for them to shake. "Welcome to America."